'Life is an incurable disease.'
Abraham Cowley

This novel is dedicated to
Barbara Boote
A 'real book' with real thanks

That fluid.

That smell.

She recognised it so well and yet her mind told her that it was impossible.

And then she was standing in it. Standing in the great, thick tide of it, watching it creep further down the corridor like a living organism.

No, this couldn't be.

But she knew that smell.

But why . . . ?

Why the open window? Where had the thick fluid come from?

She looked down at her feet, at the liquid lapping around them. The stench was starting to make her dizzy. That unmistakable odour. Cloying. Choking. The corridor was awash with it.

She was standing in petrol.

Val turned back towards the window, her eye drawn to something moving in the darkness beyond, outside. Something tiny. Something glowing red.

The match hit the petrol, spinning through the air as if in slow motion before it landed and Val opened her mouth to scream but could not force the sound out.

The petrol exploded.

The world turned a bright, searing red.

Also by Shaun Hutson

Assassin
Breeding Ground
Captives
Deadhead
Death Day
Erebus
Heathen
Knife Edge
Lucy's Child
Nemesis
Relics
Renegades
Shadows
Slugs
Spawn
Stolen Angels
Victims
White Ghost

PURITY

SHAUN HUTSON

WARNER BOOKS

A *Warner* Book

First published in Great Britain in 1998
by Little, Brown and Company
This edition published in 1999 by Warner Books

Copyright © 1998, Shaun Hutson

The moral right of the author has been asserted.

A CIP catalogue record for this book
is available from the British Library.

ISBN 0 7515 2524 3

Typeset in Palatino by
Palimpsest Book Production Limited,
Polmont, Stirlingshire
Printed and bound in Great Britain by
Clays Ltd, St Ives plc

Warner Books
A Division of
Little, Brown and Company (UK)
Brettenham House
Lancaster Place
London WC2E 7EN

One

'So, how easy do you think it would be to kill some-one?'

Amy Watson took a drag on her cigarette then blew out a long stream of smoke, watching it slowly dissipate in the air. She gently flicked the dead end into the already overflowing ashtray on the desk, glancing at a microphone in front of her, then at a small video screen to her left. In luminous green letters the words PAUL – MUSWELL HILL were blinking.

She sat forward in her seat, one carefully manicured hand moving slowly over her black Levi's, wiping away a piece of fluff and some stray ash. She took a sip from her coffee cup, aware of the impenetrable silence inside the studio, then leaned closer to the microphone.

'Come on, Paul,' she said softly. 'This is supposed to be a talk show. Talk to me. Answer the question. Would you kill someone if you got the chance? If you *knew* you could get away with it? Could you bring yourself to take another human life?'

'If that person had killed someone close to me, yes I could,' said Paul from Muswell Hill. 'If it was like my girlfriend or someone like that.'

'I don't believe you. I think that even if someone raped your girlfriend and murdered your parents and you caught that person, you wouldn't be able to kill them; you wouldn't be able to bring yourself to do it.'

'I bloody would,' Paul grunted.

'You'd get up close and knife them, would you?' Amy persisted. 'You'd stick that blade in and risk getting covered in their blood, or you'd press that gun barrel to their heads and blow their brains out, would you? I don't think so.' She reached for the pack of cigarettes lying close by, placed one between her lips and lit it. 'It isn't a pretty sight, Paul. It isn't like it is in films, you know. There's a lot of mess and pain and it smells too. It's not like Arnold Schwarzenegger mowing down the bad guys with a smile and a stupid joke. We're talking about *real* people.'

'You don't know enough about me to tell me I couldn't do it,' Paul of Muswell Hill said angrily.

'I think I do, Paul,' Amy told him and flicked a switch on the console in front of her.

Paul disappeared both from her headset and from the video screen.

She glanced at the next name. GEORGE – ESHER.

She waited a moment before connecting him.

'Crime, capital punishment, murder,' Amy said, smiling. 'That's what we're talking about at the moment. All good clean fun here on the radio. If you've got a view on those subjects or on any others, ring in now. You know the number.' She gave it out once more. 'If you've got views that you think are worth sharing, then share them with me. I might even agree with you. If I don't, then you're history.' She flicked the switch. 'Go ahead, George from Esher, you're on. Dazzle us with your views.'

'Hello,' said a faltering voice.

'Go ahead, George,' Amy said, taking another drag on her cigarette.

'Hello, can you hear me?'

'Loud and clear, George. The nation is waiting.'

'Well, what I wanted to say was that I agree with you.'

'Grovelling won't keep you on the air any longer, George. Agree with me about what?'

'I don't think the average man would be able to take a life even if it was done in revenge. That's why I think we should have capital punishment.'

'George, you know what that's called? It's called passing the buck. You let someone else murder for you.'

'Capital punishment is hardly murder, is it?'

'Strapping a man's wrists and ankles together, placing

a linen bag over his head, slipping a noose of rope around his neck, then sending him hurtling through a trapdoor to break his neck – *that* isn't murder?'

'If he's committed a murder then he's got it coming.'

'He's got it coming. Now there's the voice of a reasoned liberal-minded individual, George. And what if he's innocent? Would you be prepared to let the state snuff out the life of an innocent man?'

'The chances of an innocent man being hanged are very, very slim. I—'

Amy cut him short. 'Are they, George? Tell that to Timothy Evans and James Hanratty. What about the Guildford Four and the Birmingham Six? They'd have been executed if we still had capital punishment. People who were later found to be innocent. Would those innocent lives have been worth it, George? What if that innocent man was you, George? As you were about to go hurtling through the trap, would your last thought be "Well, never mind, at least I'm only one in a thousand; this doesn't happen very often"? I doubt it.'

'So I suppose you think that they should be let off, do you?' countered George from Esher haughtily. 'You think they should be *understood* or pitied?'

'No. I think murderers should get life but life should *be* life. They shouldn't be out in ten years.'

'Capital punishment is a greater deterrent.'

'No it isn't, George. How many states in America have the death penalty and look at their murder rates? Much higher than ours.'

'Prisons are like holiday camps now. Three square meals a day, television—'

Again she cut him short. 'What would you advocate then, George?' Amy said, blowing out another stream of smoke. 'Rat-infested cells, bread and water, floggings twice a day? You're history, George.' She flicked one of the switches on the console in front of her.

'On line four we have Wendy from Harrow. What can you add to this debate, Wendy?'

'What about child murderers?' said Wendy from Harrow. 'Would you execute them?'

'I have my own views on what we should do with child murderers, Wendy.'

'And what are they?'

'The same thing we should do with paedophiles. We should put them in a room with the parents of the child they've abused or killed, tie them to a chair, then let the parents loose on them with baseball bats and hammers. It might seem a little radical but I think it would do the job.'

'Men who kill children, and paedophiles too, they should be treated. The important thing is to find out why they do what they do. They need help.'

'And what sort of help would you give the parents of the children they had abused or killed, Wendy?'

'It would help them to cope with the loss better if they knew why it had happened.'

'Have you got any children, Wendy?'

'No, I . . .'

'Then don't get involved in arguments like this. How can you hope to understand the feelings of a parent who's lost a child if you have no children of your own?'

'I'm a social worker and—'

'Say no more. You're history.' Amy cut her off glee-fully. 'Thank you for that contribution, Wendy from Harrow. I love social workers, don't you? People who actually get paid for having no comprehension of real life. Perhaps one of the few cases where capital punishment should be obligatory. So, any social workers out there, if you're listening, why not ring in and tell me why you shouldn't all be put in a boat, towed to the middle of the Atlantic and drowned. Just call the usual number. You should know it by now.' Again Amy gave out the number of the show. 'We've got to take a commercial break but when we come back we'll be talking about a subject even more dear to my own heart. The one subject guaranteed to provoke a completely irrational response from normally stable people. Yes, we'll be discussing smoking. So, while you all get your questions and comments ready, I'm going to light up. We'll be back in three minutes.'

Amy got to her feet, pulled off her headset and dropped it on the desk.

She looked at the microphone, a smiling face drawn on its yellow foam cover, etched there with a Biro by one of the station's other presenters. On the screen to her left half a dozen calls were already waiting to be answered.

As she headed for the studio door she glanced first at her watch then at the clock above the console.

12.02 a.m.

Two

'The lines are on fire tonight,' Mike Osborne commented as Amy hurried into the control room.

He had produced Amy's show since its inception nearly eighteen months ago, and was, at thirty-six, eight years older than her. He was a tall, powerfully built man, and was dressed in a denim jacket and faded jeans, with a small rose-shaped tattoo on the back of his left hand. He'd tried to have it removed on three separate occasions using laser treatment, but the tattoo's shape was still clearly visible. Osborne always wore the sleeves of his shirts buttoned in an effort to hide the mark, believing the tattoo was somehow inappropriate for someone in his position. Whether any of his superiors thought the same he didn't know. None had ever voiced an opinion one way or the other.

The other occupant of the control room was two years younger than Amy. Joanne Parker acted as a researcher, assistant and, more importantly, a close friend to Amy. The two women had known each other for three years, having met at a party at Planet Hollywood. At the time Jo had been working as PA to a director of a firm making soft drinks and Amy was just beginning her career in radio. They had hit it off immediately with that curious kind of spiritual kinship that so rarely comes along in life.

'Can you get me another coffee, please, Jo?' Amy asked. 'I'm just nipping to the loo.'

'Make it quick,' Osborne said, glancing at his watch. 'You're back on the air in two minutes.'

'There's some mail, Amy,' Jo told her. 'Do you want to wait until after the show?'

'No, leave it on my desk inside the studio,' Amy said,

hovering by the door. 'How does it sound from here, so far?'

'It sounds good. Now get a move on,' Osborne told her.

'Are you sure?' Amy persisted.

Osborne picked up an empty paper cup and threw it at her with a smile.

'Move it,' he shouted, then grinned.

Amy hurried along the short corridor to the Ladies, one eye on her watch. Ninety seconds left.

She flushed the toilet, ran her hands beneath the hot tap, and hurried back to the studio. Swinging herself into her seat and pulling on her headset, she listened to the commercials through one earpiece while she waited for the red light to flash on to tell her she was back on the air.

There were a small pile of letters and two small packages stacked neatly on the desk next to a steaming cup of coffee. She sipped at the coffee as she began ripping open the first of the letters.

She read them swiftly.

The abusive ones she dropped straight into her wastebin. They didn't usually vary in content no matter what their source or writer. The main difference was the lucidity used to attack her. Some of the letters were short and sweet. Words like 'mouthy bitch', 'loud-mouthed tart', occasionally eclipsed by such descriptions as 'self opinionated' or 'arrogant', dependent on the source of the letter. Every now and then correspondence praising her opinions or the show in general would arrive, but Amy tended to treat those with the same scepticism she treated the more derisory correspondence. There was a number of requests for her autograph, more for signed photos. Some even included their own photos. Others sent old pictures taken of her when she was a model years ago. Some of these were accompanied by insults. Every now and then there would be a threat.

The word 'whore' had been used in one of the letters

and attached to it, a photo taken from a spread she'd done for *Penthouse* two years ago.

Amy screwed up the photo and the letter into a ball and binned them.

Above the studio door the red light came on, glowing dully in the gloom of the room.

'Welcome back,' she said, swivelling round in her chair and pushing the other earpiece into position. 'I hope you enjoyed those clumsy attempts to get you to part with your money. Now back to business.' She lit a cigarette. 'Smoking.' Amy blew out a stream of smoke. 'What is the rule now? You can only smoke in your own bedroom, under the duvet after midnight? That would be about it, wouldn't it? After all, everyone knows that smokers are to blame for everything from cancer to the break-up of the Royal Family. Cigarettes are the greatest single threat to human life since bubonic plague, and anyone who actually dares to admit they enjoy the filthy weed is lower down the food chain than plankton.' She took another drag, careful to lean close enough to the microphone so that every sound was audible. 'That tastes good and if I want to kill myself by doing it, then that's *my* choice. All you non-smokers who are always ranting on about the dangers of passive smoking should thank people like me. With the money the government screws out of smokers, it stops you paying so much tax. So, all you self-righteous do-gooders who complain about smokers just remember that.' She glanced at the video screen where several calls were already flashing green.

'Harold from Chiswick, what do you think of smoking and smokers?'

'It's a filthy habit,' Harold from Chiswick snapped.

'Have you ever smoked, Harold?' Amy asked.

'No, I haven't. It's disgusting and it's dangerous. Passive smoking causes cancer.'

'Where's your proof?'

'Any doctor will tell you that.'

'Any doctor will tell you that drinking to excess is bad for you. Do you drink, Harold?'

'Yes. What's that got to do with it?'

'Well, if I get behind the wheel of a car smoking a cigarette the chances of me killing someone are small, but if *you* go out and have a drink, drive home and hit someone then does that make them a passive driver? There are more deaths on the road every year related to drinking than smoking aren't there, Harold?'

'That's a ridiculous argument.'

'Is it? Have you ever been drunk?'

'I don't drink that much, I—'

'Have you ever been drunk, it's a simple question, I've tried to use single syllables where possible. Have you in your life ever been drunk? Yes or no?'

'Yes, when I was younger.'

'How old are you now?'

'Forty. What's that got to do with it?'

'Okay, somewhere back in your dim and distant past, dim being the operative word, you have been drunk. Correct?'

'Yes.'

'Now what do you think most people find more obnoxious, a smoker blowing smoke near them or a drunk slobbering all over them trying to tell them his philosophy on life or, if they're really unlucky, throwing up on them? Which would *you* rather have, given the choice, Harold? If you were shut in a room for twenty-four hours with either a smoker or a drunk, which would you choose?'

'That's not an argument, it's—'

'You're history, Harold.' She flicked another switch.

'Line two,' she said. 'Sarah from Wapping. Sarah, are *you* a smoker?'

'Yes I am; I'm also a nurse.'

'It's a wonder you can afford fags on the pittance you get paid. Isn't there a little bit of a double standard there, Sarah? You're a part of the medical profession, a profession dedicated to preserving health, and yet you ally yourself with one of its greatest enemies, cigarettes. How many do you smoke a day?'

'Twenty. Sometimes more.'

'And what point would you like to make?'

'Smoking is an addiction, right, but smokers get no help from the government or the media. I've seen junkies brought into Casualty suffering from overdoses; I've seen drunks brought in who've done themselves or other people damage and yet everyone wants to help them. Junkies can get methadone on the NHS to help them with their addiction and drinkers can go to Alcoholics Anonymous, but it seems as if no one wants to help smokers. It's as if everyone thinks it's our fault that we smoke.'

'How do you feel about people with lung complaints being refused treatment if they smoke?'

'I don't agree with it. Drinkers with cirrhosis of the liver are treated; they aren't told they'll be denied treatment if they don't stop drinking. I think it's unfair.'

'So do I, Sarah, and I'll tell you something else that's unfair. It's only ever cigarette smokers who are criticised. Never cigar or pipe smokers and I think we'd all agree that those things give off more and far worse smoke than a good old fag. Right?'

'Right.'

'Thank you, Sarah. Let's see what Andy on line one has to say. Go ahead, Andy. By the way, where are you calling from? I can't quite make it out.'

'I'm on a mobile,' came the reply.

'And are you smoking?'

'No, and I wouldn't go out with a bird who did.'

'A bird. Now there's a phrase you don't hear very often, Andy. Political correctness passed you by with the same speed as freedom of choice obviously. Because that's what it comes down to in the end, isn't it? *Your* freedom not to go out with a woman who smokes and *my* choice to steer clear of Neanderthals like you.'

'You think you're clever, don't you?'

'Well, I haven't had an invite to the Mensa Christmas

party yet but I do my best. Do you think *you're* clever? But then again this is supposed to be a *serious* discussion, isn't it? I beg your pardon. Back to the cigarettes.'

'Fu—'

'That's it, Andy, just stick to the reasoned arguments. They seem to work better for you.' She turned off the line. 'Well, there goes Andy into the night. Take care women everywhere, if you want a smooth-talking devil like him to romance you, then ditch those Rothmans now.'

As she spoke, Amy glanced across at the two packages on her desk, wondering what could be inside.

One was about the shape and size of a shoe box, the other was flatter, a squashed Jiffy bag.

Both bore London postmarks.

'You never see people smoking on the television any more either – has anyone noticed that?' she continued. 'On old episodes of *Coronation Street* and on chat shows people used to come on puffing away, but not any more. It's a bad influence, you see. Obviously the people who run TV are afraid that the sight of a celebrity smoking will induce millions to run out and start chain-smoking.' She glanced at the monitor.

'David from Petts Wood, what have you got to say on this subject?' Amy said, flicking another switch.

'Well, I don't smoke,' David from Petts Wood said with a slow deliberation over each word that made it sound as if he was reading from a card.

'You should try it, David,' Amy insisted.

'My father died of lung cancer.'

'I'm sorry to hear that. Did he smoke?'

'No.'

Amy ran a hand through her hair.

'So, what you're trying to tell me is that even if you don't smoke you can still get cancer, David, is that right?' she said, realising that this caller was struggling.

No need to crucify the poor bastard.

'I think so, yes.'

'Quite right, David. You could smoke fifty fags a day

and never be ill. You could steer clear of cigarettes all your life and still get cancer. In fact, you could get hit by a bus tomorrow so you might as well go out and enjoy yourself. Don't you agree, David?'

'I've got cancer.'

Shit.

'I'm sorry to hear that, David,' Amy said quietly.

Don't let them hear you're shocked.

'Is it smoking related?' Amy asked.

'The doctor said it could have been hereditary, because of my father.'

Amy looked up towards the window of the control booth and saw Osborne frantically drawing his hand across his throat in a cutting motion.

Amy ignored him.

'Do you think it's wrong for people to smoke around you if they know you've got cancer?' she enquired.

'Well, it isn't going to make me any worse.'

Amy smiled. *Thank you, David from Petts Wood.*

'David, I want you to do something for me,' Amy said, leaning closer to the microphone. 'I want you to ring this show again in a week and let me know how you're getting on. Will you do that for me?'

'I'm having some more chemotherapy tomorrow.'

'Well, then you ring back tomorrow night if you feel up to it, but do me that favour, will you, David? You keep in touch with the show and let us all know how you're getting on.'

'All right.'

'You take care of yourself, David.'

She cut him off.

In the production booth Osborne shook his head and smiled.

Amy sipped at her coffee, scanned the flashing names and selected another.

'Frankie from Upton Park in the good old East End,' she said cheerily. 'How are you, Frankie, and what's your point?'

'That nurse, earlier, right. She was wrong about what she was saying about drugs, right?'

'Which part of what she said was wrong, Frankie?'

'If you let me finish, I'll tell you, won't I?'

'I beg your pardon. Please continue.'

'If you're on drugs, right, then you can't get help from people 'cos, like, it's against the law, right?'

'This is fascinating, Frankie, do go on. And on. And on.'

'Are you listening to me?'

'For about another five seconds unless you make your point.'

'Fags, drugs, drink. It's all the same. It's all a drug but it depends what you're taking, don't it? I mean, fags, right, they ain't like cocaine, are they?'

'No, it *is* easier to buy a packet of Superkings than a bag of cocaine at your corner shop, I'll give you that. Have you taken drugs, Frankie? You sound as if you might be on them at the moment.'

'I've dabbled.'

Frankie from Upton Park dissolved into fits of whooping laughter.

'You're history, Frankie. Ian from Kilburn,' she continued, taking the next call. 'Have you ever dabbled?'

'With drugs?' the caller asked. 'Just the odd spliff, you know. Nothing like cocaine or heroin.'

'Do I detect an Irish accent there, Ian?'

'Yes. Is it that obvious?'

'Fairly. Which part of Ireland are you from?'

'Cork.'

'How long have you lived in London?'

'About ten years.'

'And what were you phoning in about?'

'Well, it's the drugs thing really. I wanted to ask a question. I wanted to ask *you* a question.'

'Fire away, Ian, or maybe that's the wrong thing to say to an Irishman. What's your question?'

'You used to be a model and I read somewhere that

catwalk models and photographic models snort cocaine because it stops them feeling hungry. So if they don't feel hungry, they don't want to eat and that's what keeps them slim. Is that how you kept your figure when you were modelling?'

Amy looked up at the clock on the studio wall.

'Congratulations, Ian,' she said, grinning. 'You are the first caller on tonight's show to mention my modelling career. A mere one hour and seventeen minutes from the beginning of the show. I think that's a world record.'

'I didn't mean to be offensive, it's just that everyone knows you used to be a model and it's something I've always been curious about.'

'Ian, you flatter me. Perhaps everyone listening doesn't know that I was a model.'

'Ah, go on. You were a model for about six years, weren't you?'

'Seven actually.'

'So, did you take drugs to stay slim?'

'Drugs were available, most models will tell you that. I've always been lucky. I don't have to watch what I eat and it was a hectic career, lots of dashing about. There wasn't always *time* to eat. Anyway, enough about me—'

He interrupted her. 'Being on the go all the time, you must have got pretty horny with no boyfriend. Did you and any of the other girls ever—'

'Thank you, Ian,' said Amy, cutting him off. 'You're history, but I'll tell you something, that attempt at a question towards the end raises an interesting point for you guys listening out there. What is so fascinating about two women having sex? Why do you always want to watch? Why do you all think that a woman's secret fantasy is to sleep with another woman? Let me know.' She gave out the number to call.

Amy took another drag on her cigarette and selected one of the many waiting callers.

'Don from Southwark. Tell us about *your* fantasy.'

'I want to rape a woman.'

Three

'Why, Don?' Amy asked, her voice even.

'Because that's my fantasy. Some women fantasise about it too.'

'Do they? Which women?'

'Women say in magazines that they dream of being raped.'

'Some women fantasise about rough sex, Don, but there's a world of difference between fantasising about rough sex and actually doing it. Just like there's a difference between rough sex and rape. Have you ever been rough with a woman you've made love to, Don?'

'Not that rough.'

'What's your definition of rough then?'

'A couple of slaps, a bit of pulling. You know, ripping her clothes off and that.'

'And the women you did this with, they agreed?'

'Well, one of them got a bit uppity about it.'

'Was this one of the women you slapped?'

'It was only a bit of fun. I'd had a few to drink. It happens, doesn't it?'

'So, she didn't want sex with a drunken slob so you slapped her? Is that right?'

'She'd been giving me the come-on all night. She was dressed in this short black dress, her tits were hanging out nearly. She was begging for it.'

'Was this your girlfriend?'

'I'd known her for a few months, we went out for a meal, hit a couple of clubs and then went back to her place. When it got round to time to do the business she bottled it. Said she wanted me to go home. Well, I wasn't having that. She'd been giving me the green light ever since I picked her up.'

'So you slapped her and had sex with her?'

'Yeah.'

'You had sex with her against her will? You raped her.'

'No. She enjoyed it after a while. I didn't hurt her.'

'You hit her. You had sex with her when she didn't want it. Wake up, Don. That was rape.'

'She enjoyed it.'

'Did she tell you that?'

'She didn't have to *tell* me.'

'Oh, I see, your incredible prowess as a lover was enough to let you know that she was satisfied. Is that right? So, Don, if that wasn't rape, what would be in your limited view? Your fantasy is to rape a woman – how would that fantasy differ from what you did to your girlfriend? You tell me what is different about rape?'

'With rape you'd have to hold the woman down, wouldn't you? She'd be spitting at you and fighting you, wouldn't she?'

'Has a woman ever spat in your face, Don?'

'No way.'

'Perhaps one should. Perhaps they should spit in your face, kick you in the nuts then stamp on your head with their stilettos. How do you think that would feel, Don? Or perhaps having your testicles shut in a vice might be more appropriate. Do you think you'd still feel like sex after that? Because that's probably how much your girlfriend felt like sex after you'd slapped her and forced yourself on her.'

'That's the sort of thing I expected you to say. I bet you'd like it rough, wouldn't you? I've seen your pictures in magazines, showing off your tits and arse. I bet you can't get enough of it—'

'Well, I've certainly had enough of you, Don, you moron. Crawl back under your stone.' Amy shook her head.

Fucking arsehole.

'Well, there goes Don into the night,' she continued.

'A plain, old-fashioned kind of guy. None of your "new man" rubbish for Don. A straitjacket might be an idea though. Let's see what our next and, hopefully, sane caller has to say. Go ahead, Emma from Camden.'

'Hello,' said Emma from Camden. 'I'd like to say firstly that I thought you dealt with that last dickhead . . .'

There was an awkward silence.

'I'm sorry, is it all right to say that?' Emma from Camden asked.

'What? Dickhead?' said Amy, smiling. 'I don't think they'll take me off the air for that, Emma.'

'Oh, good, because I thought he was a complete prat. That's just typical of some men's attitudes to women, isn't it? I mean—'

'You can make your point any time you like, Emma.'

'Sorry, yes, I was ringing in about fantasies. You know, sexual fantasies.'

'They were the ones I had in mind.'

'Well, what you said about men imagining two women in bed together – I agree with you that it's predictable but I also agree that most women would do it given the chance.'

'You think that most women would sleep with another woman if they had the chance?'

'Well, I don't think there's anything wrong with it.'

'Have you ever slept with another woman, Emma?'

'No, but my boyfriend wants me to.'

'Your *boyfriend* wants you to? And how do you feel about it? Who does he want you to sleep with?'

'My best friend, Kim.'

'Does Kim know this?'

'Not yet. My boyfriend wants me to talk her into a threesome. He's always going on about it. He says we should experiment with our sex lives.'

'That's a good idea, Emma. What's your boyfriend's best friend called?'

'Tony.'

'Well, as soon as you've persuaded Kim to sleep with

you and your boyfriend then get your boyfriend to go and arrange a threesome with him, you and Tony. How would you like that? Or more to the point, see how *he* likes that. What's your boyfriend's name?'

'Paul.'

'Well, if Paul wants to watch you and Kim having sex, tell him that you'd like *him* to watch while you have sex with Tony. How about that?'

There was a silence on the other end of the line.

Amy sucked on her cigarette.

'He says that he *needs* to do it before we get married,' Emma from Camden said. 'He says that it's his fantasy, that he needs to get it out of his system or he might be tempted to do it some time in the future.'

'So, you're thinking of getting married, are you, Emma? Has Paul made any other demands like this? Does he feel he has to sleep with an entire women's football team to get it out of his system before he gets married? Does he feel the need to fly off to Spain with his mates for one last lads' holiday before the big day? Stuff like that?'

'No, just the threesome. Do you think it's wrong then?'

'I'm not an agony aunt, Emma, but can't you see he's holding you to ransom here? He's blackmailing you emotionally. Either you arrange a threesome or he's threatening you with an affair later in your marriage.'

'But I do quite fancy Kim myself.'

There was a giggle at the other end of the line.

'Then sleep with her and tell him about it afterwards or make him a video,' said Amy, stubbing out her cigarette. 'Better still, make him a video of you, Kim and Tony. That should keep him happy for hours.'

Amy flicked a switch and went to another call.

'Hi, there, Peter from Muswell Hill,' she said, cheerfully. 'I've had a few calls from Muswell Hill tonight. There—'

'Did you get the package?' The voice was low and even.

'I've got a couple of packages here, Peter,' Amy told him. 'How do I know which one's from you?'

'It's in brown paper,' said the monotone voice, 'inside the Jiffy bag.'

'Will I like what's in it?'

'Just open it and find out.'

In the production booth Mike Osborne was already on his feet. He moved towards the glass partition, peering in anxiously at Amy.

Without a second thought and, as yet, unable to see Osborne, she pulled the package towards her.

Four

'Go on, open it.'

The voice seemed to reverberate around the studio.

'This is when you wish you were on television instead of radio, isn't it?' said Amy. 'So everyone can share the excitement.' She looked up and saw Osborne standing at the production-room window. He was pointing to the package and shaking his head.

Amy merely shrugged and reached for a pair of scissors to cut through the masking tape that sealed the top of the bag.

Beneath the brown tape, staples had also been used to secure the package.

'Do you do your Christmas presents up like this, Peter?' Amy said humourlessly.

At the other end of the line she could hear faint breathing.

'Well, ladies and gentlemen, listening out there,' she said, pulling the last of the masking tape free, 'I have undone the first part of the package. Exciting, isn't it?'

Osborne was scribbling something on a piece of card using a marker pen.

He pressed it to the glass.

It read: IT COULD BE A BOMB.

Amy read it as she prepared to undo the staples.

'Give me a clue what's in it, Peter?' she said into the microphone.

'Something for *you*,' the voice said softly. 'I listen to your show every night. I agree with everything you say.'

'Now that's my kind of man,' Amy said and chuckled.

She started on the staples using a pair of scissors to prise the metal free.

Osborne banged on the glass again and gestured even more frantically towards the sign.

Amy found that she could focus on only one of the hastily scrawled words now – BOMB.

She removed another of the staples.

'I've been listening to you for the last year,' said the voice. 'I've got photos of you. I even tape the programmes every night. And when you're on television, I videotape you.'

'What do you do for a living, Peter?'

BOMB.

Leave it there now. Leave it on the desk top.

'I haven't got a job.'

Leave the fucking package alone.

She freed the final staple.

Amy looked up at Osborne then pulled open the package.

There was a pungent smell coming from inside the Jiffy bag. A musty, familiar odour.

'Have you got it open yet?' the voice asked.

Amy used a pencil to feel inside the bag.

There was something soft in there.

She reached in with the tip of a finger.

It felt like material.

Silk.

The smell was growing stronger.

She used the scissors to cut down the side of the bag, opening it carefully and slowly, aware of both Osborne and Jo now watching her through the glass.

Why the hell was that smell familiar?

She used the pencil to lift out the contents of the bag.

'Well, Peter, just what I always wanted,' she said quietly.

The silk camisole dangled harmlessly on the end of the pencil.

Osborne placed both hands on his cheeks, a look of relief spreading across his features.

'I thought about you when I was picking them out,'

the voice told her, a note of excitement creeping into it. 'I pictured you in them.'

There was a pair of grip-top stockings in the bag too.

Both the camisole and the stockings were spattered with semen.

'That's *my* fantasy,' said the voice.

A chuckle.

Amy dropped the camisole, the stink of stale ejaculate strong in her nostrils.

'You'd look beautiful in them,' the voice purred. 'You'd look beautiful in anything. I'd like to see you in them one day. Perhaps we could meet.'

'That's very kind, Peter,' Amy said, gazing at the semen-stained stockings. 'I think I'm busy until the year two thousand and twenty.'

Another chuckle at the other end of the line.

'I like a woman with a sense of humour.'

'That isn't your first criterion, is it, Peter? I would have thought a pulse might have been top of the list. Or maybe not in your case.'

Amy lifted one of the white-flecked stockings up on the tip of the pencil so that Osborne could see it, then, with her free hand, she made a circle with her thumb and forefinger and shook them in the air.

The producer nodded.

'I'd do anything for you,' said the voice, then hung up.

'Well, it's not often someone cuts *me* off,' Amy said, pushing the camisole and stockings off the desk on to the floor.

The smell still clogged her nostrils.

'We're coming up to the news in about twenty seconds,' Amy said, glancing down at the crumpled clothes. 'Perhaps there'll be something worth talking about after we've heard it. You know the number to call.'

'*I'd do anything for you.*'

When she looked up again, Mike Osborne was still standing at the window of the production booth. He was shaking his head slowly.

Amy waved him away then glanced at the second package on her desk.

'Here's the news,' she said into the microphone. 'Listen carefully, I'll be asking questions later.'

She switched off the microphone.

When she looked back towards the window of the production booth Osborne was gone.

She reached for the other package.

Five

'Don't open it.'

Amy turned to see Osborne entering the studio, pointing at the package. 'You don't know *what* could be inside.'

'Probably more of that,' said Amy, motioning towards the pile of semen-spattered clothes beneath the desk.

'Sick fucker,' Osborne said contemptuously. 'I'll get someone in to clean it up.'

He noticed that Amy had the other package in her hand now.

'Amy, put it down, I'll call Security,' he told her. 'Let them deal with it.'

'Stop panicking, Mike.'

'It could be a bomb or anything.'

'People might not like everything I have to say but I doubt if anyone hates me enough to send me a bomb.'

'You'd be surprised,' he said, raising an eyebrow.

'Thanks for the vote of confidence. Look, it's just weirdo mail, Mike, nothing else.'

Before he could stop her, Amy had ripped off the brown paper covering to reveal a cardboard box. She shot him a challenging glance then lifted the lid.

Osborne flinched involuntarily.

'You're getting paranoid in your old age, Mike,' said Amy, smiling.

She turned the box towards him so that he could see its contents.

There was a box of chocolates inside, complete with a red foil bow stuck carefully on at one end. A small note was attached, which she read aloud. 'I love the programme, I hope you like these chocolates, lots of love, Stuart Gardiner.'

She pushed the box towards him. 'Want one? I'll save you the nut cluster.'

'Don't eat any of those,' Osborne insisted. 'They could be injected with poison or anything.'

'Have you been reading too many Agatha Christie novels, Mike?'

'Just bin the fucking things, will you? Make me feel better. Christ almighty, clothes that have been wanked on, poisoned chocolates. Who knows what—'

'No one says they've been poisoned,' Amy interrupted. 'Jesus, you *are* paranoid. But don't worry, I won't eat them. Happy now?'

'I put a trace on that last call by the way,' Osborne told her. 'The bastard who sent *those*.' He pointed towards the soiled camisole and stockings.

'What for?'

'Because he's a fucking weirdo.'

'Half the people who call this programme are fucking weirdos, Mike, you know that. The guy is harmless, trust me.'

'How can you be so sure?'

'Because I've had calls like that before, dozens of them.'

'And how many times has someone sent you clothes he's shot his load over?'

'I've been threatened with beatings, rape and Christ knows what else since this show started, and yet tonight is the first time you've reacted like this. Just cool it, Mike. The guy isn't dangerous, I'd bet money on it.' She took a drag on her cigarette. 'How long have we been doing this programme now? Eighteen months?'

He nodded.

'Nothing's happened yet and it's not likely to,' she said with an air of assurance that Osborne didn't share.

He glanced up at the studio clock.

'You're back on in fifty seconds,' he said flatly, turning towards the door. 'Don't blame me for being concerned, Amy.'

'I appreciate it, but don't worry. I can look after myself.
I'm a big girl now.'

He looked up at the clock again.

'Thirty seconds,' he said and left.

She was alone in the studio again.

Six

Amy rubbed her eyes as she sat back from the microphone, listening to the tirade of words in her headset. Reaching for her coffee she took a sip, wincing when she found it was cold.

It felt chilly inside the studio and she made a mental note to check the heating at the next break.

Meanwhile, John from Fulham forged on, his words sometimes faltering. There was passion in his sentiments, anger even, but, she decided, enough was enough.

'Okay, slow down, John, I get your point,' she said, in an effort to halt the verbal barrage. 'So, what kind of role models would you like to see for kids?'

'Well, I suppose it should be their parents ideally but it doesn't work like that, does it?'

'Did you look up to *your* father?'

'Yes, he had his own business. I used to go out drinking with him at the weekends. He was everything I wanted to be.'

'What kind of business did he have?'

'He was a baker. He worked hard six days a week then he used to go out drinking on Saturday and Sunday.'

'And you went with him? How old were you then?'

'In my early twenties.'

'Didn't you have friends you could have gone out drinking with? I mean, it's a bit odd a bloke of twenty-two or twenty-three going down the pub with his dad, isn't it? That would be like a teenage girl wanting to go clubbing with her middle-aged mum.'

'What are you implying?'

'I'm not implying anything, John, I'm just curious. Did any of the other blokes your age go drinking with their fathers?'

'I don't know what the others were doing. That was their business, not mine. I went down the pub with my dad and his friends, that was what I wanted, I—'

'Hold on, John, rewind for a second. You went down the pub with your dad and his friends. So there you were, in your early twenties, surrounded by all these middle-aged men who you couldn't possibly hope to have anything in common with.'

'We talked about football.'

'Not the most expansive topic, John. You should have been out with guys your own age, chasing women, stuff like that. Are you married?'

'Yes, I have been for thirty years.'

'Kids?'

'A boy.'

'And does he look up to you the way you looked up to your father?'

'I would imagine so.'

'John, how can you say that? What have you given him to look up to? What have you given him to aspire to? Are you a good role model for him?'

'I work hard, I'm honest. Why shouldn't he look up to me?'

'Does he live at home?'

'No, he moved out when he was twenty-two. He's married now.'

'What does he do for a living?'

'He's a musician.'

'Do I detect a note of sarcasm in your voice, John? What's wrong with that? He earns money doing it, doesn't he? He makes enough to look after his own life, doesn't he?'

'He's a dreamer. He thinks one day he'll be in a pop group or something.'

'And perhaps he will. Didn't *you* ever have dreams when you were his age? Or was your only ambition to be like your father?'

'At least my father had a trade and I wanted a trade. I

didn't daydream about some hairbrained thing like being a musician.'

'So you never had any dreams?'

'I was more practical.'

'There must have been something you always wanted. Everyone has dreams, John. Everyone has something that they secretly long to do. Very few of us ever manage it but we all have dreams. If you don't you might as well be dead.'

'That's pathetic.'

'It's true, John and, I'm afraid,' she flicked a switch, 'you're history.'

She chose line four and the next caller stuttered on to the airwaves.

'Am I on?' said a hesitant voice.

'Joe from Romford, yes, you're on. Anything to add to this debate?'

'Well, I agree with that last bloke about kids not having anyone to look up to – well, they have but the people they look up to aren't worth looking up to, if you know what I mean.'

'Well, it took a bit of deciphering but I think I get your drift, Joe. Have you got kids of your own?'

'Leave off.' A chuckle. 'I'm only twenty-three. I don't want kids yet, do I? No, I'm talking about my young brother and sister. They're eleven and twelve. The boy's older, you know.'

'And they look up to what kind of people, Joe?'

'Well, you know, like pop stars and celebrities and these bloody nobodies in soap operas, people on the telly, that kind of person. I mean, that can't be right, can it?'

'Why, Joe?'

'Well, they're nobodies, aren't they?'

'Who?'

'These soap actors and actresses. I mean, you can't open the bloody papers or turn on the telly without seeing their faces. Or the women in them are having babies and selling the pictures to newspapers and magazines for bloody fortunes. It's not right. Or then one of them comes out and says he had a drink or a drugs' problem and he sells his bloody story to the papers for a fortune too. I mean, who gives a toss?'

'The public, Joe. That's why they read newspapers. Do you know how many million people a week watch soap operas?'

'Yeah, lots, but that's not the point. What I'm saying is, they think they're big stars, don't they? But they're nobodies. I mean, if people ask them for their autographs then they have to sign the name of the character they act as, because no one knows who the bloody hell they are in real life. And they say they're fed up with being in soaps, so they chuck it in to go off to Hollywood to become big stars and then, six months later, they come crawling back wanting their old part back in the bloody soap opera because it's the only thing they can act in. They haven't got the talent to do anything else, they just think they're so high and bloody mighty when they're just nobodies. And they get paid a fortune too.'

'Do you watch soaps yourself, Joe?'

'Sometimes, but my brother and sister watch them all the time and those Australian ones are even worse and then what happens? Every Christmas, half a dozen of them come over here and do bloody pantomimes. I mean, that can't be right, can it? A bunch of bloody Aussies coming over here and their acting's worse than the prats in our own soaps.'

'What do you think of the soap stars who start singing careers?'

'Well, that's out of order, isn't it? I mean, any of these so-called celebrities who've been on telly for more than six weeks, they think they can do any bloody thing. Sing, dance, tell jokes and the biggest joke of all is they can't even bloody act. They can't even do the thing they're supposed to be good at. I mean good actors are people like that bloke out of *The Godfather*.'

'Marlon Brando?'

'No, the other one. The short bloke who was in *Heat*.'

'Al Pacino.'

'Yeah, him. I mean, he was brilliant in that *Scarface* too. He's what you call an actor, not some bloody nobody in a soap opera.'

'I think your chances of seeing Al Pacino in *Eastenders* is pretty slim, Joe.'

'I *know* that.'

'What about Robert de Niro in *Coronation Street*?'

A laugh on the other end of the line. 'Yeah, or Tom Cruise in *Brookside*. That'd be a laugh.'

'Thanks for your call, Joe,' Amy said. 'How about any other suggestions for superstars in soaps? Stallone in *Home and Away*? Mel Gibson in *Neighbours*?' She glanced at the list of callers. 'Wendy from Peckham, what do *you* think?'

'I think you've got a bloody nerve,' said Wendy from Peckham. 'I mean, you got where you are today by putting it about with showbiz types, didn't you?'

'Would you like to be more specific, Wendy,' said Amy, lighting another cigarette.

'You were a model, weren't you?'

'That's right. I'm not ashamed of it. Why should I be?'

'I didn't say you should. I'm just saying. You were a model, you met lots of famous people, you went out with a drummer in a rock band, some famous writer, a TV producer. Next thing you know, you've got your own radio show. Still, they say it's not what you know but who you know, don't they?'

'And where did you pick up all these penetrating details about my private life, Wendy?'

'From the newspapers.'

'And you believe everything you read in newspapers, do you?'

'It was true though, wasn't it?'

'I did go out with a drummer and a writer, yes.'

'And he was married, wasn't he?'

'Separated actually. We were both unattached, it wasn't an affair despite what the papers said.'

'Whatever. You slept around with people in showbiz and now you've got your own radio show.'

Amy laughed. 'I wish it had been that easy, Wendy, I'd have done it years ago. Either that or I'd have slept with an executive from Warner Brothers and I'd be in charge of a film studio now.' She blew out a stream of smoke. 'When I finished modelling I was invited on a television show as a fashion consultant, I also did a number of radio interviews and I was offered a nightly spot on one of them to talk about fashion and the fashion business. It turned into a phone-in because it was so popular and after that I was offered *this* show. I feel I worked for this, Wendy; I'm sorry you don't but you're entitled to your opinion. Just as I'm entitled to the opinion that you're jealous of what I do.'

'Jealous of taking my clothes off so that men can stare at me – I don't think so.'

'Why, is your body that awful, Wendy?'

'There's nothing wrong with my body. I just don't want the whole world seeing it. I mean, you can't have much self-respect to do a thing like that and it's hardly a difficult job, is it, nor is sitting in a radio studio talking to people.'

'What do you do for a living, Wendy?'

'I'm a hairdresser.'

'So what would you do if someone offered you fifty thousand pounds to strip off for a magazine?'

'I'd tell them to stuff the money, because I've got too much self-respect. The only person who sees *me* naked is my boyfriend, and *he* never complains. He thinks I've got a great body and I didn't sleep with him just because he's got lots of money.'

'Meaning what, Wendy?'

'Well, when women like you sleep with men, it's always the rich ones, isn't it?'

'Hey, hey, hey, what do you mean? Women like me. What kind of woman would that be?'

'Well, you knew it would further your career by sleeping with rich men.'

'I had enough money of my own, Wendy, I didn't need a rich man to pay my bills.'

'That drummer you slept with, you wouldn't have looked at him twice if he'd been a plumber. Or that writer, if he hadn't been well known, you wouldn't have gone near him. You slept with them because of what they had, not what they were. All you were interested in was the money and the fame.'

'Wendy, how is it possible to be bitter, jealous, vindictive and stupid all at the same time? I'd love you to tell me.'

'I'm not jealous!'

The words were shouted with such vehemence that Amy sat back and slipped one earpiece off.

'Okay, I'll make do with vindictive,' Amy persisted.

'You people are all the same – it's like the man before said – all these so-called celebrities, they get paid hundreds of thousands a year and then they moan because they've got a hard life. Well, if they don't like it why don't they go and do a job in Tesco's or something. They complain when they're photographed coming out of restaurants – well then, why do they always go to restaurants where they know the photographers will be? They'd be more upset if they *didn't* get photographed. They *want* people to see them. And the men are even worse. These ugly men always have beautiful women around them because they've got money, not because of who they are. If they had nothing then none of these beautiful women would want to know them. But they're too stupid or big-headed to realise that. They've got no personality, they don't need one because they've got money. Not like ordinary people.'

'So if you won the lottery and loads of men started hanging around you, wouldn't you think it was a little bit suspicious, Wendy? Wouldn't they be after you for your money?'

'But I'd have my boyfriend. I wouldn't want any other men.'

'And what if your boyfriend only stayed with you because you had money? What if he secretly despised you? He might not think that much of you now. He might just be with you because you're good in bed, or good looking. He might just be using you until another better-looking alternative comes along. How do you know he's not cheating on you as we speak?'

'He wouldn't do that.'

'Is your knowledge of men as specialised as your knowledge of showbiz, Wendy? Most men will stray given the chance.'

'Not *my* boyfriend.'

'That's very naive, Wendy. What makes your boyfriend so special?'

'He agrees with me on everything. We never argue.'

'Perhaps your lives are so empty you have nothing to argue about. Is your life lacking passion so badly, Wendy? If it is I feel sorry for you.'

'I don't want you to feel sorry for me,' Wendy from Peckham shouted angrily. 'Not you or any of your showbiz friends, those overpaid, overrated bastards. All they want to do is get their faces on television and in the papers. They take so much and give nothing back. When I have kids I don't want them looking up to scum like that. I want them to look up to nurses and doctors and teachers. People who *give* something to society instead of sucking it dry.'

The line went dead.

Amy looked towards the production booth and shrugged.

Osborne was standing close to the glass looking at her, shaking his head slowly.

She connected another caller.

'Peter from Muswell Hill,' Amy said, again looking towards the production booth, and this time her brow was furrowed. 'Twice in one night. I *am* privileged.'

'That whore who just insulted you,' the voice said flatly. 'Someone should do something about her.'

'Like what, Peter,' Amy said, smiling.

'Kill her.'

Click. The line went dead.

Seven

'Perhaps I should get a job reading the fucking weather,' said Amy, pushing the door of the production booth closed and slumping against it. She blew out her cheeks and stood motionless for a moment. Then she crossed to a table at the rear of the small room where a pot of coffee, one of tea, some milk and a plate of biscuits stood. She poured herself a coffee and flopped into one of the high-backed swivel chairs next to the table, reaching for a bourbon, which she pushed into her mouth piece by piece.

Jo Parker joined her and poured herself a coffee.

'If you can't stand the heat . . .' Mike Osborne called from behind the mixing desk where he was scribbling something furiously on to a pad.

'Up yours, Mike,' Amy called back, reaching for another biscuit.

'Another witty comeback from the queen of the airwaves,' Osborne chuckled. 'What's wrong, anyway? It was a good show tonight.'

'Yeah, after all, it's not every night I get sent some underwear, is it? Even if the bloke has wiped his knob on it first,' Amy said, lighting a cigarette.

'The bloke who sent those things must be really sick,' said Jo quietly.

'It could have been worse, Jo.' She turned towards Osborne. 'It could have been a bomb, couldn't it, Mike?' She grinned.

Carrying a sheaf of papers, Osborne joined them, topping up his own cup of coffee.

'You can laugh,' he said, pointing a finger at her. 'You had no way of knowing what was in that package. Some of the nutters who ring this show – I wouldn't put *anything* past them.'

'I'd have been sick,' said Jo, shuddering. 'I mean, fancy wanking over them.'

'He must have money to burn, the camisole looked decent quality,' Amy mused. 'Perhaps I ought to get it back from Security and get it cleaned.'

'Now that *is* sick,' said Osborne, smiling. He took a sip of his coffee and headed for the door. 'I'll be back in a minute. Jo, order cabs all round, will you?'

And he was gone.

'He says that every night,' Jo muttered. 'And every night he knows I do it before the show even starts. What does he think I am, stupid?'

Amy regarded her warily for a moment then leaned forward.

'I don't think it was a trick question, Jo,' she said quietly, a smile playing on her lips.

'Sorry, I didn't mean to snap but sometimes I think Mike gets the impression I'm some bloody YTS trainee. I have been here for nearly two years.'

'Well, *I* appreciate you.'

Jo managed a smile.

'Do you fancy going on to a club or something?' Amy asked. 'I could murder a drink.'

'No thanks, Amy. You go. I'm not in the mood. Another time perhaps.'

'Are you okay, Jo?'

'I'm fine, why do you ask?'

'Just curious. No, make that concerned. You've been quiet for the past three or four days. It's not like you.'

'Thanks a lot,' Jo said, smiling.

'You know what I mean. Is something wrong?'

Jo shook her head.

'I'm tired, that's all,' she said. 'I've got a few things on my mind.'

'But nothing you want to talk about?'

'No, but thanks for asking. I didn't know I was making it that obvious there was something wrong.'

'Like I say, if you want to talk.'

The door of the production office opened and Osborne walked back in.

He pulled on his coat.

'Come on then, you two,' he urged. 'Unless you want to spend all night here.'

'No thanks, three hours is quite enough for me,' Amy insisted, pulling on her own jacket.

Jo snatched up her handbag and coat and the three of them headed for the lift, passing framed photos of some of the station's other presenters as they made their way down the corridor. The sightless eyes followed their passage.

Amy looked at her own picture as they waited for the lift to arrive. Her hair was shorter in the photo, cut into a bob that brushed her collar. Now her blond locks reached well past her shoulders.

'Christ, I look so young in that picture,' she said. 'It's depressing.'

'You're not exactly ready to draw your pension, Amy,' Jo said, smiling.

'You look angelic,' said Osborne, chuckling. 'Almost untouched.' He cracked out laughing.

Amy punched him playfully on the arm as the lift arrived.

They rode it to the ground floor.

The security guard who sat behind the desk in the marbled foyer was reading a well-thumbed copy of *Maxim* magazine. He looked up and nodded, hitting a button on the control panel to open the electronic main door of the building.

There were three cabs parked outside.

Amy pulled up the collar of her jacket against a sudden icy blast of wind that swept across Bedford Square.

'Are you sure you don't fancy that drink?' she said to Jo but the younger woman shook her head.

'I'll see you tomorrow,' she said and scurried across to one of the waiting taxis.

'What drink?' said Osborne, watching as Jo clambered into the cab. He and Amy watched it pull away.

'I was going to drop into a club before I went home,' Amy told him. 'I fancied a drink.'

'Do you want some company then?' he asked, still not looking at her.

'Jo wanted to get home.'

'Good for Jo. Do you still want that drink?'

'I'll have one when I get home.'

'Is that a "no", Amy?'

'I didn't hear you ask, Mike.'

'Do you fancy a drink with me?'

'Not tonight.'

She squeezed his arm gently and took a step towards her waiting cab.

'You wouldn't have said "no" a year ago,' he told her.

She turned, one hand on the cab's door handle.

'A year is a long time,' she reminded him, smiling.

He watched as she climbed into the cab, watched as it pulled away, its brake lights flaring red as it turned a corner out of sight.

Osborne walked to his own cab.

Another blast of cold air swept across Bedford Square.

Eight

The first thing that struck Amy Watson was the silence. *It was always the silence.* And she hated it.

She locked the door of her first-floor flat and hung up her coat, the silence closing around her like an oppressive, invisible fist. Even before she flicked on any lights she crossed first to the television set then to the stack system and switched them both on.

She pressed the Mute button on the TV remote, glancing at the silent screen for a moment, the sound of music from the hi-fi floating on the air. Only then did she seek out the lamps dotted around the room and begin turning them on, each one making its own pool of soft light in the darkness.

Amy kicked off her boots and padded over to the small drinks' cabinet where she poured herself a measure of Jim Beam. She sipped at it, feeling the amber liquid burn its way to her stomach. It was cold outside but her central heating was timed to come on at midnight. The flat was warm and cosy.

What about welcoming?

Amy took another sip of the drink.

It would have been more welcoming with the presence of someone else.

She glanced at the television, at some cookery programme, (*who the hell would be learning to cook at 2.45 in the morning?*) then at the stack system. She crossed to it and changed the CD, slipping the latest Clannad album in. Amy lowered the volume then wandered into the kitchen, still clutching her drink. She could still hear the music in the other room but she felt sure that it would not disturb the other residents of the building.

There were five other flats in the large building in

Northampton Square. One on the same floor. Two above her and two below. She saw little of the other residents, due in part to the unusual (or ungodly, she sometimes thought) hours she worked. The flat on the same floor as hers was occupied by a divorced man in his fifties who, as far as she could remember, worked at Lincoln's Inn in some legal capacity. He was a slim, grey-haired individual she knew only as Mr Greaves. He was the longest serving resident and he'd been there when she bought the flat five years earlier.

Immediately above her were a couple in their thirties who she'd spoken to a few times. Michael and Patricia. She hadn't a clue what either of them did for a living, only that they weren't married and that Patricia had moved out for three weeks about nine months ago, presumably over some row Amy had been fortunate enough to miss.

The other flat on the second floor was occupied by one Karen Walsh, who was a year or two older than Amy. She was the marketing manager for a large cosmetics firm and was hardly ever there. The two women had spoken a handful of times, even had coffee together in Karen's flat but, apart from that perfunctory attempt at community spirit, they had seen little of each other since then.

Below her were George and Vanessa Seaton, both in their forties. They had a son who occasionally stayed with them but, as with Michael and Patricia above her, Amy hadn't a clue what the Seatons did for a living. Meetings with them had been even rarer.

The other flat, directly below her, was empty. It had been for about a year now. Previously occupied by a freelance journalist whose name she'd forgotten. Amy had discovered that the man had done a runner one night, taking all he could carry with him. Exactly why, she never did discover. She didn't really care either.

The residents of the flats, like so many in London, were living proof of how easy it was to live in close proximity to others while remaining blissfully ignorant of the details of their lives. Her fellow tenants, she assumed, were as uninformed about *her* as she was about *them*. It was a situation that suited everyone. People tended to keep themselves to themselves. Cocooned within their own little worlds, very few found the need to venture beyond.

And Amy was content to be on nodding terms with her fellow residents. She wanted no more. She *needed* no more.

So what about the loneliness?

She took another sip of Jim Beam. She was alone. Not lonely, she told herself.

Are you fooling yourself?

There had been men in the past. Too many, she sometimes thought in her more prudish moments. She'd fallen in love before. How many times? Twice? Three times?

Four long-term relationships and quite a few – *how many was 'quite a few'? It was a convenient euphemism* – liaisons.

Good word.

The surroundings, the people, the business had all contributed to her enthusiasm – *another euphemism?* – with the men she'd shared beds with over the years.

There had been no one in her life for over a year now. Certainly not on a regular basis. It was a complication she was happy without.

Wasn't it?

What the hell. She wasn't looking, but if the right man came along then . . .

She smiled to herself and moved through the kitchen without turning on the fluorescent lights. She fumbled in the fridge for the remnants of a fruit salad she'd bought the day before.

There was a Danish pastry on the top shelf but, other than that, the fridge was full of salad stuff, low calorie drinks, mineral water, low-fat cheese and lean meat. It was a culinary legacy of her modelling days. The Jim Beam hadn't always been on the menu then but Amy had always enjoyed a drink. She finished it and set the glass down on the draining board, before making her way back through the sitting room clutching a chicken leg she'd taken from the fridge. She nibbled at it as she passed the silent, flickering television, heading for the bathroom.

She turned on the shower, finished the chicken leg and dropped the remains into a small bin beside the toilet, then she quickly undressed and stepped beneath the cleansing jets of water, enjoying the feel of the stinging water against her skin.

Amy thought that she might sit and watch television or listen to some music when she'd finished in the shower. She needed something to help her sleep. She felt like this every night after the show. It was difficult to switch off. The adrenaline that flowed so quickly during the programme still coursed through her veins.

Perhaps she would read. The flat was full of books, mostly paperbacks. Most unread. She bought a lot of them but read very few. There were some in her bedroom that she tended to scan over and over again. She was confortable with them.

One in particular. It was signed and dated. That date now four years old. He'd signed it for her one night as they lay in his bed in the hotel in Mayfair. Their love-making over for that night they had talked into the small hours and she had asked him to sign a book for her. It had amused him but he'd done it, written something special on the title page for her in that sweeping scrawl of his.

The affair had lasted three years, then just petered out like the dying embers of an untended fire. One day they had lunch together, the next he was gone. She hadn't seen him, other than on television or in magazines, for eighteen months but there wasn't a day that passed that she didn't think of him.

And sometimes those thoughts were tinged with anger. She wondered *why* he'd allowed their relationship to disintegrate so rapidly. Why he couldn't at least have called her once or twice. After all, he had been the one who had pursued her so single-mindedly when the affair had begun.

When she stopped to think about it, the situation was maddening. And yet pride had prevented her from contacting him.

On two occasions she'd written to him via his publishers, never sure whether the letters had reached him or whether he'd merely chosen to ignore them. She'd even phoned there once and asked for his number. Just the sound of his voice would have been enough for her.

Wouldn't it?

She closed her eyes tightly as she felt the shower spray splashing her face.

No, it wouldn't have been enough, would it?

If she'd spoken to him again she would have wanted to see him again, wanted to touch him.

To love him again?

He had a book out at the moment; she'd seen it in a book shop a week ago. It was dedicated to his new-born son. She hadn't bought it.

Amy switched off the shower, slipped on a bathrobe and padded back into the sitting room.

The news was on television so she turned up the volume, drew her slender legs up beneath her on the sofa and watched as the stories unfolded. A child abuse ring in North London. A plane crash.

It was the final story that made her sit up.

Nine

Jo Parker sat bolt upright as she heard the sound of a key in the door. It took her a couple of seconds to realise that it wasn't *her* door but the flat across the landing. She heard muffled voices, a muted chuckle then a loud bang as the door was closed once more.

She exhaled wearily and lay back down, rolling over on to first one side then the other, eyes clamped tightly shut in the hope that this would hasten the onset of sleep.

It didn't.

She rolled on to her back, eyes now open and gazing at the ceiling, her glance alighting on a crack in the artex. She traced the black blemish as if it were a river on a map. There were other cracks in the ceiling. The room needed redecorating, she thought. In fact, the entire flat needed redecorating. She'd been meaning to do the job ever since she moved in ten months ago, but she seemed to have neither time nor inclination lately.

Jo rolled over on to her side and looked at her wardrobe, one door slightly open where a hinge was broken. Something else that needed fixing. *Everything needed bloody fixing.*

She remembered, as a child, she had had a wardrobe in her room. A big wooden antique piece of furniture that seemed to be more like an heirloom than a place to store clothes. It had, her mother told her, been in the family for eighty years. A little bit different to the flimsy IKEA structure that held most of her clothes at the moment. The only thing the two pieces of furniture had in common was that they had faulty hinges. The doors of both would not close properly and, at night, when she'd been a child, she had stared in fear at that heavy wooden door, convinced that some unspeakable creature lived within its black depths. Lurking behind the coats and dresses.

She believed it because her older brother had told her that every wardrobe had a monster inside it, especially old ones like the one in her room. He didn't have to worry because he only had a small wardrobe and two chests of drawers, but she was in big trouble with that old antique in her room.

She smiled as she recalled his words, the smile fading quickly. Danny had left home when she was eighteen, intent, as he'd put it, on seeing the world. Her parents had tried to stop him but he had saved enough money from his two weekend jobs to be able to go. He and his friend he was travelling with would find work in the places they visited. There was nothing for anyone to worry about. He'd be back in a year or two unless he settled in one of those fabulous far-off places.

Jo could remember waving him off from the airport as he and his friend caught the flight to the South of France. She had cried and he had teased her for it, then he had hugged her, told her he loved her and disappeared out of her life. Postcards had arrived with surprising regularity for the first five months from locations as exotic and far flung as Egypt, Turkey, Greece and several parts of the United States. Jo, then just fifteen, had taken them into school to show her friends. Then they'd stopped.

The next communication to arrive was an official one. It was postmarked Bangkok. Her brother was dead. He'd been working as a barman in a nightclub and been involved in a fight. His hand had been badly gashed with a broken bottle. Somehow, the communique didn't say how, the wound had become infected and Danny had been rushed into a Bangkok hospital. The treatment he'd been given had not worked. His condition had grown steadily worse.

It had taken him two months to die.

She could still remember her mother crying late into the night on most nights, while she herself sobbed in her own room, glaring at the half-open wardrobe door, thinking that whatever lurked within couldn't be anywhere near as bad as the reality she and her family were living through.

His body arrived back in England in a metal coffin.

Her younger brother, Billy, seemed less affected by the tragedy, even though it intensified an introversion that he had already displayed from an early age. Her parents gave up on him, too concerned with their own grief. Jo tried to offer her own comfort but he seemed to dismiss it. Isolated, even within the confines of such a tightly knit family, he became secretive. Self-obsessed.

Jo left home shortly after finishing college and walked straight into a job at a publisher's. She rose quickly through various positions, moved to a record company for a few months, then returned to publishing briefly before taking a job as a PA.

The job was good. The money was excellent. The opportunities for travel superb. However, when her boss told her that she should book double rooms for them for all their foreign trips, and that if she didn't follow instructions she'd be looking for another job, the offer to work with Amy Watson was one to be grabbed with both hands. The money was less but the work was enjoyable and she'd become close friends with Amy.

Everything seemed fine in her life.

Except it wasn't. Like that bloody hinge, it needed fixing.

She finally gave up trying to sleep and swung herself out of bed.

She wandered through to the small kitchen and switched on the kettle, dropping a tea bag into a mug she took from the sink.

She ran a hand through her chestnut hair, waiting for the kettle to boil. The beginnings of a headache gnawed at her skull. Her eyes felt as if someone was trying to poke them out of her head from the inside.

She looked up at the wall clock. It was 3.56 a.m.

Again she heard a key in a lock. This time it was her door.

The kettle began to boil.

She walked through into the sitting room, her face set in hard lines.

'Where the hell have *you* been?' she snapped angrily at the newcomer.

Ten

Billy Parker pulled off his jacket and tossed it unceremoniously on to the back of the sofa.

He brushed past Jo, smiling mockingly at her as he slumped down in one of the chairs facing the television. He looked at the blank screen, as if expecting it to burst into life beneath his gaze and drummed agitatedly on one thigh with the thin fingers of his right hand.

'So, what are you doing up then?' he asked, cheerfully.

'I couldn't sleep,' she snapped. 'I was worrying about you and where you might be.'

Billy coughed and got to his feet.

'No need to worry about me,' he told her, making his way into the kitchen.

He saw that the kettle was boiling.

'I'll have a coffee with you, if you're making one,' he said, taking a slice of dry bread from the loaf that stood on the chopping board. He pulled it into pieces and began pushing them, one by one, into his mouth.

'So, where have you been, Billy?' Jo persisted.

'Just out.'

'Out where?' she snarled. 'Don't get funny with me.'

'I was seeing some friends. Any problem with that?'

'What kind of friends?'

'Oh, give it a fucking rest, Jo. What do you want? Names and addresses. Friends, right. That's it.'

'I've got a right to know where you've been, Billy. While you're living here, you abide by my rules.'

He saluted mockingly.

'Yes, madam,' he chided. 'Jesus, you sound more like my fucking mother than my sister. I met a few friends, we had some drinks, something to eat. We talked. Satisfied?'

'Where have you been drinking until four o'clock in the morning, Billy? And what *with*? You've got no money,' she reminded him. 'You've got no money because you've got no job. You've been sponging off me ever since you got here.'

He stood up, digging one hand in the pocket of his jeans.

Jo watched as he pulled out some notes. She glimpsed the purple of twenties, the pale red of a fifty.

He threw the untidy bundle at her.

'There, that's this week's fucking rent, right?' he rasped.

She looked down at the money strewn across the floor and the sofa. Slowly she picked up a crumpled twenty.

'Where did you get this?'

'What does it matter to you? Just take it.'

'It *does* matter. There's more than a hundred quid here. I want to know where you got it.'

'What difference does it make?'

'You're living under my roof. Now tell me, where did you get this money?' She took a step towards him, the twenty gripped in her fist.

He looked into her blazing eyes and chuckled. It was a mocking sound.

'Oh, you look sexy when you're angry,' he said softly, a sly grin on his face.

She stepped even closer. 'Listen, you little bastard, I want to know where you got this money,' she hissed angrily. 'Where did you steal it from?'

Billy took a step back, his grin fading, his eyes narrowing.

'That's just bloody typical of you, isn't it?' he snarled. 'Just because I've got some money in my pocket, you assume I must have nicked it. You don't think I could have worked for it.'

'I know you, Billy. You've always taken the easy option and stealing's easier than working, isn't it? Anyway, where's someone like you going to get a job. Who's going to employ *you*?'

'Plenty of people. Just because I didn't go to fucking college like *you* did doesn't mean I can't get a job. There're plenty of things I can do. Plenty of people who want my services.'

'What kind of services do you offer, Billy? Pimping? Drug pushing?'

'If you don't want the money then give it back,' he snapped, holding out his hand.

'I don't want this money,' she told him, pressing the twenty into his palm. 'I don't want any of your money unless I know where it's come from.'

He snatched the note away.

'You just stay out of my fucking life then,' he told her. 'It's none of your business anyway.'

'While you're here, it *is* my business. I didn't ask you to come here, Billy. You turned up on my doorstep, remember?'

'You didn't have to let me in.'

'What was I supposed to do? Turn you away? You are my brother.'

'Yeah, don't remind me. But if it had been Danny, you'd have been pleased to see him, wouldn't you?'

'Leave Danny out of this.'

'Why? Hit a nerve, have I?'

'Leave it, Billy,' she said, glaring at him menacingly.

'You'd have welcomed *him* into the flat, wouldn't you? Would you have shared your bed with him, Jo? It wouldn't have been the first time, would it?'

'You're sick,' she said dismissively.

'*I'm* sick?' he countered.

They regarded each other angrily for a moment, the silence finally broken by Billy.

'You were the same as Mum and Dad,' he said, his voice low. 'You all thought the sun shone out of Danny's arsehole. He couldn't do anything wrong, could he? Nobody ever cared about me.'

'It's a bit early in the morning for sob stories, Billy.'

'It's true. If it had have been me that was killed no one

would have cared. But because it was Danny everyone was gutted.' He leaned closer to her. 'Fuck him, I'm glad he's dead.'

Jo struck him hard across the cheek with the flat of her hand, the sound of the blow reverberating around the flat.

Billy rubbed his cheek gently, surprised by the power of her blow.

'I'm going to bed,' she told him.

'Good. Perhaps *I* can get some sleep. If you had a decent flat at least I'd have my own room to sleep in, instead of having to doss down on your fucking sofa.'

Jo spun round.

'If you don't like it, Billy,' she rasped. 'The door's there and the sooner you walk through it, the better.' She glared at him for a moment then turned back towards her bedroom door.

She slammed it behind her.

Billy looked at the door for long seconds then set about retrieving the money from the floor. He sat down on the sofa again, folding each note as he counted it.

He smiled. A good night's work. And there would be plenty more where that came from.

Eleven

Phillip Barclay removed the plastic sheet from the corpse with the flourish an artist might use to unveil his latest masterpiece. The pathologist laid the sheet on the adjacent slab then gestured towards the body which lay before him.

'Claire Glover, aged twenty-one,' he said evenly. 'Death by strangulation.' He pointed to a particularly raw, vivid striation mark just below the larynx.

The youngest of the three men in the room leaned closer to the body, his eyes fixed on the red mark on the victim's throat.

'What did he use?' Detective Inspector David Grant wanted to know.

'Thin flex or possibly nylon string. I found fibres in the wound,' said Barclay.

'It looks deep,' Grant observed.

'Nearly three and a half millimetres,' Barclay told him. 'The killer was strong.'

'Time of death?'

'Some time between eleven and one last night, possibly earlier. I can't be more specific yet.'

'Try,' said Grant, allowing his gaze to travel over the rest of the body.

Claire Glover had probably been fairly pretty in life but her swollen features, bloodshot eyes and gashed lips made it difficult to appreciate that now, Grant thought. She was about five-three, wide hipped but a little on the thin side. She looked as if she could have done with a few good meals. Not that it mattered any longer.

'The rigor mortis would seem to indicate the early hours,' Barclay continued. 'I'm going to do a vitreous humour test to try and pin it down more exactly.'

'What's that?' the third man in the room asked.

'The vitreous humour is the jelly-like substance behind the lens of the eye,' said Barclay. 'We take it out with a fine-needled syringe for examination. We then inject water back into the eye.'

'What for?' Detective Sergeant Stuart Lawrenson enquired.

'If we didn't, the eye would collapse,' Barclay told him. 'It's a purely cosmetic exercise before the body goes off to the coroner.'

Lawrenson nodded, his eyes scanning the body.

He was three years older than his superior but the thick moustache he sported made him look older than his thirty-seven years. The flecks of grey in it, as with those in his hair, didn't help either.

Lawrenson looked first at the corpse then at Grant, who was bent close to the body, inspecting every inch of the dead girl. She had a tattoo of a rose on her right shoulder, another of a heart enclosed in barbed wire on her left thigh. There were also several bruises on her thighs.

'What about these?' Grant asked, pointing to the purple blemishes.

'As far as I can tell she got them when she fell,' said Barclay. 'She must have been semi-conscious, trying to fight. The killer pushed her down and straddled her to get some leverage.'

'Any fibres?' the detective inspector continued.

The pathologist shook his head.

'Blood?' Grant persisted.

'Only hers,' Barclay observed. 'There wasn't much blood loss from the wound around the throat. Strangulation's a pretty clean killing method if you know what you're doing.'

'And our boy obviously did,' Grant murmured to himself, his gaze still travelling over the body.

'What about semen?' Lawrenson enquired.

Barclay raised an eyebrow. 'We did rectal, vaginal

and mouth swabs,' he said. 'We found semen present in all three.'

'Busy night,' Lawrenson said.

'Well, she was a working girl, wasn't she?' Grant added.

'There were traces of KY jelly on the rectal swab and lubricant on the vaginal one, the kind you find on a condom,' Barclay continued. 'At a rough guess I'd say she saw at least seven punters last night before she was murdered. Protected *and* unprotected sex.'

'Jesus,' grunted Lawrenson. 'I can't understand why they do it without a rubber, what with AIDS and all that shit.'

'Because they can get twice as much for doing it without one,' Grant told him. 'When I was on the vice squad I knew pros who could get fifty quid for a blow job without a johnny. It's only twenty if the geezer wears one. I mean, come on, Stuart, we're not looking at some Mayfair fanny here, are we?' He made an expansive gesture with his hand over the body. 'This is King's Cross fluff. No class. No looks.' He shook his head. 'No choice. She was probably selling it to finance a habit anyway.'

'We did find evidence of amphetamines in her bloodstream,' Barclay added. 'And alcohol too.'

'Fifty quid's worth of speed goes further than twenty quid's worth,' Grant mused.

'Could she have been raped?' Lawrenson wanted to know.

'There's no bruising around the vagina or anus to indicate that,' Barclay told him.

'Kinky punter,' Grant offered. 'He goes back to her flat, gets out the rope or flex or whatever, offers her fifty, maybe even a hundred to fuck her while he's got the noose round her neck. She says yes, he gets carried away. Scratch one pro.'

'But there was evidence that she was trying to fight off her killer,' Lawrenson protested.

Grant shrugged.

'It started off as a bit of business,' he offered. 'When she realised he was going too far she got scared.'

'As simple as that?' said Lawrenson.

'Either way, I think we're going to be pulling in some overtime,' Grant murmured.

The three men stood looking at the body for a moment longer then Barclay broke the silence.

'There's something else,' he said. 'It's not relevant to the case but I thought you might like to know.'

Grant looked at him expectantly.

'She had cervical cancer,' the pathologist said. 'It was very advanced. She was dying. She might even have known it.'

'AIDS or cancer,' murmured Lawrenson. 'That's a hell of a fucking choice.'

'It didn't matter in the end, did it?' Grant observed. 'Someone made a choice for her.'

'What do you reckon, Dave?' Lawrenson asked. 'Two in four days. There has to be a link, doesn't there?'

Grant continued to gaze at the lifeless body of Claire Glover, his attention riveted on the savage red mark around her neck.

'Let's have another look at the other victim,' he said to Barclay.

Twelve

'Claire Glover,' Grant said and banged the first photo stuck to the blackboard. 'And Tessa Carr.' He tapped the second one, gazing at the assembled throng of plainclothes and uniformed police gathered in the Incident Room at New Scotland Yard.

'Aged twenty-one and nineteen respectively. Both prostitutes. Both strangled within three days of each other. Bodies found within half a mile of each other. MO in each case is identical.' He continued looking around the room, as if allowing the information to sink in. 'We could be looking at a possible serial killer, although it's too early to tell. It could stop at two but I doubt it. Whichever way this goes I want results. Got it?'

There were a few murmurs inside the room; one of the plainclothes officers got up and moved closer to the blackboard, studying the array of photos of the two dead girls more closely. The snaps showed them in both life and death but most had been taken after their murders.

Grant lit up a cigarette and waited for the burble of chatter to die down.

'There's a lot of ground to cover on this,' he said, flicking ash on the floor. 'I want to know if they were working the same patch, if they had regular customers, if they had a pimp. If they *did* I want to know his name. I want to talk to him.'

He turned to the blackboard and pointed at a photo showing the crook of Tessa Carr's arm and the track marks on it. Thick purple scabs had formed over the bruised punctures.

'This one was on smack,' Grant said. 'That means she had a dealer. I want to know *his* name too.'

'What do we know about them, guv?' asked Detective

Constable Dennis Schofield. He was tapping a pen gently against the palm of one large hand.

'Claire Glover was from Coventry,' Grant told him. 'The usual shit with her. Didn't get on with her parents, thought the streets of London were paved with gold. Did a runner when she was sixteen. Couldn't get work and ended up going on the game about four years ago.'

'She was picked up four times by vice between then and her death,' Lawrenson added. 'She also had convictions for shoplifting.'

'Tessa Carr was from Croydon,' Grant continued. 'She spent most of her life in foster homes and children's homes. Her parents are being traced now, for what it's worth. She'd been on the game since she was fourteen. She did three months in Holloway for possession of pot when she was eighteen. She had a suspended for assault too. Some punter got a bit rough with her, she stuck a steel comb in his arse.'

A ripple of laughter ran around the room.

'Are you sure that wasn't a request, guv?' someone shouted from the back of the room.

More laughter.

'Well, whoever he was he didn't get as rough as the geezer who strangled her, did he?' Grant said flatly. 'Anyway, check him out.'

'Was the same weapon used in both murders?' Schofield wanted to know.

'No,' Grant told him. 'The MO was the same but Tessa was strangled with thin flex, possibly from a lamp or something like that. Claire was done with nylon string according to the pathologist.'

'Were either of them raped?' someone called.

'There's no evidence of it in either case,' said Grant. 'There is also no evidence of fingerprints at either crime scene. Not on the bodies at any rate. Any prints that were found are being processed at Hendon as we speak but we're not expecting much more than those belonging to the victims.'

'Where were they found, guv?' Detective Constable Keith Friel enquired.

'Tessa was found under Maiden Lane bridge behind King's Cross,' Grant informed him. 'There's a strong possibility that she was killed somewhere else then dumped there. Claire had a flat she used in Argyle Square. The rent was paid on time on that place every month, so it's my guess that someone else was paying it, I doubt if she had enough money to keep up the payments. This means either a pimp or a friend. Another girl working that area, maybe even a punter. Some of the silly bastards get that attached to a particular girl. Whoever it was, find them.' He took another drag on his cigarette and regarded the other occupants of the room challengingly.

'I've requested plainclothes *and* uniforms on this one,' Grant said. 'It's going to be a big job. Let's just hope it doesn't get any bigger.'

There was a heavy silence broken by Grant himself.

'On a personal note, I know there are some of you in this room who don't think I should be in charge of this case,' he said, drawing on his cigarette. 'Some of the – how shall I put it – more senior among you. Senior in years, I mean.' He looked slowly around the room. 'Well, that's tough shit I'm afraid. I got the promotion on merit and anyone who doesn't like being told what to do by a younger man can walk out of here now.' He gestured towards the door. 'This is my first big case as DI and I don't want anyone fucking it up, got that? Some of you might think I've got something to prove. Well, that's fine because I'm going to prove it by nailing this bastard. And I'm going to do it with your help. All of you. I couldn't give a fuck who does or doesn't like me. This investigation is all that matters. I'm going to push you all hard but I'm going to push myself even harder.' He dropped his cigarette and ground it out on the floor. 'Like I say, I want results and if *I* think someone's not pulling their weight then I'll have them off this fucking case like that.' He snapped his fingers.

Someone coughed but, other than that, his tirade was met with silence.

'I'm glad you all understand the position,' Grant said quietly. 'Are there any more questions?'

There weren't.

'Until we know about these girls in more detail,' Grant continued, 'or the people they mixed with at any rate, the motive for these killings is anyone's guess, but it might be worth checking out some of the local clap clinics because, according to the pathologist's report, Tessa Carr was suffering from non-specific urethritis *and* syphilis. The murderer could be a punter who caught a dose off her and decided to take it out on a few other pros as revenge.'

Grant glanced at his watch.

'Right, let's get moving on this,' he said. 'Like I said, I want this bastard and I'm going to get him, no matter what it takes.'

Thirteen

The imposing figure at the lectern stood motionless apart from barely perceptible movements of his head. All around him shouts of approval or disapproval resounded, reverberating off the oak-panelled walls of the House of Commons.

Home Secretary David Albury gazed around impassively, first at the opposition benches then back at his own party, many of whom were nodding their heads in a gesture of solidarity.

Albury waited for the noise to die down, brushing one sleeve of his Armani suit as he waited.

He was a tall, powerfully built man with greying hair and deep lines across his forehead and around his eyes. Although well into his forty-eighth year, the advance of time had brought to his appearance distinction rather than the weariness that seemed to reside in the features of so many of his colleagues of the same age. And, he noted, with a degree of smugness, some even younger.

He glanced down at his notes as the chamber was quiet once again.

'Despite the protestations of my learned colleagues opposite,' he continued. 'The decline in morals and standards in society is not attributable simply to lack of housing, bad schooling or shortage of jobs.'

There were more shouts, cheers and challenges.

Albury again waited patiently for the rumblings to subside.

When it finally did he looked around him again.

'There is a more insidious cause,' he continued. 'Insidious because it is so accessible and so powerful. I speak of course of the media. In particular of films and video. The constant diet of violence, sex and obscenity which we see paraded on cinema screens and, even worse, on our own television screens, is without doubt a contributory factor in this horrific decline in moral standards that we are experiencing not just in our own country but throughout the world.'

Another chorus of approval from behind him.

'All one needs to do is look at the list of top ten films showing around the country or the list of the ten most popular videos being rented or bought,' he continued. 'It is a catalogue of violence, sex, perversion, blasphemy and filth. No deviation is too foul. We have films and videos glorifying the taking of heroin, delighting in the after-effects of car crashes, showing in close-up the effects of violence. We are assaulted with images of sex, not just wholesome sex but perverted sex. Incest, child molesting, lesbianism. There seems to be no limit to the depths to which some film makers will stoop in an effort to shock us. And they call this entertainment.' He took a sip of water. 'Is it right that the public should be subjected to this constant barrage of horror and obscenity? Surely there is enough violence in the world already without having to portray it on screen.'

More cheers.

'But the ones I feel most for are the children,' said Albury, lowering his voice slightly until it had an almost reverential tone. 'I feel sorrow that their young lives are being blighted by these people who call themselves artists and entertainers. Because it is children who are most susceptible to the kind of filth which these film makers choose to pollute our screens with.'

There was a sustained round of applause.

Albury nodded, raising a hand to quiet his approving audience.

'When children see violence glorified on screen, is it any wonder they feel that it is right?' he persisted. 'Is it any wonder that they imitate it? And yet those film makers who continue to produce these kind of films choose to ignore the consequences of their actions. The only allegiance they have is to the god of money. They care nothing for what they are doing to young minds, they have just one interest. The pursuit of wealth and if innocence and morals are to be sacrificed in this quest for riches then their response would seem to be, so be it.'

He reached for a sheet of paper and held it up.

'The top ten films in the country at the moment,' Albury snapped, pointing to the list. 'Sex, violence, profanity and perversion in every one. Where is there a family film in this list? Where is the kind of good wholesome entertainment that we enjoyed years ago? Instead there are films here about bank robberies, murder, sexual perversion. They contain scenes of torture, nudity and crime, and every one is further blighted by gutter language. Do we want to hear the language of the terraces when we are sitting in a cinema? Do we want to see what should be reserved for the bedroom splashed across the screen before us? Is there any need to show us beatings and shootings in such lurid detail? The answer, I'm sure you'll agree, is no.'

There was another round of applause. A number of the members of the House stood up to add their support.

'And these film makers tell us that this is the *real* world,' Albury continued. 'This is supposed to be the world *we* live in. Well, I don't know about you but it's not like any world *I* am aware of. And, furthermore, I don't think the public wants to see this so-called reality on the screen when they visit the cinema or watch their televisions. I don't believe they want to see nudity or hear bad language. These have no place in what should be works of entertainment.'

He took another sip of his water.

'Many cases can be cited of individuals imitating what they have seen on the screen, be it a cinema or video screen,' Albury insisted. 'And yet still the defenders of these vile films cry that they are not to blame. I say that is rubbish. I say that the public must be protected from this kind of corruption. The public in general but, in particular, children. Video reaches all too easily inside homes these days, children have access to material they should never see but these film makers and those who defend them, don't consider that or, if they do, they choose to ignore the implications. Well, *I* will not ignore the implications. *I* will not stand by and watch while these films contribute even more to the breakdown of our society. *I* will not look on dispassionately while the public is subjected to this continuing stream of filth and corruption. That is why I believe this Bill that I propose must become law as quickly as possible. That is why I propose a complete re-think on the obscenity laws and how they are applied to films and video. A new form of classification must be introduced and these vile films must be controlled and, if necessary, banned. A committee must be set up immediately to look into this. For the sake not just of the children of this country but for all right-minded people everywhere. It is our duty to protect and that is what we must do.'

The applause was deafening.

Fourteen

Anita Bishop reached for the remote control and hit Mute so that all she could see was the picture of the House of Commons. The camera had zoomed in on the face of David Albury. She could see the triumphant look on his face as he took the applause of colleagues and opponents. She was sure she could detect the vaguest hint of a smirk on his thin lips. During the nine months she had worked as his secretary, she had come to know that expression well. Of course, those not so familiar with him would not notice such a minor muscular mannerism, but she prided herself on her powers of observation. That was one of the many things Albury himself had taught her.

She had first met him while working for a local paper in her home town of Brighton. The death of the local MP had threatened to cut the government's majority and Albury had decided to contest the seat on behalf of his party. They had crossed paths at a series of press junkets and then later in more intimate circumstances when she had interviewed him for a feature her paper was running on the forthcoming by-election.

From the first meeting she had found him to be charming and, unusually for a politician, relatively sincere. Either that or he was even more practised at duplicity than the rest of his colleagues. However, Anita had given him the benefit of the doubt and she'd found him to be a witty and warm man. Despite his wealth he seemed at ease amongst those less privileged than himself. Something else few of his colleagues were very adept at faking.

Anita was no stranger to wealth herself. Her father had owned a chain of greetings' card shops before he retired to live on the Côte d'Azur with her stepmother. That had been six years ago, two weeks after Anita's twenty-third birthday. She heard from her father every three or four months, occasionally she flew out for a few days holiday when work permitted but, they had never been a close family, even when her real mother was alive.

Despite representing his Brighton constituency, Albury spent most of his time in London where he had a flat in Kensington. His family home was in Sussex. She'd visited it once and met his wife and daughter.

She'd visited the flat in Kensington too on more than one occasion.

Since starting work for Albury as a secretary-cum-PA, she had discovered that he was something of a workaholic and, when he didn't feel like working in the confines of his office at the Houses of Parliament, he was just as likely to suggest they continue their work at the Kensington flat. The dwelling reeked of good taste and money. A little like Albury himself.

When he'd offered her the job as secretary she had accepted without a second thought. She had never held particularly strong political views, even as a student, but she had been captivated more by Albury the man than by the politician. She admired his determination. She envied his passion and she was more than a little in awe of his power. Besides that, for a man twenty years her senior, he was extremely attractive. Power and wealth were potent enough attributes in themselves but combined with his physical appearance, they were positively dynamic.

She knew that his ambition was to be Prime Minister before he was fifty, and such was his self-belief he had convinced her that it was only a matter of time until that happened. That ambition, however, was something he only ever spoke about when they were alone. Even Albury didn't intend letting personal goals interfere with the overall well-being of the Party. It was something else she respected about him.

Anita continued looking at the screen, noticing that Albury had stepped away from the lectern. She could see him seated in his familiar position on the front bench, pulling at one cuff and smiling as the Prime Minister leaned close and said something to him.

She switched off the set and turned her attention back to her work. There were some dates to be fitted into his diary. Rumours were rife that an election was due in less than six months. There weren't many empty spaces left in that diary.

She smiled then scribbled a note on one of the pads on her desk. When he returned to the office there was something she wanted to ask him.

Fifteen

Amy Watson drove her foot into the punch bag, her teeth gritted as she felt the impact. It felt good.

She stretched, took a step back then drove another powerful kick into the hanging bag, shouting as she did. *Christ, that felt good.*

She twisted around on her shapely legs and kicked twice with her right foot, the shuddering impacts both creating harsh thuds as they connected with the leather. Her red leotard was already dark with sweat, her blond hair hanging like snakes' tails from so much exertion. Her bare feet were taped across the insteps, around the ankles and under the arches and she paused momentarily to fasten some of the tape, massaging the toes of her right foot as she did so.

Close by, clad in a black leotard and white leggings, Jo Parker was lifting some five-kilo weights, inhaling and exhaling, gazing at her own reflection in the huge mirror that ran the full length of the rear wall. She could see her biceps bulging as she lifted each weight up to her chest then lowering it again in repetitions of ten, pausing only briefly between each set to reposition herself.

The gym smelled of sweat and damp hair.

The two women had been coming to the place together for the last six months, Amy for even longer. She had always worked out whenever she found the time when she was modelling, now she found she did it because she wanted to. Kick-boxing particularly was something both she and Jo had taken to immediately. The other attraction of this gym, run by an ex-boxer who was known to all and sundry only as Gus, was that it was rarely busy at the time Amy and Jo wanted to use it. Indeed, on this particular day, there were only three other people using the facilities.

A man in his fifties was pedalling happily on one of the exercise bikes on the far side of the room, a Walkman clipped to his shorts.

A man in his thirties, dressed in an immaculately clean adidas tracksuit was using one of the three stairmasters in the gym while a third man, in his late twenties, sat about ten yards away, dressed only in shorts and trainers, lifting weights Amy guessed must be close to twenty pounds each. He'd obviously been doing it for some time too because his entire upper body was bulging with overdeveloped muscle. There was no careful body sculpture going on, she mused. He had set out to build huge muscles and he'd succeeded. He looked ungainly, his head appearing too small for his body.

Perspiration was running in rivulets between his huge pectoral muscles. Every now and then he would cast a furtive glance at Amy and Jo. His appreciative gaze travelled over the sweat-stained women, pausing to enjoy the sight of Amy's slender legs and taut buttocks constrained so exquisitely by Lycra leggings or of Jo's breasts pressing against her leotard. He watched as Amy drove several more kicks into the punchbag, hurriedly averting his gaze as she turned towards the bottle of Evian she'd left propped beside the mat. She took a large swig and offered some to Jo, who shook her head and continued lifting, sweat trickling down her face.

Amy stood there with her hands on her hips watching her companion, seeing the muscles bulge on her forearms and biceps.

'If you don't watch it, Jo,' Amy said, smiling, 'you'll end up looking like Hercules over there.'

She made a movement with her eyes in the direction of the musclebound man who was busily fixing another five kilos to each of the weights he was lifting.

'He's watching us,' said Jo, still lifting steadily.

'What?' Amy said and chuckled.

'He's been watching us ever since we got here,' Jo went on, gritting her teeth as she continued lifting.

'There's no law against him looking, Jo,' Amy told her, running a hand through her hair.

'He was watching us while we were on the bikes and he's been watching us ever since we came over here.'

Jo dropped the weights, the loud clang reverberating around the gym.

'I've had enough of this,' she hissed. 'I'm going. I've got things to do anyway and I can do without that fucking idiot staring at me all the time.'

As she spoke she turned the full fury of her gaze in the direction of the musclebound man, who saw the malevolence in her eyes and wondered what had provoked it.

'What the fuck are you looking at?' Jo rasped at him.

'Jo, for Christ's sake,' said Amy, stepping in front of her. 'Just leave it, will you?'

'What's wrong with you?' the man asked innocently, his voice shaky, unprepared for the verbal onslaught aimed at him.

Jo stepped towards him. 'Had a good look at us, have you?' she snapped.

'I don't know what you're talking about,' said the man, continuing to lift the weights, looking away from Jo now. His face was flushed and not all of it was from the effort of lifting.

'Are you coming?' Jo said, looking at Amy who merely shook her head.

Jo spun away, heading for the changing rooms. 'I've got things to do, I've got to go,' she said.

'Jo, we've got to talk,' Amy said, gripping Jo's wrist. 'What's wrong?'

Jo shook loose.

'Not now, Amy,' she said, the knot of muscles at the side of her jaw pulsing angrily. 'I'll see you tonight.'

She turned and stalked away.

Jo watched her go then turned back towards the punchbag.

'What's wrong with your bloody friend?' said the musclebound man. 'Time of the month or something?' He smiled crookedly.

Amy looked at him disdainfully.

'She should be *grateful* people are looking at her,' the man continued. 'She's got a good body – she can't expect people not to look. Touchy cow.'

'Well, at least she's given you an excuse to exercise your *right* arm a little more now, hasn't she?' Amy said dismissively, watching as the smile slipped from the man's face.

Amy spun round and drove three powerful kicks into the punchbag.

It swung gently back and forth on its chain, the imprint of her last kick still visible on the leather.

Sixteen

Jo Parker dropped the sports bag in the hallway of the flat then turned to lock the flat door. She stood with her back against it then she sucked in a deep breath, held it a moment and let it out in a long sigh. She could hear music coming from the sitting room and she sighed again when she heard how loud it was.

As she strode into the room the sound seemed to envelop her. There were CD cases strewn over the carpet in front of the stack system, some of the discs out of their cases.

She picked her way through the debris and immediately switched off the thumping sound system.

'I was listening to that,' said Billy Parker who was seated at one end of the sofa, a cigarette jammed between his lips.

He used the remote control to reactivate the hi-fi, the sound filling the room once more.

Jo jabbed the Off button once again and stood with her back to the player, glaring at her brother.

'You're home early, aren't you?' Billy asked, flicking ash into an overflowing ashtray.

'Is this what you've been doing since I left?' Jo demanded. 'Sitting around on your arse wasting time?'

'I went out to get a sandwich. You didn't have fuck all worth eating.'

She saw three empty cans of Stella by the sofa.

'Is that when you got those?' she demanded, pointing at the cans.

'Man cannot live by bread alone,' he said and cracked out laughing.

Jo glared at him. 'You were supposed to be out looking for a job,' she reminded him.

'I had other business.'

'Yeah, I bet you did.'

He sniffed the air exaggeratedly. 'Good work-out?' he asked. 'It smells like it.' He grinned. 'What's wrong, were the showers broken?'

He stubbed out his cigarette and reached for another can of Stella.

'Did you make the appointment?' Jo asked.

'What for?'

'Did you?'

'What's the fucking point? No one cares anyway.'

'Don't start with the sob stories again, Billy, I'm not in the mood.'

'Don't pretend you care, Jo. You don't care and neither do Mum and Dad.'

'If I didn't care I wouldn't have let you stay here, would I?'

'Do Mum and Dad know I'm here?'

'I spoke to Mum about a week ago. She knows.'

'Did she send her love?' he asked, his voice heavy with scorn. 'I bet she didn't even ask how I was, did she? If they cared that much they wouldn't have thrown me out in the first place.'

'You didn't help yourself, Billy.'

'It's not my fault, the way I am.'

'Nobody said it was.'

'They blame me and do you know why? Because it doesn't go down well with their friends at the Rotary Club or the fucking Round Table. They lost points when the truth came out.'

'What the hell are you talking about?'

'They've been doing it all their lives, Jo. Scoring points off their friends and using us to do it. Their life is one big competition. All their friends' kids went to grammer school so we had to go to *private* school. It put them in front on points.'

'You're being ridiculous.'

'Am I? Why do you think they pushed you to go to college? Because all their friends' kids were going to college.

They couldn't be left out of the game. That would have killed them. So, when you went they got more points. When Danny was killed it was like rolling a double six. All that fucking sympathy. None of their friends could hope to compete with that, could they? They were in front. They had an unassailable lead, but then it all went wrong with *me*, didn't it?' He took a swig from the can. 'When I told them I was gay, that was it, and once their friends found out, it was all over for them. Slide down the biggest ladder back to square one and miss a turn.'

Jo sat down opposite him.

She was the one who broke the silence.

'Please make the appointment, Billy,' she said quietly. 'I'll come with you.'

'To hold my hand? No thanks.'

'You've got to know.'

'Why? There's a better-than-average chance I'll be positive.'

'You can't be sure but even if you *are*, you can get help.'

Billy laughed mockingly.

'The experts always say that, don't they?' he chided. 'Take an AIDS' test, put your mind at rest. What a fucking joke. If you take it and you're positive then all that tells you is that you're going to die soon. Who wants to know *that*?'

'But there are drugs that could help you, Billy.'

'Help, not *cure*, Jo. Do you know what ZCT and all those other fucking pills are? They're not help, they're a stay of execution. Well, if I've got it, I don't want to know.'

He took a last swig from the can and crushed it in one fist.

'But I'll tell you something,' he continued. 'If I *am* positive, if I have got AIDS, then I'll make sure I'm not the only one. I'll take as many with me as I can. If *I'm* going to die, then so are a lot of other people.'

Seventeen

Detective Inspector David Grant switched off the engine of the Montego and sat in silence for a moment gazing at the house ahead of him. The house in Paddock Road was similar to many in this and other roads like it in Dollis Hill. Modest but comfortable the estate agent had called it. For some reason Grant could still remember his words but then again, he mused, remembering things was part of the job after all. The ability to recall the smallest and seemingly most insignificant detail was a prerequisite in his work as a detective. It was normally something he prided himself on but it occasionally irritated him that his capacity for recall extended not just to things of importance but also to bullshit.

'*Modest but comfortable.*' That was in the file marked bullshit.

He picked up his briefcase from the passenger seat, locked the car and made his way to the front door. A light was on in the sitting room and another upstairs. Tina was home.

He let himself in and when he heard the television headed straight for the sitting room, but as he entered the room, he found it was empty. A comedy programme was on, the canned laughter loud in the background. He switched channels and found the news before heading into the kitchen to get a cup of water, which he gulped down like a man who has just emerged from a trek in the desert.

The air smelled of cooked food. The table was laid for one. He assumed she'd already eaten.

Grant wandered back into the sitting room and flopped into one of the armchairs.

'Hey, you.'

He looked up as he heard her voice, managing a weary smile as Tina padded into the room wearing just a pair of jeans and a baggy white sweater.

She crossed to him and sat on his lap, kissing him, and he inhaled deeply, savouring her scent.

It was warmth and freshness. She always smelled as if she'd just bathed.

He slid one hand up inside her sweater, feeling how smooth her skin was. She giggled and writhed on his lap as he closed one hand around her unfettered right breast.

Tina pulled free of him and retreated to the kitchen.

'Calm down, Tiger,' she called, the merest trace of a northern accent in her voice. It had been stronger when they'd first met, the Yorkshire twang having softened during the intervening five years. For three of those five years they had been married.

He followed her out to the kitchen where she was pulling a cottage pie from the oven, spooning some on to a plate for him.

'I'm not hungry, babe,' he said apologetically. 'Sorry.'

'Eat something, Dave,' she advised. 'You'll be ill if you don't.'

'I've only been home two minutes and you're lecturing me already,' he said, smiling.

He sat down at the carefully laid place and picked dutifully at the food.

Tina got herself a Diet Coke from the fridge and sat down opposite him.

'What time did you get in?' he wanted to know.

'About eight. I got a Chinese on the way back.'

'You didn't cook this especially for me?' he said, jabbing the cottage pie with his fork.

'Took it from the freezer and heated it up with my own fair hand.'

'How did the show go today?' he asked.

'Well, apart from the bloody photographer being late it was fine. The usual thing – organised bedlam – but then fashion shows usually are. Still, we got some good shots, especially of the new Galliano and Conran stuff. We're running a big feature on those in the next issue.'

He nodded dutifully.

'I'm pleased *somebody* had a good day,' he said wearily.

'I wasn't too impressed with some of the new Versace dresses,' Tina continued, oblivious to his remark. 'But they showed us some trouser suits and they were gorgeous. I wish I could afford their prices.'

Grant pushed food slowly into his mouth, watching her as she swigged from the Diet Coke can.

'Another girl was found dead this morning,' he said quietly. 'Another prostitute.'

'Well, they ask for it, don't they? Doing a thing like that, I mean, they don't know what kind of weirdos they're picking up, do they?'

'That's two he's killed in a week. I think it's the same guy.'

'Do you want a drink with that?' she asked, getting to her feet and crossing to the fridge.

Grant exhaled deeply. 'I'll have a beer.'

She put down the can beside him and sat again, watching as he continued to prod at his food.

'If you don't want it, don't eat it,' she said finally.

He dropped the knife and fork on to the plate and pulled open the ring pull on the can, taking several deep swallows. With the back of his hand he wiped his mouth and shook his head.

'You couldn't give a shit about my work, could you?' he said, looking directly at her.

Tina picked up his plate and began scraping the leftovers into the nearby pedal bin.

'I don't particularly want to hear about it over the dinner table.'

'You don't want to hear about it *anywhere*, Tina.'

'Don't start, Dave.'

She dropped the plate into the bowl and ran hot water on it.

'I'm not starting,' he protested. 'But it's true, isn't it? You're not interested.'

'I don't want to hear about people who've been shot or cut up or beaten to death.'

'But it happens and I have to deal with it. It's my work.'

'Then leave it in the office at New Scotland Yard, Dave.'

'Jesus Christ. I wish it was as easy as that.' He sucked in an angry breath. 'I can't "leave it at the office", Tina. I carry it with me all the time. Twenty-four hours a fucking day it's here.' He tapped his forehead.

She took the plate and cutlery from the bowl and began drying them up.

'Leave the bloody drying up, will you?' he shouted. 'Just for once stop with your tidying and cleaning.'

'Look, just because you've had a shitty day, don't come home and start taking it out on me.'

'Sometimes I just want to talk. That's all. But you don't want to listen, do you?'

She was standing at the sink staring at him.

'Sometimes I need to get things off my chest,' he continued. 'But you're not interested, are you? And yet I have to sit here and listen when you talk about *your* job.'

'Sorry if I bore you, Dave.'

'You know what I mean,' he hissed. 'You'd be interested if I was talking about kids, wouldn't you?'

'Yes I would,' she snapped. 'If you were to come home one night and say "Tina, I've changed my mind, I *do* want kids" I'd be *very* interested. But that's not likely to happen, is it, Dave?'

'We've been over this time and time again. What's the point?'

He got to his feet and wandered into the sitting room. Tina followed him.

'What's the point?' she repeated angrily. 'I'll tell you what the bloody point is. You're being selfish. *You* don't want kids. You never stopped to consider how I might feel.'

He flopped into one of the armchairs, his eyes on the television.

'We've been through this.'

'So that's it? We've discussed it a couple of times so you've had enough? Well there are still things we *haven't* talked about.'

'A couple of times? Christ, it's all we *ever* talk about. We agreed at the beginning that our careers should come first.'

'No, Dave, you wanted *your* career to come first and it has. I've always respected that. All I'm asking now is that you consider *my* feelings.'

'I can't understand you, Tina. You've got a bloody good job with that fashion magazine. You've got a career. But you'd be willing to give all that up to be up to your knees in shit and nappies twenty-four hours a day. It doesn't make sense.'

'It doesn't make sense to you,' she snapped. 'Because you can't see any further than the next promotion.'

'So now you're pissed off because I want to get on?'

'You're a detective inspector. How much further do you want to go? When is this obsessive desire to better yourself going to stop, Dave? When you've got the bloody commissioner's job? Who the hell are you trying to impress? You've done what you set out to do. You're at the top of your profession. Why are you still so resistant to having kids?'

'We've got a good life together, Tina. We live well. We're both successful at what we do. Why let a kid spoil that?'

'Why do you always see a child as an obstacle? You never even consider what it could give us, do you?'

'I see it disrupting our lives, making demands on us. I'm not ready for that, Tina.'

'How can it disrupt *your* life, Dave, you're never bloody here. I never know what time you're going to walk in at night. I don't even know *if* you're going to walk in. Take a close look at us. What life have we got for a child to spoil? We haven't even got a life together. We don't go anywhere because of your work and if we do then you're always on call. We spend most of our time apart. You're working or I'm working. We're like two lodgers sharing the same house.'

'And a baby would change all that, would it?'

'Probably not,' she said wearily. 'Perhaps it's too late for that. Perhaps it's too late for anything to save this marriage.'

Eighteen

'Who does this sanctimonious bastard think he is?'

Amy sat back in her seat, a copy of *The Standard* open in front of her.

David Albury's speech had been well reported and the paper had even run an editorial that, for the most part, backed the views of the Home Secretary. There was a photo of Albury with his wife and daughter on one page and another of him in the House of Commons on the other. On the opposite page in a column headed THE DIRTY DOZEN were twelve films or videos that Albury had singled out for attention during the speech.

> *Natural Born Killers*
> *Lethal Weapon IV*
> *Man Bites Dog*

Amy continued down the list, shaking her head.

> *The Last Temptation of Christ*

'He's a bit out of date on most of these, isn't he?' she said mockingly.

'You're back on air in ten seconds, Amy,' said Mike Osborne from the production booth, his voice sounding robotic over the microphone.

Amy took a sip of coffee and fumbled for a cigarette, one eye on the studio clock.

'Five seconds.'

Amy lit up and took a long drag.

The red ON AIR sign flashed on.

'Welcome back,' she said. 'For those of you just joining

us we're talking about free speech and censorship. I don't know about you but I think we have far too little of the former and far too much of the latter in society today. But today, Mr David Albury, who you may or may not know is Home Secretary, proposed plans for an all party committee to look into the – as he put it – "appalling and ceaseless stream of filth that we are all subjected to every time we visit the cinema, switch on our television sets or rent a video." His words, not mine.'

She hit a button and connected one of the waiting callers.

'Sarah from Richmond. Have you been exposed to any streams of filth lately, Sarah?' Amy asked, smiling.

'I do agree that there's too much violence on television now.'

'Do you watch violent programmes, Sarah?'

'Well, you don't always know they're going to be violent when they start, do you?'

'What sort of TV do you watch then?'

'Soaps, costume dramas, stuff like that.'

'They're violent, aren't they? Soaps have wife beating and car crashes and vandalism. That's violent, isn't it?'

'Yeah, but it's not guns, is it?'

'Oh, I see, so violence only counts if it entails guns. What about knives? Axes? Chainsaws? Rocket launchers? Don't they count as violent? Or how about good old-fashioned fists. They can be pretty lethal sometimes.'

'I don't think people want to see violence on television all the time.'

'Do you watch the news, Sarah?'

'Yeah.'

'Well, there isn't a more violent programme on the TV than the news and that's all *real*. Isn't that worse?'

'But that's real life. They're just showing you what goes on, aren't they? I mean, in films, it's not realistic.'

'Have you ever seen anyone shot, Sarah?'

'No.'

'Then how do you know it's not realistic?'

'Well, they do it to make the heroes look good, don't they?'

Amy shook her head despairingly.

'What do you do if a violent scene comes on the TV, Sarah? Do you watch it?'

'I suppose so.'

'Why don't you turn the TV off? If you hate violence that much, why not exercise your right to freedom and switch off?'

She smiled.

'Because that's what I'm going to do to you right now, Sarah,' Amy said. 'You're history.' She cut the connection and flicked another switch.

'Alan from Notting Hill. What do you think? Are violent films and videos to blame for the ills of our society?'

'Well, no, and I'll tell you what really pisses me . . .'

There was a momentary pause.

'Hello, Alan,' said Amy.

'Hello, am I still on?'

'You're still on. The world is waiting for your pearls of wisdom.'

'Like I said, what really . . . gets to me is all these bloody do-gooders trying to tell people what they should and shouldn't watch. Like you said, it's supposed to be a free country.'

'So you don't agree with the Home Secretary's plans?'

'What plans?'

'He wants to re-classify films, bring in stricter censorship. What do you think of that, Alan?'

'I think he should mind his own business. They should all mind their own business. All these old gits are so out of touch with everyday life they don't know what goes on anyway. You get these do-gooders telling people to stop watching violent films and then one of them . . . that old prat with the bald head. What's his name? You know? The one that's always visiting murderers in prison and saying they should be let out.'

'I think I know who you mean, Alan.'

'People like him, or that stupid old cow who's always complaining about stuff on the telly. What's her name? You know? They should just shut up and let people live their own lives. I mean, they wouldn't like it if people started coming round their houses and telling them what to do.'

'Quite right, Alan. Thanks for your comments,' said Amy. 'I think the real problem is that these self-appointed guardians of our morals aren't even elected by members of the public. No one voted them into a position where they have any right to speak for anyone other than themselves. They are expressing their own views, not the views of the vast majority.'

She glanced across at the screen and saw half a dozen more callers' names flashing.

'I read the Home Secretary's speech as it was reported in the paper,' said Brian from Southwark. 'And I have to say, I agree with what he said. I have children and I don't want them exposed to this kind of thing.'

'How old are your children, Brian?'

'I've got a boy of twelve and a girl of ten.'

'Well, then they're not going to be exposed to any of the films David Albury mentioned, are they, because all of those films had "eighteen" certificates.'

'They could get them from a video shop.'

'Any video shop renting "eighteen" certificate films to kids under age is liable to be fined. Besides, Brian, what happened to parental responsibility? Isn't it *your* job to make sure they don't see material you feel is unsuitable.'

'I can control my children when I'm with them. I don't know what they're up to when they're round friends' houses. Perhaps not all parents are as conscientious as I am.'

'So you're blaming the *parents* of your kids' friends if your kids get to see these films?'

'If these films were banned in the first place then they wouldn't be able to see them, would they?'

'Have you actually seen any of the films that the Home Secretary listed as those he wanted banned, Brian?'

There was a moment's silence.

'No I haven't seen them,' said Brian of Southwark.

'Then how can you comment on them?' Amy asked.

'I've read reviews of them, I know what they're about.'

'I've seen photos of Adolf Hitler, it doesn't make me a fascist. You can't comment on something you haven't seen, Brian.'

'I've spoken to people who've seen them.'

'Is all your information on every subject secondhand, Brian? Do you watch television?'

'Not often.'

'Do you read?'

'Yes, I read a lot.'

'Then presumably you'd like violent books banned as well? Because they'll probably be the next target of someone like David Albury. He'll start with films and videos, move on to TV then books. If these new laws of his are as Draconian as he would like, then no branch of the entertainment business will be safe.'

'I don't see it as a bad thing. I'd ban violent books too, I mean, they're even easier for children to get hold of.'

'So what would you start with, Brian? Which books? The Bible? The complete works of Shakespeare? *The Iliad*?'

'That's ridiculous.'

'No, it isn't. There are few books in print more violent than the Bible or Shakespeare. Surely they should be amongst the first banned?'

'The works of Shakespeare are art. You can't ban art.'

'Anything creative, to a degree, is art, Brian. Art and creativity should not be banned, no matter what their subject matter. Do you feel the same about sex as you do about violence?'

'What do you mean?'

'Would you ban sexually explicit material as well as violent material?'

'I think sex is a different matter.'

'So, in your opinion, it's fine for children to watch two people having sex but not to watch two people shooting at each other? Don't you realise that *your* life is being controlled too by these self-appointed moral guardians, Brian. Doesn't it bother you that you have no control over your own life?'

'I'm perfectly in control of my own life.'

'No you're not. There is censorship in every walk of life. Things that you are told you cannot do because the law says you cannot do them. That is a form of censorship, Brian. But perhaps that suits you because it means *you* don't have to make responsible decisions. *You* don't have to make choices because those choices are made for you by faceless bureaucrats and self-important people more concerned with voicing their own opinions than caring about those of others.' She took a drag on her cigarette. 'I just wondered if I was the only one to have remembered that there's an election due soon. The kind of public hysteria David Albury is trying to whip up is useful for vote-catching. It deflects public attention away from things like government policy failures. Basically, a campaign like this is using films as a scapegoat. Films are blamed for problems that have already been created by the state of our society – with its poor housing, joblessness, domestic violence and a general sense of hopelessness felt by a large majority of the population. It's a bandwagon to jump on and Albury's inviting anyone who wants to jump up there with him.'

She glanced up at the studio clock.

'We're going to take a break for the news,' said Amy. 'Then we'll carry on with this fascinating topic. I want to hear from all the do-gooders and those who hate them. Let's have a balanced view. And, if you're out there listening, David Albury or any of your cronies, give me a call. If you've got the guts.'

She flicked off a switch and the music that introduced

the News began to fill her headset. She pulled it off and glanced at the screen. At the flashing names.

One of them looked familiar. *Why?*

She frowned as she gazed at it.

PETER FROM MUSWELL HILL

There was something . . .

'Amy.'

She heard Mike Osborne's voice from the production room.

'That next call,' he said, a note of concern in his voice. 'Don't take it.'

Again she looked at the screen. At the name.

'Can you hear me, Amy?' he persisted. 'Don't take that call.'

Nineteen

'Peter, we're going to have to stop meeting like this.'

Amy leaned close to the microphone and blew out a stream of smoke. Then she glanced up and saw Osborne standing at the large window that separated the studio from the production room. His arms were folded, his face set in hard lines. Amy thought that she could see him shaking his head gently.

'I bet you don't agree with censorship, do you, Peter?'

'No,' said Peter from Muswell Hill. 'I agree with what you said.'

'About everyone having the right to watch what they want to watch?'

'About everything you said.'

'What kind of films do you watch, Peter?'

Silence.

'Peter,' she persisted. 'Can you hear me?'

'There's nothing wrong with violent films,' he said quietly.

'Do you watch violent films, Peter?'

'I watch all kinds of things. I'm not prudish.'

Osborne was still standing sentinel at the glass partition. Amy watched him for a moment as she listened to the caller.

'I find them liberating,' Peter continued.

'In what way, Peter?'

'Violence happens in everyday life, you can't hide from it. Sometimes it's necessary.'

Amy blew out a long stream of smoke.

'In what circumstances is violence necessary, Peter?' she asked.

Silence.

'Have you ever been violent to anyone, Peter?' Amy asked.

'Sometimes you have to hurt people,' he told her.

'What would make you *want* to hurt someone, Peter?'

Silence.

Amy looked across at Osborne who was imitating a cutting action across his throat.

Amy shook her head and leaned closer to the microphone.

'What I do, I do for you,' Peter said suddenly.

'What *do* you do for me, Peter?'

'I tell people about you. I tell them to listen to you, to what you have to say.'

'Thank you very much, Peter, I appreciate that.'

'Did you get the present I sent you?'

'Yes, I told you that last time you called the show.'

'No. This is something else. Something new. It's a surprise.'

'What is it?'

'If I told you that it wouldn't be a surprise, would it?'

The laughter which she heard raised the hairs on the back of her neck.

'I like to give surprises,' he continued.

More laughter.

Again she felt those icy fingers at the back of her neck.

'How will I know it's from you if you don't tell me what it is?' said Amy.

'You'll know,' he said flatly.

'Will I like it?'

'Wait and see.'

He hung up.

'The guy is a fucking nutter,' said Mike Osborne. 'He should be reported to the police.'

Amy stretched in her chair and took a sip of her coffee.

'He's harmless,' she said dismissively.

'How the hell do you know that?' Osborne protested.

'Jesus, you don't know what's going through his mind. He's fixated on you. Obsessed.'

'What do you think, Jo?' Amy asked, looking across the production room at the younger woman.

Jo shrugged. 'I'm no psychiatrist, Amy, but I think Mike's right about him being obsessed with you.'

'What's your problem, Mike?' Amy said. 'He hasn't made any threats against me, he hasn't said he's going to kill me.'

'That might just be a matter of time,' Osborne insisted. 'What if you reject him? What if he turns against you?'

'How can I reject him? I haven't even met him and I'm not likely to either.'

'And what if he turns up at the station one night? What then?' Osborne demanded. 'I'm telling you, Amy, the police should know about this guy. Before it's too late.'

Amy shook her head and got to her feet.

'You worry too much, Mike,' she said, pulling on her coat.

'And maybe you don't worry enough,' he snapped irritably.

Amy held his gaze for a moment then headed for the door, Jo close behind.

The two women walked to the lift in silence, Amy jabbing the Call button. When it arrived they rode it to the ground floor.

'What if Mike's right about this bloke being crazy?' Jo said, as the doors slid open.

'Don't you start too.'

They walked to the main entrance, Amy raising a hand to the nightwatchman who nodded back in acknowledgement, watching as the women stood on the pavement outside chatting for a moment. Then he returned to his magazine.

Amy looked across at her waiting cab then glanced at her watch. Before she could speak, Jo was already heading towards her own taxi.

'I'll speak to you tomorrow,' said the younger woman, as she slid on to the back seat of the vehicle.

Amy nodded and looked around Bedford Square. Tall buildings towered over her from all four sides, only the odd light burning in windows here and there.

She shuddered slightly and walked to the cab, clambering in.

As the vehicle moved away from the kerb a dark shape moved in the shadows thrown by the building behind.

A form that seemed to be a part of the blackness itself.

The figure watched the taxi disappear around a corner then melted back into the gloom as soundlessly as it had emerged.

Twenty

Christ, it was cold.

Even inside the Montego with the heating on, Detective Inspector David Grant shivered as he brought the vehicle to a halt outside number six Wenlock Road. The wind was whipping wildly around the car and the street, sending spilled rubbish flying from a nearby dustbin. A crisp packet stuck to the windscreen momentarily before another gust of wind sent it spinning into the air.

Grant switched off the engine and glanced out. The sky filled with huge, bruised clouds threatening to unleash a downpour any second. Not all the streetlights were working but the slowly turning, blue lights of the ambulance parked across the pavement outside number six illuminated the early morning somewhat.

In addition to the emergency vehicle, there were also two marked police cars parked nearby and a blue Saab, which he recognised as belonging to Detective Sergeant Lawrenson. It had been Lawrenson who had called him about fifty minutes ago.

Grant swung himself out of the car and headed towards number six. He flipped his ID at the uniformed man standing at the top of the narrow staircase that led down to the basement flat, noticing how red the man's face was. The uniformed man was shivering. He stepped aside to let the detective inspector through.

As he reached the front door, the paint chipped and peeling, Grant noticed that there was a window-box on the sill but it seemed to consist only of dried earth. Any flowers that may have flourished there were long dead. Cat shit lay in one corner of the paved area at the bottom of the steps.

Grant wandered into the hallway, and could hear

voices inside the flat. As he entered, he noticed that the walls were bare; no posters or prints brightened up what was a distinctly dismal abode. Two pairs of dirty trainers lay discarded close to the door, and a leather jacket was hanging from a coat hook to his right, the material worn and scuffed in places. He turned and glanced at the door. The hinges were intact. The lock didn't seem to have been smashed.

'No signs of forced entry, guv.'

He recognised the voice immediately as belonging to Lawrenson.

The detective sergeant was smoking a cigarette, flicking ash on to the worn carpet.

'I've already checked the doors and windows,' Lawrenson continued.

Grant nodded. 'Let me see what we've got,' he muttered, following his companion through into the sitting room.

It was small anyway but the presence of three men made it look even more cramped. As in the hallway, the walls were bare. A single light hung from the ceiling, its bulb illuminating the scene below. The fact that the shade which surrounded it bore pictures of Marilyn Monroe made it seem all the more bizarre. A two-seater sofa had been overturned and lay on its side close to a chair and a small portable television which, Grant noticed, for some reason had no plug on.

There was a fireplace housing a two-bar electric fire and, on the mantelpiece above, a radio. He saw a stack system, which had only one of the speakers attached.

And he saw blood. Splashes of it littered the carpet and fireplace and, as Lawrenson stepped aside, Grant saw where it had come from.

The body sat in the chair was a man in his late twenties. He was naked apart from a pair of underpants, his long legs stretched out in front of him as if he was warming his feet in front of the fire. His face was tinged blue, his eyes open and bulging in their sockets, the whites spattered

red. A dark patch stained the front of his pants. As Grant stepped closer he could smell urine and the stronger, more pungent odour of faeces. As well as these odours, the coppery smell of blood filled the room.

It was everywhere. The red fluid covered most of the dead man's upper torso and it looked as if his arms, from the elbows down, had been dipped in the stuff. There was more of it around his mouth, some having congealed on his lips and chin. Several vivid striation marks ran around his throat as though someone had drawn on his flesh with a red Biro.

On the other side of the chair, the pathologist Phillip Barclay leaned close to the body, running expert eyes over each injury in turn.

'How long's he been dead?' Grant wanted to know.

'I'd say about seven hours,' Barclay told him.

'Cause of death?'

'Strangulation.' The pathologist pointed to the marks around the throat. 'Performed with thin flex or string.'

'Like the other two?' Grant murmured.

Barclay nodded.

'From the nature of the wounds and the pressure exerted, coupled with the angle of the attack, I'd say—'

'Same killer,' Grant finished the sentence.

Barclay nodded.

'So who's our boy?' Grant nodded towards the corpse.

'His name's Harvey Dwyer,' Lawrenson filled him in.

'What do we know about him?'

'More form than Desert Orchid. Robbery, aggravated assault and he ran a little sideline too.' The detective sergeant produced a small plastic bag from his jacket pocket and held it up. 'We found this in the kitchen.'

Grant looked at the brownish-white powder. 'Heroin.'

Lawrenson nodded. 'There are syringes in there too. We found more in the bathroom and there was other stuff in the bedroom. Coke, Es, speed. He was a walking pharmacy.'

'There are track marks on his arms and thighs,' Barclay added.

'You say there was no forced entry, Stuart?' Grant said, still peering at the body.

'No, and as far as we can tell, nothing was taken. No personal effects, not the drugs. There was still money in his wallet.' Lawrenson nodded towards the mantelpiece, where a black leather wallet lay untouched.

'No forced entry means he could have known his killer,' said Grant.

'He was dealing as well as using,' Lawrenson offered. 'Maybe someone didn't like the prices he was charging.'

'Then why not take the drugs too?' Grant said. 'Robbery's not the motive. Someone wanted him dead, it's as simple as that.' He pointed to the blood-drenched arms of the corpse. 'What happened there?'

Barclay raised an eyebrow.

'Something *I've* never seen before,' the pathologist said. 'The wrists were cut after strangulation using a *very* sharp knife. A Stanley knife or something similar. Look—' He pointed to a cross-shaped incision on each wrist. Both were gaping open like gasping mouths. '—The ulnar and radial arteries were then pulled out. Not just cut. The killer literally ripped them out of Dwyer's arms.'

Twenty-One

'Perhaps it was symbolic,' said Detective Constable Keith Friel, 'ripping the veins out. Perhaps it was meant to mean something.'

'Like what?' Grant challenged.

His words echoed in his office as he looked around at his colleagues, searching their expressions.

Lawrenson stifled a yawn and ran both hands through his hair.

Friel lit up a cigarette and puffed anxiously on it.

Detective Constable Dennis Schofield was glancing at the photos of the dead man and shaking his head.

'Come on, for fuck's sake,' hissed Grant. 'Somebody give me *something*. Why has he changed his MO?'

'The pathologist's report says that all three victims were strangled the same way, guv,' Lawrenson offered. 'Who says he has changed it?'

'This business with the veins, it might just be some kind of sick joke to put us off the scent,' Friel added.

'What fucking scent?' snapped Grant. 'We haven't got a scent yet. We've got three bodies, all strangled and no motive. That's all we've got. No motive, no links.'

'It's going to take a bit of time,' offered Schofield.

'We haven't *got* time,' rasped Grant.

'Two pros and a drug pusher,' said Lawrenson. 'Perhaps the killer is wiping out low-lifes.'

Grant shrugged.

'We do know that Claire Glover bought drugs from Dwyer,' said Friel. '*That's* a link.'

'What's the word on the street?' Grant asked. 'Is anyone talking?'

'*Everyone's* talking,' Schofield informed him. 'It's just

that what they're saying isn't helping much. They're scared but they're *more* scared of us.'

'You're not talking to the right people,' Grant snapped.

'We just need some luck,' Schofield protested.

'Then get some,' Grant demanded.

A heavy silence descended on the room, finally broken by Grant.

'All right, this business of him pulling the veins out of Dwyer's arms, perhaps it *does* mean something,' he mused. 'But what?'

'It was done after Dwyer was killed,' Friel said, 'so the killer wasn't torturing him. It has to have a meaning.'

'It doesn't *have* to,' Grant said. 'The killer was just making sure.'

'If he wanted to be sure he could have cut Dwyer's throat, stabbed him through the heart – anything,' Lawrenson said. 'This business with the veins is a bit elaborate, isn't it?'

'So,' Grant conceded, 'the *act* itself probably does have meaning. But who is it sending a message to? Us or to other people like Dwyer?' He flipped through the pile of papers on his desk. 'By the way, who found the body?'

'Dwyer's landlord,' said Lawrenson. 'His statement's on your desk. He heard raised voices about eleven; he said it sounded like an argument.'

'But he didn't go down to the flat until nearly five hours later,' Grant observed. 'He didn't intend getting involved, did he? Have we eliminated him as a suspect?'

'His wife was with him all night; besides, he had no hassle with Dwyer. He said his rent was paid on time every month. He hardly saw him,' Lawrenson continued.

'So, other possible suspects?' Grant mused. 'Another drug dealer trying to muscle in on Dwyer's customers?'

Friel nodded. 'That's *my* bet.'

'That explains his death but not the other two,' Grant reminded the younger man.

'Maybe he was into pimping too,' Schofield offered.

'There's nothing in his past form to indicate that,' Grant said. 'But I'm inclined to think it was someone who knew all three victims.'

'Why?' Friel asked.

'Because at all three murder scenes there was very little or no sign of a struggle. There was no forced entry into Dwyer's place last night.'

'Perhaps it was one of his customers,' Schofield suggested. 'The deal could have cut up rough and the buyer topped him.'

'Then why not take the gear that was lying around the flat? Another user would have taken the coke and smack we found and used it or sold it on. But nothing was taken. Christ, whoever killed him didn't even bother going through his fucking wallet.' He sat back in his chair, hands behind his head.

Another heavy silence fell upon the four men.

'What I can't understand is why Dwyer didn't fight back. He was a big geezer, he should have put up a decent fight,' Lawrenson said.

'Perhaps he was already out of his head on smack when the killer attacked him and took him by surprise,' Grant surmised. 'The pathologist's report shows traces of heroin in his bloodstream.'

Lawrenson reached for the report and ran a finger down the carefully typed sheet. 'It also says he was suffering from septicaemia and hepatitis B. He was a sick man.'

Grant nodded. 'And now,' he said quietly. 'He's a *dead* man.'

Twenty-Two

Amy heard the shout before she heard the crash. An angry yell followed by a loud bang and then a voice once again, muttering.

She locked the door of her flat and peered over the banister, spotting several wooden crates in the hallway.

She could still hear the voice but, as yet, she couldn't pinpoint its owner.

Amy dropped her keys into her jacket pocket and made her way unhurriedly down the stairs, glancing over the banister as she went.

She saw the back of the man's head first. He was kneeling in the hallway picking up saucepans, and was muttering to himself as he dropped the pans back into a packing crate.

He was wearing a leather jacket and jeans; his hair, an inch or two over his collar, was thick and lustrous.

As Amy approached the bottom of the stairs she saw another half a dozen or so crates and boxes of various shapes and sizes piled outside the door of flat number one. The door was slightly ajar but she couldn't see into the flat.

The man dropped the last saucepan into the box, straightened up and turned just as she reached the bottom step.

'Having trouble?' said Amy, smiling as he looked at her.

His own smile was immediate and welcoming and she found herself momentarily gazing into his steel-grey eyes.

'You could say that,' he said and chuckled. 'I suppose that's what I get for being cheap and moving myself. I should have hired Pickfords.'

'Are you moving in to number one?'

Again he nodded. 'You might not have known if I hadn't dropped those bloody saucepans,' he said and grinned. 'Sorry if I disturbed you.'

'You didn't. Besides, it looks as if we're going to be neighbours; I live in the flat above.' She extended her right hand. 'Amy Watson.'

He shook the offered hand and she felt the strength in his grip.

'Jake Webber,' he replied, holding on to her hand a fraction of a second longer than necessary. Long enough to look into her green eyes. 'Nice to meet you.'

'I had no idea anyone was moving in. I hadn't seen or heard anyone looking round. No estate agents or anything like that.'

He shrugged then bent down to pick up one of the boxes. 'Well, I'd better get on.'

'Look, I was just going to get some shopping. Is there anything you want? You seem to have your hands full, if you'll excuse the pun, moving in.'

'Actually, could you get me a sandwich and some teabags if you're going anywhere near a supermarket. I haven't eaten since seven this morning. I'm starving.'

Amy smiled broadly. 'No problem. Do you want me to help you carry this stuff into the flat?' She moved towards one of the crates.

Webber spun round, his eyes blazing. 'Leave it!' he snapped.

Amy took a step back, stunned by the vehemence of his tone.

Immediately his smile returned. 'They're heavy,' he explained. 'Thanks anyway.'

'Okay, I'll go and get the provisions then.' She paused as she got to the main door. 'Don't drop anything else, will you. You might disturb the neighbours.' She grinned, then was gone.

He too smiled broadly, watching her as she left.

As soon as he turned around the smile disappeared.

He lifted the box with ease, despite its weight, pushed his way into the flat, then returned for another. He wanted them all inside before she returned.

Amy checked her watch as she opened the door into the hallway. It was 2.30 p.m. She'd been gone less than an hour.

The hallway was empty of boxes, the door of flat number one firmly closed.

She hadn't bought too much food for herself, just enough to last until the weekend when she would spend up to three hours in the supermarket replenishing her depleted fridge and cupboards. She actually enjoyed the trek up and down the aisles. For now, she had only two carrier bags. Inside one were two packs of sandwiches.

She knocked on the door of number one and waited.

Webber opened it almost immediately and she held up the bags in front of him.

'Meals on wheels,' she said chuckling, and handed him the sandwiches. 'I didn't know what you wanted, so I got a mixture.'

'How much do I owe you?' he asked.

'Call it a house-warming present.'

They both smiled. She gave him the teabags too. Still he was standing in the doorway, leaning against the frame.

'Look, I would ask you in, but the place is a tip.'

'So is mine and I've lived there five years.'

'I haven't had time to unpack much yet and . . .'

She held up a hand to silence him. 'Don't worry about it.'

'Some other time perhaps?'

She nodded.

'I'll leave you to get on then,' Amy said, again looking into his eyes. 'If you want anything, like I said, I'm in the flat directly above.'

'Before you go, I've got a confession to make,' he said, that faint smile still creasing his lips. 'When you introduced yourself earlier, I knew you were Amy Watson.

You've probably heard this so many times but I used to collect your photos when you modelled. I even had one of your calendars. Sorry if that embarrasses you.'

'I'm very flattered.'

'You did a spread for *Penthouse*, didn't you? A couple of years ago.'

She nodded.

'I've still got it,' he said almost guiltily.

She smiled broadly. 'Well, you've got me at a disadvantage, Jake,' she said. 'All I know about you is your name. You even know where my birthmark is.'

Webber cracked out laughing.

'I feel like some teenager who's been caught wanking,' he said, feeling his cheeks colour. 'I listen to your radio show too.'

'Now you're grovelling.'

'Look, thanks for these,' he said, holding up the sandwiches. 'Next time, *I'll* buy.'

'I'll hold you to that,' said Amy and turned towards the stairs. 'See you around, Jake.'

He waited until she was halfway up the stairs then closed the door.

Amy was on the top step when she heard a low clunk.

The door of number one had been bolted.

Twenty-Three

The only sound in the incident room was the low hum of the air-conditioning. David Grant walked slowly around the deserted room, drawing on his cigarette, glancing at the array of photos tacked to the noticeboards at one end of the room.

Claire Glover.

Tessa Carr.

Harvey Dwyer.

There were half-a-dozen photos of each victim. One taken in life, the others in death.

Was this it? The existence of three people reduced to black and white ten-by-eights and a handful of files.

They all had families somewhere. People to grieve for them. People who loved them.

Didn't they?

Each one a son or daughter.

Each one now a statistic.

Nothing more.

For Grant they were a means to an end. In death they would tell him much more than they ever could while they'd lived. The examinations, the post-mortems should give some clues as to who had snuffed out their lives so brutally.

But *why* had those lives been snuffed out?

Come on, think.

He moved closer to the pictures and gazed into the blank, monochrome eyes. *What can you tell me?*

He stared at the pictures of Claire Glover. Stared into those eyes. At the livid complexion. At the deep gouges around the neck and the bruises on the face.

Who did this to you?

In the post-mortem photos of Tessa Carr her eyelids were open wide enough for him to be able to see her glazed eyes. Like those of a fish on a skillet. People used to believe that the last thing imprinted upon the eye of a murder victim was the identity of the killer.

Grant smiled.

Look into those eyes.

There was bruising around the left one. A slight tear in the lower lid of the right.

What did you see?

He peered at those of Harvey Dwyer.

As the life was being throttled from you, did you look into the face of your killer?

Grant examined a separate set of photos that showed just Dwyer's forearms, the veins and arteries torn out.

He exhaled wearily and turned his back on the pictures. A headache was beginning at the base of his skull and he used one hand to massage the tight knot of muscles there. A glance at his watch told him that it was 10.56 p.m.

Time to go home?

He'd rung home two hours ago to tell Tina he'd be late. He'd left a message on the answerphone just like he'd done so many times before, and he knew that she'd listen to it with the same weary resignation she had listened to other similar messages he'd left.

Time to go home?

There were files on the desks in the incident room. Statements. Medical reports. Post-mortem notes. He picked up the first of the manilla files and sat down at one of the desks.

He lit another cigarette and began reading.

She knew as soon as she closed the front door behind her that he wasn't home. As soon as she saw the red message light flashing on the answering machine she knew that he had called.

Tina Grant didn't even bother to check the message. She kicked off her shoes and left them in the hall, before heading upstairs, switching on the lamp at the bottom of the staircase as she passed.

She made her way up to their bedroom and undressed

quickly, slipping on a T-shirt. Then she wandered into the bathroom, brushed her teeth and headed back to bed.

Back to *their* bed.

It was cold beneath the sheets. It was always cold these days, she thought.

She stretched, realising how tired she was. She didn't know what time he'd be home. Even if he would be home.

She glanced at the clock then set the alarm, settling herself once more.

Rolling on to her side, one hand almost unconsciously strayed to the empty side of the bed where her husband should be lying.

It felt so cold.

She closed her eyes and sleep was upon her in minutes.

Amy sat up in bed, muttering irritably to herself. *Jesus Christ. Was it too much to ask for a few hours sleep?*

She sat in the gloom for long seconds before finally reaching across and flicking on one of the bedside lamps. She hated the darkness when she was alone.

She yawned. *You're tired. Why can't you sleep?*

For the last eighteen months she had found it difficult to sleep at night. A few hours here and there. She'd always been able to function on a surprisingly small amount of sleep but, lately, it was becoming more of a hindrance. She rarely rose in the mornings feeling refreshed.

The sleepless nights had begun when the affair had finished. Whichever way she chose to look at it, she was faced with the inescapable fact. She missed him.

Missed having him close to her at night.

Missed the knowledge that they would meet, however infrequently.

Him. Him.

Can't you even bring yourself to say his name?

She looked across to one of the bookshelves on the far side of the room. Several of his books were displayed there.

John Howard.

She'd felt safe with him.

There had been a time during their affair when she'd confided in him that she'd been suffering bad dreams on an almost nightly basis. One night, as they'd drifted off to sleep, he'd whispered to her to wake him if those bad dreams returned.

She had slept soundly in his arms that night and on every occasion she'd seen him. Usually exhausted by the intensity of their lovemaking, she had rested safely with him and the dreams had not returned.

He had driven them away. She'd convinced herself of that.

And where was he now? Lying in bed with his wife? Or with another woman perhaps?

He'd cheated with *her*, why should he stop?

Amy wondered what he was doing and she was angry with herself for even entertaining those thoughts.

Angry with *him* because she could not rid herself of them.

Of his image.

Of the memories. Because now memories were all she had.

She ran a hand through her hair and exhaled deeply.

The bang came from below her. A loud impact of wood on wood.

A door being slammed?

Amy swung herself out of bed as she heard the sound of a key in a lock, the silence of the night acting as an amplifier for the smallest noise.

She crossed to one of her windows and peered out into the street. There was a lamp directly opposite, the sodium glare casting deep shadows. Someone had emerged from the flats and was making their way across to the other side of the street, walking swiftly, hands dug into their pockets. The figure was unmistakable.

Amy glanced at her bedside clock then back out into the street to see the figure being swallowed up by the gloom.

She frowned. Where the hell was Jake Webber going at 3.22 in the morning?

Twenty-Four

'Dirty bastard,' muttered Nancy Kendall, bending low over the sink.

She coughed loudly, hawked and spat into the dirty basin, spinning both taps afterwards. She watched the mixture of phlegm, semen and water swirling around the plughole, as if mesmerised by it, then she straightened up and inspected her reflection in the cracked mirror.

She leaned closer and put out her tongue. God, she hated it when they came in her mouth.

'Dirty bastard,' she said again, reaching inside her handbag for a small jar of Listerine. She swilled a capful of the liquid around her mouth and spat again. Then she splashed her face with water and smoothed her hair away from her forehead. She had a spot just above her right eyebrow. It looked red and angry against the paleness of her complexion. She prodded it with her index finger before swigging more of the Listerine.

The taste was beginning to fade now. That horribly familiar salty, oily flavour, which she had come to know only too well during the last four years. The first time a punter had come in her mouth she'd nearly vomited, spitting out most of the ejaculate, much to the man's fury. She'd spattered his trousers with it.

Nancy grinned as she remembered the incident, the grin fading slightly as she remembered too how hard he'd hit her. He'd knocked out one of her teeth.

Bastard.

That was how she'd met Simon. Both of them had been sitting in Casualty at The Royal North Hospital that Saturday night – she, wondering if her jaw had been broken and he, awaiting stitches for a cut hand.

He'd started talking to her, even introduced her to the

girl he was with. She'd been fifteen then. She'd guessed he was in his early twenties.

They'd become lovers a week later.

Two days after that he was pimping for her. But he was doing it, he kept reminding her, because he loved her and he didn't want any harm to come to her on the streets. She would be safe with him because he was careful. He only worked with three other girls and he didn't allow them to get into trouble. He looked out for them. Just like he'd look out for her.

She looked at her reflection once more and, running a comb through her long dark hair, smiled as she thought of him. It was only a short walk to their flat from where the punter had dropped her off. She'd taken the money from him then headed for the all-night café near St Pancras Station to wash out her mouth. To swill the taste of him away. It was in that toilet she now stood.

It had been a good night. She'd made over seventy pounds. Simon would be pleased.

She took a five-pound note from the wad in her purse and gazed at it for a moment before slipping it beneath her right foot, and pressing it into the high-heeled shoe she wore. She'd tell him she used some money to get a taxi home. He wouldn't mind. He wanted her to be safe. He cared about her.

She walked out of the café toilet, through the clutter of tables, where two or three taxi drivers sat talking and drinking coffee, and out into the night.

The wind was whipping along Euston Road, hurling rubbish before it. A discarded McDonald's container tumbled past her, propelled by the breeze. Nancy pulled up the collar of her jacket and began walking, grateful that she hadn't got far to go.

She passed St Pancras town hall and headed down Judd Street, noticing that one of the doorways contained what looked like a discarded bundle of clothes.

As she drew alongside the bundle moved and an unwashed face glared out at her. A man in his twenties?

It was hard to tell his age. He muttered something under his breath, annoyed at being woken by the clicking of her heels on the pavement, then he rolled over, pulled his filthy sleeping bag more tightly around him and tried to sleep again. Nancy could smell the acrid stench of urine emanating from the man, wafting on the breeze like an invisible cloud.

She walked on, turning into Cromer Street. Several of the streetlights were out and the thoroughfare was in virtual darkness.

A car parked close to the kerb suddenly started up, the sound of the engine making her jump. She peered into the gloom inside the car but couldn't make out the face of the driver. The engine spluttered and died and she heard grunts of anger from inside as the occupant tried once more to get the car going. As she crossed the road she could still hear the whining of the engine behind her.

The church opposite towered above her, its spire thrusting up into the dark sky. The building was dark and it appeared as if it had been hewn from the blackness itself, part of the deep gloom that covered the street.

She could hear creaking and, as she drew nearer, realised that the wrought-iron gate that led up to the main door of the church was moving in the breeze, the hinges groaning.

She reached into her handbag and pulled out a key, happy that she'd reached her destination.

Simon would be glad she was back.

She pushed the key into the door and stepped into the tiny hallway.

Nancy heard laughter coming from the sitting room. The door was slightly ajar and she realised that he had the television on. That was where the laughter was coming from.

She smiled. He'd waited up for her. God bless him. He must have missed her.

She pushed open the door, a smile spreading across her face.

It vanished rapidly as she began to scream.

Twenty-Five

In her dream someone was knocking on a door. Banging insistently. Someone she couldn't see.

The knocking was getting louder.

Inside her head it was deafening.

Amy wanted to clap her hands to her ears, to shut out the sound, to stop the dream.

She sat bolt upright. The banging continued.

She blinked myopically, looked around her.

The banging?

She was awake and yet the noise continued. She sat in bed listening, gradually realising that the sound wasn't part of a dream but was happening below her.

It wasn't banging. There was no one banging on a door.

She had heard the door to number one being opened and closed. There was movement below. Amy could hear someone moving around.

She shook her head as if to clear the lethargy. An attempt to separate dream from reality.

Amy rubbed her eyes and looked at the bedside clock. 4.36 a.m.

Jesus Christ.

It was still dark outside. Dawn was another hour or more away. And yet, below her, Jake Webber was moving about as if it was midday. It had been *his* door she had heard. Not some imagined, dreamlike intrusion. As she slowly lay back down she heard the sound of his shower running.

Amy closed her eyes, surprised at how tired she was, at how easily the drowsiness washed over her as she rolled on to her back.

Below her, the hiss of Webber's shower continued.

She glanced again at her clock and pulled the duvet up more tightly around her neck to keep out the cold.

Her eyelids began to close. Sleep was a welcome invader. She felt herself drifting off.

Where had Webber been?

She exhaled deeply.

Where?

She stretched, luxuriating in the warmth of her bed.

What kept him out in the early hours?

Perhaps she'd ask him.

'Jake. Where were you . . .'

Outside the wind was growing stronger. Amy slept.

Twenty-Six

The lift bumped to a halt and the doors slid open with a soft whirr.

Detective Sergeant Lawrenson shuddered involuntarily.

'It's always so bloody cold down here,' he said as he and Grant set off along the corridor.

Grant chose to ignore his colleague's remark.

He reached the door marked PATHOLOGY and pushed it open. The strong smell of chemicals swept over the two men like a wave. It was a smell both of them were well acquainted with.

A man was seated at a desk inside the outer office. He looked up and nodded cursorily at the two detectives as they passed.

'He's just finished,' he commented, watching as the men headed through another door.

'How long had Costello been pimping?' asked Grant without looking at his companion.

'Seven or eight years,' Lawrenson told him. 'He started young.'

'He finished young too, didn't he?'

Grant pushed open a set of double doors and the two men entered the main pathology lab.

Banks of fluorescents set into the high ceiling reflected their cold light off the white-tiled walls and floor and also on the cold steel surfaces of six worktops inside the lab. Only one of these was occupied.

The two men crossed to it immediately.

Phillip Barclay looked up from the corpse, wiping his hands on his apron which was already flecked with blood. Simon Costello's body was naked. Exposed to any prying eyes that cared to look.

Grant pointed at the throat. At marks that were becoming all too familiar.

There was a deep, angry crevice about half a centimetre thick in the flesh of the neck. Just above the larynx. There was dried blood around the mouth and, Grant noticed, at the base of a nostril. Several dark bruises showed up vividly against the pallid skin, most of them around the tops of the arms and the shoulders.

Lawrenson looked on with similar interest, trying to avoid looking at the huge Y-shaped cut that ran from Costello's sternum to his pelvis. The flesh had been folded back and the internal organs were exposed.

A set of scales hung above the autopsy table and, in one of the dishes, Lawrenson noticed two huge reddish-pink lumps of tissue, which he recognised as lungs. Close to Barclay, alongside a trolley that bore his implements, was a smaller dish also containing some human offal. A more shapeless discoloured object glistened beneath the bright lights. He had no idea what it was. The smell coming from the lungs and the open abdominal cavity of the corpse threatened to overpower him, and combined with the smell of chemicals, was almost intolerable.

'Go on then, Phil,' said Grant, looking at the pathologist. 'Surprise me. What did you find?'

'It's the same MO as the other three.'

Grant smiled and nodded. 'Murder weapon?'

'The lead of a lamp inside Costello's flat.'

'Why is there so much blood around the mouth?' Lawrenson enquired.

'There's always a certain amount of internal bleeding within the windpipe itself during a strangulation,' Barclay explained. 'The rupturing of blood vessels due to pressure, that kind of thing. In this case he bit his own tongue off too.'

'What about the bruising?' Grant asked.

'It's where he fell or was dragged by the killer. As I told you when we found the first two victims, this killer is very strong. However, in this case, he might have found the job a little easier.'

Grant looked puzzled.

Barclay pointed at the lungs dangling in their metal dish above the body.

'The lungs are diseased,' he said flatly. 'Costello had a chronic bronchial condition. At the time of his death he was in the early stages of emphysema. He was using an inhaler most of the time. It was found in his flat, as I'm sure you know.'

Grant nodded.

'It's not so difficult choking to death a man who can hardly breathe anyway,' Barclay added.

'There were no signs of forced entry, just like the last one,' said Grant. 'So, again, I'm wondering if he knew his killer.'

'Pissed-off punter again?' Lawrenson offered.

'Did Costello know any of the other victims?' Grant asked, his gaze still riveted on the corpse.

'Some tart we spoke to thinks he used to pimp for Claire Glover at one time,' Lawrenson informed his superior. 'But that was a while ago. He had a small stable. Three, four girls tops, including his own bird, the one who found him.'

'Time of death?'

'Early morning,' Barclay informed him. 'I'd say between two and five.'

'What kind of person would know a drug pusher *and* a pimp well enough to be able to walk into their flats and attack them without arousing their suspicions,' Grant mused. 'It had to be someone they trusted. Someone they'd both dealt with before. Either that or the entry *was* forced.'

'There was no sign of that at Dwyer's place or Costello's,' said Lawrenson.

'I don't mean he kicked the fucking door down,' Grant snapped. 'I mean, what if they had no choice but to let him in. There's a knock on the door, they answer it and someone's standing there pointing a gun at them. Open the door or I'll blow your head off. It's not out of the question.'

'Then why go to the bother of strangling them once they were inside?' Lawrenson insisted. 'If the killer used a shooter to gain entry then why not just use it on them?'

'Because guns are easier to trace than ropes or flex. And they're noisier. If the killer had shot them, Christ knows who might have heard. He could have been spotted leaving the scene. But if he only used a gun to get *into* the flats then he could have taken his time, chosen how he did them. Neither of them were going to fight back with a gun stuck in their face, were they?'

Lawrenson stroked his chin thoughtfully.

'Come on,' snapped Grant. 'At least admit the *possibility*.'

'Fair enough, guv,' said Lawrenson. 'But that still doesn't give us a motive, does it?'

'How many statements have been taken regarding this case?' Grant wanted to know.

'So far, nearly seventy and we've still got fuck all. We've had men out round the clock, like you said. We've tried all the usual sources.'

'Then try them again.'

'We're stretched to the limit already.'

'Bollocks,' Grant hissed. 'Someone somewhere knows something. And I want them found. If we don't stop this bastard soon we'll be up to our necks in corpses. He's on a roll and I'll tell you something, he's not going to stop until we get him.'

Twenty-Seven

David Albury sat back in his seat and pulled gently at his cuffs, a smile hovering on his lips as he listened to the tirade of words being flung at him from a member of the audience. Albury looked directly at the man, who was now on his feet, pointing angrily at the Home Secretary. He thought how grubby the man looked, dressed in his cheap shirt and jeans.

Judith Maddison, presenter and host of *Late-Night London*, moved closer to the furious man, trying to ensure that his words were heard through her microphone while at the same time not allowing him to rip the implement out of her hands.

The rest of the audience were either gazing at the speaker or looking at the stage area where Albury sat. Opposite Albury were two men in their twenties, one of whom was dressed in a suede jacket and black cords, the other looking somewhat ridiculous in a waistcoat and black trousers, a key-fob hanging from the pocket of the waistcoat. His greying hair was pulled back in a ponytail and, when he looked at Albury, it was through thick bi-focals.

The man in the audience finally sat down and Judith Maddison hurried towards Albury. 'How do you respond to that, David?' she asked the politician. 'How do you justify your new Bill to limit the availability of violent or pornographic films and videos? Isn't it an infringement of freedom?'

Albury waited a moment then adopted his much-practised and patronising tone.

'Judith, this isn't about freedom of speech,' he said earnestly. 'My Bill is to prevent the kind of so-called freedom granted to film makers and video distributors who are more concerned with making a fast buck with sensationalism than trying to use their medium for more useful purposes.'

'So what kind of films would *you* like to see being made?' Judith asked him.

'That isn't the issue here, my personal opinion isn't important. What I care about is ordinary people, families and, more particularly, children.'

There was a muted round of applause from some audience members.

'We've already seen the damage some of these videos can do,' the Home Secretary continued. 'For instance, if *Child's Play 3* had never been made then perhaps a little boy would still be alive today in Liverpool. His killers admitted committing their crime after seeing that film.'

'That was never proved,' said the man with the ponytail.

'The killers themselves said it,' Albury countered. 'Are you prepared to see more innocent lives affected by the kind of mindless horror which brought about the death of Jamie Bulger?'

'What do you say to that, Tim Newton?' Judith asked the man with the ponytail. 'Would there be less crime if this kind of film was banned?'

'There is no empirical evidence that violence in films is linked to violence in real life,' said Newton, shifting in his seat.

'I wonder if you could look the mother of that murdered child in the eye and say that,' Albury said, leaning towards Newton. 'Could you comfort that woman by telling her that?'

There was more applause from the audience.

Albury realised he was in a stronger position now and he pressed on, raising a hand to silence Newton when he tried to speak.

'I must say, Judith,' said the MP wearily, 'I feel something close to pity for Mr Newton if he refuses to see the effects of this kind of film. Do you have children, Mr Newton?'

'I don't think that's relevant.'

'*Do* you?' Albury persisted.

'No, but—'

'Well, one day you might and then perhaps you will understand the fear which so many parents in this audience feel,' the Home Secretary continued. 'We all want the best for our children and I don't feel that subjecting them to an endless diet of violence and sex on film and video is the best we can offer them. Do you?' He smiled condescendingly, the smile broadening as a loud round of applause swept from the audience.

Newton twisted in his seat again, his face darkening.

'But children don't see violent films or sexually explicit films because of our certification standards, they—'

Albury interrupted him again. 'That's rather naive, isn't it?' he said, his head on one side as if he was addressing a naughty child. 'As long as these films are freely available then children will find some way of seeing them. Violence begets violence. What people *see* they will copy.'

Another round of applause.

'But people have a right to see what they choose to see,' Newton responded angrily.

'And you would give them that freedom irrespective of the risks, would you?' Albury smiled that patronising smile again.

Newton opened his mouth to say something but it was drowned beneath another round of applause.

The Home Secretary pulled at his cuffs once more.

'You're talking about bringing in tougher ratings for films,' said Newton irritably. 'This has nothing to do with kids, you'll be depriving *adults* of the right to see films they want to see if you try to ban everything.'

Albury shook his head wearily. 'The Bill I am proposing,' he said disdainfully, 'will ensure that the kind of violent and pornographic film I am opposed to, I and the vast majority of right-thinking members of the public, will not be so widely released. This kind of film will be cut more heavily to make it more acceptable, although how anyone can find violence acceptable I really don't know.'

Judith Maddison stepped forward towards the man sitting on Newton's right.

'Stephen James,' she said. 'You run film festivals that specialise in showing horror films and violent films, don't you?'

James looked perplexed by his sudden inclusion in the debate. He swallowed hard and managed to nod.

'What kind of films do you show at these festivals?' Judith Maddison persisted.

'Zombie movies,' James began. 'Cult horror stuff.'

'Such as?'

'*The Texas Chainsaw Massacre, Suspiria, Cannibal Ferox*, that kind of thing.'

'And are these festivals popular?' the interviewer asked.

'Yes, very popular,' said James. 'We've been doing them for about five years now.'

'And what kind of people come to see films like that?' Judith enquired.

'Just normal people,' James said.

'What is your definition of normal,' Albury interjected scathingly. 'I think that people who would pay good money to watch that kind of garbage must be rather pathetic and possibly dangerous.'

There was laughter from the audience.

Newton and James squirmed angrily in their seats.

James shouted something at the Home Secretary and gestured furiously at him but Albury merely turned away, smiling evenly at the audience.

People were standing up in the audience now, anxious to make their point.

Hidden from the prying eye of the four cameras, standing in the gloom at one side of the set, the producer smiled and looked at Albury.

'He's very good, isn't he?' he said, nodding in the Home Secretary's direction.

'Yes, he is,' Anita Bishop agreed, smiling. '*Very* good.'

Twenty-Eight

As Amy stepped from the cab she dropped her Puma sportsbag on the pavement and fumbled in her handbag, reaching for her purse.

She glanced at the meter and handed the driver a ten-pound note.

'Keep a couple for yourself,' she said, watching as he counted out the change.

He gave her one last appraising look then pulled away.

'Carry your bag, miss?'

The voice startled her and she spun round. Jake Webber was standing behind her, grinning broadly.

Amy smiled. 'You scared me,' she said, laughing.

She thought how fresh he looked considering how late he'd returned home. Apart from some stubble he looked as if he'd had more sleep than *she* had.

'I saw you arrive,' he told her, allowing his gaze to travel swiftly over her – the trainers, tracksuit bottoms and the white T-shirt covered by a leather jacket.

'Spying on me, eh?' she said, smiling. 'I've been to the gym.'

'And now?' he asked, picking up her bag.

'Now what?'

'Any plans?'

'No. Why?'

'I was just about to get some lunch. I wondered if you'd join me?'

'Sandwiches?'

'I can run to beans on toast.'

She laughed, looking deeply into his eyes. 'Thanks, Jake.'

'Let's go,' he said and they started walking.

*   *   *

DEE-DEE TEAS was a small café on the corner of Percival Street. Immaculately clean, it was more a miniature restaurant than a café, the menu boasting everything from sausage, beans and chips to cannelloni.

'I've lived here for four years and I never knew this place was here,' said Amy pushing a forkful of pasta into her mouth.

Webber smiled.

'How did you find out about it? You're not from around here, are you?'

He shook his head. 'I hear things.'

'Where *are* you from, Jake?'

'Originally? Hertfordshire. Hatfield, that way. What about you?'

'I was born in London. Hackney.'

'It's not a very strong accent.'

'It's still there sometimes. You know what they say? You can take the girl out of Hackney but you can't take Hackney out of the girl.'

They both laughed.

'I suppose jetting around the world modelling helped lose that accent,' he observed, sipping his coffee.

'Maybe.'

'Why did you give it up?'

'I was getting too old for it. It's a bit depressing when you're sharing a changing room with girls young enough to be your . . .' she shrugged. 'Younger sisters.'

She smiled and found the gesture returned.

'*How* young?' he enquired.

'Thirteen or fourteen sometimes.'

'That's disgusting. They're still kids.'

'That's the kind of model designers want to use. No curves. No shape. Skinny. They say most male fashion designers are gay, the clothes they design would look fine on young boys, so they choose girls with no waists and no tits. Girls who have bodies like boys. Boobs can be a handicap with some designers.'

'So who did you model for?'

'Most of the big names. Versace. Westwood. Calvin Klein. Are you impressed?' She grinned.

'Very. Why did you pack it in?'

'You just asked me that. I told you, I was getting too old.'

'Bullshit.'

'Jake, in case you hadn't noticed, once you hit twenty-five, everything starts heading south. Boobs, bum, the lot. I got sick of fighting gravity.'

'Don't you miss it?'

'Sometimes. I met some good people. Had some laughs. I met some arseholes too though.'

'Go on then, spill the beans. Give me the gossip.'

'Oh, photographers were the worst. If I had a pound for every one who's tried to get me into bed I could retire.'

'I can sympathise with them.'

She grinned. 'I think that's a compliment, isn't it?'

He nodded.

'Didn't you want to become an actress or a writer?' he asked. 'Most of these bloody models seem to think they've got gifts in those directions.'

'Do I detect a hint of cynicism there?'

'Sorry.'

'Don't be. I agree with you. No, I enjoy doing the show. That's enough for me.'

She sipped her Perrier and regarded him over the rim of the glass.

'Well, that's *my* life story,' she quipped. 'Your turn.'

He smiled.

'I don't even know what you do for a living,' she told him.

'As little as I can get away with,' he said, holding her gaze.

'Is it such a big secret, Jake?'

'I didn't offer to buy you lunch so I could talk about myself for two hours.'

'You're a very unusual man then. Most I've met can't

wait to talk about themselves. This is like having lunch with a spy.'

He chuckled. 'Perhaps I'm just a good listener. And it helps because you're a good talker.'

She punched him playfully on the arm.

'Hey,' he said, feigning annoyance. 'That was a compliment too.'

'You're full of compliments, Jake. Or full of shit.'

'Now who's being cynical?'

'How are you settling in?'

'Fine. I haven't seen much of the other tenants though. What are they like?'

'To tell you the truth, I haven't seen much of them either. Fortunately no one's suggested a residents' committee yet.'

They ate in silence for a moment, Amy occasionally looking at her companion. He was an attractive man, she had to admit. As she studied his features she saw a scar running from the corner of one eye across towards his ear.

'Where did you get that?' she asked, boldly tracing the outline of the scar with her finger.

He looked up as he felt the smooth flesh against his skin.

They looked deeply into one another's eyes, her finger still brushing against his face.

'Does it matter?' he asked.

'I was just curious.'

'You seem to be curious about a lot of things, Amy.'

'If you told me more about yourself I wouldn't need to keep asking.'

'There's not much to tell. There's a lot less to me than meets the eye.'

'I find that hard to believe.'

'Trust me.' He winked at her.

Amy laughed. 'That is so corny, Jake.'

Webber looked at her. The smile illuminated her features.

'You're very beautiful,' he told her.

'And *that* sounds even cornier but thanks anyway. Listen, are you doing anything tonight? I was wondering if you'd let me cook you dinner. I know that sounds a bit forward, doesn't it?'

'I'm not complaining, am I? I'd like that. Promise not to rag me if I don't spend the whole evening talking about myself. What time do you want me?'

'About eight? But don't expect anything fancy, will you?'

'Formal dress? Casual?' he said, grinning.

'Whatever you want.'

'I'll get the bill,' he said, reaching into his pocket for his wallet. Flipping it open, he pulled a couple of notes free.

Amy saw pictures inside the leather container. There were two of a young child.

She sipped at her drink, trying not to make it obvious that she'd spotted the snaps.

Another mystery?

He snapped the wallet shut and re-pocketed it.

Who was the child?

Webber was looking at her and smiling.

Amy returned the gesture, her eyes never leaving his.

Only when she finally glanced down did his smile fade.

Twenty-Nine

Jo Parker pushed the flat door shut with her back and dropped the four plastic carrier bags.

She ran a hand through her hair, wincing as she inspected the red marks across her palms where she'd been lugging the weight of the shopping. She hadn't been able to get a taxi from the supermarket and she'd got sick of waiting for a bus so, despite the weight of her load, she'd walked and now, as she rubbed her hands, she was regreting that decision.

The flat seemed almost unnaturally quiet as she headed towards the kitchen with the shopping.

No television. No hi-fi.

'Billy,' she called.

No answer.

She passed through the sitting room and saw a couple of T-shirts and a pair of jeans scattered wantonly on the sofa and the floor. One sock had also been tossed unceremoniously into a nearby armchair.

Jo exhaled wearily as she saw the scattered clothing.

There was a duffel bag beside the sofa, more clothes spilling from it like stuffing from a ripped toy.

Lazy bastard, she thought as she glanced irritably at the discarded clothes.

She could only guess where her brother was. He'd been sitting watching a video when she'd left nearly two hours ago. She'd asked him to clear away the clothes then, on her way out.

She shook her head in dismay, wondering whether or not to leave them and let *him* tidy them up when he returned. Whenever that might be. But one more glance at the untidy, dirty garments and she decided she'd clear them up herself.

But first the shopping had to be attended to.

She took it from the bags and began placing it in cupboards or freezer or fridge, moving with practised, almost robotic movements.

Since Billy had been staying with her, the bills had almost doubled. She earned a decent salary but Billy would prove to be an even more considerable drain on her resources if he stayed much longer. And not just on her financial reserves. His constant presence or, more particularly, his attitude were pushing her close to breaking point.

She tried to tell herself that blood was thicker than water and that, in his condition, he needed her, needed someone close. But, even the string of clichés she presented herself with didn't seem to justify having him stay with her indefinitely. At times like this, as much as she disliked admitting it to herself, she found it easy to understand how her parents could have rejected him so easily. She didn't blame them for not wanting him around if he behaved the same way he'd behaved since he arrived unannounced on her doorstep.

Would it have been different if it had been Danny?

She knew the answer without asking the question. Billy had been right. She would have welcomed her older brother with open arms. Told him he could have stayed as long as he wanted.

But that was not to be.

It was *never* to be. Not any more.

She stopped what she was doing for a moment, the thought of Danny catching her unawares, the momentary vision of his face flashing into her mind making her feel disorientated.

Jo swallowed hard and the image vanished. She finished unpacking the shopping and headed back into the sitting room.

Angrily, she snatched up the clothes from the sofa and floor. She'd give him another week then he was out.

You won't throw him out.

She'd help him look for a place if he'd let her or perhaps even have a word with her parents and see if they'd take him back.

They don't want him. No one wants him around. Not even you.

The T-shirts needed cleaning; she wrinkled her nose as she smelled perspiration. She balled them up.

One minute you're talking about throwing him out, the next you're getting ready to do his washing.

She picked up the sock and jammed it, along with the T-shirts, into the duffel bag before reaching for the jeans.

As she picked them up something fell from one of the pockets.

Jo knelt and inspected the object. It was a bottle with a child-proof lid. A bottle for pills.

The label had been scratched off. Whatever this bottle contained, she suspected, was not a prescription drug.

She held the plastic container in the palm of her hand for a second longer then pushed it back into the pocket of the jeans before checking the other pockets.

In one back pocket there was a piece of paper.

She unfolded it and scanned what was written there. It looked like a mobile number.

But whose?

She rummaged in the other pocket and found a handkerchief. It gave off a rank, familiar odour. Stale semen.

She winced and stuffed it back into the jeans.

She sucked in a weary breath.

She hurried across to the notepad next to the phone and wrote down the number on a sheet about halfway into the pad. Then she returned the slip of paper to her brother's jeans and jammed the whole lot into the duffel bag.

She made her way to the bathroom and washed her hands thoroughly, the smell of soap replacing the musty scent of semen.

Phone numbers. Pill bottles. What the hell was Billy up to?

One part of her wanted to confront him, to force the truth from him. Another told her to wait.

It could be innocent.

Could be?

She studied her own reflection in the bathroom mirror.

She would wait.

For now.

Thirty

Jake Webber watched the candle burning lower, its flame wavering as a draught caught it.

Amy watched him across the table, the dull yellow glow of the flame casting deep shadows.

'Penny for them,' she finally said.

Webber looked up and smiled, shaken from his aimless gazing by the sound of her voice.

'I'm sorry,' he said quietly. 'I was miles away.'

'Charming.'

He grinned broadly. 'I was just thinking what a beautiful meal that was. Thank you very much. It beats the shit out of a Birds Eye Ready Meal For One.'

'You sound like an expert, Jake. Do you eat a lot of them?'

'You know what it's like. When you're on your own you don't always bother cooking for yourself, do you? I usually end up with a take-away or a microwave dinner.'

'Didn't your mother ever tell you how important it is to eat properly?' she said, smiling.

He raised an eyebrow. 'She didn't tell me much about anything really.'

'Do you still see her?'

'She died twelve years ago. A stroke.'

'I'm sorry.'

'Don't be. It happens, doesn't it. My old man was killed in a work accident two years later.'

'What kind of accident?'

'He was a roofer by trade. Him and some other bloke were working on a church roof in Kentish Town. The bloody thing collapsed under them. The other bloke broke his back, he's been paralysed ever since. My dad was killed.'

'Were you close?'

'You're doing it again.'

'Doing what?'

'Asking questions.'

'I'm trying to find out about you, Jake, that's all. There's nothing sinister to it, you know.'

'I thought I'd done well, we got through most of the meal without you probing.'

'If it bothers you . . .'

He raised a hand. 'Like I told you this afternoon,' he said softly, 'there's not much worth knowing.'

'We've spent over three hours sitting and talking and eating and I still don't know any more about you apart from the fact that your parents are both dead. All we've done is talk about *me*. My life. What I've done.'

'It's more interesting.'

'Are you always this secretive with women?'

He laughed. 'Why do you think I'm being secretive just because I'm not rabbiting on about myself all the time?'

'Are you always this mysterious with your girlfriends?' she enquired, pushing her wine glass towards him.

He refilled it then repeated the procedure with his own.

'What makes you think I had any?' he said flatly.

'Jake, you're a good-looking guy. I think I'd be pretty safe in assuming you'd had some kind of contact with the opposite sex.' She raised her glass and sipped from it.

'I could be gay,' he said, grinning.

She shook her head.

Webber laughed again.

'Look, you're the model. How come there's no man in your life? I'd have thought there'd have been blokes queuing up to take you out.'

'Did you pass them on the stairs?'

'So, what's your secret? Why no man?'

'I'm a dyke.'

'Got any pictures,' he said, chuckling.

She picked up her discarded napkin and threw it at him.

'You went out with a drummer from a rock band,' he told her. 'I remember seeing it in the paper and then some writer. What was his name? Howard, that was it. John Howard.'

She nodded slowly, the brightness fading from her face. She took another sip of her wine.

Yes. John fucking Howard.

He watched her intently, aware that mention of the name had struck a nerve of some kind.

'No one on the scene at the moment?' he continued.

She shook her head. 'What about you. Anyone "on the scene"?' There was a hint of scorn in her voice which she tried, but failed, to conceal.

They looked at each other across the table, the flames of the candles still flickering.

'Come on, Jake,' she said, 'you know all about *me*. Tell me something about yourself.'

'Like what?'

'Like who's the kid?'

He looked surprised.

'At lunchtime, when you were paying for the food, I saw some photos in your wallet of a kid,' she told him. 'I assumed it was yours.'

'Yes,' he said sternly. 'She was mine.'

'So, is there a wife somewhere too? Is that why you're so secretive? What's going on? Let me guess. You're going through a divorce, she's kept the house, kicked you out and you see your kid only occasionally. Right?'

'I'm not on your fucking show, Amy,' he snapped. 'I'm not one of those sad bastards who call you asking for advice or spilling their fucking problems for the whole world to hear and laugh at, so don't treat me like one of them.'

The vehemence in his tone shook her.

'Am I right?' she persisted, her voice softer.

'Would it matter if you were?'

'I'm interested in you, Jake. Is that such a crime?'

He swallowed what was left in his glass and refilled it.

'There's no wife,' he finally said. 'There never has been. There've been women. Enough of them.'

'And the child?'

'She was mine,' he said, his voice cracking slightly. He cleared his throat, reaching into his pocket for his wallet. He flipped it open and pulled the two photos free, pushing them towards Amy.

'She's beautiful,' said Amy, inspecting the snaps. 'How old is she?'

Webber swallowed hard. 'Eighteen months when those were taken,' he said quietly, filling his glass again. 'Her name was Samantha.'

'So, where is she?'

'She's dead.'

Amy looked first at the snaps then at Webber who was staring blankly ahead.

'Those were taken about a month before it happened.' Again his voice cracked.

'How?' Amy asked.

He took the pictures back, cradling one in the palm of his hand, gazing at the tiny smiling little face captured there.

'I was living with someone,' he began, not taking his eyes from the picture of his child. 'Her name was Kim, she worked for a cosmetics firm. It was a good job, good prospects. She was very career-minded. She never wanted kids.'

'Did you?' Amy asked softly.

'They were all I ever wanted,' he confessed. 'I suppose after my parents died it got worse. Some fucking shrink would have a field day with the Freudian implications no doubt.'

'What about your girlfriend? Did *she* know how badly you wanted kids?'

'We never really talked about it. She was on the pill, she had no intention of coming off it, no thoughts of giving up her career to become a mother.' He gazed more intently at the photos of the child.

'So, what happened?'

'Kim had a bout of food poisoning. She was sick a lot. The pill never worked. She got pregnant. It was an accident, as simple as that.' He took a sip of his wine. 'I was fucking ecstatic when I found out.' A smile hovered briefly on his lips. 'Kim was pissed off. All she could think about was how having a baby would ruin her career.'

'Didn't she think about an abortion?'

'She might have thought about it but she never mentioned it to me. That was never an option as far as I was concerned.' He shrugged. 'So she had the baby. I was there for the birth. I was the first one to hold Sam. She was premature. Christ, she was tiny.' He took a sip of his wine. 'I took them home three days later. Within the space of a week, Kim was looking for child-minders. She just wanted to get back to work. She couldn't get on with breast-feeding or the sleepless nights. I think she started to hate Sam. I did everything I could to help but, as far as Kim was concerned, it was never enough.'

'Did she go back to work?'

'Part-time. She missed out on a promotion because of that. She started taking it out on Sam.'

'Did she hit her?'

'Not as far as I know but she was sharp with her, she had no patience with her. I think every time she looked at Sam she resented her.'

'How did she die?' Amy asked, reaching out with one hand to gently touch Webber's arm.

'She was crawling around on the landing one day and she fell down the stairs. Broke her neck.' He clenched his teeth.

Amy saw the tears welling in his eyes.

'The fucking stair-gate was open, Kim should have shut it, she should have been watching her,' Webber rasped. 'Sam was dead before we got her to the hospital.'

'Jake, I'm so sorry.'

'Yeah, so am I,' he hissed, the knot of muscles at the side of his jaw throbbing angrily. He had one fist clenched tightly and was bumping it gently against his chin. 'At the funeral, Sam's coffin was so small I carried it on my own. It was like a little white shoebox and it had a white bouquet on top with a silk bow; as if she'd been gift-wrapped.'

He lowered his head.

'Kim and I split up a month later,' he said. 'I'll never forgive her for what happened.' He looked directly into Amy's eyes and the rage and sadness burning there transfixed her. '*She* deserved to die too,' Webber snarled. 'I should have done it then. I should have put her in the fucking ground next to Sam.'

Thirty-One

They sat in silence, either unable or unwilling to speak, as if any utterance would be an intrusion. Then Webber carefully slid the photos back into his wallet. It was he who broke the silence.

'I haven't been back to the grave since Sam was buried,' he said in a quiet voice.

'Why?'

'Because I can't face it,' he snapped. 'I can't face *her*.'

'You *need* to go back, Jake.'

'Why? So I can relive all the memories again? So I can go through all that pain again?'

'You'll never cope with her death if you don't face it.'

'Don't patronise me, Amy. I cope with it, in my own way.'

'It's tearing you apart. Don't tell me you don't want to go to see her grave because I won't believe you.'

He eyed her warily.

'Very professional,' he said, scathingly.

'Oh, for Christ's sake, I'm not trying to psychoanalyse you, I'm trying to help you. Stop being so bloody defensive, Jake.'

'How much more do you want to know about me, then? Isn't what I've told you enough?' He finished what was left in his glass and banged it down hard on the table. 'Perhaps I'm scared. There, I've said it. Satisfied? Perhaps you're right, perhaps I can't cope with it. How the hell would you know what it feels like? No one can unless they've been through it.'

'What are you scared of?'

'I let her down too, Amy,' he said, his voice quivering. 'I blame Kim for Sam's death but perhaps I was as much to blame. I was there when it happened and I couldn't stop it.'

'It was an accident, Jake, how could you have stopped it?'

'I knew Kim didn't give a shit, I should have kept a closer eye on Sam myself. Maybe that's why I don't want to go to visit the grave. Because it would make me confront my own guilt, my own part in her death.'

'Would you go if I came with you?'

Webber looked fixedly at Amy.

'Why would you do that for me?'

She shrugged. 'I'm just trying to help.' She got up, walked around the table, and sat beside him, squeezing his hand, feeling him respond, feeling the strength in his grip.

Almost without thinking, she leaned forward, her face close to his.

'If I go with you, will you go?' she whispered, one slender finger tracing a pattern across his cheek.

He slid a hand around her shoulders and pulled her closer and their lips brushed. Lightly at first, then with more urgency. She snaked her own arms around his neck and, as she did, she felt his tongue pushing urgently against her lips, then her teeth. She responded fiercely, sliding her own tongue into his mouth.

They remained locked together for seconds that seemed to stretch into an eternity.

Amy allowed one hand to drop to his thigh, her fingers trailing across the material of his trousers, feeling the muscles beneath. He gripped her arm, his strong fingers digging into her soft flesh, but in that strength there was tenderness. The strength was replaced by a feather-light gentleness as his hand moved slowly across to first brush then cup her right breast, and then his thumb brushed one swollen nipple.

She shuddered.

They broke the kiss and sat looking intently at each other, both of them sucking in deep breaths.

He touched her lips with a finger and she flicked out her tongue to moisten the end of the digit. Webber drew that slippery finger across her bottom lip with excruciating slowness, her own saliva glistening in the candlelight. Then he repeated the process on her top lip, feeling her ever-willing tongue once again slide around the probing fingertip. She kissed it lightly.

She was stroking his thigh gently, rhythmically, and still they continued to gaze into each other's eyes.

'I've got to go,' he said, leaning forward, kissing her lightly on the lips.

'Why, Jake?' Her voice was low and shaking.

She kissed him again and this time she felt his hand on her thigh. Stroking. Kneading the smooth flesh just below the hem of her short dress.

'You don't have to go,' she told him breathlessly.

He got to his feet and she rose with him.

'I know I don't,' he whispered, leaning forward so that his mouth was pressed right against her ear.

She felt the warm breath against her tender lobe.

'This seems so pointless, Jake,' Amy said. 'You leaving.'

'There'll be other times.' He raised an eyebrow. 'Won't there?'

She smiled and nodded.

He paused at the front door, turned and they kissed again.

'I'll see you tomorrow,' he said.

'Think about what I said,' she told him. 'About Sam.'

He nodded then headed for the stairs.

As she closed her door she heard his footsteps receding away, heard his own door open and close.

Amy stood against her door, her breath coming in shallow gasps.

Things moving a little fast aren't they?

She sighed then walked back into the sitting room, glancing across towards the dining area. To hell with it, she'd clear up in the morning.

You hardly know the bloke and you are trying to seduce him.

There was half a glass of wine left and she picked it up, sipping at it.

Time for a cold shower before bed?

She smiled to herself and crossed to the window of the flat, looking out into the street. It was deserted out there. People were either out partying or tucked up in bed.

Lucky bastards.

She could still taste him on her lips.

Frightening, isn't it, how quickly feelings overtake you?

The streetlight opposite was flickering again, threatening to die completely. Amy wondered if anyone had reported it to the relevant authority. For what it was worth.

She finished her wine and was about to move away from the window when she saw him. Crossing the street, hands dug in his pockets in that familiar stance.

It was Webber.

He had changed into jeans and a leather jacket.

Going where?

She glanced at her watch.

1.23 a.m.

By the time she looked back he'd disappeared into the night.

Thirty-Two

Ralph Harker knew there was going to be trouble. It might just be an argument, a few threatening words hurled back and forth but, whatever the final outcome, he was sure that there was going to be trouble.

He fumbled in one pocket of the dirty overcoat he wore and felt the short-bladed knife he always carried. It felt reassuringly sharp against the pad of his thumb. In his other pocket was a half-bottle of White Horse. He patted that lovingly. He'd stolen it only hours earlier from an off-licence in Shaftesbury Avenue. Some he'd already drunk but he still had three-quarters of a bottle left, and now all he wanted to do was drink it in peace. Drink it and sleep, if he could in the chill wind. Sleep in his usual spot but, at present, someone was occupying his usual spot.

That was why Ralph was convinced there was going to be trouble.

He'd lived on the streets of London for the past eighteen months and that nomadic existence had taken its toll on his body both internally and externally. His face bore lines and creases that made him look older than his forty-two years. His body was thin and undernourished. Every few days he took a trip to the Centre Point Hostel and got what passed for a square meal but, most of the time, he did as others like him did. He scavenged in wastebinds and skips, he begged and, when necessary, he stole.

There had been nowhere for him to go when he'd finished his latest five-stretch in Wandsworth. No home to return to. No family to shelter him. One of his sisters had written to him on a regular basis while he'd been inside but she'd made it clear that she didn't want him knocking on her door when he was released.

One of the screws had said 'See you soon' as he'd walked free and, at times, Ralph wondered if there was not only an inevitability about those words but also a kind of salvation. At least inside he was warm, well fed and reliant only on the screws. Outside it was more difficult.

He'd tried to get jobs but who the hell was going to employ him with his form? His parole officer had offered to help but he'd done nothing. No one wanted to offer Ralph anything, not even washing up in some greasy fucking café.

Bollocks to them.

He'd manage. It wouldn't be the first time he'd been on the streets.

He coughed and rubbed his chest. The fucking pain was worse now. It always hurt more when he coughed. The quack inside had said something about a bronchial condition, and possible liver damage. He'd said that Ralph should drink less when he got out.

Fat fucking chance. He patted the bottle of White Horse once again and advanced steadily towards the figure sleeping in his spot.

The lights that usually illuminated the canopy of the Phoenix Theatre in Charing Cross Road were off. It was darker than normal in the small passageway that ran alongside. There was a dry riser inlet close to the stage door. That was Ralph's spot. It had been for the last six months and now there was someone in it. Cheeky fucker.

Ralph looked down at the dark shape covered with blankets, and coughed.

The shape didn't stir.

He prodded it with his toe.

'Oi,' he said, his hand closing around the knife.

One of the dirty blankets was pulled down to reveal the face of a youth in his early twenties, his face pale, his eyes heavy with sleep.

'Move,' said Ralph. 'This is my fucking patch.'

The youth rubbed his eyes and blinked myopically at Ralph.

'Come on,' Ralph insisted more loudly.

The youth looked him up and down. 'I'd just got to sleep,' he complained.

'I couldn't give a fuck, move it or I'll move you,' Ralph hissed.

'I don't want to fight about it—'

'Then move.'

The youth gathered the blankets around him and got to his feet.

'Go on, fuck off!' said Ralph dismissively.

The youth stood there for a moment longer gazing at Ralph.

The older man pulled the knife free and brandished it before him. 'You want a bed for the night?' he snapped. 'I'll put you in a fucking hospital bed. Now piss off.'

The youth turned and walked away briskly.

Ralph settled into his space over the dry riser and wrapped his coat more tightly around him, digging the whisky out of his pocket. He couldn't carry on living like this. He'd go and see some of his old contacts tomorrow, see if there were any jobs he could do. It didn't matter what he had to do, he had to get off the streets. Someone might even have a job lined up. He hadn't lost his touch, he was sure of that. If they needed a little muscle he could help. If they wanted someone to keep an eye open he could do that. He could even drive if they'd let him. Ralph took a swig from the bottle. Maybe crime didn't pay but it was better than sleeping on the fucking streets.

He never saw the figure approaching him from behind.

Never heard the footsteps.

All he felt was something being slipped around his neck but he had no time to protest.

The wire was jerked hard.

So hard it lifted him off his feet.

The whisky bottle fell from his grip and shattered at his feet, the amber fluid racing away into a drain.

Ralph's eyes bulged in their sockets as the wire was tugged more tightly. It felt as if his head was swelling, threatening to burst like a balloon.

Then, nothing mattered any more.

Thirty-Three

David Grant slammed the newspaper down on the desk top and looked around at his companions. The other men in the Incident Room looked on impassively as Grant held up another of the papers lying close by, pointing to the headline.

SERIAL KILLER ON THE LOOSE?

it screamed.

'See it?' he snarled, reaching for another.

POLICE BAFFLED BY LATEST KILLING

He hurled that one across the room.

'There are details in all of these fucking papers about the murders,' Grant rasped. 'Details I have gone to great lengths to suppress.'

He picked up another of the tabloids. 'There are even details of the killing method,' he said angrily.

He eyed the men in the room challengingly. 'Now what I want to know is who leaked this information? Who gave the press this story?'

Silence.

'It had to be someone on this team,' Grant persisted. 'Only the officers working on this case knew the kind of details printed in these fucking rags. I've had reporters on the phone all morning asking me to confirm whether or not there is a serial killer at large in London. A serial killer who is strangling his victims. Something they couldn't possibly have known without inside information and I want to know where they got that information.'

'Why would anyone on this team release those details?' asked a voice from the back of the room.

Grant looked up to see that the question had been asked by Detective Constable Friel.

'You tell me,' snapped Grant. 'My guess is this is personal. Someone wants me to fuck up this case. Someone wants me to look like a idiot in front of the press and the Commissioner. Somebody's got a grudge and I'd lay money it's someone in this room.'

Again he scanned the rows of faces.

'Why would anyone want you to fail, guv?' Lawrenson wondered, puffing on his cigarette.

'Jealousy,' Grant told him. 'I knew when I got this promotion that there were some people who resented me for it. Well fuck them. I can put up with envy but what I won't tolerate is this.' He reached for one of the papers and held it up, waving it accusingly in the air. After a moment he threw it down again. 'This investigation isn't just about me, it's about this entire department. Whoever's leaking this stuff to the press isn't just making *me* look bad, they're making all of *you* look bad too.' He pointed at the watching officers.

'I think your paranoia's showing, Dave,' said a voice from the back.

'Leech. I should have expected that from you,' said Grant, aiming his ferocious gaze at an older man seated on a chair towards the rear of the room. Ronald Leech was in his late forties. A powerfully built man with a full head of almost pure white hair.

'You're looking for someone with a grudge?' Leech said defiantly. 'You might as well get the fucking phone book out and work your way through.'

'Perhaps I don't need to look any further than you, you bitter, twisted old bastard,' Grant snapped. 'I know you wanted this position. You'd been suck-holing the Commissioner long enough before he gave it to me.'

Leech got to his feet. 'I don't have to listen to this.'

Grant stepped in front of him. 'Yes, you do,' he rasped. 'Remember who's in charge here, Ronnie. Now sit down.'

The two men glared at each other for long seconds then the older man returned to his seat.

'If I find out you were behind these leaks I'll see to it you're back on a fucking beat in a month,' Grant threatened.

'What would I have to gain by going to the press?' Leech demanded.

'What would any of us have to gain, guv?' Schofield added.

'I told you, it discredits *me*.'

'But it makes us all look bad, like you said. It makes no sense,' Schofield persisted.

'I told you when I took over this investigation that there were people in this department who wanted to see me fail,' said Grant.

'I can't believe that,' Lawrenson added.

'Believe what you like, *I* know it's true and I'll tell you something else, the way this fucking investigation is going at the moment they must think they're on to a good thing.'

'There's nothing out there, guv,' Schofield said, puffing on a cigarette.

'There's a fucking murderer out there who's killed five people,' snapped Grant angrily. 'Five killings and we still haven't got shit. Who the hell have you been interviewing?'

'We've been working round the clock on this one, guv,' Lawrenson said. 'You know that.'

'Then where are the results?'

'We've asked all the usual,' said a voice from the back.

'Then ask the *unusual*,' Grant said. 'The media think we don't know what we're doing and I'm beginning to think that some of you *don't*.'

'So what's your theory?' Leech asked.

'I still think the killer knew his victims,' Grant said.

'We have to find out how he knew them, how he *found* them because when we find out how he found them, we find him.'

'Just like that?' said Leech disdainfully.

'Do whatever it takes,' Grant snarled. 'But I want someone and I want them quick.' He turned to the blackboard behind him where the photos of the murder victims hung. 'Otherwise this lot are going to have company.'

Thirty-Four

Amy Watson puffed on her cigarette, listening to the rantings of the latest caller, occasionally looking towards the window of the control booth where Mike Osborne was standing. He was sipping from a mug of coffee, watching Amy intently.

'I blame the police for these killings,' said the caller indignantly. 'Things like this didn't happen years ago. There used to be bobbies on the beat, you could talk to them, they knew everyone by name but—'

'Does the name Jack the Ripper ring a bell?' Amy interrupted.

'What?' the caller asked, bemused.

'You said things like this didn't happen years ago. I mentioned Jack the Ripper. And what about Haigh, the acid-bath murderer. Christie. Crippen. Peter Manual. George Joseph Smith. These are men who've gone down in criminal history. Don't try to say that the serial killer is just a *modern* phenomenon.'

'But all those men were caught.'

'That wasn't much help to their victims, was it? Are you suggesting that this murderer won't be caught, then?' She looked at the name flashing on her screen. 'Is that what you're saying, Maurice?'

'They might get him but they haven't done much so far, have they?' Maurice from Enfield continued. 'He's killed five people and they haven't even arrested anyone.'

'Do you work for the police?'

'No? What's that got to do with it?'

'Then how do you know they haven't arrested anyone yet?'

'It would have been in the papers and on the television.'

'So where do *you* think the police are going wrong then, Maurice?'

'There aren't enough of them walking a beat now. They sit around in those cars, none of them want to get cold by getting out. The policemen these days are lazy, and even when they do catch criminals they're out of prison in no time.'

'The sentencing isn't the fault of the police, Maurice, it's the judicial system that's to blame.'

'Well, I still think the police are—'

She flicked a switch. 'You're history, Maurice,' Amy said, smiling, taking another call.

'Bob from Lewisham,' she said. 'What do you think about these killings? Do you think the police will get their man?'

'I read somewhere that the conviction rate is ninety per cent,' said Bob. 'So they probably will.'

'Do you think they do a good job?'

'On this case or in general?'

'Both.'

'I've got no gripe with the police. I think they do all right. I mean, they're undermanned and all that, aren't they? I reckon they'll get this bloke, but I just reckon he'll kill a few more before they do.'

'What makes you think that, Bob?'

'Well, I've read books about these serial killers, blokes like that Sutcliffe geezer and the other one who buried them under the floorboards, you know, Nelson.'

'Nilsen,' she corrected him. 'Denis Nilsen.'

'Yeah, him. Well, they get sort of addicted to the killing, don't they? They get a buzz out of it. A sexual thing. If this bloke's killed five already then he must be enjoying it. He's not just going to stop, is he?'

'But you think the police are doing their best to catch him?'

'Yeah. I think that last bloke was out of order trying to blame them for not having got him yet. I don't blame the police. I blame the media.'

'For not catching the killer?'

'No. For making someone like that in the first place.'

'I'm not with you, Bob.'

'Well, these geezers are a bit funny in the head, aren't they? I mean, that bastard who shot those kids at Dunblane, that Hamilton bloke. I mean, he was weird, wasn't he? But he knew that if he shot loads of kids that his name would become famous. Like the geezer at Hungerford. Ryan. They knew that their names would be all over the media, and ever since it happened the press haven't let it drop, have they? I mean, there's things in the papers saying we mustn't forget what happened but some nutter reading that could think "Hold on, if I kill a few people, I'll get my name in the papers. I'll be famous." If the media dropped the coverage I reckon there'd be less of these serial killers around.'

'That's an interesting thought, Bob,' said Amy, blowing out a stream of smoke. 'Do you think that's why *this* killer is doing what he's doing? For fame?'

'You can never tell with these nutters, can you?'

'Quite true, Bob,' she said, smiling. 'Let's see if our next caller agrees with you.' She hit a button. 'Roy from . . .' She could see no location on the screen. 'Where are you from, Roy?'

'I'm speaking on a mobile,' the voice told her softly.

'Do you agree with what Bob just said? Is this killer in it for the fame? Should the police have caught him by now?'

Silence.

'Can you hear me, Roy?'

'I don't care why he's doing it,' said the caller quietly. 'Those he's killed deserved to die and there will be more deaths. There are plenty more scum out there to be removed.'

Thirty-Five

Amy looked at the screen where the name was flashing, the caller's words still echoing in her ears, his low breathing audible over the phone lines.

'Why do they deserve to die, Roy?' she asked, glancing up to see Osborne had again come to the window of the production booth.

There was silence on the other end of the line.

'Roy. Can you hear me?' she persisted.

'You need to ask me that?' he said scornfully. 'But then I suppose you would, wouldn't you? You weren't that different to *them*, were you?'

'I'm sure you're making a very interesting point here, Roy. I just wish I could understand what you're on about.'

'The ones who died. They had no self-respect, no morals, no shame. They didn't deserve to live. Prostitutes. Pimps. Drunks. Drug pushers. They're all scum.'

'Why do you include me with *them*, Roy?'

'You have no morals either. You take your clothes off. You flaunt yourself.'

'Not any more, Roy.'

'You *did*,' he roared. 'You tempted men with your body. You exposed your body for everyone to see. You had no shame.'

'Did I tempt *you*, Roy?'

Silence.

Osborne was standing waving frantically at Amy now, trying to attract her attention.

'Did you find the pictures of my body exciting, Roy?' she persisted.

Osborne was drawing his hand across his throat in a cutting motion but Amy merely shook her head.

'Do you think there's something wrong with the human body, Roy?' she continued. 'Do you think it's dirty?'

'What *you* did was filth,' the voice rasped.

'I was a model, Roy. That's all. Do you think that all models are like me?'

'Others show their bodies too. They're whores. *They* deserve to die.'

'Are you married, Roy?'

Silence.

'I thought not,' Amy murmured.

'I don't trust women,' he told her.

'Have you been hurt by a woman in the past, Roy? Is that why you don't trust us?'

'Whores. I see them on television, in the streets, in magazines. Flaunting themselves.'

'And because of that they deserve to die?'

There was a hiss of static on the line.

'You said that *all* the murder victims deserved to die,' Amy continued. 'Three of them were men.'

'Scum.'

'We quibble over terms,' she said, chuckling.

'Don't laugh at me, you bitch,' he hissed, the vehemence in his tone enough to raise the hairs on the back of her neck. 'I'll call you again, after the next one dies.'

He hung up.

Amy was momentarily stunned but she sucked in a deep breath, composing herself.

'I'll be back after the news,' she said. 'So, pay attention.'

She pulled off her headset and slumped back in her seat. 'Fuck,' she murmured under her breath.

Osborne appeared in the doorway of the studio, his face set in stern lines.

'I'm going to call the police,' he told her.

'And tell them what, Mike? That another nutter called the show? They're hardly likely to be surprised, are they?'

'He made threats, Amy,' Osborne insisted.

'It was some arsehole having a laugh.'

'Well it didn't sound very funny from where *I* was,' Osborne snapped. 'This could be important.'

She held up her hands in supplication.

'If you want to call the police, Mike, then call them,' Amy said irritably. 'Do what you like.'

'What the hell's wrong with you? What if he's serious? What if that *is* the killer? You heard what he said before he rang off. He'd call you back after the next one. The police should know about that call.'

'You couldn't trace it – what good will it be to them now?'

'He threatened you.'

Amy shrugged. 'He wouldn't be the first,' she said quietly, sipping at her coffee. She inhaled wearily. 'Look, if you call the police in you might scare him off. If he calls again, perhaps I can get some information out of him.'

'Calls again?' Osborne murmured. 'After someone else has died?'

They locked stares then Osborne shook his head gently, reaching for the door handle.

'This is a hell of a fucking game you're playing, Amy,' he said angrily. 'I hope to Christ you know what you're doing.'

And he was gone.

Amy reached for her cigarettes and lit up another.

'So do I,' she murmured.

Amy stepped from the cab and thanked the driver, shivering as a breeze swept down the street. She hadn't realised how cold it had become. Emerging from the warmth of the studios into the chilly clutches of the night, she pulled her collar up as she headed for the front door of her building.

She fumbled for her key as she drew closer, glancing up to see that there were lights burning in Webber's flat.

She looked at her watch.

2.03 a.m.

Perhaps he couldn't sleep.

She found her key and let herself in, ensuring that the front door was securely locked again, then she glanced across at Webber's door.

From inside she could hear movement.

She felt like talking and wondered if Jake would too. Besides, apart from a brief meeting that morning, she hadn't spoken to him all day.

Missing him?

She smiled to herself and crossed to his door, knocking lightly. There were still sounds of movement from inside.

She knocked again. No response.

Again she tapped, a little more urgently now.

'Jake,' she called.

The door remained firmly closed. And yet, inside, she could hear his voice.

His voice.

She heard only a low droning sound, she couldn't pick out words. Maybe he was on the phone.

She knocked again.

Silence.

She pressed her ear to the wood but his voice was silent now.

'Jake,' she called again, her face close to the frame of the door. 'It's me.'

Nothing.

She waited a moment or two then began to climb the stairs, looking back towards his door.

She could hear the muffled sound of him speaking again but, as before, she was unable to pick out individual words. Only his tone. It was angry.

Thirty-Six

David Grant heard the door behind him open and he turned slightly, taking his eyes from the pile of papers on the coffee table.

Tina Grant padded into the room dressed in just a T-shirt, her hair unkempt. She crossed to the chair opposite her husband and sat in it, drawing her legs up beneath her, folding the hem of the T-shirt over her toes.

'Sorry if I disturbed you,' said Grant.

'I wasn't sure if you were coming home tonight.'

He ran both hands through his hair and sat back on the sofa.

'I got sick of staring at the office walls,' he told her. 'I thought a change of scenery might mean a change of luck. A flash of inspiration.'

She eyed the documents disinterestedly.

'I didn't get in myself until ten,' Tina said. 'A few of us went out for a drink when we left the office.'

He nodded.

'One of the photographers is off to the Maldives tomorrow on a shoot,' she continued. 'It was a kind of farewell drink. His name's Carlo.'

'Carlo. He sounds like an Italian waiter.'

'Actually he's very good at what he does,' she said, defensively.

'I'm happy for him,' Grant said scornfully.

'And he's very attractive – most of the girls in the office fancy him.'

'And what about *you*? Do you fancy him?'

'Dave, I didn't come down here to pick a fight.'

'Then don't tell me about this good-looking wop waiter. I'm not interested.'

'Interested? You sound jealous.'

'Do you *want* me to be?'

She eyed him malevolently.

'I don't expect anything to distract you from your work,' she sneered. 'I wouldn't want it to. Even if I told you I was fucking him I doubt if that would make much of an impression, would it?'

'Are you?'

'I might as well be. When was the last time *we* had sex?'

'I don't keep a fucking diary, Tina and, quite frankly, at the moment, I've got more important things to think about.'

'Like your case?' she said mockingly. 'You can't let anything get in the way of that, can you? Especially not your marriage.'

'Give it a rest, I've got work to do.'

He turned his attention to the papers in front of him. Statements. Pathologists' reports.

'You've always got work to do,' she snapped, getting to her feet.

She crossed to the video and pushed a tape into the machine.

'Well,' she said, handing him the remote control. 'If you can find time away from your work perhaps you'd better look at this.' She pressed the Play button while he held the control in his hand. 'It looks like someone else is taking an interest in your work.'

'What the hell is this?' he said, looking at the screen.

'It was on the news, I taped it for you. I thought you might be interested. After all, it is to do with your work.'

She slammed the sitting-room door behind her.

The picture on the video screen flickered slightly then settled and Grant leaned forward, raising the volume on the set simultaneously.

'. . . claimed five victims and yet there has still been no official word from New Scotland Yard . . .'

Grant frowned as he saw that the source of the words

was a well-dressed, attractive woman in her mid-forties. She was sitting in a large office, the camera pointing at her while a reporter, out of shot, listened to her speak and fed her more questions.

'I realise the difficulties facing the police in a case such as this,' the woman continued, and Grant now saw that a caption at the bottom of the screen had identified her as Charlotte Kilbride.

He wrote her name on a piece of paper.

'That's why I think they should accept my offer,' she continued.

'What exactly *are* you offering the police?' the reporter asked.

'My help,' Charlotte Kilbride said smugly. 'I've had my own practice here in Harley Street for over ten years now. I feel that my insights as a psychiatrist would be invaluable to the officer in charge of this investigation. I think his name is Detective Inspector Grant . . .'

'You fucking bitch,' whispered Grant, his gaze fixed on the screen.

'. . . Furthermore, I think that Detective Inspector Grant and his team would be foolish to ignore the help I can offer as they are obviously having problems catching this killer.'

'Fucking bitch!'

He rewound the tape, the picture spinning backwards, then he hit Play again.

. . . obviously having problems catching this killer.'

He studied her every feature.

Rewind. Hit Play.

'. . . problems catching this killer.'

Rewind. Play.

'. . . problems catching this killer.'

He hurled the remote furiously across the room.

Thirty-Seven

Jake Webber slumped into the passenger seat of the black Vectra and gazed blankly through the windscreen.

Amy slid the key into the ignition and looked across at him.

'Are you okay, Jake?' she asked, starting the engine.

Webber nodded slowly, his eyes still fixed ahead, drawn for some inexplicable reason to a slick of bird shit on the glass.

'I don't know why I'm doing this. I don't know if I *can* do it.'

For the first time he looked at her and she saw something behind his eyes.

Anguish?

Fear?

He hadn't spoken more than half-a-dozen words since she'd knocked on his door five minutes earlier. She'd stood there and watched as he'd muttered to himself, snatching up first a denim jacket, then discarding it in favour of a leather one, pulling the jacket on and shrugging at her that he was reluctantly ready. His hand had shaken as he'd locked the door.

Now she guided the car skilfully through traffic, glancing at him occasionally, reaching across once to stroke his thigh with her left hand.

Webber looked down at the hand and for fleeting seconds he gripped it tightly. Again she saw that look in his eyes.

Fear?

'Thanks,' he said quietly.

'For what?'

'For coming with me.'

'You would never have gone if I hadn't.'

'Do you blame me?'

'You can't hide from it for ever, Jake. You shouldn't try to shut it out. What happened, happened, and God knows I can never even imagine what it must feel like to lose a child, but not visiting her grave isn't going to solve anything. It isn't going to change the way you feel.'

'You don't know *how* I feel,' he snapped.

An oppresive silence followed before Jake continued.

'I don't even know if Kim visits the grave. I don't know if *anyone* does. That was why I changed my mind, I'd never thought before that no one might go to visit Samantha's grave. I couldn't bear to think of her being so alone there. Does that sound stupid?'

Amy shook her head.

She glanced across at him and saw something else mixed with the fear in his expression. It was a vulnerability that touched her deeply. A facet of his character which she realised he was always careful to hide both from others and, she guessed, from himself.

You've known the bloke less than a week.

She noticed he was gazing blankly out of the side window.

How can you hope to know what he's thinking. Jesus, you don't even know what he does for a living let alone how his mind works.

Webber shifted uncomfortably in his seat, tapping on his right knee with an index finger.

'What about her Grandparents on her mother's side?' Amy asked. 'Wouldn't *they* visit?'

He could only shrug.

'I just don't know, Amy,' he said a little irritably. 'For all I know, I might have been the last person to see her grave the day we buried her.'

She drove for the next few miles in silence, unable to find the right words to comfort him, Webber unwilling or unable to speak. If he was feeling something other than what showed in his troubled gaze then he was keeping it to himself.

Thirty minutes stretched into forty-five then into sixty.

She thought about turning on the radio to break the increasingly heavy solitude, but contented herself with concentrating on driving and looking at her companion every now and then.

Just leave him alone.

He lit up a cigarette and wound down the window slightly to let the smoke escape.

Alone with his thoughts?

'Mind if I join you?' she said finally, nodding towards the Marlboro.

He lit one for her and pressed it to her lips. She took a drag then exhaled.

'I've got to get petrol,' she said, spotting a Texaco station up ahead.

She swung the Vectra into the forecourt, stubbed out the cigarette and hauled herself out of the car.

A moment or two later Webber also clambered out. She watched as he walked across the forecourt towards the small shop. Along with a rack of newspapers, there was an array of Cellophane-wrapped flowers. Small bunches from which Webber selected two. She watched as he went inside and paid, striding back towards the car with his purchases.

He brandished them over the roof of the car.

'I knew there was something I'd forgotten,' he said, attempting a smile.

He climbed back into the Vectra.

Amy continued filling the tank.

They should be at the cemetery in another fifteen minutes.

Thirty-Eight

Grant looked fixedly at the house in Harley Street, his face set in firm lines. He took a drag on his cigarette and blew out a long stream of smoke.

'Is that the one?' asked Lawrenson, nodding towards the three-storey Georgian building. It was indentical in numerous ways to so many of the other dwellings along the street. Large edifices that had been homes to the wealthiest families in London in an earlier century were now host to a similarly affluent financial group. The doctors, psychiatrists, psychoanalysts and consultants who worked in this famous centre of healing plied their trades for considerable reward.

Grant looked at the array of expensive cars parked up and down the street and wondered which belonged to patients and which to practitioners. He also wondered which one belonged to Charlotte Kilbride.

Fucking bitch.

He took another drag.

Interfering fucking jumped-up bitch.

'Guv, I said is that—'

Grant cut his colleague short. 'I heard what you said,' he muttered, nodding. 'That's the one.'

Lawrenson prepared to swing himself out of the car but Grant shot out a hand and gripped his shoulder.

'You wait here. I'll deal with this.'

The detective sergeant watched as his superior clambered out of the vehicle and strode across the pavement and up the four stone steps that led to the ornate front door of the building.

Grant noticed several buzzers on a panel, each one accompanied by a name.

'Doctor Charlotte D. Kilbride,' he read aloud, pressing his finger on the buzzer and keeping it there.

After a second or two there was a metallic crackle and the intercom spat into life.

'Hello.'

'I'm here to see Doctor Kilbride.'

'Do you have an appointment?'

'Just open the door, I want to speak to her.'

'She has appointments all—'

'Open the door, I'm a police officer, this is important.'

The intercom went dead and Grant peered through the small window in the door and saw a middle-aged woman making her way down a narrow hallway.

As she opened the door he stepped through without waiting for an invitation, pulling his ID from his pocket and pushing it towards her for inspection.

'I want to see her now,' he demanded, making his way up the hallway.

The secretary or receptionist (*whatever the hell she was*) scurried along behind him, her face flushed.

To his right was a waiting room and he peered in quizzically. The room was huge, its centre-piece an enormous marble fireplace and an open fire which was crackling away merrily, sparks jumping from the coal. Decorated in a soft green and beige, the room possessed a high-vaulted ceiling and was immaculately furnished with leather chairs and a couple of two-seater sofas. In the centre of the room was a large oak coffee table, magazines lying in rows of almost unnatural neatness on its highly polished surface. He saw the latest copies of *Go*, *Sight and Sound*, *Four Four Two* and *Time Out* amongst others. No dog-eared, out-of-date copies of fucking *Reader's Digest* here, thought Grant.

Paintings hung on the walls. Copies in most cases.

He recognised a couple. *When Did You Last See Your Father?* by Yeames. *1814* by Meissonnier.

No AIDS posters plastered to cracked and peeling walls. Money bought better medical care and also better waiting rooms it seemed.

Two people were inside the waiting room, both in their

late thirties. A man in an Armani suit who was doing his best to hide behind a copy of *The Times* and a woman with a pinched face and sad eyes who looked blankly at Grant then returned to her laptop computer.

Grant stepped back out of the waiting room and glared directly at the receptionist. 'I want to see Doctor Kilbride now.'

'That isn't possible,' the woman told him. 'I've already told you that. She has appointments and—'

'Is she with a patient now?' he demanded.

The woman shook her head.

There was a white-painted door at the end of the hall and Grant headed towards it.

'She's on the first floor,' said the woman wearily. 'First door on your right. I'll tell her you're coming up.'

'Don't bother, I'll surprise her.'

He gripped the handrail and began to ascend. As he reached the top of the stairs he glanced back and saw the receptionist was still standing at the bottom looking up at him, her face still flushed. He held her gaze until she retreated back towards her desk out of sight.

There was a window on the landing that looked out into the street and Grant crossed to it, peering out at the scene beyond. Lawrenson was now out of the car, leaning against the driver's door, puffing agitatedly on a cigarette and glancing occasionally at his watch. Waiting.

Grant waited a second longer then spun round, knocked once on the door to his right and walked in without invitation.

Dr Charlotte Kilbride was seated behind her desk. If she was surprised by the sudden intrusion, it barely registered on her face.

'Can I help you?' she asked.

Grant ran appraising eyes over her. Early forties, shoulder-length brown hair cut in a bob. She was wearing an immaculately pressed black jacket and skirt over a white blouse. She looked better in the flesh than she did on the tape last night, thought Grant.

That fucking tape.

He produced his ID once more and pushed it towards her.

'Detective Inspector David Grant, Murder Squad,' he announced. 'I want to talk to you.'

'How can I help you?' she asked, a slight smile on her lips.

'You *can't* help me, that's what I'm here to tell you.'

She nodded. 'You saw the interview last night?'

'Yeah, I saw it and like I said, you can't help me. I don't *want* your help, I don't *need* your help.'

'At least have a seat.' She gestured to one of the leather chairs in front of her desk.

'This isn't a social call,' he reminded her. '*Or* a consultation.' He looked around the room at the shelves lined with books, the brass lamps, the leather furniture.

'Then what can I do for you?'

'I'm here to tell you to keep your nose out of police business.'

'I wasn't aware I was interfering with police business, Inspector.'

'*Detective* Inspector,' he reminded her. 'I'm talking about that bullshit interview you gave last night.'

'I was asked for my views, I gave them, I'm sorry if they caused you any offence.' She turned in her chair to face him, uncrossing her slender legs, brushing a fleck of dust from one thigh.

'You tried to make me look stupid,' he snapped.

'I merely spoke my mind. I offered help, I offered my expertise. If you don't want it—'

'I don't,' he snapped.

'If you think it undermines your authority, then perhaps you have a different kind of problem.'

'Don't try to psychoanalyse me,' he sneered. 'I'm not one of your fee-paying nutcases.' He crossed to a filing cabinet beside her desk. 'Perhaps they're the ones I should be checking up on. You treat nutters, don't you? How do I know one of *them* isn't the killer?'

'My patients are suffering from various psychological problems,' she said calmly.

'So let me check some of their files.'

'Those files are confidential.'

'Not if I come back with a warrant they're not. How do I know you're not protecting one of them?'

'What goes on between myself and my patients is my business,' she said irritably.

'And this murder case is *mine*,' Grant rasped. 'So keep your nose out of it otherwise I'll be back with a warrant and I'll grill every one of your *patients*.' He slapped the filing cabinet.

'Are you frightened of my offer of help, Detective Inspector? Afraid I might be useful to you? Worried that I *could* help you catch this killer?'

He turned towards the door.

'Stay out of it,' he warned. 'I'll get him and I don't need help from *you* or anyone else.'

As he reached the door he paused again, pointing an accusatory finger at her. 'And stay away from the press and television.'

'Is that a warning, Detective Inspector?' she asked, getting to her feet.

Again he ran his gaze over her figure.

'Just do what I said,' he snapped. 'Keep out of it.'

And he was gone, slamming the door behind him.

She heard his footsteps receding down the stairs then, a moment later, the front door banging shut.

Charlotte Kilbride crossed to the large picture window close to her desk and watched as Grant climbed into the waiting Montego, which pulled away rapidly.

For a moment longer she stood there gazing out into the street then she turned to the filing cabinet closest to her and, carefully, pulled out the file she sought.

Thirty-Nine

As Jake Webber pulled himself reluctantly from the Vectra, he glanced up at the sky. A watery sun hung against the cloud-smeared heavens, offering little warmth.

'I'm cold,' he said under his breath.

Amy walked around the car and took a firm grip of his free hand.

'Ready?' she asked softly, squeezing his hand.

He nodded none too convincingly and they began walking, the gravel path crunching beneath their feet.

The vast necropolis that was Norwood Cemetery stretched out before them, lines of headstones and stone markers standing like frozen sentinels. In some places they were in arrow-straight lines, in others, in irregular configurations. There was a wide central walkway and dozens of smaller paths leading off it, some man-made, others merely tracks worn in the grass by the passage of so many weary and sorrowful feet.

A single sparrow was singing cheerfully in the lower branches of one of the nearby trees but as Amy and Webber approached it flew off and Amy became aware again of the heavy silence that enveloped the resting place. The only sound was that of their feet on the pathway.

Webber paused for a moment and looked around, his already strained expression showing signs of increased distress.

'I'm not sure where it is,' he said quietly.

'Take your time, Jake,' Amy told him softly.

'I should be able to remember where my own fucking daughter is buried,' he snapped, his tone hardening.

He shifted the bunches of Cellophane-wrapped flowers from hand to hand, the wrapping crackling in the stillness.

Ahead of them was a small ridge topped by a carefully tended privet hedge and a row of small conifers. Webber headed up the incline, Amy trailing in his wake.

Something here looked familiar to him.

Amy hurried along behind him, reaching the top of the incline. More graves stretched away before them. To the left, about twenty yards away, a woman in her fifties was filling a watering can from one of the many taps dotted about the cemetery. To the right was a small willow tree, its lower branches draping over the ground like a net.

Amy noticed a number of graves close to the tree. The grass around them was uncut. Long and untended.

Webber had frozen and was standing still, staring towards the willow tree and the overgrown plots.

Amy saw how pale his face was and she reached out and gripped his arm.

'Jake,' she whispered.

'I can't do this, Amy,' he said, turning to look at her and she saw that there were tears in his eyes.

'Is she over there?'

He swallowed hard.

'Is Sam buried there?' Amy persisted gently, nodding towards the weed-infested graves.

One single tear rolled from the corner of his eye and trickled slowly down his cheek.

He wiped it away angrily. 'Let's go. I should never have listened to you in the first place.'

'Jake, you're here now. You've come this far.' She kept a firm grip on his arm.

She saw the knot of muscles pulsing at the side of his jaw.

'Do it for *her* sake, for Samantha,' Amy continued.

He looked at Amy then at the bunches of flowers he was gripping tightly in his powerful fist, almost crushing the stalks. He closed his eyes for a moment. Jesus. Had it really been so long since he'd been back here?

Ten yards. You only have to walk ten yards.

He looked into Amy's eyes again.

Ten lousy stinking yards.

He felt as if someone had opened a hole in his stomach. The feeling of emptiness there seemed to be spreading until it filled every limb, every fibre of his body, every pore.

Turn and walk.

Amy wanted to say something, to tell him that it would be all right, that she was with him, but whenever she tried to speak the words wouldn't come.

What the hell do you say to him?

She saw the pain in his expression. A deep-rooted torment the like of which she could never remember seeing before. As if, before her eyes, she was seeing a man having his soul ripped apart. Then he turned and headed towards the grave and she walked beside him, holding his arm as he moved inexorably closer to the plot he sought.

So small.

The grave was less than three feet long, the grass and weeds having covered it like unruly invaders. Leaves that had fallen from the willow were also scattered across it. A metal plaque was set in a small square of marble at the head of the grave. Amy tried to read it through the overgrown grass and the grime that stained the brass.

She watched as Webber knelt, pulled a handkerchief from his pocket and wiped the plaque clean.

Finally, she could read it.

> SAMANTHA JOANNE WEBBER
> AGED EIGHTEEN MONTHS
> ASLEEP IN THE ARMS OF GOD.

Amy felt tears welling up in her eyes as she watched Webber looking helplessly down at the grave.

'Hello, babe,' he said softly, his voice cracking. 'It's Dad.'

He wiped his nose with the back of his hand and began

pulling at the weeds covering the grave, hurling them angrily to one side.

Amy waited a moment then began helping him. She could see the tears rolling down his cheeks as he tore at the intruding weeds, ripping them free furiously.

'It doesn't look as if it's been touched since she was buried,' he said angrily, sitting back on his haunches for a moment and regarding the plot, taking every detail in.

'What about the plaque?' Amy asked, still pulling weeds and grass away. 'Who would have put that there?'

He could only shrug.

'Kim maybe. That's probably why my name is there – she didn't even want to be associated with Sam when she was gone,' he said bitterly. 'Well that's fine. I'd rather people knew she was *my* daughter.'

He continued to stare down at the plaque.

'When she was buried,' he said, his tone more even now, 'she was buried with one of her toys. Some kind of little dog. She loved that. She always had it in her pram or her cot. I thought she should have it with her for ever.'

Amy moved towards him as his head dropped forward and tears ran down his cheeks.

Amy felt helpless to stem this tide of grief, angry with herself that she could offer no comfort. She merely snaked her arm around his waist and pulled him close, wiping a tear from her own cheek.

'Oh Christ, Amy,' he said, the desolation in his voice making her shudder. 'Why her? Why my baby? She didn't deserve to die. There are so many in this fucking world who should be lying there instead of her.'

He shook loose of Amy's comforting grip and continued clearing the grass and weeds away.

Amy stepped back and watched him, watching until the plot was exposed, the plaque clean and gleaming for all to see.

She didn't move towards him, merely watched as he wiped his dirty hands on his handkerchief then gently laid the flowers on the grave. Amy was reluctant to intrude upon his grief. She stood with her hands clasped in front of her.

The slight breeze that had sprung up rustled the Cellophane that encased the flowers.

'Dad's got to go now, babe,' Webber said, gazing down at the grave, wiping away another tear with a muddy hand. 'Sleep tight.'

He sobbed uncontrollably, his entire body shaking as he stood at the graveside.

Amy bowed her head, warm tears flowing from her eyes. She felt his pain but she knew that nothing she could do or say would ease it and that realisation brought only fresh tears.

A bird which had been sitting in the branches of the willow took flight, rising into the sky, heading away from the two distraught figures below as if it could no longer bear the sight of such devastating sorrow.

Forty

Amy had turned to glance at Webber a number of times and, on every occasion, she had found him staring blankly out of the side window. Once or twice she thought about speaking but couldn't find the words.

What the hell could she say to him?

They sat in traffic, the silence inside the Vectra growing more oppressive by the minute.

Webber allowed his head to loll back against the headrest, his eyes closed.

Amy wondered if he was trying to sleep. Perhaps with sleep would come the chance to blot out the memories.

Perhaps.

'Do you believe in God?'

The words took her by surprise. He hadn't spoken for more than thirty minutes and she hadn't expected him to utter a sound perhaps until they reached home.

She looked across at Webber and saw that his eyes were still closed.

'Did you hear me? I asked if you believed in God.'

'I've never really thought too much about it, Jake,' she confessed. 'I believe there's *something* but I don't know whether I'd call it God.'

'Someone once said that God is a sadist but probably doesn't even know it.' A bitter smile creased his lips. 'I don't believe. Not any more.'

'I think lots of people who've lost relatives think like that, they—'

'I'll tell you why I don't believe,' he interrupted. 'Because none of it makes any fucking sense. It isn't logical.'

'What isn't?'

'Life. Death. God. None of it makes sense. Why did

my little girl have to die when there are all kinds of fucking scumbags walking the streets?' he rasped. 'They're the ones that deserve to die, not her. The pimps, the pushers, the slags, the fucking junkies. The garbage. They're the ones who should have died, not *her*.' He exhaled deeply. 'Eighteen months old,' he murmured. 'It's not fair.'

'I'm sure the parents of other children feel the same as you,' Amy offered. 'Those who lose kids must think it's unfair too.'

'What do *you* think?'

She looked puzzled.

'Do you think it's fair that there's so much scum walking the streets when my child is dead?'

Amy felt helpless, unsure of what to say.

'Jake, I feel sorry for you, you know that.'

'I don't want your fucking pity,' he hissed. 'I asked if you thought it was fair.'

'No,' she admitted. 'All right, it's not fair, is that what you want to hear? It's not fair that people die in wars or famines or floods or plane crashes.'

'Because it's always the *wrong* people. It's always *decent* people,' he told her angrily. 'Do you know what would be fair? If a plane load of junkies crashed. Five hundred of the bastards packed into a 747 going down in flames. Now *that* would be justice. If that happened, even *I* might start believing in God.'

There was a vehemence in his tone that unsettled her and yet, deep down, she told herself she could forgive his bitterness and his rage. To have a life he cherished so much snatched from him so cruelly, she believed, at least gave him the right to his anger.

They drove some way in silence then she placed a hand on his knee, wondering what kind of response it might elicit.

'Why don't you come to the show with me tonight, Jake?' she asked.

He looked at her blankly.

'Come to the studios with me. We'll have a meal first and—'

'No,' he said, interrupting her, some of the anger having left his voice. 'I think I'm better off on my own tonight.' He managed a wan smile.

'You'll sit around brooding.' You shouldn't be on your own tonight.'

'I think that's *exactly* what I should do. I'm not going to be very good company.' He squeezed her hand. 'Besides, I've got things to do.'

'Such as?'

He didn't answer, merely squeezed her hand more tightly.

'Jake, what's so important?' she persisted.

'Leave it, Amy,' he said, fixing her in a cold stare. 'I'm better off alone.'

She held his gaze a second longer then returned her concentration to the road.

Webber fumbled in his jacket pocket for his key and let himself in, turning to face Amy, who was standing on the threshold.

'Are you sure you're going to be okay?' she asked him.

He nodded. 'I'll be fine.'

He stepped forward and kissed her gently on the lips. 'Thanks for coming with me,' he said quietly. 'For making me go in the first place. Thanks, Amy.'

They kissed again, more urgently this time, their tongues slipping and sliding against each other as they pressed their bodies hard together. She draped her arms around his neck and felt his strong hands gripping her waist.

When they finally parted, Amy was breathing heavily.

She touched one of his cheeks gently. 'I'll be home about two. If you're still up, what about a night cap?'

'Sounds good to me.'

'Just come up when you're ready.'

He nodded and pushed the door a little. 'I'd better let you go,' he said.

Why did she feel he was pushing her out?

'See you later?' she said but it sounded more like a question.

'Yeah, more than likely,' he told her, his smile looking a little strained.

She stepped back.

'Thanks again, Amy,' he said, and he pushed the door shut.

She was left staring at the wooden partition.

Shut out.

She stood staring at the door then turned and slowly, almost sadly, made her way up the stairs towards her own flat.

Inside his flat, back pressed to the front door, Webber heard her ascend.

Only when he heard her key in her lock did he move.

Forty-One

She rarely thought about death. Despite the fact that she'd been working in St Angela's Hospice in Camden for the past six years, confronted by the dark spectre on a daily basis, Valerie Hardy seldom stopped to consider either her own mortality or that of those she cared for.

Those who knew her found it strange that such an environment did not precipitate feelings of fear within her; the constant closeness to death that she experienced so often seemed to negate rather than reinforce any contemplation of her own life and death.

Valerie had found the first year something of a struggle, the inevitability of losing so many patients had been hard to bear to begin with but she had gradually come to terms with it. There was sadness, she didn't deny that and, in the small hours, when she was doing her rounds, she sometimes shed tears for a particular patient who had died. But the overwhelming feeling she had from working at St Angela's was one of satisfaction. She rejoiced in the knowledge that the care administered by herself and her colleagues to those within the walls was first class and helped to make the last few months or days of a patient's life not just bearable but almost enjoyable.

The hospice wasn't a place of sadness and depression. The staff did their best to see that it was one of good spirit. Val never ceased to be amazed at the fortitude with which some of the residents faced their predicaments. It was humbling. She felt privileged to tend to their needs, proud to be their friend.

Prior to joining St Angela's she had worked in the Intensive Care Unit at St Barts. A job that required a completely different frame of mind and was, in its own way, perhaps even more depressing than working with those she knew were going to die. In ICU there was the distant hope that a patient would survive, would recover from some horrendous injury, or wake from some deep coma. And often that happened but when death struck, to the nurses working in the unit, the blow was somehow harder to take than the inevitability of death she faced at St Angela's. Here she was working with men and women who *knew* there would be no miracle recovery, no unexpected cure. There were no false hopes here, just the unavoidable conclusion both patient and staff could only wait for.

Val found it curiously reassuring.

The hospice (although she hated the word and the connotations it carried) held about fifteen patients at any one time, mostly in their late sixties and upwards. She knew them all. Knew their lives as well as she would know their deaths.

Val and five other nurses, plus three doctors, were on constant call to tend to the needs of these special people who lived what little life they had left with a zest that sometimes put others to shame.

She checked her watch and continued with her rounds. The night shift was easier as far as work load was concerned. Walk the corridors, check on each patient, ensure they were comfortable. She would administer some sleeping pills to those who had difficulty sleeping if they requested them or, sometimes, she would just talk to them. That was all they wanted at times. To talk.

The silence inside the building was one not of oppression but of overwhelming peacefulness.

Val checked on three patients. Two stricken with cancer, the other with advanced multiple sclerosis. All three were sleeping soundly. Val stood looking at them with the same love in her eyes that a mother reserves for her sleeping child.

She moved around the hospice assuredly and swiftly, shivering as she felt a chill sweeping down one corridor. She checked the central heating and saw that it was set at Normal. Val pressed one hand to a nearby radiator and found it was warm.

She eased the temperature up a few notches and then crossed to the first room, easing the door open and entering.

Mrs Bridgeman was snoring quietly.

Val tucked in the corner of a blanket that had come loose on the woman's bed then glanced around her room. There were two vases of flowers in the room, one of which smelled a little rank. Val made a mental note to change the water in the morning before she went off duty.

Photos were scattered all around the room. Mrs Bridgeman's son. Her granddaughter. A sepia tinted one of her husband.

Val leaned forward and gently slipped the Mills and Boon from the sleeping woman's hands, sliding her bookmark into the appointed pages and placing the paperback on the bedside unit. Then she backed out of the room quietly and closed the door, moving across to the next patient.

Mr Cross was in his late sixties. The cancer had spread rapidly from his lymph glands to virtually every other part of his body. No one gave him more than a month but he was almost unbearably cheerful, and again Val found herself overwhelmed with love. None of the patients, in fact none that she could remember during her six years at St Angela's, had ever expressed the slightest hint of bitterness or self-pity at their condition.

Humbling, indeed.

He stirred slightly as she wandered around the room. She waited, ensuring that she hadn't disturbed him but realising that the high dose of morphine he was given every night would secure his uninterrupted night's rest.

She moved out into the corridor once more. Again she felt the cold breeze and, this time, she saw that it was coming from the end of the corridor. The sash window was open five or six inches, allowing a chill wind through. Who had opened that?

Val headed towards it, shaking her head irritably. The window should be kept closed.

Only as she drew closer did she realise that the floor was slick with moisture. No, not slick. It was *swimming* with fluid. Thick, dark fluid that gave off a pungent and immediately recognisable smell. The entire corridor was filled with it, as if it had seeped through the open window. In places it had run beneath the doors of patients' rooms.

That fluid.

That smell.

She recognised it so well and yet her mind told her that it was impossible.

And then she was standing in it. Standing in the great, thick tide of it, watching it creep further down the corridor like a living organism.

No, this couldn't be.

But she knew that smell.

But why . . . ?

Why the open window? Where had the thick fluid come from?

She looked down at her feet, at the liquid lapping around them. The stench was starting to make her dizzy. That unmistakable odour. Cloying. Choking. The corridor was awash with it.

She was standing in petrol.

Val turned back towards the window, her eye drawn to something moving in the darkness beyond, outside. Something tiny. Something glowing red.

The match hit the petrol, spinning through the air as if in slow motion before it landed and Val opened her mouth to scream but could not force the sound out.

The petrol exploded.

The world turned a bright, searing red.

Forty-Two

Amy knew immediately that it was Webber heading across the street. From her position in her bedroom window she saw him approaching the flats, hands dug deep into his pockets.

She looked at the clock. It was 3.17 a.m.

She'd knocked on his door as she returned that morning but had received no answer. In fact, she had convinced herself, even as she stepped from the taxi that there would be no one home when she banged the door.

'Things to do.' That was what he'd said, wasn't it? He had 'things to do'.

Until this time?

As she watched him drawing closer she tried to see his face in the gloom, through the deep shadows, but she couldn't. As usual she could only guess at what was going on behind his eyes.

She had seen his pain that afternoon and she had felt unbearably, infuriatingly helpless to ease that pain. If only she could have found some words, no matter how clichéd or bland, to say to him as he'd stood at his daughter's graveside. But instead all she had been able to do was stand there impotently while he gave vent to so much pent-up emotion.

Amy had been surprised at how deeply his display of grief had affected her. She couldn't remember the last time something had touched her so profoundly.

And why? You've known the bloke a week.

She exhaled deeply and reached down for another cigarette, lighting it up, the lighter flame dancing in the gloom of the bedroom.

Only a week. You know nothing about him except that he lost a daughter.

She heard his key in the front door, then in the lock of his flat. The door was closed and then there was only silence.

Amy waited a moment then got to her feet, slipping on a pair of Reeboks, not bothering to fasten the laces. She brushed some ash from her jeans then walked through the sitting room towards her own door.

She hesitated a moment. Should she go down and see him now? Probably all he wanted was to be alone with his thoughts. The last thing he needed was company.

She looked at the door. Wondering.

Go to him.

She left her blouse untucked, slipped the latch, pocketed her key, then she made her way quickly and quietly down the stairs towards the door of flat number one.

She felt nervous. A stupid almost adolescent anxiety.

Frightened he's going to turn you away?

She tapped softly on the door and waited.

No answer.

He doesn't want to know.

Again she knocked.

The door opened almost immediately and she found herself looking into his eyes.

'Did I wake you?' he asked, a note of weariness in his voice.

She shook her head.

'I was waiting for you,' she told him. 'I heard you come in.'

He smiled weakly, as if the gesture was forced.

'If you want me to go I will, Jake,' Amy told him.

'No. Come in.'

He stepped back, ushering her inside.

Amy hesitated a moment longer, almost surprised at the invitation then she stepped past him and wandered through towards the sitting room, hearing the door close behind her.

He followed her in.

'Have a seat,' he told her, motioning towards the sofa.

She did so, glancing around the room surreptitiously, anxious not to make it too obvious that she was inspecting its contents. Christ, the place was almost spartan. A sofa, one chair, a small coffee table, a television, a portable music system and a couple of cabinets. And that was it. No pictures on the walls. No ornaments. Just what she saw.

He emptied his jacket pockets and she saw him lay some loose change, some keys, a pack of Rothmans and a box of matches on the coffee table.

'Is vodka okay?' he asked her.

'It's fine.'

'I've got some lemonade in the fridge, and some ice if you like.'

'It's fine as it comes, Jake,' she assured him, taking the tumbler from him and sipping the clear liquor.

He took a swallow from his own glass and refilled it immediately

'How did the show go tonight?' he asked.

'It went well, you should have come.'

'I told you before, I don't think I'd have been very good company.' He swigged more vodka. 'Look, I need to have a shower, make yourself comfortable. I won't be long.'

He headed off towards the bedroom and through into the bathroom. After a moment or two, Amy heard the sound of running water.

She got to her feet almost immediately, walking slowly around the sitting room.

She pulled open the cabinet that supported the television and found a video inside and a handful of CDs which she flicked through. Nine Inch Nails. Metallica. Enya. Garbage. Roxette.

She smiled.

Eclectic tastes to say the least.

She moved across to the cabinet where the bottle of vodka was standing and pulled it open. It contained

half-a-dozen glasses, some cocktail sticks and a cork-
screw.

The sound of running water was still coming from the
bathroom.

She moved into the kitchen. A table and two chairs.
An electric kettle on one of the work tops. Tea and
coffee caddies. She checked the cupboards in there too,
not really sure what she was looking for. There were
some tins of food, a couple of Pot Noodles, some instant
milk and more teabags but not much else. The fridge was
similarly bare. Half a carton of milk, some out-of-date
sausage rolls. A couple of microwave pizzas. The flat
might be home to Webber but it seemed more like a
place to stop off rather than one to settle in. It was
hardly welcoming.

She moved into the bedroom. Again it was sparsely
furnished, only a chest of drawers and a small MFI
wardrobe occupying any space near the bed. The bed
was unmade from the morning.

Amy crossed to it and pulled up the duvet.

What the hell are you doing?

She smiled at her own actions.

What are you looking for? Why are you prying?

As she held the duvet she could smell him on it.

His jeans lay discarded close to the bathroom door,
which was ajar. She crossed to it, carrying her drink
and paused there, listening to the sound of running
water. Then, slowly, she pushed it open and stepped
in.

She could see the outline of his body through the
shower curtain and for a while she watched him as he
stood beneath the spray.

A small stool stood just inside the door. On the wall
there was a medicine cabinet with mirrored doors and
she caught sight of her own reflection briefly.

'How do you feel now?' she asked, raising her voice
above the gushing water.

There was silence for a moment then Webber pulled

back the shower curtain slightly and looked at her with an expression of surprise and delight.

'Sorry to barge in.'

'Feel free,' he told her and let the curtain slip back again.

She sipped at the vodka, still studying his shape through the almost transparent plastic curtain.

'I hope you didn't feel as if I pushed you into visiting Sam's grave today.'

'I'm glad you did. If you hadn't, I would probably never have gone,' he admitted. 'I owe you for that.'

'I did it because I care,' she told him. 'I care about *you*.'

The shower curtain rings rattled as the flimsy divide was pulled open. Amy stood naked before Webber, her clothes discarded on the bathroom floor.

Without a word she stepped beneath the water with him and he pulled her to him, welcoming her into his arms, pressing her slender body against his.

She lifted her arms around his neck, their lips pressing together, tongues seeking each other almost frenziedly as the water bounced off them from the stinging spray. They were joined by the passion of their kisses until she pulled away slightly, her breath coming in low gasps.

He traced a rivulet of water as it coursed down her chest towards her nipple, using his thumb to further tease the already stiff bud, then he bent his head and flicked his tongue around the sensitive flesh, allowing it to swirl around the puckered skin. His saliva mingled with the water as he drew his head away and repeated his actions on her other breast. With his free hand he gently cupped first one buttock then the other, allowing one index finger to probe tentatively towards the top of her legs.

Amy felt his penis stiffen as her hand closed around it, coaxing it to full erection with firm caresses. She rubbed her thumb over his glans and felt him shudder.

They kissed again and she allowed herself to be pushed

back against the wall of the shower, his stiffness now nudging against her belly.

She pulled him harder against her, enjoying the feel of that rigid shaft, knowing that his excitement was as great as her own.

He broke the kiss and nibbled at her earlobe, then her neck, then slid down towards her breasts taking each nipple in his mouth in turn before allowing his tongue to trace a pattern across her belly, through the water, which still lashed them. Finally, he was on his knees in front of her, his tongue stirring the soft downy hair of her pubis.

She thrust her pelvis towards him as the pleasure grew and stroked his wet hair. She felt his tongue slide over her throbbing clitoris before trailing gently over her distended and slippery outer lips.

He tasted her moisture there and savoured it, using both hands to massage the flesh of her slim thighs, his tongue now working expertly around her swollen clitoris, pausing every so often to probe her wet cleft.

Amy pressed her back harder against the shower wall as he kept up this exquisite action, pushing her closer to ecstasy. She opened her legs a little wider, allowing him better access to her most sensitive areas and she shuddered as he used his tongue and fingers so expertly. She could feel the pleasure building to a crescendo and she gripped his shoulders hard, circling her hips as he concentrated his efforts. Clenching her teeth, she felt his expertise driving her closer to orgasm.

When he pulled away for a moment she almost cried out with disappointment, but the feeling was only temporary and a second later she felt his tongue between her legs again. He moved more urgently now as he sensed her release was near – but, despite her pleasure, she wanted him more fully. Wanted to feel that stiffness inside her – wanted his liquid pleasure deep within her – but then she surrendered to the feelings enveloping her. A warmth started to spread from between her legs and across her belly then up to her breasts until the skin there and across her chest flushed pink.

His tongue flicked incessantly across her swollen clitoris and she cried out as the first wave of orgasm swept through her, her whole body shuddering.

She felt him gripping her hips, her thighs. Jesus, there was such strength in those hands. She held him there as the sensations swept through her. The water bounced off her hardened nipples and ran down her quivering body as she gasped out her pleasure, and her own moisture glistened on his chin as surely as the shower spray.

She kept her eyes closed, wanting the ecstasy to continue.

And it did.

Forty-Three

When Amy woke she could hear Webber's low breathing beside her, feel the gentle rise and fall of his chest beneath her arm. She moved closer to him for a moment, pressing herself against him, allowing one hand to trail up his thigh.

Webber stirred slightly and Amy smiled to herself as she propped herself up on one elbow and looked down at his sleeping form.

The intensity of their lovemaking had exhausted them both and, as she moved, she felt the residue of his liquid between her legs. He had carried her from the shower, wrapping her in a towel as easily as a parent wraps a child and she had been amazed at the strength in his arms.

He had made love frantically, almost frenziedly, but that had served only to heighten her own pleasure and she had responded with equal passion. Within that fury there had been tenderness that was almost incongruous. A selflessness on his part that did not seem to sit naturally with the intensity of his lovemaking.

Was this to be the first of many such nights?

Was it to be as it had been with John Howard?

She closed her eyes briefly, as if to banish the image of the writer. The lover. She had never felt anything the way she had felt it with Howard.

Until tonight?

And yet, as she kept telling herself, what did she know of this man whose bed she now shared? Other than his anguish at losing his only child, she knew nothing of his character and yet she still felt strangely drawn to him, and she knew the feeling was reciprocated. There had been other men in the past she had shared a bed with and known nothing about, but they had not mattered.

She had been with them for one or two nights as *she* chose but they had meant nothing to her.

Webber *mattered*. This man, who was still so much a mystery to her, mattered.

She brushed a hair from his face then swung herself carefully out of bed, anxious not to wake him. It was warm inside the flat so, still naked, she padded through into the kitchen to the fridge and retrieved a carton of milk. Then she went to the cupboard where she remembered he kept some glasses, blew the dust from the bottom of one and filled it with the white liquid.

She drank deeply, illuminated only by the dull light from within the fridge.

She pushed the door shut and padded back towards the bedroom carrying the rest of the milk.

She paused at the bathroom and decided to relieve herself. Tugging the light cord, she was about to sit down when she noticed that the mirrored doors of the medicine cabinet were slightly open.

She pushed them shut but one swung open again and, when she couldn't shut it the second time, she opened the door fully to see what was blocking it.

There was a plastic bag full of cotton wool jutting out half an inch or so, preventing the door from closing.

She lifted it out, intent on shutting the cupboard. A box was behind the cotton wool. It was plain brown cardboard. About five inches long, half that across. There was black stencilled writing on the front:

50 CARTRIDGES
9mm BALL NATO M882 LOT WCC92D043 – 002
OLIN CORPORATION

Amy swallowed hard and reached for the box, hefting it before her.

She turned it over and read the back: WARNING: These cartridges are loaded to military velocity and pressure . . .

'My God,' she murmured, undoing one end of the box.

There was a piece of Styrofoam inside and, within each segment of it was a gleaming, brass-cased 9 m.m. round.

She looked down at the bullets uncomprehendingly.

Bullets. Dear God, do you realise what you're holding?

She took out one of the shells and turned it slowly between her thumb and forefinger.

Bullets. Real live, fire from a gun, fucking bullets.

She hurriedly replaced it in the Styrofoam, pushed the container back inside the box and replaced it in the medicine cabinet, her hand quivering slightly as she did so.

Bullets. What the hell was Webber doing with a box of bullets? And if there were bullets wouldn't there be a gun?

'Shit,' she said, her voice quivering. 'Shit.'

Her head was spinning. What did this mean? What the hell was she getting herself into? The rational part of her mind told her that there was a good reason for this unexpected find. That if she asked Webber he would explain why he had a box of 9 m.m. ammunition in his medicine cabinet.

But should she ask?

What if there *wasn't* a rational explanation?

This man, who you don't know, has live ammunition in his flat.

Why?

She swallowed hard.

Ask him.

'Amy.'

She heard him calling her.

Amy closed the cabinet door hurriedly, startled by the sound.

'I'm coming, Jake,' she said, trying to mask the confusion in her voice. 'I won't be a minute.'

He was sitting on the edge of the bed when she re-entered the bedroom.

'Are you okay?' he asked.

She nodded.

Come on, be convincing.

'I was thirsty,' she told him, holding up the glass of milk.

He lay back, patting the mattress beside him. A signal for her to join him which she did, allowing herself to be enveloped in his broad arms.

Ask him.

'I thought you'd walked out on me,' he said, grinning, and she felt one of those strong hands stroking her hair tenderly.

Ask him about the fucking bullets.

'Why should I?' she murmured as he pulled her closer, kissing her forehead. She felt his free hand slide down her back and cup one of her buttocks, kneading the smooth flesh. His penis was stiffening against her belly as he felt her warmth.

'Just hold me,' she said softly, kissing him tenderly on the lips.

He did and in a few moments he'd drifted off to sleep again, his low breathing stirring her blond hair as he exhaled.

Amy felt the strength of his embrace and she closed her eyes.

The bullets.

She would ask him when the time was right.

And when would that be?

It was a long time before she slept.

Forty-Four

Grant had smelled burned human flesh before but never as powerfully as this. That unmistakable sickly sweet odour of charred skin and scorched bone seemed to fill the air, clogging in his nostrils, even at the back of his throat. Twice he coughed, hawked and spat into his handkerchief while other officers around him also toiled amidst the vile stench.

Lawrenson actually had a handkerchief tied around his nose as he moved amongst the blackened debris that was once St Angela's Hospice. The smell of burned flesh mingled with the equally pungent stink of scorched wood and incinerated plaster. There was a gaping hole in the roof where the flames had roared upwards through the building, finally escaping through the tiles, blowing them aside.

At least half of the building had been reduced to a shell by the ferocity of the flames. Despite the fact that the fire brigade had responded so quickly, the fire had taken hold with a speed that surprised even those firemen still wandering through the wreckage. It had swept through St Angela's like some kind of blazing whirlwind, destroying everything it touched, incinerating both wood or flesh with the same ease and vehemence.

The floor which he walked on was swimming with water from the firemen's hoses. Filthy, blackened water that formed huge inky puddles on the remains of the scorched floor. He felt it splash around his feet, ducking to avoid a fallen beam, which was still smouldering, still giving off some heat.

Grant paused, hands on his hips, and glanced around at the destruction. Away to his right, on a patch of grass, twelve black plastic body bags were lying in a neat row. All of them filled.

'Eleven patients and one member of staff,' said Lawrenson joining him, and glancing at the row of bodies.

'What about the rest?' Grant asked.

'Two more patients are suffering from slight burns. The other two have been taken to hospital – they're being treated for shock.'

'And the staff?'

'One nurse is badly burned – she's in Intensive Care at University College Hospital. A male nurse was hit by falling masonry, he's stable.'

'Are there men with them?'

Lawrenson nodded.

Grant continued walking along the corridor, its walls scorched black by the fire, its floor deep in filthy water. There was a watch lying on the debris-strewn floor in front of him. He knelt and retrieved it on the end of his pen. It was old, the gold yellowed and worn.

The back bore an inscription:

TO MY DARLING LILLIAN ON OUR ANNIVERSARY

He shook his head. 'Lillian,' he repeated slowly, softly.

'Mrs Lillian Potter, she's over there,' said Lawrenson nodding towards the line of body bags.

The watch had no winder, probably hadn't worked for years.

Grant laid it carefully on top of a nearby radiator that had been stripped of paint by the searing flames.

'The response time of the fire brigade was less than five minutes once they'd got the call,' said Lawrenson. 'The call was logged at just after two this morning.'

'Who made it?'

'One of the staff, just before they got out.'

Grant walked on, passing firemen pulling the remains of a burned bed from the shell of a bedroom. In what was left of the bedroom there was a large wooden wardrobe, most of which had been incinerated in the blaze. But, still hanging inside it were a selection of suits, strangely undamaged by the raging flames. On the wall, also untouched by the fire, was a small metal crucifix. There were scorch marks all around the icon but it remained untarnished.

'What about the physical evidence?' Grant wanted to know.

'A petrol can, found outside one of the windows,' Lawrenson told him.

'Any prints?'

Lawrenson shook his head. 'Whoever it was wore gloves,' he informed his superior.

'What about footprints?'

'The paths around the hospice are all gravel. Even if the fire brigade *hadn't* been stomping all over them we'd have had trouble finding anything, as it is . . .' He allowed the sentence to trail off, shrugging his shoulders.

'So the petrol was poured in through a window and then ignited,' Grant mused.

'That's about the size of it, guv.'

'I want a full report from forensics within the hour – I'm going back to the Yard.'

'Who the fuck would want to torch a hospice?' Lawrenson shaking his head in bewilderment.

'You tell me.'

'As if it isn't bad enough that we've already got *one* nutter out there, now *this*.'

'What makes you think it isn't the same killer?'

'Where the hell's the motive *this* time?' Lawrenson protested. 'How the fuck can there be a link between this and the other murders?'

'I think there is,' murmured Grant. 'And what's more, I think I know *what* it is.'

Forty-Five

'This fire wasn't started to destroy property,' Grant began. 'It was intended to kill. We're lucky it didn't kill more people than it did.'

'Twelve's enough, isn't it?' called a voice from the middle of the incident room.

Grant looked around the group of weary, bleary-eyed policemen gathered before him and saw that the comment had come from Leech. The older man was seated on a desk puffing on a cigarette.

'Someone carried, or dragged, a three-gallon can of petrol to that hospice and emptied it through one of the windows,' Grant continued.

'Somebody bloody strong must have done it then,' said Friel. 'Those things are heavy.'

'Someone strong,' Grant repeated. 'That would be consistent with what we've got on the other murders, right?'

'What the hell has this got to do with the other murders?' Leech demanded. 'This can't be related. It—'

Grant didn't let him finish his sentence. 'Someone drove to the hospice, carried that petrol through the grounds without even leaving a fucking footprint, emptied the contents through a window then set fire to it.'

'What physical evidence have we got?' Schofield asked.

'Sod all. Not a fucking light, if you'll excuse the pun . . . The killer wore smooth gloves. There are no prints. Forensics say that any fibres left behind were burned up in the fire. So, we're even further up shit creek and no bastard is chucking us a paddle yet.'

'I still don't see the link between this fire and the other killings,' Leech persisted. 'The other victims were low-lifes. These victims were . . .' He struggled for the word.

'Normal?' Grant offered.

'Somebody kills a couple of pros, a pimp, a druggie and some dead-beat on the streets – fair enough,' said Leech. 'But why would the same geezer burn down a hospice? It doesn't make any sense.'

'It depends on motive,' Grant said. 'And I reckon we might have one at last.'

A heavy silence fell upon the room, all eyes riveted on Grant as he turned towards the blackboard behind him.

'The victims so far,' he said, pointing at photos of each murdered soul. 'Leech is right – at first this looked like a clean-up campaign – that's what I thought too. The killer was wiping out scumbags. As simple as that.'

'So what made you change your mind, guv?' Friel asked.

'These killings tonight – but there was a note on the coroner's report about the last victim, Ralph Harker, that started me thinking too.' He tapped the photos. 'Two tarts, a drug pusher, a pimp and a small time criminal who happened to be an alky. MO identical in every case. Suspects? None.' He looked around the room at the questioning faces of his colleagues. 'The murderer's physical and psychological profile indicates a very strong man with possibly some kind of deluded moral motive. To clean up the streets.'

'So what's the link with what happened tonight?' Leech asked impatiently.

'Illness,' Grant told him.

'The killer's sick,' Leech persisted.

'Not the *killer*, the *victims*,' said Grant and again he turned to face the photos pinned to the blackboard, tapping each one in turn. 'Tessa Carr was suffering from cervical cancer when she was murdered. Claire Glover had syphilis and non-specific urethritis.' He drew on his cigarette. 'Harvey Dwyer – hepatitis B, septicaemia and arteritis. Simon Costello – emphysema and a bronchial condition so bad that he needed an inhaler. Ralph Harker – cirrhosis of the liver and an advanced form of Bright's disease. It damages the kidneys of heavy drinkers. And now tonight eleven residents of st Angela's Hospice, all terminally ill with cancer. There's your link, there's your motive.'

'So you're saying that these people have been killed because they're *ill*?' Leech queried.

'As far as the perpetrator is concerned, these aren't murders, they're mercy killings,' Grant continued.

His comment was again met by silence.

It was finally broken by Schofield. 'But how would the killer know that the victims were ill?' he asked.

'He wouldn't have to be a doctor to work it out, would he?' Grant snapped. 'Two King's Cross tarts, probably poxed up to the eyes. It's a reasonable assumption, most of them are. A drug user – a fair bet he's shared needles, infected his blood. The killer could have *seen* Simon Costello using an inhaler. An alky living on the streets, a more than fair chance he'd have a fucked-up liver at the very least, and as for the hospice patients . . .' Grant shrugged and allowed the sentence to trail off.

'So what kind of killer are we looking for now?' Friel asked.

'Someone whose family could have suffered from cancer or one of these other diseases possibly,' said Grant.

'So what do we do next?' Leech asked disdainfully. 'Put everyone with the flu, a stomachache or a fucking hangover under guard in case the murderer tries again?'

There were a number of ironic laughs inside the room, hastily silenced by a withering stare from Grant.

'This shifts the entire focus of the investigation,' he said. 'It gives us a whole new set of leads to follow.'

'It puts us right back at square one,' Friel said wearily.

'We hadn't got *past* square one, even before tonight,' Grant said.

'You still don't know if your idea about illness being the motive is right,' Leech said.

'Have you got a better suggestion?' Grant snapped.

Leech hadn't.

'What about the nurse that was killed tonight?' Schofield asked.

'She was in the wrong place at the wrong time,' Grant said. 'Simple as that. The killer was after the hospice residents, not the staff. They were just unlucky.'

'Maybe the killer is ill,' Friel offered. 'Perhaps *he's* got some kind of disease and he wants to take as many with him as possible.'

'Then why take out people who are going to die anyway?' Grant countered. 'No, like I said, this fucking maniac thinks he's doing his victims a favour by ending their suffering.'

'All the victims were dying, were they?' Schofield interjected. 'I mean, they all had terminal illnesses?'

'I think syphilis can be a killer if it isn't treated,' said Grant, looking at the picture of Claire Glover. 'What's your point?'

'So it's reasonably safe to assume he's not going to have a crack at someone with a cold?' Schofield continued.

Grant nodded.

'But there are so many diseases that are *potentially* fatal,' said Schofield. 'Meningitis – pneumonia – angina. How the hell do we know who's a potential victim?'

Grant had no answer. He looked around at the faces of his colleagues in the smoke-filled Incident Room and they all showed the same expression of bewilderment.

'No one is safe until we nail this fucking headcase,' Grant said flatly. 'No one.'

Forty-Six

'Why did you hit her?'

Charlotte Kilbride's words seemed to echo around her large, high-ceilinged office. Suspended there like the motes of dust that twisted and turned gently in the rays of sunlight poking intrusive fingers through the windows.

Andrew Chapman shifted uncomfortably in the antique leather chair, the worn material creaking beneath him. He was in his mid-forties. A tall, imposing-looking man with a round face that looked somewhat out of place atop his thin neck and wiry frame. He pressed his fingertips together then the flat of his hands as if in prayer. Perhaps seeking some divine inspiration in his search for an answer to the question she had asked him.

'I didn't *want* to hit her,' he said finally, hauling himself to his feet and wandering across to the closest window.

He gazed out into Harley Street, his eyes blank, his mind fixed on the recollection.

'She laughed at me,' he continued.

'Why did she laugh?'

'She was just some cheap little tart. Eighteen or nineteen. It annoyed me that she was laughing.'

'You haven't told me *why*?'

'I was in Leeds on business. There was some kind of conference. I had to go on behalf of the bank where I work. One of the barmen at the hotel told me that prostitutes used the hotel to pick up customers. He even pointed a couple out to me.'

'And you picked one up?'

'She was pretty. Brown hair, cut in a bob. She was only about five-two but she had really long, slim legs and she was wearing a short skirt and black high heels – suede ones. And she had this yellow jacket on – I remember it because it was so bright. And underneath she just wore a kind of body suit. A black one.'

'So you took her back to your room?'

He nodded.

'She asked me if I wanted a girlfriend for the night,' said Chapman, grinning crookedly. 'When we got back to my room she told me how much it would cost. Thirty pounds for straight sex with a condom. Fifty without. Twenty pounds for a blow-job with a condom. Forty without. If I wanted her to stay the night then it would be a hundred.'

'And what did you tell her?'

'I laid the magazines out on the bed.'

'The pornographic magazines?'

'They weren't really pornographic. Just *Club International*, *Men Only* and *Mayfair*. They only have pictures of girls in. I told her I wanted to look at the magazines while she masturbated me, that was all. That was when she laughed.'

'Why?'

'She asked why I needed a real woman when I could just have a wank myself. She said I was wasting her time, that she could earn more money with someone else. I offered her ten pounds but she laughed even more. That was when I hit her.'

'Did you hurt her?'

'I only used the back of my hand but she started shouting. She even took a swing at *me*.' He smiled again. 'I threw her out of the room.'

He turned away from the window, looked directly at Charlotte Kilbride. The psychiatrist saw his smile widen but it never touched his eyes.

'That's the trouble,' he continued. 'It's never the same as it is in my magazines or films. Real life is never like that.'

'What makes the women in the magazines and films better, Andrew?'

'They're fantasies, aren't they? They always do what you want them to do. You can control a fantasy. You can't control a real woman the same way.'

'Is that really what you want? To control them?'

He turned away, back to the window, as if his answer lay somewhere out there in the street.

'I just want to look at them. When I look at sex magazines or watch porno videos, it's like I own those women. They're mine. They do exactly what I tell them to do. They're all there for *me*.'

'How many magazines do you buy a month?'

'Six or seven, sometimes more.'

'And videos?'

'Three or four at a time.'

'Where from?'

'A shop in Soho. Always the same shop.'

'And you've never thought of mentioning them to your wife? Asking if she'd like to look at the magazines too, or watch the videos with you?'

'She wouldn't do that,' he snapped. 'She thinks they're disgusting. She'd think *I* was disgusting if she knew.'

'And would that bother you, if she thought that?'

'Of course it would. I've got a family too.'

'A boy and a girl, isn't it?'

He nodded.

'Perhaps my wife is right,' he murmured. 'Perhaps it *is* disgusting. But I can't do without it.'

'You will, in time,' Charlotte said confidently.

'I'm not so sure,' Chapman said. 'I've been coming here over a year now, spending eighty pounds an hour to tell you that I buy sex magazines and videos like other men buy cigarettes. And for what?'

'So I can help you. Why did you come in the first place?'

'I wanted to stop. I wanted to stop feeling so pathetic.' There was a note of anger in his voice. 'So *reliant* on these magazines and videos. It's like a day doesn't pass when I don't have to look at one. I sneak them into my office in the bank and look at them when everyone else is out at lunch. I lock my office door and I turn those pages and I masturbate while I imagine what I'd be doing to the girls on those pages. And I can't stop myself looking and then when I've come I feel angry. With *them* and with myself. *I* feel disgusted. That was why I hit that prostitute in Leeds. She made me feel disgusted with myself.' He began pacing back and forth across the room.

Charlotte watched his steady progress, smoothing her skirt, brushing fluff from it.

'You've been with other prostitutes, Andrew,' she said. 'Did you feel the same with them?'

'The others did as I told them but I still don't like them. I caught VD from one. Filthy slag. Disease-ridden bitch. She told me she was clean. I shouldn't have trusted her.'

'Did your wife find out about the venereal disease?'

'No, I took the antibiotics the doctor gave me and it cleared up quite quickly.'

'What do you think your wife would have done if she'd found out? Do you think she'd have left you?'

'Perhaps. Do you blame her? I could have brought that infection home, given it to *her*.'

'What about your magazines? Your videos? You take those home, don't you?'

'I hide them.'

'What do you think your wife would say if she found them?'

He shook his head.

'What would *you* do if she found them?'

Chapman continued to gaze out of the window, his eyes blank.

'She mustn't know, just as she mustn't know that I come here for help,' he said quietly. 'I'd die if she ever found out. I'd be humiliated – but perhaps that's what I deserve.'

'You shouldn't hate yourself, Andrew. At least you're looking for help. You've come a long way. You should give yourself some credit for that.'

'And how much longer is it going to take? How much longer before I'm *cured*.' There was scorn in his voice. 'Before I don't have to look at those magazines and those videos. Before I don't have to visit disease-ridden whores any longer? How long before I can look myself in the eye without feeling ashamed. Disgusted? You tell me. You're the expert.'

'If you want to help yourself then you will. I'm here to aid that process. It's like healing, Andrew. Like a pain that has to be soothed. It's just that I can't give you a bottle of pills to cure you. In the end you have to cure yourself. It's the same for all my clients, irrespective of what they feel is their problem.'

'Do you know what it's like to feel self-hatred?' he demanded. 'To feel repulsed by your own feelings. No, you don't and you never will. You should be grateful for that.'

She glanced surreptitiously at the clock on her desk. His time was nearly up.

'I know,' said Chapman, as if reading her mind. 'Time to make another appointment. Time to leave. Time for the next eighty-pound-an-hour meal ticket to come in.'

'It isn't like that, Andrew, and you know it,' she said serenely.

He turned back to the window and continued to stare out, his face set in hard lines.

Charlotte Kilbride watched him and noticed that his fists were clenched at his sides, the knuckles white. She knew there was so much rage inside him, so much fury. What bothered her was where that rage would manifest itself. And against whom. She wondered if it already had. Such self-loathing would require an explosive outlet.

She looked again at his clenched fists.

Forty-Seven

Amy glanced at her watch then at the clock on the wall of the studio. They both told her it was almost midnight.

She stifled a yawn as she listened to the latest caller droning on, nodding her head as he ranted and raved about how wrong it was that women had abortions so easily.

'So you'd allow hundreds, even thousands, more unwanted children into the world every year, would you, Mark?' Amy asked. 'You'd take away a woman's right to choose whether or not her life is wrecked by an unwanted child, would you? You'd play God if you had the chance?'

He was about to say something when Amy flicked a switch.

'You're history.'

There was a flatness, an indifference in her voice which she was all too aware of but also felt helpless to disguise.

She wasn't surprised when she looked up towards the production-booth window to see Osborne standing there first pointing at her then shrugging his shoulders. The producer looked a little angry and, Amy reasoned, he had a right to be.

But he doesn't know what's on your mind, does he?

She lit up another cigarette and took another call, listening with the same undisguised uninterest.

She had a pen on the desk in front of her and, as Karen of Tower Hamlets continued the debate about abortion, Amy began doodling. She wrote the word:

BULLETS

Then, beneath it:

GUN

Ask him about the bullets when you get home tonight.

She exhaled deeply.

If he's there.

'I had two abortions when I was at school,' said Karen from Tower Hamlets. 'I mean, if I'd had those kids who would have looked after them?'

'Have you got kids now, Carol?' Amy asked.

'Karen.'

'Sorry?'

'Karen. My name is Karen, not Carol.'

'Excuse me.'

Amy checked on the screen beside her.

Come on, get a grip.

She looked up to the production-booth window again and saw Osborne shaking his head irritably.

'I've got two kids,' Karen continued. 'But I had them when I wanted them. I don't think it's right for people to judge women who have abortions. Especially men.'

'I agree with you.'

'I mean, I know some kids use it like bloody contraception, don't they? They get pregnant and nip off down the clinic for an abortion. I don't agree with that but they should at least have the choice.'

'Life's all about choice. I agree with you, Karen. Thanks for your call.' Amy pressed a button then leaned closer to the microphone. 'We're taking a short break for the news now but join us again in fifteen minutes for more scintillating chat and stunning insights into the modern world with me, Amy Watson, your friendly neighbourhood insomniac. I hope there are plenty more of you out there.'

She pushed the microphone away and got to her feet, dropping her headset on to the console then heading for the studio door.

As she emerged into the corridor, Osborne stuck his head out of the production room and gestured to her.

'Have you got a minute, Amy?' he asked briskly.

She joined him in the control room.

'What the hell is wrong with you tonight?'

'What are you talking about?'

'You know bloody well what I'm talking about. This is a talk show, right? Well, you're not talking. The poor sods who are ringing in might as well be talking to a brick wall. Show some bloody interest, Amy. It's unprofessional.'

'It's not *that* bad.'

'It *is* that bad. If I was listening as a punter I wouldn't be wasting my time ringing in to some bitch who's not interested in what I've got to say.'

She regarded him balefully for a moment.

'Bitch, eh?' she said sarcastically. 'So, it's worse than unprofessional, is it? I'm a bitch too.'

'Just show some interest, will you,' he snapped.

'Bitch,' she repeated.

'You might be pissed off but there's no need to let the world know about it. What is it, time of the month?'

'Oh, fuck you, Mike.'

'Not for more than a year,' he said scathingly.

'Then get over it,' she told him. 'I'm going to the toilet.'

'That's where this fucking show's going if you don't get a grip.'

She barely heard the end of the sentence as she stepped back out into the corridor and headed for the Ladies.

What was she supposed to do? Tell him what was *really* on her mind? *Sorry if I'm not quite my usual perky self, Mike, but the guy I'm sleeping with happens to keep bullets in his medicine cabinet. Okay?*

She pushed the door of the Ladies and walked in.

Jo Parker turned from one of the sinks and faced her, and immediately Amy saw how wan her friend looked. The younger woman swiftly looked away as Amy headed for one of the cubicles.

'Couldn't you stand it either?' Amy said, shutting the door and seating herself.

'Stand what?' Jo asked, wiping her face.

'Osborne's moaning about the show. About me.'

Jo didn't answer.

'Are you all right, Jo?'

Still no answer.

Then Amy heard the unmistakable sound of crying. Soft, almost childlike weeping.

She dressed hastily and hurried out to find Jo wiping tears from her eyes.

Amy embraced her and felt Jo return the gesture.

'What is it?' Amy asked.

Jo shook her head. 'I'm sorry,' she said tearfully. 'I didn't want to say anything.' She stepped back, wiping her eyes with her fingers. 'I didn't want to bother you with my bloody problems.'

'What are friends for?' Amy said, smiling. 'You know I'd bother you with *mine*.' She attempted a grin but it was wasted, Jo was too distraught.

'It's my brother,' Jo began. 'He's been living with me for the last few weeks. I think he's in trouble.'

'What makes you think that?'

'I found a bottle of pills and some phone numbers in his clothes the other day.'

'What kind of pills?'

'Well, there weren't any in the bottle, it looked as if he was just using the bottle to store them.'

'But how do you know that, Jo?'

'Because I know *him*. He's used drugs before.'

'And you think he's using now?'

'Pills, needles. I don't know what he's on. He hardly ever comes back to my flat any more. He's out all the time. He stays out all night most nights, never tells me where he is or who he's with.'

'It might be innocent, Jo, you—'

'Not *him*. He's always got so much money too and he isn't working. How else could he be getting money, Amy, if he's not dealing?'

More tears began to flow.

Amy hugged her again.

'You don't know for sure, Jo,' she said softly. 'You might be jumping to conclusions.'

Just like you don't know for sure the significance of the bullets?

'I'm frightened of what he might do,' Jo continued. 'Or of what might happen to him. I don't want to lose another brother.'

Amy held her friend close.

'What the hell is he mixed up in?' Jo whimpered. 'I've got to know.'

Forty-Eight

12.31 a.m.

Amy sipped at her coffee and connected a caller named Roy.

'Where are you calling from, Roy?' she asked, noting that there was no location for the source of the call.

Roy. Why did that name ring a bell?

Silence.

'I asked where—'

'I told you I'd call again after the next murder.'

Amy felt a shiver run up her spine, icy fingers tickling the nape of her neck.

'Where are you calling from, Roy?' she persisted.

'You won't be able to trace this call – I won't be on long enough. You need twenty-nine seconds for a trace, don't you?'

'Very clever, Roy,' she said sardonically. 'What's your point?'

'I want to talk about death,' the voice said, and again Amy felt the skin of her neck puckering.

'Whose?'

'No one specific. Not yet.'

'Did you mean those people who were killed in that fire yesterday?'

Silence.

'Roy?'

'Time's up. I'll call you back.'

And he was gone.

Before Amy had time to react, his name flashed brightly on the screen again and she looked up to see both Osborne *and* Jo looking in at her.

She connected him again.

'Welcome back, Roy,' she said. 'Are you going to do this all night? Talk for twenty-odd seconds then hang up?'

'I'm on a mobile now. You can trace the signal but not pin down the location.'

'What makes you think I really *care* where you are, Roy?' Amy said defiantly.

'Because you care what I've got to say about these killings.'

'They're nothing to do with me and, for all I know, they're probably nothing to do with *you* either. You might be one of these nutters who gets his rocks off confessing to murders he hasn't committed. You just want to sound important, Roy.'

She puffed on her cigarette.

'Twelve bodies recovered from that fire,' he snapped.

'You could have read that in the newspapers. Am I supposed to be impressed?'

'Two prostitutes, a pimp, a drug pusher and a tramp before them,' he continued.

'*That* was in the papers too. Tell me something I don't know.'

'There'll be more.'

Icy fingers.

'That's a reasonable assumption – hardly privileged information though.'

Tracing chilly patterns over her neck and shoulders.

'One of them could be *you*.'

'Oh, yes, you disagreed with my work in the past, didn't you, Roy?'

'It wasn't work. Work is done by honest, clean-living people. You sold yourself. Sold your body. Sold your morality.'

'So, you're going to kill me because I've got no morals, Roy? That means you'll have to kill half the population of the country too.'

A long silence.

'Why were the people killed last night, Roy?' Amy continued. 'What kind of moral code had *they* broken? They were sick people, that was all.'

'Then they were released.'

'From what?'

'From suffering. From this world and its corruption – and it's been made corrupt by people like *you*. People with no sense of decency – no standards or concepts of morality.'

'You should have been a politician, Roy,' she said with a sneer. 'You like the sound of your own voice.'

'You don't like it because you know I'm telling the truth,' he countered angrily.

'I know you're a sad, self-important little man who thinks he's being profound but you're not. You should be pitied. But not by me, Roy. I just find you irritating. You're history.'

She severed the connection.

As she glanced across she could still see his name flashing madly on the screen but she went to the call below it.

'Dennis from Golders Green,' Amy said. 'You're not going to threaten to kill me, are you?'

'I couldn't believe what that bloke was going on about,' said Dennis from Golders Green. 'You should sue him for threatening behaviour.'

'Roy is too insignificant to waste time on, Dennis,' she said, still watching his name flashing on the screen. 'What point would *you* like to make?'

'Well, it is to do with these murders.'

Roy's name continued to flash.

'I wonder if they might be racially motivated,' Dennis mused.

'In what way, Dennis?'

'Well, all the victims have been white, haven't they?'

'So, what's your point?'

'Well, the blacks are always going on about how everyone is against them and that and, well, it might be a black killer trying to get back at us whites.'

'An interesting theory, Dennis. Not much evidence to back it up though.'

'Well, I mean, most blacks have got a chip on their

shoulder, haven't they? I mean, if they don't like the way they're treated then they should go home. Same with the bloody Pakis. I mean, they come over here by the boat-load and—'

'Have we got your location right, Dennis?' Amy interrupted. 'You are calling from Golders Green, aren't you?'

'Yes, why?'

'I thought you might be calling from Auschwitz. I think your kind of bigoted viewpoint belongs there.'

'I say these blacks are too powerful . . . they—'

'You're history, Dennis,' she hissed, dismissing him. 'Get back to your copy of *Mein Kampf*.'

On the screen the name ROY was still flashing.

Amy looked towards the control booth but there was no sign of Osborne.

She connected Roy again.

'Go ahead, Roy,' she said. 'Give us more pearls of wisdom.'

This time she saw Osborne standing there with his arms outstretched and his head back in an attitude of resignation.

Silence on the line.

'Come on then,' she chided. 'Gone shy on me?'

'You're dead, bitch,' he hissed. 'DEAD!'

The final word was roared with such ferocity that Amy was forced to slip one earpiece off.

The line went dead.

She watched as his name dimmed and faded on the screen. Empty screen. Dead line.

That icy caress moved once more over the back of her neck.

When she reached for her coffee her hand was shaking.

'Are you sure you're going to be okay?' asked Amy, placing one hand on Jo's shoulder.

The younger woman reached up and touched the hand softly.

'I'm not the one who was threatened,' Jo said. Then she nodded. 'Yeah, I'll be fine.'

'You can come and stay with me for a couple of nights if you like,' Amy persisted.

'Thanks for offering but I'm going to be thinking about Billy wherever I am and, who knows, he might even come home. I want to be there when he does.'

'It might not be what you think, Jo.'

The younger woman could only shrug as she headed for the waiting taxi.

'If you need me, call me. It doesn't matter what time,' Amy said, watching as her friend climbed into the cab.

The driver guided it out into traffic and it pulled away.

Amy pulled the collar of her jacket up, finished her cigarette, then, before she climbed into her own taxi, she glanced around, squinting in the gloom.

If there was anyone skulking around in the shadows she couldn't see them.

Skulking in the shadows? Imagination running away with you?

Who would be?

Roy's words echoed inside her head. '*You're dead, bitch.*'

The wind was getting stronger, it whipped her hair around her face as she stooped to get into the cab.

'*You're dead, bitch.*'

Forty-Nine

Despite the soothing warmth of the water she was lying in, Amy was irritated that the drowsiness that precedes sleep as yet eluded her. She rarely felt tired after a show, never felt like coming straight in and flopping exhausted on the bed. The adrenaline was always coursing too strongly through her veins. Particularly if it had been a good show and the callers had been challenging.

But tonight she felt that her unwanted alertness, even at such a godforsaken hour (it was approaching 2.35 a.m.) was due more to the thoughts tumbling through her mind than to any stimulating conversation she'd had with those who called her show.

Amy drew the flannel through the bathwater, wrung it out, then laid the cloth across her face. She wished that cutting out the light would also cut out her thoughts, and she cursed the fact that so much seemed to be tormenting her at present. Fragments of sentences. Of ideas. Of suspicions. They all whirled around inside her head, unwanted but so difficult to remove. Like stains on her consciousness.

Webber.

The bullets.

She had glanced at his door as she'd entered the building, thought about knocking, then decided against it.

Roy (if that was his real name) and his rantings. His threats against her. *Death* threats. Jo Parker's distress and fear for her brother. The entire twisted, unfathomable mess lodged in her mind like a splinter in soft skin.

She pulled the flannel from her face, exhaled deeply and raised one leg, washing it gently.

Webber. *What was he doing now?* Was *he* thinking about *her*? *What* was he thinking? Probably thinking about his dead daughter.

Amy remembered the soul-wrenching grief he'd shown

at the child's graveside, and her own feeling of help-lessness to ease his suffering at such a terrible loss. His gratitude to her for helping him overcome the pain, even though they both knew it would take a long time, perhaps longer than either of them could imagine.

Then she thought of the bullets. Bullets equal gun. It was a simple equation. Gun equals violence and possible death. Was that equation quite so cut and dried? She thought not.

Was Webber a killer? Having a gun doesn't make him a killer? Why would he want a gun?

'You don't even know he's got one,' she said aloud, answering her own unspoken question.

She washed the other leg.

And Roy? Was he a killer? *The* killer? A psychiatrist would call his maniacal rantings and threats a craving for attention. Threats to be treated with contempt or scorn? Or to be received with trepidation and fear?

'You're dead, bitch.'

Perhaps she should tell Webber about Roy's threats. So he can use his gun on him?

Amy shook her head, irritated with herself, with her own train of thought.

She soaped her hands and washed first one breast then the other. She sucked in a deep breath and decided she wouldn't mention the threats to Webber when . . .

She felt it to the right of her left nipple. Beneath the soft flesh she felt the lump.

Amy froze, her hand on her breast, her fingers probing the lump. The lump in her breast. The words screamed inside her head. The lump in her breast.

She probed it with shaking fingers, recoiling from the pain as she pushed too hard.

'Oh God,' she whispered, her throat already dry.

She looked down, trying to inspect the lump more fully.

The lump.

She was amazed at how quickly the panic spread through her, like a forest fire through dry timber it engulfed her, the word and its connotations hammering inside her brain like a jack-hammer.

The lump in her breast.

As she felt around it as calmly as she could, she realised it was about the width of a fifty-pence piece. The circumference was more difficult to gauge.

But what the hell did size matter? The size of a pea, the size of a grapefruit. She had a swelling there. A collection of cells that had formed into a firm and painful knot beneath the smooth flesh. Cells that could, even as she touched and probed, be cannabalising others. Growing.

The word seared through her consciousness. *Growth.*

Others followed it. Tumour. Cancer. Breast cancer. This was how it started, wasn't it?

She checked her nipple for any signs of discharge, any blood.

There was none. At least none she'd noticed. Had she just failed to see it in the past few days? How long had it been there?

Amy felt faint.

She hauled herself up and out of the bath, pulling her robe on, dripping water on the tiled floor. For a second she thought she was going to be sick but the sensation passed and she realised that the feelings were caused not by the (*The what? The growth? The tumour? The lump?*) knot of cells in her breast but by her own panic.

She sucked in several deep breaths, trying to calm herself, fighting to find reason in this madness of fear. Many women, most women, found lumps in their breasts, the vast majority of which were benign, harmless. They gave no pain, they . . .

But this lump hurts.

She caught sight of her face in the mirror as she passed it, her features strained, the colour gone from her cheeks.

She hurried into the sitting room and poured herself a brandy but, as she raised it to her lips she felt sick again. Sick with worry. She couldn't drink it.

Amy reached for the phone. She needed to tell someone.

Needed to hear some words of comfort. She was trapped alone in her flat with this lump in her breast and her thoughts of breast cancer and mastectomy and death and she felt as alone and frightened as she'd ever felt in her life.

She dialled Webber's number and waited. And waited. *Be there for me.* And waited. No answer.

She jabbed out the digits of Jo Parker's number.

Ringing.

Please, Jo, pick it up. Let me hear a voice.

No answer.

She *was* alone.

Amy put the phone back gently, her panic now receding slowly, her heart rate slowing somewhat.

She sat on her sofa, head back, gazing blankly at the ceiling. The voice of reason tried to batter its way through the wall of fear and riotous imagination.

'Call the doctor in the morning,' she said aloud, hoping that the sound of her own voice would drive away the terror.

She could feel herself becoming more calm and she sucked in several more deep breaths to speed the process. Her heart had stopped battering against her ribs.

She closed her eyes for a moment, almost meditatively.

That's it. Calm down.

Benign. She clung to the word like a drowning man clings to a lifebelt. Benign.

She used it to push away that other word. That word that sounded so terrifying in *any* context.

Malignant.

She fought to force that word from her mind but the battle was a mighty one and the malignancy of her fear clung as surely as the possible malignancy of that lump in her breast.

She ran a hand through her hair. See the doctor tomorrow. He'll tell you it's benign.

She nodded to herself, the initial panic over.

It was then that she started to cry.

Fifty

The limousine waited outside number six, Drayson Mews, its engine idling, its tinted windows occasionally reflecting some of the many faces outside the three-storey Georgian house.

The small thoroughfare, just two minutes from Kensington High Street, was normally quiet, but this particular morning there were up to a dozen journalists and at least three film crews arrayed along its length. Many of those present were looking around at the other dwellings around number six, and more than one comment was made about being able to 'smell the money'.

From some of the windows of other houses in Drayson Mews, faces appeared and looked out almost disdainfully at the clutch of media thronging around the front door of number six. Some residents objected to the intrusion, others accepted that this kind of invasion would happen periodically when they shared a street with the Home Secretary. One or two even welcomed the cameras and the jabbering horde. It gave them a feeling of importance themselves, as if living in the same street as a member of the cabinet somehow gave them a vicarious importance and re-emphasised the social heights to which they had risen.

David Albury had already seen the newsmen and women outside his house and he stood watching them from behind his curtains for a moment, before finally heading towards the front door.

'Who *are* those people, Daddy?' asked his daughter, Harriet, also looking out at the gathering throng. She was twelve years old, a tall, gangling child who looked, with her pinched features and large eyes, more like her mother than Albury.

When she spoke it was with a voice shaped at expensive

kindergarten, honed at Roedean and polished at St Paul's. But if she had her mother's looks, she had her father's manner. A slightly superior air that seemed to sit quite comfortably on such young shoulders.

'Why are they outside our house?' Harriet continued.

'They want to speak to your father,' said Louise Albury, emerging from the kitchen clutching a cup of tea. 'He's very popular at the moment.'

'Some of them look rather common,' Harriet observed. 'One of them is smoking.' She wrinkled her nose.

'Your father will handle them, won't you?' Louise said, turning her attention to her husband.

If Albury caught the edge in her tone he didn't react to it. Instead he headed for the front door, waited a second, then pulled it open.

Immediately, the reporters outside surged forward calling out questions, and a barrage of cameras went off.

'Mr Albury, over here.'

'What kind of impact do you think this Bill will have?'

'Are you glad that the legislation has been passed?'

Albury raised a hand, as if to force back the throng then he stood silently until the chorus of voices died away.

'I'll answer your questions,' he finally said. 'But keep them brief, I'm due at the House of Commons within the hour.'

More cameras snapped.

Microphones and mini-tape recorders were pushed closer to him. The cyclopean eye of a television camera fixed him in its unblinking stare.

'What exactly do you expect this Bill to achieve, Mr Albury?' asked one of the journalists.

'It will make it more difficult for children and other impressionable people to view offensive material,' Albury replied.

'What do you class as offensive?'

'That's a very difficult question to answer,' Albury said almost dismissively. 'I think most right-thinking people will be able to discern what gives offence and what doesn't.'

'Is it aimed specifically at violence in films and video?' asked another reporter.

'The measures included in the Bill also take into account the gratuitous amount of sex seen in films and on television. It is a very wide-reaching piece of legislation.'

'Someone said that the censorship laws were strict enough already. Why strengthen them?'

'You only have to look at society to realise that those laws were *not* sufficient,' Albury countered. 'The increase in violence and sex in films and on video has led to a steady decline of values in day-to-day life. Moral codes have been eroded by this particular branch of the media.'

'How do you respond to the suggestion that the measures proposed in your Bill aren't just strict but Draconian?' a television reporter challenged.

'Society has to be protected against this kind of thing. People have to be protected, for their own good,' Albury said condescendingly.

'What about freedom of expression? Doesn't that extend to film makers or artists of any kind?' someone else asked.

'This Bill doesn't attempt to stifle creativity,' Albury chided. 'It will ensure that the creativity of which you speak is kept within guidelines – moral guidelines.'

'Is it true that it extends to the closure of stripclubs and sex shops?' another reporter enquired.

'There is provision within the Bill for certain establishments to be closed if they are not working within the parameters outlined *in* the Bill,' Albury explained.

'Aren't you afraid you'll force the video industry underground?'

'Film makers, video distributors, publishers or anyone else affected by the Bill would have no need to fear it if they were making and producing suitable products for public viewing or consumption,' Albury stated.

'By that, do you mean films and books that *you* approve of?' asked the same journalist.

'I speak for a huge majority of people in this country who are sick and tired of being subjected to the filth served up to them by film makers, video distributors and other so-called artists,' Albury said with an air of superciliousness.

'Isn't this just a good vote-catcher with an election coming up? That's why it's being rushed through Parliament, isn't it?'

Albury ignored the question.

'For too long now this country has lost sight of family values.' He began to sound sanctimonious. 'It was my wish that this Bill would help to restore those values.'

'So, it's nothing to do with the election coming up, then?' the reporter persisted.

'Is it true that the Bill includes provision for the banning of certain films and videos that have already been released?' somebody called from the back of the throng.

'A number of films and videos will be withdrawn from circulation – yes,' Albury answered. 'Once again, in the public interest.'

'What's the point if these films have already been viewed?' the same journalist persisted.

'No more questions,' said Albury, raising both hands.

'When will the Bill become law?'

Albury merely waved, turned and headed back inside his house.

He emerged a moment later carrying a briefcase, with his wife and daughter on either side of him. They were both smiling fixedly as the cameras snapped away.

Albury bent and kissed his daughter on the cheek, then he moved through the throng of press towards the limousine.

The driver sprang from behind the wheel and opened the back door, standing between Albury and the press.

He slammed the door, the tinted windows making it impossible to see inside the vehicle.

Albury relaxed back into the leather seat and exhaled deeply. Sitting across from him, smiling, was Anita Bishop.

Albury returned the smile as the car pulled away.

Fifty-One

'I thought *I* was supposed to be the quiet one.'

Amy looked up from her plate, momentarily disorientated by the words. She saw Webber gazing at her, a slight smile on his lips.

Apart from a man who sat alone reading the *Telegraph*, they were the only ones in the small restaurant off Portland Street. Most of the other lunchtime customers had long since left. Staff had been clearing tables for about twenty minutes now and those that weren't busy were standing around the till or in the kitchen chatting, content to let their last patrons finish their meals in peace.

Outside, traffic rushed past in a noisy haze but inside the restaurant and particularly inside Amy's head the world seemed to be barely moving. It was as if time had been slowed, as if everything moved in slow motion. Including her own thoughts. Her world had narrowed to the tiny space she and Webber now occupied at the corner table.

And to the lump in her breast.

A cone seemed to have descended around them, shutting out the rest of the world, focusing their own problems in that one small area.

'Sorry, Jake,' she said, trying to shake herself from her thoughts.

'It's okay, I should be used to it by now, you've been like it all through lunch,' he said, still smiling. 'What's wrong?'

'Nothing,' she lied.

Apart from the fact I found a box of bullets in your medicine cabinet and, last night, while you were out at 3.30 in the morning, I discovered a lump in my breast, everything is just fine. Honest.

Webber raised an eyebrow.

'You know that expression about not bullshitting a bullshitter?' he said.

She nodded.

'I'm smelling bullshit. What's on your mind?'

She sipped her drink, watching the slice of lemon bobbing up and down in the Bacardi when she prodded it with the cocktail stick.

'If you want me to mind my own business I will,' he continued. 'If you don't want to talk about it, that's fine. I just wondered if I could help.'

'I wanted to talk last night, Jake,' she said a little too vehemently. 'But you weren't there.'

He eyed her warily.

'Just like you're not there most nights,' Amy continued. 'You're out somewhere in the small hours doing Christ knows what.'

'I thought this was about *you* not *me*,' he said evenly.

'It is,' she snapped.

'So tell me. What did you want to talk to me about last night that you can't talk to me about today.'

'It doesn't matter.'

'It matters to me,' he said through clenched teeth and she saw how his eyes blazed as he looked at her.

'I found a lump in my breast,' she blurted out.

His features softened and he reached across the table to touch her arm.

'Why didn't you tell me earlier?'

'It's taken me this long to tell you *now*.'

'And you called me last night?'

She nodded. 'I called you then I called Jo.'

He looked vague.

'Jo Parker, a friend of mine,' Amy elaborated.

'And what did *she* say?'

'She wasn't there either. I just wanted to talk to someone, Jake, to *tell* someone. It's not the sort of information you want to keep to yourself, believe me.'

He squeezed her hand.

'I wanted someone to talk to *me*, to tell me that everything was going to be all right,' she continued.

'I'm sorry I wasn't there when you needed me.'

'You weren't to know.'

'Listen to me, whatever I can do to help, just tell me.'

'I don't know *who* can help.'

'How bad is the lump? How big?'

'Big enough.'

'Have you seen a doctor yet?'

'I only found out last night.'

'You should have been at a doctor's first thing this morning.'

'I'm frightened. I know I've got to go, I know that's the only way they can help me, but I'm scared shitless, Jake. Do you blame me?'

He shook his head.

'You didn't say anything the night we spent together,' he observed. '*I* never felt anything.'

'Perhaps there was nothing there then. Perhaps this is some kind of quick-growing cancer that—'

'You don't know it's cancer – don't say that,' Webber said, cutting her short.

'What else could it be, doctor?' There was scorn in her voice.

He fixed her in an unblinking gaze, surprised at the anger in her voice.

'Don't you think I haven't considered every possible alternative?' she said challengingly. 'I spent all of last night doing that, Jake. It's called clutching at straws. Trying to talk myself into believing that whatever it is it isn't cancer. The trouble is, every time I come back to the same conclusion – breast cancer.'

'Listen, Amy. You make a fucking appointment and quick, got it? And no matter where or what time, I'll come with you.'

'Jake, you don't have to.'

'I know that. I *want* to. I want to help you the way

you helped me. Without you I'd never have gone to see Samantha's grave. I owe you for that at least.'

'Don't feel you have to repay me, Jake.'

'I care about you. I care about what happens to you. This isn't a fucking favour, Amy. Don't shut me out. Not now.'

He squeezed her hand more tightly and she saw the concern in his eyes.

She reached across the table and gently ran a finger over his stubbled cheek.

'Thank you,' she said, her voice almost a whisper.

'Make the appointment.'

Fifty-Two

Police Commissioner Alex Hayward sat back in his seat, fingertips pressed together meditatively. Every now and then he would nod sagely but, not once during the twenty minutes that David Grant had been in his spacious office, had the older man's face betrayed even a flicker of emotion.

For such a small man, Hayward had a commanding presence that seemed to inspire a combination of respect and foreboding amongst his bigger built subordinates. Few people had ever witnessed him losing his famed temper but those who had spoke of such an incident in almost reverential tones. And yet, Hayward was an approachable and personable character, as likely to be found in a patrol car with a couple of uniformed officers as at a high-level meeting. He usually travelled with a mobile unit once a month. He was fond of telling his companions that it kept him in touch with the streets. It also put the fear of Christ into which ever unit he picked to act as his escort that particular day. Even so, the men seemed to appreciate that someone in so lofty a position as the Commissioner should still be interested in the day-to-day workings of uniformed men. It didn't lessen their trepidation however.

Hayward had said little since Grant entered the office. Pleasantries had been exchanged, Grant had been congratulated on his promotion, quizzed on the nature of the current investigation and even asked about his family. He'd lied and said that everything was fine at home.

The family was another pet concern of the Commissioner. He preferred family men working close to him. He felt that the family gave a man stability and a sense of responsibility. These were things that his family had done for him; he felt it only natural the same should apply to his subordinates.

He had also asked Grant if he had any kids or *planned* to have any.

Grant lied about that too.

Grant sipped the tea he'd been offered upon entering the office, winced when he found it had gone cold and replaced the cup.

He was finished. He had said what he had to say.

Now he waited.

Hayward remained in that fixed position, fingertips pressed together, eyes looking through, not past, Grant.

Grant shifted uncomfortably in his seat, wondering for a moment if the little Scot had even heard what he'd said.

Finally Hayward spoke. 'No,' he said bluntly. 'I'm afraid I will have to deny your request for extra men on your investigation.'

'But, sir, the men I've got aren't enough.'

'Every officer on the force says that, Grant. I can't spare any more men.'

'But the investigation has taken a completely different turn since the burning of that hospice. The men I've got can't cover the ground quickly enough. They—'

'How many are you using?'

'Sixty, sir. In plainclothes, undercover and uniform.'

'And you can't crack a case with sixty men, Grant?'

'I'm trying my best, sir.'

'Then try harder.'

'With all due respect, sir, you tell me a more important investigation that's going on at the moment,' said Grant with barely suppressed anger. 'The press are having a pop at us every day for not getting results, the media are crucifying us.'

'Not *us*, Grant,' the Scot corrected him. 'They're crucifying *you*.'

The younger man glared at his superior.

'Do you know one of the things I don't like about my job, Grant?'

Grant shook his head.

'I have to delegate,' the Scot continued. 'I have to let other people do what I would rather be doing myself. That means I have to trust other people and I hate trusting anyone. Now I'm having to trust *you* to wrap up this investigation and I have faith in you to do that. So don't let me down.'

'So, no more men, sir?'

'You're lucky I'm not taking them away from you, never mind assigning you more.'

Grant looked vague.

'You asked me if there was a more important investigation going on at the moment,' Hayward said with a touch of weariness in his tone. 'I don't think there is. Unfortunately, the Home Secretary doesn't agree.'

'I'm not with you, sir.'

'Starting this morning – and this comes direct from the horse's mouth, or arse depending on your views – all available officers are to be used to implement the Albury Bill. The fax came through this morning just before *you* arrived.'

'What the hell has that got to do with *my* investigation, sir?'

'It means, Grant, that any spare men are going to be running around bloody stripclubs, clip joints, video shops, book stores and anywhere else our esteemed Home Secretary tells me to send them. Just so this Bill of his can be *seen* to be having some sort of effect.'

'And he thinks that takes precedence over a murder investigation?'

'It wouldn't matter to Albury if someone had shot the Queen and stabbed the Queen Mum. The only thing he cares about is this Bill of his. That's why you can't have the men you request. You take your orders from me. I take mine from him. Neither of us has any choice in this, Grant. We've both just got to get on with it. Like it or not.'

A heavy silence descended, finally broken by the Commissioner. 'Was there anything else?' he asked, glancing at his watch.

'No, sir,' said Grant, getting to his feet. 'Thanks for your time.'

He turned to go.

'Grant.'

Grant turned.

'I know it's not much consolation,' Hayward told him, 'but if it was down to me, you'd have the men you need.'

'Thank you, sir.'

'You get this bastard,' the Scot said. 'And you do it as quick as you can. If you don't get him, when the press crucify *you*, they might just decide to nail *me* up beside you. Understand?'

Fifty-Three

Amy Watson struck the punchbag with her right fist.

Bang.

The shock travelled up her arm but it felt good, she enjoyed the feeling of strength.

She struck again. And again.

Concentrate.

She took two steps back and swung her foot at the heavy bag.

Force every other thought from your mind.

The kicks she drove into it were of thunderous power and she could see the muscles in her thigh bulging with each impact. She shouted as she kicked, sweat pouring down her face, flying in salty droplets from her soaking hair. The sound echoed around the gym but was lost beneath the sound of pumping music.

It was later in the day than normal for her workout and more people were present than usual. One or two of them cast quizzical glances in her direction as she laid into the punchbag with renewed ferocity.

Force every other thought from your mind.

She kicked.

Every one.

And kicked again. Spun round, changed legs, kicked again. It was done now. There was no going back.

She gritted her teeth with the effort of working herself even harder.

Do it. Do it.

She sucked in another deep breath. The insteps of her feet were red from the continual pounding on the bag but she felt no pain. The adrenaline rush that such strenuous exercise brought nullified everything else.

Concentrate. Her mind seemed to be emptying.

Force the fear out.

She kept kicking. Another ten minutes, then she'd shower, drive home and prepare herself for the night's show.

Amy wiped sweat from her eyes and prowled around the swinging bag like a cat stalking a bird, waiting to strike.

She unfolded a slender leg and kicked with devastating power. The appointment with the doctor had been made. She had come to the gym directly after making it.

Amy kicked again. Shouted in anger. She would be at his surgery at ten the following morning.

'Rack them up again.'

David Grant watched as the black ball disappeared. He chalked the end of his cue as Lawrenson retrieved the pool balls and slotted them into position.

At a table close by two youths in their late teens sat watching, one of them sipping at a pint as if it was his first. He was watching the two policemen intently, occasionally glancing at his watch. Sometimes he would lean across and speak to his companion, shielding his mouth with the back of his hand as if he feared that Grant was some kind of lip-reader.

Grant saw the furtive whisperings and looked at the taller of the two youths dismissively.

All around them, the pub was a mass of noise. Voices and the non-stop cacophony of sound expelled by a number of fruit machines and electronic games and the steady soundtrack provided by the juke-box. The air was thick with cigarette smoke.

Grant watched as Lawrenson slammed the cue ball into the triangle and sent balls spinning in all directions.

'So, that's the story,' he said, bending down to take his own shot. 'We get no help and that's official.'

He dropped a colour.

The tall youth whispered something to his companion.

'We have to find this fucking maniac with the men we've got now,' Grant continued.

He potted another colour.

'I'm beginning to think we're pissing in the wind, guv,' Lawrenson told him. 'No leads. No suspects. Just seventeen corpses.'

'But we have an MO and we have a motive,' Grant reminded him, potting another colour. 'Perhaps we should be grateful for *that* much.'

Lawrenson was unimpressed. He watched as Grant potted the remaining balls then stepped back.

'Another one?' Grant said. '*I'm* in no rush to get home.'

'One more, double or quits,' Lawrenson said.

The taller of the two watching youths got to his feet and stepped towards Grant.

'Look, mate, we've got our name down for a game,' he said. 'How much longer are you going to be?'

Grant regarded him contemptuously.

'Patience is a virtue,' he said flatly, his eyes boring into the youth. 'You'll have to wait.'

'Well, speed it up a bit, will you, you've been on there an hour already.'

Grant took a step towards him and the youth backed away, suddenly alarmed by the look in the policeman's eyes.

'Don't bother me, sunshine,' Grant hissed. 'I've got enough on my mind already. Got it?'

The youth moved further back.

Lawrenson took a step towards his superior, glancing at the white-faced youth.

'Your break, guv,' Lawrenson said.

'Your fucking mate's off his head,' the youth said to Lawrenson as Grant got down to take his shot.

'You could be right,' Lawrenson told him, not a trace of emotion in his expression.

The white slammed into the other balls with a loud crack.

It reminded Grant of breaking bone.

David Albury reached for the mobile phone and pressed

the keys for the number he required. He sat back in the plush leather seat of the Jag and waited for his call to be answered.

The driver guided the vehicle expertly through the maze of traffic, glancing down every now and then to re-check his destination.

Albury was due to address a meeting of the National Viewer's and Listener's Association that evening and the driver was making sure his passenger wasn't late.

Every now and then he glanced at Albury in his rear-view mirror and saw him with the phone still pressed to his ear.

When it was finally picked up, Albury's expression didn't change.

'It's me,' he said. 'I'm on my way now.'

The driver tried not to make it obvious that he was eavesdropping by gazing out of the side window every time the car stopped at lights. Besides, he wasn't really interested in his passenger's conversation.

A taxi cut in front of him and he was forced to brake a little sharply.

He caught sight of Albury's disapproving glance in his rear-view mirror.

'I don't know what time I'll be finished,' Albury said. 'No. I'll get something to eat before I come home. Give Harriet a kiss for me. Okay.'

The Jag wound its way through the steady stream of traffic.

'See you later,' said Albury and switched off the signal.

He waited a moment then pressed more digits.

When he spoke again his voice was muted – whispering almost conspiratorially.

The driver noticed that he was smiling too.

'I'll pick you up at the same place tonight,' Albury said.

The driver glanced at him in the mirror, and saw his smile spreading wider.

'Business first,' Albury grinned. 'Yes. Same time too. See you later.'

He switched off.

Andrew Chapman parked the Audi in the multi-storey car park in Brewer Street. Same car park as usual. Almost the same space as usual. Second level, close to the exit ramp.

He made sure that the doors were locked and stood watching the blinking red eye of the immobiliser for a second before heading towards the narrow flight of steps that would lead him out into the street.

The night was aglow with neon. The whole street was ablaze with multi-coloured signs. Beckoning.

He looked at his watch.

9.46 p.m.

He pulled free his tie, rolled it up and stuffed it in the pocket of his jacket.

He stood on the pavement for a moment, glancing up at the sign that blazed above him. Then, reaching for his wallet, he headed into the first of the stripclubs.

'Are you going to be here when I get back?'

Jo Parker stood in the doorway of her flat staring back at her brother who was sprawled on the sofa watching television.

Billy didn't answer, but merely took another swig from a bottle of Becks.

'Did you hear what I said?'

'I don't know if I'll be here,' he told her. 'I doubt it.'

'Where are you going?'

'Where are *you* going?'

'I'm going to work.'

'So am I,' he countered, a grin spreading across his face.

Jo hesitated a moment knowing it was futile to continue pressing him for answers.

'Break a leg,' he called. 'Or what ever they say in showbiz.'

As she closed the door behind her she heard his hollow laughter.

Fifty-Four

As Amy slipped her blouse back on and tucked it into the top of her jeans she could hear the sound of running water.

She stepped from behind the screen to see Dr Alan Davidson washing his hands in the small sink on the far side of his room. It was a large room, made to look larger by the fact that there was so little furniture in it. A large desk, occupied by a computer and its printer, two chairs, a filing cabinet and a couch were the only objects to fill the space. The walls were similarly bare except for some photos behind Davidson's desk. One showed him and two small children; Amy guessed they were about three and four. The other showed him, his wife and his children all smiling beatifically for the camera.

Davidson dried his hands on a paper towel and returned to his desk where he sat down and began scribbling some notes on a piece of paper.

'Have a seat,' he said cheerfully, motioning to one of the two that stood before his desk.

'I'd rather have a cigarette,' said Amy.

Davidson looked up, a smile spreading across his face.

He was a good-looking man in his mid-thirties with, Amy had noticed, extraordinarily large but gentle hands. She'd been particularly grateful for his expert touch during the examination. The lump in her breast had been tender when his probing fingers had found it and it ached now as she sat down.

'Well, Miss Watson,' he said and began scratching his chin. 'You don't need me to tell you that there is some lumpy tissue present in your left breast as you indicated. Exactly what it is I don't know yet.'

'How soon before you do?'

Davidson shrugged. 'The quicker we get it biopsied, the quicker I'll be able to tell you what we're dealing with.'

'And how soon can you do that?'

'We can have you in before the end of the week.'

'What *could* it be, doctor?'

'It could be a lot of things.'

'Such as?'

'Mastitis. A build up of fatty tissue in one part of the breast.'

'Or cancer.'

'It's possible,' he told her honestly. 'I'd be lying to you if I said that wasn't one of the possibilities, but there are several harmless conditions that imitate the symptoms of breast cancer. Many lumps turn out to be fibromas or papillomas. Innocent tumours.'

Tumour. The word made her shudder.

'Can you cure it if it is cancer?' Amy persisted.

'Any kind of cancer can be treated if it's caught early enough.'

'What kind of treatment would be involved?'

'Miss Watson, we haven't even ascertained whether or not it *is* cancer yet.'

'Please tell me, doctor. What would you have to do if it *was*?'

He sighed wearily. 'If the tumour was found to be malignant it would be removed, depending upon its size.'

'What if it spreads.'

'Then a mastectomy might be necessary.'

She felt a cold chill spreading through her, as if someone had injected iced water into her veins.

'You mean I could lose a breast?' Amy said softly.

'If that was necessary to stop the spread of the disease, yes.'

Amy saw something behind his eyes but couldn't decide whether it was compassion or pity.

'What else would you have to do?' Amy continued.

'To ensure the disease had been removed – X-ray treatment, chemotherapy and a course of other drugs might be necessary.'

Amy nodded slowly.

'Look, this is all academic until we get the results of the biopsy,' Davidson said in his best optimistic voice. 'As soon as we do then we'll know where we are. I'm not going to say don't worry because I know you will anyway. It's a natural reaction but, as I said, even if it is cancer then we'll have caught it early.'

'Better a breast than my life, if I have to lose something, then?' she said quietly.

Davidson nodded.

'One woman in fourteen develops some kind of breast cancer during her life, Miss Watson,' said the doctor. 'I wish I could tell you different but you wanted the facts.'

'I appreciate your honesty, doctor.' She smiled weakly. 'I think.'

'We'll have you in on Friday, get that biopsy done.'

She got to her feet and ran a hand through her hair.

'I'll go and have a fag now, calm my nerves,' she told him, smiling.

'I should tell you off for even thinking about it,' Davidson said, a grin also flickering across his lips.

She thanked him again then stepped out into the corridor. One of the fluorescents in the ceiling was faulty and it kept flickering on and off. When it went off, the corridor seemed oddly dark and foreboding. Amy hurried up towards the welcoming light of the waiting room.

Webber got to his feet as he saw her and crossed to her immediately.

'I need a drink,' she said.

Fifty-Five

Amy gazed blankly out of the window while Webber fetched two coffees. Two young women, a little younger than herself, were passing the café, laughing and joking. Not a care in the world, thought Amy. For one fleeting second her self-pity overcame her and she envied those young women. Envied them their laughter, their lack of apparent worry.

How do you know what's going on in their lives? They could be worse off than you. Snap out of it.

Her own mental rebuke didn't seem to have the desired effect though. Clouds of depression hung over her as dark and threatening as they had been all morning.

Webber returned with the coffees and set them down. He'd even brought them a Danish pastry each.

A little comfort in a time of need?

She managed a smile at his gesture.

'When I said drink I was thinking of something stronger,' she said, looking into his eyes.

'How *much* stronger?' he asked, grinning. 'This coffee looks like creosote.'

She laughed. *Forced* a laugh. Manufactured a grin.

'He didn't say it *was* cancer, Amy?' Webber offered. 'You told me that yourself.'

As soon as they'd left the surgery she'd repeated, more or less verbatim, what the doctor had said to her and Webber had listened, one of his strong arms around her shoulders.

Now he watched as she spooned sugar into her coffee and stirred it.

'I'm trying to be realistic, Jake,' she told him. 'Trying to prepare myself.' She sipped the coffee. 'The big C.'

'You don't *know* that.'

'If it is,' she began, raising a hand to silence Webber as he opened his mouth to speak, 'there's a sort of horrible irony about it, don't you think?'

'What do you mean?'

'Well, I used to model, I used to make a living out of showing my breasts and now I might lose one. Perhaps it's fate. Perhaps it's some kind of payback.'

'Now you're talking shit.'

'A guy's been phoning the show lately and saying that I degraded myself, flaunted myself when I posed nude. Perhaps he's right. Perhaps this is God's way of paying me back for that.'

'For Christ's sake, Amy. That's bollocks and you know it.'

'Is it, Jake? They say what goes around comes around. God pays back in other ways, that sort of thing.'

'You didn't do anything wrong and that bastard phoning in was probably one of the ones wanking over your pictures. You shouldn't listen to shit like that.'

'So you don't think God's paying me back for flaunting my body?'

'God's got nothing to do with this because there is no fucking God.' He sipped his coffee. 'What kind of God would take an eighteen-month-old child? What kind of God would invent cancer and AIDS? Or meningitis or heart disease? God's an invention of the Church. That's it. End of story.'

Amy studied his grizzled features for a moment then reached out and touched his hand.

'Did you feel like this after Samantha died?' she asked gently.

He grunted.

'Who wouldn't?' he snapped. 'When you've just carried your own daughter's coffin through a fucking graveyard and stuck her in the ground, wouldn't you begin to wonder if God was as wonderful as everybody tells you?'

Amy gripped his hand.

'I lost the only thing in this life that I ever cared about thanks to *God*,' he rasped, emphasising the last word with disgust.

She broke a portion of the Danish pastry off and nibbled at it.

Webber exhaled deeply then looked into her eyes once more, his expression softening.

'Who else knows about . . .' he said, the sentence trailing off.

'Jo, I told her last night, and Mike Osborne, my producer,' she said quietly. 'That's it.'

'What about your family?'

'My mother lives in Canada with her sister – I don't even know where my father is.'

'What happened?'

'He left home when I was fourteen. He was an alcoholic. It wasn't much of a loss. My mum left for Canada about eight years ago. I haven't seen her since she left.' Amy chewed more of the Danish. 'She never really approved of what I did anyway. I've had a couple of letters but that's it.'

'No brothers or sisters?'

'No.'

She reached for her cigarettes and lit one.

'To tell you the truth,' she said, 'I don't think my mum ever forgave me for having an abortion.'

'You had an abortion? When?'

'When I was eighteen. It's a long story, Jake.'

'I've got time.'

He pulled his hand away sharply.

'What's the matter?' she asked, surprised at his reaction.

'Tell me about it,' he demanded.

'I just did. I was eighteen. I got pregnant. I had an abortion.'

'Who was the father?'

'What the hell *is* this?'

'I asked you a question. I'm curious. I want to know.'

His expression had darkened. His eyes were boring into her.

'A guy I was going out with at the time,' she snapped. 'Satisfied?'

'Why did you get rid of the baby?'

'I couldn't have looked after a child when I was eighteen, Jake. Besides, there were other considerations too.'

'Like what?'

She met his gaze, decided she didn't like the vehemence in his eyes and looked down at her coffee cup.

'I'd just been offered a modelling contract with a magazine,' she said quietly. 'Steady work. Well paid. It was a big break for me. I had to think about my career too.'

'You killed a child because of your career.'

'Don't be so melodramatic, Jake. I had an abortion because I *had* to. For practical and financial reasons.'

'You killed a child for the sake of your career,' he repeated. 'Mine died, Amy.' He raised his voice suddenly, attracting the attention of one or two people in the café. '*I* had no choice whether she lived or died. You did. I would have done anything for my daughter. I'd do anything now to bring her back and you sit there and calmly tell me that you *could* have had a child but you didn't want it. It wasn't convenient.' He snarled the words furiously.

Amy regarded him warily as he continued to glare at her, one hand balled into a fist.

Fleetingly, she thought he might hit her.

'Jake, I'm sorry you feel this way,' she said evenly, trying to calm him. 'I understand why you're angry—'

'No you don't,' he rasped. 'No one does.'

Suddenly he got to his feet.

'Where are you going?'

'I think I'd better go,' he said. 'It might be best if I wasn't around you for a while.'

'I'll see you later,' she said, reaching out for his hand.

He shook loose and she turned in her seat to see him storm out of the café.

Curious eyes turned in her direction and she met them

defiantly for a moment before sipping at her coffee. Lying opposite her was Webber's disposable lighter. She reached across and picked it up, dropping it into her handbag. She remembered the look in his eyes. That furious rage. The way he had looked at her – as if he loathed her. She could think of one word to describe his venomous glance and it made her shudder.

He'd looked murderous.

Fifty-Six

There was more mail than usual, Anita Bishop thought, as she opened yet another envelope addressed to David Albury. Since the successful passing of his Bill, the Home Secretary's correspondence had doubled, as had demands on his time. Most of her day was now spent fielding media enquiries as well as the usual tasks she'd always performed so efficiently. It involved working longer hours; during the past week or so she'd only managed anything resembling a lunch hour once. But Anita seemed to revel in the increased work-load as much as her employer did in his heightened profile.

The passing of the Albury Bill had catapulted the man even more strongly into the public consciousness. Whether people liked him or despised him, they couldn't ignore him.

She continued to wade through the mail. An invitation to address the Oxford Students' Union. An offer to appear as a guest on a special edition of *Newsnight* that would discuss the Bill from all angles.

She expected Albury to accept the invitation from the Students Union but doubted if he'd take up the *Newsnight* offer. He'd had several run-ins with its presenter before. She put the letter to one side.

The phone had barely stopped ringing either. More requests for interviews with newspapers and magazines.

Some were calling the Bill the single most important piece of legislation for five years. Others had branded it the worst intrusion into freedom of choice and expression since the 'Spanish Inquisition'. Anita smiled at that particular recollection. The article had been sent from a small magazine that she'd never heard of, a film magazine specialising in horror films. They'd sent a petition with the issue. Four thousand names objecting to the Bill.

It had been consigned to the waste bin.

She was about to open the next pile of letters when the office door opened and Albury walked in.

Anita turned and smiled at him, noticing that, as usual, he looked immaculate. His Armani suit was pressed to perfection, the creases in his trousers razor sharp.

He returned the smile and crossed to her, glancing at the huge expanse of mail both opened and unopened.

'Fan mail?' he said, grinning.

She laughed.

'Anything important?' he asked, inspecting some of the correspondence she pushed his way.

She told him about the Oxford Union invitation. The requests for interviews.

'You've had a busy morning, Anita,' he said, still scanning the letters. 'You should let me buy you lunch. You need a break.'

She blushed slightly. 'That's very kind,' she said demurely.

'And I think you should leave early tonight,' he continued. 'It hasn't escaped me that you've been working long hours lately and I appreciate it. But, all work and no play, as they say.'

'It has been hectic lately,' she admitted.

He sat down at his desk.

'I'll deal with the interview requests as soon as you decide which you want to do,' Anita told him.

Albury nodded, still reading one of the letters.

'I've had a woman on the phone three times this morning from a radio show. They want you to appear.'

'What kind of show?'

'A chat show, a late-night phone-in. It's hosted by a woman called Amy Watson.'

'Never heard of her.'

'They want you to answer questions about the Bill.'

'Doesn't everyone?'

'I said I'd ask you.'

'I'll think about it. I did intend spending some time with my family for at least the next *two* evenings, so if anything else comes up don't call me at home unless it's important.'

She nodded.

'What will you do tonight, Anita?' he asked, looking at her over the envelopes and letters.

'Put my feet up,' she told him. 'Take it easy while I can. Have a bath. Read. Phone some friends.' She smiled.

'Am I prying?' he asked.

'Not at all.'

'I'm curious. It's a politician's way. That's *my* excuse anyway.'

She began to open more letters when he got to his feet.

'That's enough,' he told her, smiling. 'Lunch beckons.'

He picked up her jacket from the back of her chair and held it for her, watching as she slipped her arms in.

'Where would you like to eat?' he asked, holding the door open for her.

'I'm in your capable hands,' she said, smiling.

'I hope you trust me.'

'I should do by now,' she confided.

He pulled the office door shut behind her and locked it.

They walked down the corridor together, his hand brushing lightly against her arm.

As they waited for the lift she leaned forward and carefully removed a stray hair from the lapel of his jacket.

Albury smiled.

Fifty-Seven

Billy Parker rubbed one hand repeatedly up and down his left arm in an effort to generate some warmth. It wasn't the coldest of days but he felt an uncomfortable chill creeping through him and the thick flannel shirt he wore over his black T-shirt was doing little to help.

He fumbled in the top pocket of the shirt and pulled out a crumpled box of Rothmans, delighted to discover that there was one inside. He jammed it between his lips and looked to his companion.

Brian Healy was a year or two younger than Billy – a thin, lean-faced youth with pitted skin who looked as if he hadn't had a good meal in weeks. He was wearing a leather jacket that still smelled new – possibly something to do with the fact that it had only been stolen that morning.

He pulled a lighter from the pocket and flicked it, lighting Billy's cigarette. The two of them huddled in one of the doorways of the Piccadilly theatre, glancing up and down Sherwood Street occasionally.

Two American tourists passed and gave them desultory looks, one of them wrinkling his nose at the aroma that seemed to surround the two young men.

'What the fuck are you looking at?' Billy snapped as they passed, realising that the smell came from the bundle of clothes and rags curled up in the next doorway. Only an unkempt head poking out of the pile even marked it out as a man. He asked the tourists for change as they strode by but got nothing except a disdainful look.

'Can you trust this bastard?' Billy asked, puffing on his cigarette.

'He's cool, Billy, honest,' said Healy, the words spilling out quickly.

'Then where *is* he?'

'He'll be here, he said he'd be here,' Healy babbled, shifting constantly from one foot to the other.

Billy checked his watch.

'I can give him a call if you want me to,' jabbered Healy, reaching into his pocket and pulling out a mobile phone which had been stolen the day before.

'Leave it another five minutes,' Billy murmured.

'He's coming, look, he's coming.'

Healy was pointing up the street in the direction of Golden Square.

'That's him, there, look. See, I told you he'd be here.'

The rapidity of his speech seemed to have increased to the point where the stream of words almost became a continuous drone.

'I knew he'd come. I wouldn't mess you about, Billy, I wouldn't.'

The man heading towards them was in his mid-twenties. He walked as if he was trying to take strides longer than the length of his legs would allow.

Trying to look the hard man, thought Billy, puffing on his cigarette.

As the man reached them, he nodded towards Healy then gave Billy an appraising, almost contemptuous, look.

'All right, Elvis,' said Healy excitedly.

The older man nodded.

'What did you call him?' said Billy, a grin on his face.

'Elvis, I called him Elvis, you know,' Healy gushed.

'Elvis? Is he joking?' Billy asked.

'No, he's not fucking joking,' snapped the newcomer.

'Your name's Elvis?' Billy continued.

'Yeah.'

'What, as in—'

'Yeah, as in Elvis fucking Presley. You got a problem with that?'

'You poor sod, how did that happen?' Billy enquired.

'My dad was a fan, right.'

'Elvis what?' Billy persisted.

'Elvis Thorpe. Happy now?'

Billy couldn't suppress a chuckle.

'What is it with this bastard?' said Thorpe, glaring at Billy.

'I told him about you, Elvis,' Healy babbled. 'I said you were cool.'

'Fucking right, I'm cool,' Thorpe said, adjusting the sleeves of his jacket.

He looked at Billy.

'Now, are we doing business or not?' he said irritably.

'If you've got what I want,' Billy told him.

'You got money?'

Billy reached into the pocket of his jeans and pulled out a wad of notes half-an-inch thick.

'That enough for you?' he said defiantly.

'My man is loaded,' Thorpe said, grinning.

'So, what do you want, Billy?' Healy said. 'I mean, Elvis has got it all.'

'On you?' Billy wanted to know.

'What kind of bloke do you think I am?' Thorpe said. 'I've got it back at my place.'

'Where's that?'

'I've got a pad in Flaxman Court. You tell me what you want and I'll sell it to you.'

Billy took a final drag on his cigarette then dropped it, grinding out the butt.

'Let's go then,' he said, digging his hands into his pockets.

The three of them turned and set off back up Sherwood Street.

'I've known Elvis for years, Billy,' said Healy, trying to walk alongside the other two men but forced, instead, to scurry along in the gutter.

'I haven't seen you around before,' Thorpe told Billy.

'I'm new in town,' Billy said, grinning.

Billy walked along, his eyes scanning Thorpe. He pushed his hands deeper into his pockets and, as he did so, his right hand brushed against the hilt of a flick knife.

Fifty-Eight

As Andrew Chapman parked the Orion outside number fifteen Beverley Road he could see that lights were on in the sitting room and one of the rooms upstairs.

His stomach rumbled and he patted it soothingly. He hadn't eaten much that day. A sandwich at lunchtime and that had been about it. Not that he'd *felt* much like eating. A rumour about threatened redundancies had been circulating within the bank for a week or two now, gradually building momentum until the reaction had gone from one of mistrust and concern to almost outright hysteria. Twenty jobs were to go, someone had said. From top management, right down to cashiers. No one was safe. Everyone was worried.

Not least Chapman.

He sat in the car looking at the house and he felt his stomach contract. They'd bought it three years ago, just after his promotion. Property in Chiswick was never cheap but, with his increased salary, Chapman had felt more than confident about investing in a place that many had thought too expensive.

Investment. That was the word that kept cropping up while they were considering the move. 'A bigger house would be an investment.'

As long as you had a good job perhaps it was. At the moment, the word millstone sounded more appropriate to Andrew Chapman. What with the mortgage, the school fees for their two children and his consultations with Charlotte Kilbride (*thank God Laura didn't know about those*) and, not forgetting his little obsession (there was a porn video in his briefcase now, along with two magazines) the financial drain on his resources was becoming considerable.

The threat of redundancy was almost too terrifying to contemplate. He hadn't mentioned it to Laura. No sense in alarming her unnecessarily. Not yet anyway.

He locked the Orion and made his way towards the front door, pausing to check that the lock on his case was secure.

He could watch the film tomorrow morning.

Laura was going shopping and taking Joe with her. Fiona was playing netball for her school and would be gone all day. He should have at least three hours to sit and watch *Cum Sluts*.

Even the thought was beginning to give him an erection.

He let himself in and wandered into the hall, sticking his head around the sitting-room door.

'Another day, another dollar,' he said as cheerfully as he could.

His wife was sitting at one end of the sofa, a book open in front of her, a news programme on the television.

'You're late,' she said sympathetically.

He crossed to her and kissed the top of her head. Her hair smelled as if it had been freshly washed.

'Sorry, the meeting went on longer than I expected and then a couple of the others suggested we go and have a drink, so . . .' He allowed the sentence to trail off, satisfied that the lie had sounded convincing.

'Who went with you?' Laura asked, without looking up from her book.

'Oh, just a couple of guys from investment,' he said. 'Are the kids in bed?'

His attempt to change the subject seemed successful enough.

'Fiona said she was going to read for an hour,' Laura told him. 'I said it would be okay.'

'Her light's still on.'

'She's probably dropped off. I'll switch it off when we go up.'

He sat down on the sofa beside her, glancing at the television.

'What time are you leaving in the morning?' he asked without looking at her.

'About ten, like I always do. Why?'

'Just asking.'

He reached across and took the book from her, carefully replacing her bookmark.

'I hadn't finished that chapter,' she said in mock protest.

He slid one hand on to her thigh and up beneath the hem of her skirt.

'What's got into you?' she said, grinning, then noticing that his erection was straining against the material of his trousers.

Should he tell her that the bed show he watched less than an hour ago had excited him? He thought not. Best not to mention how he had paid five pounds to gain entry to the show in Dean Street, then another twenty for two of their overpriced drinks while he had watched two girls writhing around licking each other's bodies.

Some things were best left unsaid, weren't they?

'Fancy an early night?' he said, his hand still beneath her skirt, his finger gently stroking across the gusset of her knickers.

'Yes, I'm shattered,' she said, grinning.

He pulled his finger away, his expression darkening.

'Andy, what's wrong?' she asked, wearily.

He was sitting bolt upright staring at the television screen.

'Andy.'

She looked at him then at the television. The face that filled the screen was that of Charlotte Kilbride.

'You look as if you've seen a ghost,' Laura said. 'What's wrong?'

'Nothing,' he lied. 'That woman was talking about these murders. I thought there'd been another one.'

'No, she was on earlier, saying that the police should

have caught him by now. She's a psychiatrist or something.'

I know, I visit her.

'Since when did you get so interested in murderers?' Laura wanted to know, smiling.

'This one is important,' he said sternly, his eyes never leaving the screen where Charlotte Kilbride was still being interviewed.

He barely heard what she said though. Seeing her there was like being on the end of some kind of spiritual visitation. It was as if she had appeared to remind him of his guilt. His secret. As if she could see out of the television set and was looking directly at *him*.

Only when she had disappeared from view did he seem to emerge from his trance-like state.

Laura prodded his arm. 'Welcome back.' She swung herself off the sofa and headed for the kitchen. 'I'm going to make a cup of tea – do you want one?'

He shook his head.

'Andy?' she called.

He crossed to the drinks cabinet. He needed something stronger.

Fifty-Nine

David Albury read the article in the *Guardian*. Then the one in *The Times*. Both were lengthy pieces about his own Bill, and about him.

He smiled smugly as he folded the paper and pushed it to one side, reaching for the *Independent*.

'Aren't you sick of reading about yourself?'

The voice came from the other side of the sitting room.

From Louise Albury. She was sitting at the antique writing desk that occupied one corner of the large lounge, a notepad and several reference books spread out before her.

As Albury looked across he saw that her eyes were still on the law books. She was scribbling as she spoke, not even affording him a glance.

'Urgent case tomorrow?' he said sniffily.

'Just making some final notes,' she told him. 'I think it's important and so does my client. I know it's always been a bit of a joke to you though, hasn't it, David?'

'You handle clients on legal aid for God's sake.'

'What's so wrong about that?'

'You should be using your talents on *better* cases. Better paid anyway.'

'I like the people I work with.'

'Council-house thugs and drug dealers. How delight-ful.'

'They're still people, David. Not everyone is as lucky as we are.'

'It's a waste of talent.'

'I studied law because I wanted to help people and that's what I'm doing. I'm sorry it doesn't comply with *your* grand scheme of things.'

Albury began reading the article in the *Independent*.

'Perhaps it's a good job *both* of our careers aren't so newsworthy,' said Louise, still writing. 'You've certainly got your pound of flesh from the papers, haven't you?'

'What are you talking about?'

'You love this attention, David. Don't try to deny it.'

'If a Bill that I propose happens to make the news that's fine,' he said dismissively. 'But I didn't propose it for my *own* interests.'

'David, everything you *do* is for your own interests,' said Louise, finally looking at him with an expression close to distaste.

He looked at her silently for a moment, considered saying something but his thoughts were interrupted.

The telephone was ringing in the hallway.

Albury got to his feet and wandered through to answer it.

Louise watched him disappear out of the room then returned to her scribblings.

Albury reached the phone on its third ring, hoping that it hadn't disturbed Harriet, who was sleeping upstairs.

He glanced at his watch as he picked up the receiver.

11.14 p.m.

He frowned.

'David Albury.'

He recognised the voice at the other end immediately.

'What do you want at this time of night?' Albury said irritably, his voice dropping in volume. 'I told you not to call me here tonight.'

He leaned across and pushed the sitting-room door shut.

'I can't, not tonight,' he said, answering the caller's question. 'You'll have to wait,' he continued, lowering his voice further, his tone softening slightly. 'All right, when?' He waited a moment, listening to the caller, one eye on the sitting-room door. 'Yes, tomorrow then. Yes. We'll arrange something. Yes. Listen, I've got to go.'

He pressed his fingers down on the cradle and then

replaced the receiver, sucking in a deep breath before walking back into the sitting room.

'Who was it?' Louise asked, without looking up.

'Another reporter,' he lied.

'At this time of night?'

'Well, as you said, I appear to be newsworthy. The press are no respecters of time or privacy, you know that.'

She studied him silently for a moment, then returned to her work.

Behind his paper, Albury swallowed hard. His heart was thudding a little too hard against his ribs.

Sixty

The first spots of rain were striking the window panes. They beat out an irregular tattoo against the glass, the sound growing louder as the rain became heavier.

Within the stillness of the bedroom the sound was intensified, and Andrew Chapman rolled over on to his side to watch the droplets rolling down the glass. Far away he heard the first distant rumble of thunder. Perhaps it would clear the air. The night was unbearably muggy.

He moved uncomfortably beneath the thin sheet that covered him, grunting quietly as he did so. His erection throbbed between his legs. Uncomfortably stiff.

Two girls. One blond. One brunette.

Chapman tried to control his breathing.

In their mid-twenties. As they had been before.

He pushed the sheet down a little, his right hand sliding down his body, fingers playing gently over his shaft.

They were usually the same two girls at the bedshow he visited.

He couldn't get the vision out of his mind. Their slender bodies. Busy hands.

Lying on his back, he stared at the ceiling, the rain still bouncing off the windows, but there was a softer counterpoint to that sound. Next to him he could hear Laura's low even breathing as she slept.

He turned his head and looked at her. Her mouth was open slightly, lips parted.

Like the blond girl as she felt the tongue between her legs.

Chapman slid closer to his wife, feeling the warmth from her body. He moved his face to within inches of hers, studying her features in the gloom, inching nearer until he rested his right hand on her thigh.

She stirred slightly but didn't wake.

Chapman slid closer so that his erection was pressing against the top of her leg, his right hand now brushing through the soft down of her pubic hair.

He nuzzled her ear, then her neck, his fingers now probing more urgently. He pressed his finger against the fleshy outer lips of her vagina, moving his own body so that he was squashed close and tight to her.

Laura opened her eyes and blinked myopically.

'Oh, Andy,' she murmured, her voice thick with sleep.

He kissed her cheek.

'It's late,' Laura sighed, her eyes only half open.

He had his eyes closed.

The blond girl had her head thrown back in ecstasy now.

He took Laura's hand and placed it on his throbbing erection, feeling her fingers envelop his shaft a little half-heartedly.

Gently, he rubbed between her legs.

She let go of his penis and touched his cheek gently.

'Tomorrow,' she said sleepily.

He took her hand and replaced it on his erection.

'Andy,' she murmured, aware now that the pressure he was exerting between her legs was growing. As she looked at him she saw that his eyes were still closed. He was breathing heavily, pushing his body more insistently against hers.

'Andy, leave it, will you?' she said wearily, wincing slightly as his fingers scraped a little too hard across her most sensitive area.

His eyes snapped open. 'Why?' he demanded.

'I said it's late. Besides, we'll wake the kids.' She smiled.

'Fuck the kids,' he rasped, and she was surprised by the vehemence in his tone.

He pressed harder against her, his hand still rubbing furiously between her legs.

She grabbed the hand and tried to pull it away but he would not stop his persistent movements.

'Andy, please.' Her voice wavered slightly.

'Come on,' he insisted, looking down at her face.

Outside, a louder rumble of thunder was followed by a flash of sheet lightning, which lit the entire room and momentarily illuminated his features with cold, white light. His eyes were blazing.

'Not now, please,' she pleaded, swallowing hard.

He glared down at her.

The blond would have begged him for it.

He pulled his hand from between her legs and pressed his fingers to his mouth.

'Nothing,' he hissed.

She watched him in silence, her heart thumping a little harder. When she tried to swallow, it felt as though someone had filled her mouth with chalk.

'Don't I excite you any more?' he demanded, pushing the fingers against her own lips. 'Nothing.'

His breathing was harsh and guttural as he looked down upon her almost contemptuously.

'I'm just tired,' she whispered, glancing quickly towards their bedroom door. 'And I don't want to disturb the kids. Maybe another—'

'Forget it,' he said, swinging himself out of bed.

He pulled on his dressing gown and stalked out of the room. She heard his footsteps crossing the landing, heard the sound of the toilet door opening and closing.

Laura finally managed to swallow. She lay on her back, heart beating fast, her tiredness now replaced by something else. Fear? She had never known him like this before and she didn't like it.

Outside there was another angry rumble of thunder.

Laura closed her eyes but sleep eluded her, driven away by the recollection of his anger, the force of his hands on her.

She shuddered.

The rain continued to batter at the windows.

Sixty-One

Amy stood before the full-length mirror in her bedroom and gazed at her reflection. She ran her glance from head to toe but, each time, she found herself dwelling on her breasts. More particularly the left one. The one with the lump.

The lump.

She swallowed hard and closed her eyes, her stomach fluttering even at the thought of it. She would go for hours at a time without the problem forcing its way into her mind, or at least not into the forefront of her thoughts, then suddenly, all the fears and terrors would come rushing in like a river suddenly freed from the restraints of a dam. When that happened she found herself almost paralysed with terror. Nauseous and fearful of what consequences her awful discovery may hold. What was the ultimate conclusion that could be reached? What if the lump was malignant? What if it had already begun to spread? What if they could not treat her in time? What if?

The answer was a chilling one and one which again made her feel a little faint because it was so damning in its simplicity. So inescapably final. If they could not treat her, she would die.

That was it. As simple as that.

Amy sucked in a deep breath and tried, again, to push this most terrifying conclusion to the back of her mind.

Outside, the storm seemed to be reaching its height, sheet lightning illuminating the sky with savage regularity, the ever-present crashing of thunder like a constant artillery barrage.

Amy moved away from the mirror and looked out of her window, watching the heavens being torn apart by the lightning. The power of that great elemental force was awesome. Unstoppable.

Like cancer?

She closed her eyes tightly, angry that she'd allowed the thought to intrude, to force its way back into her consciousness.

Wait for the biopsy. Wait for the results.

'Get a grip,' she whispered to herself, her voice wavering a little.

As she turned she glanced across towards her bookshelves, her eyes focusing on a number of books there. *His* books. John Howard.

What would *he* say if he knew of her problem? How would he help her to cope with it? It didn't matter. Howard didn't know and never would.

She checked her watch. It would be time to leave to do the show soon. The prospect didn't fill her with joy. She had her own thoughts to contend with. The thoughts of those who phoned in were of little consequence to her at present.

The phone rang.

She looked again at her watch, frowning, then picked up the receiver.

'It's me,' the voice said. 'I need to talk to you, Amy. Now.' Webber sounded subdued.

Amy hadn't seen or heard him since he'd stormed out on her that morning.

'I'll come down,' she told him without hesitation.

When she reached the bottom of the stairs she saw that the door to flat number one was already open.

Come into my parlour, said the spider to the fly . . .

She hesitated at the entrance, the brief remembrance of that look in his eyes earlier in the day still fresh in her mind. Then she took a step inside and closed the door behind her.

'Jake,' she called quietly.

She found him in the sitting room, perched on the arm of one chair, a glass of Jamesons in his hand.

'I know you're off to do the show,' he said. 'But I had to talk to you.'

'What's wrong?' she asked.

'Me. *I'm* wrong.'

She looked vague.

'This morning,' he elucidated. 'I shouldn't have blown up at you like that. You must think I'm a fucking nutcase.'

She smiled weakly.

'I've been sitting here thinking about it,' Webber continued. 'It just seemed so . . . wrong. I can't think of any other way to describe it.'

'My abortion was wrong, you mean?'

'Not wrong but unjust, when you think about what happened to my own child, even though that wasn't *your* fault, I . . .' He raised his hands. 'Fuck it, I don't even know how to say what I'm trying to say.'

'I think what you're trying to say is sorry.'

She took a step towards him, watching as he put down the glass. They embraced, Webber holding her tight to him, Amy clutching at him almost frenziedly. She wanted his arms around her. Needed them.

'I'm sorry,' he whispered, kissing her forehead.

The loud knocking on the front door startled them both.

Webber looked puzzled, the lines across his forehead deepening.

He left her in the sitting room, wandered out to the hallway and heard the knocking again. Louder, more insistent.

He reached for the handle and opened it.

'What the hell do *you* want here?'

Amy heard his words from the sitting room and moved nearer the door, curious about his late-night visitor.

'I wasn't expecting you,' Webber said to the newcomer. 'You'd better come in.'

David Grant accepted the invitation.

Sixty-Two

As Grant walked into the sitting room, Amy ran appraising eyes over him. He did the same to her, a crooked smile touching his lips.

'I can see why you didn't want to answer the door,' Grant said as Webber joined them.

Amy looked at him then back at the stranger. Whoever he was, he was wearing what looked like an expensive suit, she thought.

'Aren't you going to introduce us, Jake?' Grant asked, never taking his eyes off Amy.

'Just tell me what you want, will you?' Webber said irritably.

Grant ignored the comment and extended his right hand in Amy's direction.

'Detective Inspector David Grant,' he said, smiling.

She shook the offered hand.

'Amy Watson.'

Again she looked at the two men. First one then the other.

Detective. What the hell was a policeman doing here at this time? She wondered if her fears about Webber had been right. Was this man here to arrest him?

And yet he'd used Webber's first name. She was puzzled.

'Does she know?' asked Grant, nodding towards Amy as if she couldn't hear him.

'Know what?' she demanded.

'She doesn't, does she?' Grant continued.

'I didn't think it was necessary,' said Webber.

Amy's bewilderment was turning to anger.

'Somebody tell me what's going on,' she demanded.

Webber looked sheepish. 'I should have told you,' he began. 'I'm sorry I didn't.'

'Told me what?' she said angrily.

'I'm a policeman,' he confessed.

She stared at him for a while, then at Grant, then back again at Webber.

'I know I should have told you, I'm sorry if it's a shock.'

'A shock,' she blurted. 'It's a relief.'

It was Webber's turn to look puzzled.

'I was beginning to think *you* were the killer,' Amy told him.

'Why?'

'Jake, you haven't exactly been up-front with me, have you? You wouldn't tell me what you did for a living, you were out most nights until the small hours, you never said where. And then I found bullets in your bathroom and I was terrified that you were the killer.'

'Why didn't you say something to me?'

'Like what "Excuse me, Jake, but could you explain where that box of ammunition in your medicine cabinet came from?"'

'If you thought I was the killer why did you carry on seeing me?'

'Because I wasn't sure. I didn't *want* to believe what my mind kept telling me. I had to know the truth.'

'And now you do.'

She nodded.

'Sorry to interrupt this little lovers' conversation,' said Grant sarcastically, 'but this isn't a social call, Jake.'

'So he's your boss?' Amy continued, pointing at Grant.

Grant smiled. 'Jake and I are more like brothers than colleagues, aren't we, Jake?'

'Yeah, most brothers hate each other,' Webber snapped.

'We went through basic training together,' Grant told her. 'We were even partners for six years in the Vice Squad. Until we both moved on.' He grinned.

'Until you fucked me over, you mean,' snapped Webber.

'You wouldn't have wanted the promotion anyway,

Jake. You were never the ambitious one out of us two, were you?'

'Some of the credit would have been nice.'

'Life's a bitch, isn't it?'

'What happened?' Amy enquired.

'Let *him* tell you,' Webber sneered.

Amy held up both hands.

'Wait a minute,' she said, looking at each man in turn. 'I still don't get this.' She turned her attention to Webber. 'Jake, you moved in here because of this killer?'

He nodded.

'At the time, most of the killings had happened within a five-or six-mile radius of here,' he told her. 'It was a good base to operate from. There are three or four other undercover men set up in different locations like me.'

'All at the taxpayer's expense,' Grant added. 'So you'd better hope it works. It's costing *you* money.'

Amy sat down.

'Jesus Christ,' she murmured. 'I don't believe this.'

Webber crossed to her and rested a hand on her shoulder. 'I'm sorry I couldn't tell you the truth,' he said quietly.

All she could do was nod.

'Everything clear now?' Grant said sarcastically. 'If you wouldn't mind, your boyfriend and I have got business to discuss.'

'The investigation's stalled,' said Webber. 'I know that.'

'This is police business, Webber. No one else's,' snapped Grant, nodding towards Amy.

'You can't catch the killer, can you?' Amy said flatly.

'That's nothing to do with you,' Grant told her.

'We've got no leads,' Webber said.

'I might be able to help,' Amy told them.

Both men looked at her in surprise.

'I think he might be calling my show,' Amy explained. 'I think he's been contacting *me*.'

Sixty-Three

Webber glanced at his watch.

12.36 a.m.

He took a sip of his coffee, then got to his feet and crossed to the glass partition that ran the length of the production booth. Through it he could see Amy sitting at her console, leaning forward towards her microphone as she chatted to another caller. The sound of their conversation was being relayed through two speakers inside the control room.

Amy was talking to a man called Wayne from Beckton who was rambling on about why private education was a bad thing.

Webber stood there for a moment longer then returned to his seat next to Jo Parker. He smiled at her as he sat down.

Mike Osborne watched him carefully, not for the first time since he'd arrived at the studio.

'So, they ring in, give their names and addresses and you put them through to Amy?' Webber repeated, watching the console in front of Jo flashing with a dozen red lights.

'They don't give their addresses,' she told him. 'Just the area they're calling from.'

'Does she get many crank calls?' Webber asked Osborne.

'It's that kind of show,' the producer said condescendingly. 'You have to expect the odd weirdo.'

'Or killer,' Webber murmured to himself.

He listened to a moment or two more of Wayne from Beckton's tirade then got to his feet again.

'This guy that rings in claiming to be the killer,' he said does he ring at the same time every night?'

'No, he doesn't ring every night.' Osborne said.

'But when he does? Is it at the same time?'

'No,' the producer explained. 'He's not *that* predictable.'

Webber caught the disdain in the other man's voice.
Jumped-up little prick, he thought.

Webber turned and walked back to where Jo was
sitting. He looked at the screen and saw the names
flashing in luminous green. As a new call came through
on her headset, she typed in the name and location.
They would be relayed to Amy in the studio via her
own screen.

'Is it mostly men or women who ring in?' Webber
asked.

Jo shrugged. 'Mostly men,' she said. 'Guys on shifts.
Someone with something to get off their chest. People
who just want to talk. We get about thirty per cent
women callers though. Look.' She pointed to the screen
where the legend KAREN. QUEENSWAY was flashing.

Jo smiled up at Webber who returned the gesture.

She held his gaze for a second then returned to typing
in the names of new callers.

'What exactly are you hoping to find here, Mr Webber?'
Osborne asked him.

'A straw,' said Webber, gazing out of the production-
room window at Amy.

Because that's what I'm clutching at.

Osborne looked puzzled and, again, looked the policeman up and down.

'Am I bothering you?' Webber asked without looking
at the producer.

'What makes you think that?' Osborne said.

'Just curious,' Webber told him, lighting up a cigarette.

Osborne glared irritably at the policeman's broad back.

Amy raised a hand and waved when she saw Webber
standing watching her.

He smiled back at her, listening to her conversation
over the speakers in the production room.

'. . . I think it's bloody crazy, the amount these so-called stars get paid,' said Gary from Hanwell. 'I mean, you get five dozy tarts singing some crap song and the next thing they're making a bloody film or advertising drink. It's mental.'

'Do you think everyone in showbiz is overpaid, Gary?' Amy asked him.

'Most of them. I mean, you've got your real superstars like Madonna, people like that, I mean, they deserve their money and some of these actors too, they deserve it but most of them they just get a load of money dumped in their lap for doing sod all. I bet *you're* on a bloody good wage for just sitting there and talking every night.'

'Well, thanks for your concern, Gary. I do okay. There *is* a bit more to it than just talking, you know.'

'Yeah, but before that you used to get paid for taking your clothes off, didn't you? I mean, that's hardly difficult, is it?'

'No, taking your clothes off is easy but modelling is hard work.'

'Getting flown to all different parts of the world. Having all your hotels paid for, all your food bought for you. If that's hard work, I reckon *I* could do that.'

'So what's stopping you? If you think it's so easy, why not have a go yourself.'

'Don't be stupid, I couldn't do that.'

'You just said it was easy.'

'I've got a proper job.'

'What do you do?'

'I'm an electrician.'

'So, why is your job any more worthwhile than a model or a singer or any other kind of entertainer?'

'Because I work hard for mine. I support a wife and kid on my money. I have to watch every penny. I can't just run out and buy a ten-thousand-pound watch when I feel like it, like some of these bloody so-called celebrities do. They've got so much money it's obscene. There are ordinary people struggling to make a living and you've got these rich bastards pissing away money they don't even deserve. There's no justice in this world.'

He hung up.

Amy looked up at Webber who merely shrugged.

In agreement perhaps?

Amy took the next call.

'Holly from Tottenham,' she announced. 'Anything to add to what the last caller said or did you want to make a different point?'

In the production room Webber was smiling.

'They get pretty heated, don't they?' he said. 'What happens if anyone swears while they're talking to Amy? How do you cut it out?'

'There's a four-second delay on each call,' Osborne explained.

'I should think you'd need it with some of them,' Webber continued, puffing on his cigarette.

'Well, people get passionate about things they care about,' Osborne said. 'Isn't there anything *you're* passionate about?'

Webber opened his mouth to say something but Jo suddenly raised a hand to attract his attention.

'Detective,' she said. 'I think I've got him.'

Webber crossed to her and looked at the screen.

'Are you sure?'

'That's the only way he ever identifies himself,' Jo explained.

She typed in one word and they both watched i glowing on the screen:

ROY

'I'm sure it's him,' Jo said.

'All right,' Webber instructed her, 'put him on.'

Sixty-Four

'It's been a long time, Roy,' said Amy. 'Where have you been? I've missed you.'

'Don't lie to me,' said the voice that had become all too familiar.

'Sorry, I didn't mean to add lying to my list of crimes. What are they? Would you like to run through them again for the benefit of those listeners who didn't hear you ranting last time.'

Silence.

'Come on, Roy,' she chided. 'You reeled off a long list of things I'd done wrong. Tell me again what they were.'

'You know.'

'Oh yes, I remember now. I'm immoral, aren't I? I have no standards. I have no self-respect and now you're calling me a liar too.'

'Does he always use a mobile?' asked Webber, listening to the conversation over the speakers.

Jo nodded.

'No way of tracing it. Crafty bastard.'

He straightened up and looked through into the studio, watching Amy.

'So, why are you calling, Roy?' she asked him. 'Afraid we might have forgotten who you are?'

'You think you're so funny, don't you? You think you can humiliate me on your little show.'

'I wasn't trying to humiliate you, Roy. What gives you that idea?'

'I've been watching you,' Roy said flatly.

Amy shuddered involuntarily. Those icy fingers were laying across her neck again.

'And what have you seen?'

'I've seen you come and go.'

'Where do I live then, Roy?'

'A flat.'

Her flesh rose in goosebumps. 'Whereabouts?' she demanded.

'You wouldn't want me to tell *everyone*, would you?'

'Do you think he's bluffing?' Jo asked Webber.

'He could be,' Webber said.

'And if he's not?' Osborne added.

'Are you planning on killing anyone else then, Roy? That's what you usually ring up to tell us, isn't it? When you're going to kill someone.'

'You don't listen properly,' he said angrily. 'I've never said *when* I'm going to kill, only that I will.'

'So the murders are going to go on, are they, Roy?'

Silence.

'Come on, talk to me. Who are you going to kill next?'

'You.'

She swallowed hard.

'I told you I would,' he continued. 'That's why I've been watching you. Tracking you.'

The laugh that rolled down the phone line froze her blood.

'Can't you do anything?' Osborne said angrily.

'Like what?' Webber demanded.

'You can do voice prints, can't you?'

'Chances are he's using some kind of electronic scrambler to disguise his voice. A little bit more sophisticated than a hankie over the fucking mouthpiece,' snapped Webber. 'Besides, I don't think he's kosher.'

'How can you be sure?' Osborne demanded.

'Gut feeling.'

'Policeman's instinct?' chided the producer.

'Something like that,' Webber replied, trying to ignore the scorn in the other man's voice. 'Besides, Amy told me on the way here that she'd asked this geezer about the killings before but that he couldn't give her any details. Nothing specific. I'd bet money he's just trying to frighte her.' He spun round. 'How can I speak to her now, while she's got him on the line?'

'This microphone is connected to her headset,' Osborne told him, indicating a small mike close to his console. 'It works like an earpiece – she'll be able to hear you but the listeners won't.'

'Work it for me,' Webber said, leaning closer to the microphone.

Osborne looked indignant.

'Just do it,' Webber snapped.

The producer complied.

'Amy, it's Jake,' she heard in her headset. 'Ask him what colour hair the first prostitute he killed had.'

'Roy, those prostitutes you killed,' she began. 'Did you kill the first one the way you're going to kill me?'

In the booth, Webber frowned. *What the hell was she playing at?*

'That would spoil the surprise, wouldn't it?' Roy said.

'What colour hair did she have?' Amy persisted.

'Who knows? It could have been dyed. Everything about her was false. She deserved to die.'

'So you don't know?' Amy said disparagingly.

'Ask him whose wrists he cut,' Webber's voice persisted.

'Jesus,' murmured Osborne. 'I thought the victims were strangled.'

'They were. But one of them was cut too. Only the killer would know which one. The papers just mentioned mutilations.'

'Whose wrists did you cut?' Amy asked, doing as she was instructed.

Silence.

'He doesn't know,' murmured Webber.

'Roy, can you hear me?' Amy said more urgently.

'Details aren't important,' the voice said finally.

'Because *you* don't know them,' she said damningly.

'I'll cut *your* wrists,' he said.

He hung up.

'You're putting her at risk,' Osborne said angrily. 'Making her talk to this maniac.'

'She wouldn't do it if she didn't want to,' said Webber, watching Amy through the glass partition.

He noticed that she was reaching for another cigarette. What he couldn't see was that her hands were trembling.

Sixty-Five

'It's getting out of control.'

Andrew Chapman ran a hand through his hair in a gesture of near desperation. He sat in the leather chair for a moment, then stood up and began pacing Charlotte Kilbride's office, finally crossing to the window, peering out into Harley Street.

'I thought I was learning to get a grip on it out . . .'

The psychiatrist looked at him, noticing how pale his skin was. The dark rings beneath his eyes stood out even more starkly against the pallor.

'You *are* learning to control it, Andrew.'

He shook his head. 'I can't,' he said, a note of defeat in his voice. 'I'm weak, I know that.'

'It took a tremendous amount of strength for you to come here in the first place. Even more so to come here today. By admitting to yourself that you've got a problem you're showing strength, not weakness. Don't be ashamed.'

'I'm *not* ashamed,' he snarled angrily.

'How did you manage to get here today?'

'I called in sick.'

'Does your wife know?'

'She doesn't know I'm *here*. I've told you before, if she found out about me coming to you it would kill her.'

'Why? What's so bad about you seeking help?'

'You don't understand, do you?' He turned to face her. As he did, he found his eyes drawn to her legs. They were crossed, her skirt riding up towards her thigh.

Aware of his probing gaze, Charlotte shifted position, smoothing the material of the skirt, brushing a thread from it.

He's watching you.

'It's as if I live two lives,' he said wearily. 'As if I'm two people in here.' He tapped his forehead. 'Even *I'm* beginning to lose sight of who's the *real* one.'

He wandered back towards the leather chair and sat down.

'I can't think straight any more,' he said. 'I try to work, I function day-to-day but it's like it's a robot, not me. Like I'm looking at myself from the outside. Detatched from what I do. I feel as if I'm losing grip on what's real and what's not. There are so many things going round in my mind, I can't seem to focus on one thing for more than a few seconds at a time.'

She sat listening, watching, never taking her eyes from him as he spoke.

'And I'm frightened,' he told her.

'Of what?'

'What I might do.'

Charlotte scribbled something on the notepad before her, aware that he was following her every movement.

'Afraid that you might hurt someone? Yourself even?'

'I wouldn't hurt myself but I might hurt someone else.' He lowered his head slightly. 'It wouldn't be the first time, would it?'

Charlotte held his gaze, her heart beating a little faster.

'Who else have you hurt, Andrew?' she enquired, her tone softening.

'You know.'

'The prostitute you told me about?'

He was tracing patterns on the arm of the chair.

'There have been others too,' he said finally.

'Who?'

He looked straight at her, his eyes boring into her.

'Help me before I hurt anyone else,' he said. There was a note of pleading in his voice.

'Tell me about the others you've hurt, Andrew. I can't help you unless you do.'

She was trying to keep her voice calm, trying not to let the professional mask slip, but beneath her apparently relaxed exterior she felt as if every muscle in her body was knotted.

He sat there silently.

Charlotte wanted to grab him and shake it out of him, *force* him to tell her the truth.

Stay calm, let him speak in his own time.

'Andrew,' she prompted softly.

He looked at his watch. 'I can't talk, not now,' he said, getting to his feet.

She rose with him, unable to restrain herself any longer.

'Who else have you hurt?' she asked.

He would only shake his head, then he looked her directly in the eye again and she wilted beneath that stare.

He turned towards the door, anxious to be out of the room, as if the atmosphere was suffocating him.

'Thanks for your time,' he said, then he was gone.

Charlotte stood behind her desk gazing at the closed office door, listening to his footsteps receding down the stairs.

'Shit,' she murmured, looking down at his file. She sat down and began flicking slowly through it.

'Help me before I hurt anyone else.'

His words echoed inside her mind.

Sixty-Six

Blurred visions.

Dreams?

Some kind of waking nightmare?

Amy closed her eyes again and tried to roll over, tried to escape the dream. She felt pain in her chest, particularly around her left breast.

Oh God, had the cancer begun to spread more rapidly?

She tried to remember what had happened to her, more convinced now that this *wasn't* a dream. The smell of disinfectant was strong in her nostrils and she could feel linen beneath her fingers. She was in a bed. But where? The thoughts, the remembrance came with difficulty at first. Incidents, words and visions tumbled through her mind in a disordered stream.

She opened her eyes again, saw white walls, indistinct outlines.

She had arrived at the hospital at eight that morning carrying just an overnight bag containing a change of clothes, toothbrush and some make-up. That kind of thing. Everything had moved so quickly. She had been shown to her room. Then she changed into a surgical gown. She vaguely remembered talking with a doctor but she couldn't remember what about.

Amy blinked hard and tried to focus. *Still so tired.* She couldn't remember the doctor's face. *Why won't my head clear?*

She tried to swallow but her throat was dry. *Anaesthetic wearing off.*

Her eyes jerked open. *The operation. The biopsy.*

The moment of savage clarity passed and she closed her eyes again.

She lay on the bed, every muscle tight despite the after-effects of the anaesthetic because with the realisation of where she was came the fear of what might happen to her. She exhaled deeply and tried to clench her fists, to force herself from this immobility. She felt warm flesh against her own.

A hand closed over her forearm and squeezed gently.

She turned her head to one side and saw a blurred shape and, as she stared, it began to take on detail.

She rubbed her eyes with her free hand and looked towards the bedside.

'Hello, you,' said Jake Webber softly.

He reached forward and brushed some hair from her forehead, allowing his hand to stroke her cheek.

'How long . . .' The words disappeared in the dryness of her throat.

Webber reached across to the bedside cabinet and handed her a beaker filled with water. There was a straw sticking out of it and he pushed it towards her mouth. She sucked the fluid down, swallowed, then drank some more.

'Thanks,' she murmured as he took it away.

'How do you feel?'

'I don't know,' she said, managing a wan smile. 'How long have I been out?'

'Two hours.'

'And how long have *you* been here?'

'About two hours. I was here when they brought you back from surgery.' He smiled. 'I told them I was your boyfriend. They said it was okay for me to wait.'

'My boyfriend,' she said, squeezing his hand.

He watched her as she lay there.

'I'll go if you want to rest.'

She shook her head.

'I don't want you to go,' Amy reassured him, and Webber leaned forward and planted a kiss on her forehead. 'Unless you have to.'

'I rang Grant this morning, told him about that call last night,' he said.

'Do you still think Roy isn't the killer?'

'He didn't seem to know enough details about the murders. I've got a hunch he's just some sad bastard who's enjoying the attention. On the other hand he could be cleverer than any of us think. The calls might be some kind of double bluff. Make us believe he *doesn't* know anything.'

'What did Grant say?'

'He said to play it by ear, if you'll pardon the pun. Don't dismiss the bastard, just in case.'

'Just in case he really *is* going to try to kill me?'

'Grant said I should keep an eye on you.'

'So that's the only reason you're here,' she said sleepily.

He squeezed her hand more tightly then kissed her on the lips.

The door opened and they both looked over to see who had entered.

Dr Alan Davidson crossed to the bed, scribbled something on the clipboard he was carrying, then hung it on the end of the bed.

'So, what's the news, doctor?' Amy asked.

'The biopsy went without any problems, we took a sample of the tissue. The next step is to get it analysed. We'll take it from there once we know what we're dealing with.'

'How long will that be?'

'Three or four days,' Davidson said.

'So what do I do in the meantime?' she asked. 'Sit around and worry myself even sicker?'

'We can't do the tests any quicker, I wish we could,' said Davidson apologetically.

'When can I go home?'

'Tomorrow.'

'How about tonight?' she said, sitting up.

'If you insist but I wouldn't recommend it,' he told her. 'You've had surgery, you shouldn't risk splitting your stitches.'

'What if I promise not to carry any sacks of cement around? Can I go home then?'

Davidson smiled. 'I suppose so,' he relented. 'But be careful.'

'I'll make sure she is, doctor,' Webber added.

'I want to go back to work as soon as possible,' she said defiantly.

'I would recommend rest for two or three days,' Davidson said.

'If I have to sit around with nothing to think about except what might be wrong with me I'll go insane,' Amy insisted. 'My mind's working overtime now.'

Davidson exhaled wearily. 'Again, I can't say I approve, but if you feel capable.'

'I've got to go back. I told you why.'

The doctor could only nod. 'I'm not going to try to stop you,' he said. 'I get the feeling I'd be fighting a losing battle.'

He turned to leave.

'What are the odds on me being okay, doctor?' Amy asked as he reached the door. 'On it being cancer?'

Davidson held up his hands in a gesture of surrender.

'What can I say?' he said. 'The tissue is either benign or malignant. That's all anyone can tell you at the moment. I wish I could tell you more. You'll have to wait. I'm sorry.'

'Thanks,' she said, trying to force a smile.

Davidson nodded then left.

'I don't want to die, Jake.'

'You're not going to die,' he said, squeezing her hand reassuringly, the look in his eye almost convincing her.

'If Roy is the killer then it looks like I've got a choice,' she said humourlessly. 'Either *he* kills me or the cancer does.'

'I told you, Amy. You're not going to die. I won't let you. I've already lost one thing in my life I loved. I won't lose another.'

She squeezed his hand and, as she did so, a single tear trickled from the corner of her eye.

Sixty-Seven

As David Albury swung the Jag into the multi-storey in South Audley Street he glanced down at the dashboard clock. In the gloom the green digits glowed.

10.56 p.m.

He guided the car up the entry ramp, the wheels squealing slightly in the silence as he steered it up towards level two. The place was practically deserted. Barely a dozen cars could be seen on each level. He hadn't even spotted an attendant in the payment area when he'd entered.

Perfect.

Albury pressed a button and the driver's side window rolled down with an electronic whirr. Immediately the smell of oil and petrol spilled into the car, and he wrinkled his nose at the cloying odour. The sound of the engine reverberated off the cold concrete walls and low ceilings as he drove.

Finally, he brought the vehicle to a halt in one of the bays towards the rear of the level. There were four or five other cars parked there. Otherwise, the place was silent.

He looked down again at the dashboard clock, thinking that time seemed to be moving slowly. He'd agreed to meet at eleven and there were less than three minutes until that appointed time.

He looked at his watch, as if that simple act would accelerate time.

Finally, he swung himself out of the Jag, the bones in his knees cracking loudly in the process. He winced and stood up, massaging the back of his neck with one hand and scanning the darkened car park for any signs of movement.

Fluorescents were set into the low ceiling but they

burned with such a cold, faltering light that they seemed barely adequate for their task. All around the meagre puddles of vague luminosity they gave off were oceans of blackness.

Again Albury looked at his watch then scanned the level.

Below him he heard something. The sound of footsteps from the lower level seemed deafening in the stillness. He heard voices. Someone laughed. A high-pitched feminine laugh. He heard two doors slam then the sound of an engine being started.

He stood motionless beside the Jag, listening to the car on the lower level pull away, tyres whining. The sound gradually died away and Albury let out a somewhat shaky breath.

The figure emerged from behind one of the concrete pillars close to him.

Albury spun round as he heard footsteps, his heart racing momentarily. Then, gradually, a look of recognition spread across his face.

'You're late,' Albury said. 'Get in.' He motioned to the passenger side.

Both Albury and the newcomer slid into the leather seats and sat for a while, in the blackness and the silence. 'I told you not to call me at home.' Albury finally broke the silence. He was staring straight ahead, gazing out of the windscreen. 'I asked you not to use my private number unless it was important. I thought you understood that.'

He felt a hand on his thigh. Resting there.

At last he turned and looked at the newcomer, whose features were still partially obscured by the gloom inside the car park.

The hand on his thigh moved higher – fingers were stroking gently across his groin now.

'I have to be careful,' Albury whispered as the movements of the fingers became more urgent. 'You know that.'

The figure leaned across and Albury moved to meet the advance.

'I have to be careful,' he said again, aware now of his erection throbbing beneath the skilled fingers that continued to knead him through his trousers.

His protestations were stifled by a kiss.

Tender at first then more persuasive.

When Albury finally sat back his breath was coming in gasps.

'We'd better go,' he said, smiling as he started the engine.

The figure nodded and slid down further into the passenger seat.

Sixty-Eight

Amy Watson rolled over and stretched, suddenly aware of a slight pain in her left breast. *The stitches.*

She sat up, lifting up her T-shirt slightly, inspecting the dressing that covered the breast.

No blood.

She had wondered what might happen if the stitches split during the night but she was relieved to see that there had been no such mishap.

Beside her, Webber stirred and turned his head to see what she was doing.

'Are you okay?' he asked, his voice sleepy.

She nodded. 'Just panicking again,' she told him, attempting a smile.

He reached across and touched the smooth flesh of her thigh, smiling as Amy lay down again and moved closer to him. He felt the warmth of her body against his and they kissed gently.

'Thanks for staying last night,' she said.

'What did you think I was going to do, drive you home from the hospital and leave you?'

She laid her head on his chest and felt him stroking her hair gently. The slow, rhythmic rise and fall of his chest was somehow reassuring and she pulled herself closer, one leg draped over his thigh.

'Are you really going in to work tonight?' he asked.

'I've got to, Jake. If I sit around here I'll go mad. What about you? Are you coming with me?'

'It depends what Grant wants me to do.'

'What is it between you and him?'

'I don't like him.'

'I gathered that.'

'I don't like the bastard and I don't trust him.'

'When he was here the other night, you said he'd fucked you over. What did he do?'

Webber sighed. 'We worked together in the Vice Squad,' he said wearily. 'We were a pretty good team. We had the record for most arrests two years running. Most of it was just bullshit stuff, little things, but one success was breaking up a paedophile ring that was trading by computer. Fifteen guys went down for that and related incidents.' As he spoke he continued to stroke her hair.

'So what went wrong?'

'There was a club owner in Soho who'd been dealing in snuff videos. Grant and I had been after him for years but we couldn't nail the bastard on anything. Then we got a sniff that he was dealing drugs too. I went over to Amsterdam to check out his supplier. Grant stayed here and kept his eye on the club owner. While I was out there, I found out that they sent the drugs back *inside* the video cases. Inside the cassette itself. The cases are always empty anyway.'

'What do you mean?'

'When porn is shipped into this country from abroad it doesn't come in the way you get it from sex shops. The spools and the tape are separated and carried in cases. Customs can't nick somebody for being in possession of miles of half-inch tape and fifty spools. It's all re-set and spooled up when they get it into this country – that's why the picture and sound quality on a lot of porn is shit. The cassette cases are shipped separately.'

Amy listened intently, trailing her fingers across Webber's belly.

'I found out these cassettes were filled with heroin,' Webber continued. 'I notified Grant and he was waiting for them when they arrived in England. Case closed. The club owner got ten years. Grant got promoted to detective inspector and I got fuck all.' He chuckled.

'Didn't Grant tell anyone you'd tipped him off?'

'What do *you* think?'

'I can understand you being mad.'

'He was right, *I* didn't want the fucking promotion. It pissed me off more that he could take the credit without even mentioning *me*. I didn't want any bloody medals. I just wanted him to admit that he couldn't have cracked it without me.'

'Why did you leave the Vice Squad?'

'I moved over to Murder Squad when Grant moved.' He chuckled again. 'Perhaps I just can't bear to be away from him. I've been working undercover for the last two years.'

She looked up at him.

'Anything else you want to know?' he asked, smiling.

She was about to say something when the phone rang. Amy rolled over and picked it up.

'Hello,' she said, feeling Webber's finger weave a pattern over the small of her back.

'Amy, it's Jo,' the voice at the other end said. 'I was just ringing to see how you were. I saw the papers. I didn't know it was that bad. I'm sorry.'

'Sorry, Jo, I've lost you. What are you talking about?'

'There's a half-page in the *Sun* saying that you underwent major surgery,' Jo told her. 'There's more in the *Star* and the *Mirror*. The *Star* mentions breast cancer.'

Amy swallowed hard. 'Today's papers?'

'I thought you knew.'

'I'll call you back, Jo. Thanks for letting me know.'

'Amy, if there's anything I can do . . .'

'I appreciate it.'

Amy replaced the receiver and sat motionless, staring ahead blankly.

'What is it?' Webber asked, sitting up.

'Jo says it's all over the papers about this,' she looked down at her breast. 'How could they know?'

'Amy, people know your face, anyone could have seen you going into hospital and called one of the papers. It might even have been one of the nurses or doctors.'

'What happened to confidentiality for the patient?' she

said, a note of distress in her voice. 'How can those bastards run stories about this?'

'You know what the press are like. They couldn't give a fuck. You're news, Amy. It's as simple as that.'

'But not about *this*, Jake,' she said, turning to face him. 'I don't want people to know what's wrong with me. Except that now it seems as if half the fucking country knows.'

The tears he saw forming in her eyes were of rage.

Sixty-Nine

'She's a target now.'

Webber lit up another cigarette and blew a stream of smoke in Grant's direction.

'If your theory's right, about the killer going after people with illness,' Webber continued, 'then she's prime material.'

Grant nodded.

'A celebrity. Not some fucking low-life wino or pro,' Webber continued. 'If he goes after *her* and he gets her, that's one hell of a scalp for him.'

'What if he hasn't seen the papers today?' said Lawrenson.

'Do me a favour, Stuart,' grunted Webber. 'Three tabloids ran stories on her, three of them printed topless pictures. Even the fucking *Independent* ran a couple of columns. He can't have missed it.'

'I agree with Webber,' said Grant, getting to his feet. 'He can't have missed it. He's no fool.' Grant looked at Webber. 'We need to get some surveillance into that studio, trace those calls from this geezer who keeps ringing in.'

'Roy,' Webber told him.

'It's not easy to trace a mobile,' Lawrenson interjected.

'I'm not saying it's going to be easy, but it can be done,' Grant insisted. 'I *want* it done.'

'I'm not sure he's the one,' said Webber. 'He's too vague about the killings.'

'Well it's the only fucking lead we've got and I want it followed up,' Grant snapped. 'Besides, I would have thought you'd have been anxious to protect your girlfriend, Jake.'

Webber glared back at him.

'Stuart, go and see about that surveillance, will you?' Grant said, looking at Lawrenson, who nodded and left the office.

When Grant looked back, Webber was still glaring at him.

'You've got good taste, Jake, I'll give you that. Used to be a model, didn't she? Topless. Full frontal. The full monty, wasn't it? You're a lucky man.' He grinned crookedly. 'She's slumming it a bit with you though. I heard she'd been out with rock musicians, writers and Christ knows what else. Did she fancy a bit of rough?'

'Fuck you, Grant.'

'No, fuck *you*, Jake. Remember who's the fucking boss here.'

'How could I forget, *Detective Inspector*.' He emphasised the last two words contemptuously.

'So, what happens when you move out?' Grant wanted to know. 'Are you going to carry on seeing her?'

'I came in here to talk about this murder case, not my fucking love-life.'

'I'm just curious, Jake. I mean, you see these models in the papers and in magazines. It just makes you wonder if they put it about like they say.'

'She hasn't modelled for over six years.'

'She still looks good though. I bet she knows her way around.'

Webber got to his feet.

'You worked vice too long, Grant,' he said dismissively.

'I bet she's great in bed, isn't she? Pity about the operation. I mean, if it *is* cancer, they'll have to take her tit off, won't they?'

Webber suddenly lunged forward across the desk, hands reaching for his superior.

Grant stepped back raising his fists.

'Any time, Jake,' he snapped.

'I'll see you when this is over,' Webber snarled and spun round, heading for the door. When he got there he paused. 'By the way, who's your missus fucking these days?'

And he was gone.

Seventy

Andrew Chapman walked briskly through the bustling hordes that thronged the pavements of Soho. He walked with purpose, unlike so many others who meandered along the narrow, neon-soaked thoroughfares gawping into the windows of shops, or peering almost guiltily through the doorways of peep shows or strip clubs. Some even parted the doors of hanging multi-coloured plastic strips, the only barrier between the outside world and the forbidden pleasures beyond.

Chapman saw three youths doing just that, laughing to themselves, anxious to enter but not finding the courage. One of them said something to a young woman standing close to the door of 'The Pirate Club' who was handing out fliers. She ignored him and his inane remarks, looking past him towards others who filed by.

A couple of Ann Summers' shops he passed had been forced to cover their windows with black tape or shutters (one of the more noticeable effects of the Albury Bill, he thought) but it didn't deter prying eyes.

He saw a couple looking intently at the rubber and latex wear on display in one window, the young man gently stroking his companion's buttocks as they stood watching, talking in hushed tones. He heard the girl laugh softly and saw her move closer to her boyfriend.

The sidestreets were darker than the main thorough-fares – like furred veins running from the main arteries of light. A tall man in a worn suit stood at the door of a club whose sign was flickering, threatening to go out perma-nently. He called out something out Chapman ignored it. He had no desire to visit *that* club. He remembered it as being dirty. The women who danced inside it were older. Past their best. Not what he wanted.

Music spilled from many of the doorways as he passed other shops and clubs. With so many restaurants and bars amongst them, the area was always busy, and the constant chatter of so many diners and drinkers mingled with the unceasing music to form one unholy din.

There was a loud argument going on between two men outside one pub on the corner of Old Compton Street and Wardour Street. Chapman saw fingers being pointed angrily and hurried past the scene. Others loitered close by, slowing their pace as if expecting or anticipating the possible violence that might come from the exchange.

Chapman had no interest in watching two men fight. He had other things on his mind.

He turned a corner, ignoring a man who was sitting on the pavement playing an accordion, a blanket between his legs with loose change scattered across it. He heard a call for change but dismissed it.

Up ahead he saw the place he sought.

The doorway was lit by flashing neon strips in the shape of a pair of pursed lips. Beside the entrance there were several framed but faded pictures of young women in varying stages of undress. They pouted alluringly at those who would look.

Beyond the main entrance there was a small desk, a little like the check-in desk at an airport. The man who sat behind it took Chapman's money without speaking and gave him a small ticket that looked as though it had been torn from a raffle book.

PRIVATE BOOTHS a sign to his left announced.

Chapman smiled and walked in.

Seventy-One

Charlotte Kilbride was halfway home when she realised she'd left her Filofax in the office.

At first she decided that it wasn't such a problem. She had no calls to make when she got home. It could wait until the morning. No harm would come to it locked up in her office. Then she realised she'd left her mobile phone there too.

She'd left later than usual, determined to write up some case notes that had been left untouched for a week. That, she told herself, was the reason for the aberration. She was normally so organised, so methodical. To forget one item was annoying, to forget two was simply stupid. She felt she had no choice but to go back.

Wearily, she turned the car as soon as she could and began driving back towards Harley Street. By the time she finally got home, she reasoned, it would be too late to eat. She wouldn't want food by that time. She decided to leave the car outside the office and dine out. It had been a while since she'd done that, and, besides, after the workload she'd got through that evening, she felt she deserved a little pampering. The prospect of being waited on, sitting in a bistro sipping wine and enjoying good pasta suddenly seemed to override her annoyance at having to turn back.

The traffic, she was delighted to find, wasn't as heavy heading back to the office and less than half an hour later she pulled up in front of the building again.

She pulled the keys from her jacket pocket, locked the car, then headed up the steps to the front door and let herself in.

Silence greeted her as she walked in, enveloping her

like an invisible hand. That was wrong. *Why wasn't the alarm going off?* Had she forgotten to set *that* too?

Charlotte hesitated in the long narrow hallway for a moment, thinking back to when she left the office. She was sure she had set it.

Positive?

She looked at the panel beside the door. No blinking red lights. Perhaps she *had* forgotten. Perhaps working so late and so hard was something to be avoided in the future, she thought, smiling to herself as she moved through the darkened hall towards the stairs.

Only at the bottom did she bother to slap on a light, then she ascended swiftly, the stairs creaking beneath her. Had she not been in such a hurry she might have noticed that one of the paintings that hung on the wall had been knocked askew. Even if she had seen it, she might have simply assumed that the cleaner had done it accidentally.

She reached the landing and flicked on the light switch there. It clicked but no light was illuminated. The landing remained in darkness. The bulb would have to be changed, she noted.

Charlotte selected the key to her office door and inserted it. The door swung open as she touched it.

She saw that paint had been scraped off around the lock, even pieces of wood were scattered across the threshold.

She took a step towards the partition, her heart thudding hard against her ribs.

Get out now.

The door swung further open to reveal what lay beyond.

Don't wait. Just get out. Call the police.

But she was transfixed by the sight before her. Her office had been ransacked. No, that was a barely adequate description. It had been demolished.

Her desk was overturned. Banks of filing cabinets had been toppled. Books swept from their shelves. Pictures had even been ripped from the walls, glass from their frames lay across the floor like crystal confetti. The scale of the destruction was breathtaking. It was as if every single item and object in the room had been either broken or disturbed in some way.

Get out.

She turned to leave.

Something hard struck her across the face. The impact lifted her off her feet and sent her toppling backwards into the ruined office, blood spilling from a cut on her cheek.

She raised a hand to protect herself and felt another thudding impact against her wrist. The pain and the accompanying crack told her that it had been broken. She tried to force out a scream but it seemed locked in her throat.

In the darkness of her office she found it difficult to focus on her assailant. A task made impossible as she was struck again across the bridge of the nose. A blow that shattered bone and sent blood spewing into the gloom.

She dropped to her knees and tried to lift her head. A thunderous blow hit the top of her skull and consciousness began to slip away. The room was becoming darker but somehow she clung to her senses and dragged herself to her feet, her head spinning, blood now pouring warmly from several cuts. Charlotte was gripped by a sudden and uncontrollable fear. A vice-like conviction that she was going to die, despite every effort to save herself. A powerful blow broke her jaw, smashed teeth and sent two of them tearing through her top lip.

She reeled, tears flowing as well as blood.

Then powerful hands gripped her wrist and she felt herself being swung round, helpless in the grasp of her attacker. Consciousness didn't desert her quickly enough now.

She realised she was being flung towards the window.

The glass came hurtling towards her as her assailant finally let her go.

She struck the window, crashed through it and seemed to hang in the air, suspended like a puppet on invisible strings. Then she plummeted towards the ground. The ground rushed up to meet her.

Below, spiked railings at the side of the pavement gleamed wickedly in the street light. She hit them first. Two of the points punctured her body, ripping through her heart and lungs, tearing the breath and life from her. Gouts of blood like crimson geysers rose into the air from the wounds. Glass from the broken window showered down over her and shattered into even tinier fragments as they struck the concrete. In the light of the street lamps they sparkled like tears, their lustre finally extinguished as several thick streams of blood covered them.

Inside her office, one floor up, a figure peered quickly out at her impaled body then turned and left as stealthily as it had entered.

Its work was done.

For now.

Seventy-Two

Amy slipped off her headphones and sat back in her chair. Across in the production-booth window Webber was standing, arms folded, cigarette dangling between his lips.

She shrugged.

'He's not going to call, is he?' Jo Parker commented, glancing at her watch.

Webber didn't answer, merely consulted his own time-piece.

1.06 a.m.

'He doesn't call at a specific time, does he?' said the detective, not taking his eyes from Amy.

'We're off the air in ten minutes,' Mike Osborne reminded him.

'Where are you, Roy?' murmured Webber, still gazing at Amy, who was preparing to take another call.

'She's got four callers left,' Jo told him. 'Then that's it.'

Webber nodded.

'It looks like all that surveillance equipment you had brought in was a waste of time,' Osborne observed.

'Perhaps he'll call tomorrow,' Webber said, ignoring the barbed comment.

'Maybe he knows that you were waiting for him,' Osborne said. 'He might be cleverer than you think. He might know you're waiting to trace him.'

Webber took another drag on his cigarette, blowing the smoke out slowly, watching it dissipate in the air, his eyes never leaving Amy.

'Yeah,' he whispered, his eyes narrowing, 'maybe he *does* know.'

Seventy-Three

Dear David,

This note probably won't come as a surprise to you. It probably won't even bother you that much. I've taken most of my clothes, I'll be back for the others in the next few days but I don't suppose I'll see you. I know you're busy. You're always busy. That's one of the reasons I'm leaving . . . There's a number on the back where you can reach me, if you want to. I hope you do.

Tina

David Grant read the note again, turning the paper over to check the number she'd mentioned. He gazed at it for a moment then crumpled up the paper and dropped it into a nearby ashtray.

He was about to pour himself another drink when the phone rang.

Seventy-Four

As Webber ducked beneath the red and yellow tape he saw the bloodstains. The dark blemishes on the pavement outside the house in Harley Street had been covered by what looked like cling-film to prevent them being contaminated. The railings above had been draped in a similar material and he saw that they too were spattered with crimson. A man in a dark suit worn at both elbows was inspecting the railings, taking samples of material and fibre from them with a pair of tweezers. Webber passed him and moved on into the house itself.

In the hallway there were more plainclothes officers, most of whom he took to be from Forensics.

As he drew level with the spacious waiting room he peered in and found two more men in there. One was dusting for fingerprints on the smooth surfaces.

'Where's Grant?' Webber asked the other man.

'Upstairs,' Schofield told him, then looked up and recognised Webber. 'How you doing, Jake?' he added, smiling broadly.

'I've been better, Den. What happened here?'

'He'll tell you,' Schofield answered, pointing towards the ceiling.

Webber made his way up the stairs, pausing to allow another Forensics man past him. He was carrying two small plastic bags.

He reached the landing and turned to his right, spotting more movement through the open door there. Grant was standing close to the window, watching as small pieces of glass were removed from the frame and bagged for examination.

He glanced around at the destruction that had been wrought in Charlotte Kilbride's office. And at the blood.

There were splashes of it in several places. A long slick near his feet, spreading across the expensive carpet. A splash on the wall close to the broken window. More on the desk top.

Grant finally turned and saw Webber looking around.

'Looks like a hell of a party, doesn't it?' Grant commented flatly.

'Who found her?'

'A taxi driver saw the body dangling from the railings. He called it in.'

'What time was she killed?'

'Barclay reckons somewhere between ten and twelve last night. He's doing the full autopsy down at the Yard now. The fall killed her.' Grant nodded towards the shattered window and Webber peered out, looking down at the railings.

'Did the killer give her a belting first?' Webber asked.

'Yeah, with a chair leg, Barclay reckons.'

'Not our man, then?'

'I don't know yet.'

'Come on, the MO couldn't be much more different, could it? Beating someone almost to death with a chair leg then slinging them out of a window doesn't quite have the finesse of strangulation, does it?' Webber muttered. He looked around the room, particularly at the paintings on the wall and some of the ornaments, many of which had been scattered in the struggle. Others, however, still remained in their original positions, including a pair of expensive-looking vases on a shelf near the door.

'The killer disabled the burglar alarm,' said Grant. 'Then he broke in through a ground-floor window at the back.'

'Any prints?'

'Smooth gloves. He knew what he was doing but . . .' Grant smiled '. . . the bastard cut himself on the glass getting in. We've got a sample, it's being typed.'

'Nothing taken by the look of it,' Webber noted. 'Do

you reckon he broke in to kill her and just made it *look* like a burglary?'

'No, something *was* taken.'

'Money? Jewellery?'

'Files.'

Grant walked across to one of the overturned filing cabinets.

'About twenty of them,' Grant continued. 'Patient files. Obviously there was something in one of them that he didn't want anyone to see. When she first contacted me and offered her help she must have thought that the killer might have been one of her patients. It looks like she was right.'

'Any way of finding out which files have gone missing?'

'Her secretary came in this morning, she said they keep copies of every file. The killer obviously didn't know that or else he had to leg it before he had the chance to look for them. Probably after he killed her.'

'So you reckon the geezer who killed Charlotte Kilbride is the one we're looking for?'

'I'd bet money on it,' Grant said smugly. 'As soon as we've got the list sorted out properly, I want to start interviewing them. I've already narrowed it down to eight. The rest are too old, too young or women. The ones I've eliminated don't match up to what we've got on our killer.'

'Which isn't very much'?' Webber reminded him. 'Who's left?'

'A cross section,' Grant said. 'But there is one *very* interesting file. It belongs to Mister, or should I say, the Right Honourable David Albury.'

'The fucking MP?'

Grant nodded.

'She treated him about six months ago for depression,' Grant continued. 'Only a couple of consultations but we'll follow it up anyway.'

'Christ, if the papers got hold of that he'd be a laughing stock,' Webber observed.

'Well, it wouldn't exactly help his public profile, I'll give you that, but I doubt if Albury's our man. I've got a pretty good idea who might be though. I'm going to see him when I leave here.'

Webber was about to ask who when he was interrupted by a shrill bleeping.

Grant dug into his jacket pocket and pulled out his mobile phone, pressing it to his ear.

'Yeah, go on, Phil, what have you got?' he said into the mouthpiece.

While Grant spoke, Webber wandered slowly through the wrecked office running his gaze over the destruction, pausing beside the overturned filing cabinets.

He looked up and saw a number of framed diplomas and certificates on the wall behind her desk. There was a splash of blood on one of them.

He heard Grant snap the mouthpiece of his phone shut and turned to face the other man.

'Barclay's finished the autopsy,' said Grant.

'Did he get a grouping on the blood from the killer?'

'Type O.'

'Great. The most common group. That narrows it down to forty-six per cent of the population. Shit.'

'It narrows it down a lot further than that,' Grant told him. 'Barclay said that there were traces of viral contamination in the blood.'

'What kind of virus?'

'AIDS.'

Seventy-Five

'Should you be doing this?'

Jo Parker glanced across at Amy Watson who was pedalling the exercise bike with steady and powerful strokes of her shapely legs.

Amy wiped perspiration from her face and looked at Jo. There were two other people in the gym, both men, both working with weights on the far side of the room. The only other sound, apart from the steady churning of the bike wheels, was the loud pop music crouching from the speakers set on the gym wall.

'Doing what, Jo?' Amy asked, still pedalling.

'You're not well,' Jo said. 'Wouldn't you be better off resting?'

'Sitting around worrying about how ill I might be, you mean? Moping around my flat thinking about cancer and Christ knows what else.'

Jo regarded her silently, pedalling herself. They had been at the gym for over an hour now and both were stained with perspiration from their exertions.

'I'm sick of people trying to wrap me in cotton wool,' Amy retorted angrily. 'First the doctor tells me I should rest, then Jake says I shouldn't work. Osborne wants me to take it easy and now *you*.'

Jo lowered her gaze. 'I didn't mean any harm,' she said apologetically. 'I asked because I care about you. Sorry if that bothers you.'

She swung herself off the exercise bike, pulled her towel from the handlebars and headed towards the changing rooms.

Amy exhaled wearily then followed her, catching her as she reached the gym exit.

'Jo, I'm sorry,' said Amy, following her friend into the

women's changing room. 'I just wish people would stop treating me like some kind of invalid.'

'But you're ill, Amy,' Jo reminded her, sitting down on one of the wooden benches, pulling off her trainers and socks and dropping them into her sports bag.

Amy also began to undress.

'But I'm not a cripple,' she said gently. 'I appreciate people's concern, but the more they go on about what might be wrong with me the more it makes me think about it.'

She slipped off her leotard and stood there in just a pair of Lycra leggings, towelling the sweat from her torso.

Jo looked at her breasts, in particular the left one. It was still bandaged but not so heavily.

'Does it hurt?' Jo dared to ask.

'Only when I think about it,' Amy smiled.

Jo slipped off her leggings and T-shirt and stood naked, close to Amy. 'I ask because I care,' she said softly, taking a step closer.

Her face was flushed, her hair plastered to her smooth skin and Amy could feel the heat from her naked body.

Jo reached out and touched Amy's cheek with her finger. The touch was electric.

Amy found herself gazing deeply into Jo's eyes.

She reached out and brushed a hair from her friend's cheek, then stepped back slightly and slid off her leggings.

They stood naked, inches from one another.

'If there's anything I can do, you *will* tell me, won't you?' Jo said quietly.

Amy nodded.

Jo leaned forward and kissed her friend tenderly on the left cheek.

'I care, Amy,' she said again, then turned away and began to pull on her clothes.

Amy blinked hard, as if awaking from a trance, aware but unconcerned that she was standing naked in the changing room. She looked at Jo for a moment longer then she too reached for her clothes, slipping on her bra first, as if anxious to hide the diseased breast.

Diseased?

She shook her head and continued dressing.

'Shall we go and get a drink?' she said, pulling on her jeans. 'I *need* one.'

Seventy-Six

Andrew Chapman looked up as he heard the knock on his office door.

'Come in,' he called.

'There's someone to see you, Mr Chapman,' his secretary told him. 'A Detective Inspector Grant. He says it's important.'

Police.

Chapman's heart jumped several beats.

'Send him in,' he said, his voice cracking. He coughed.

Grant entered, a thin smile on his lips.

'Andrew Chapman,' he said and it came out as a statement rather than a question.

'Yes, please sit down,' Chapman said, gesticulating wildly towards the chair that faced his desk.

Grant ignored the invitation momentarily and crossed to the large picture window that ran the full length of Chapman's office. He looked through the blinds, gazing down on to a view of Piccadilly Circus. An open-top sightseeing bus was passing by, tourists were pointing cameras and camcorders enthusiastically.

Chapman turned in his seat to watch the policeman. The banker's heart had slowed a little but it was still pounding with such force he feared the detective would hear it.

'How can I help you, Detective Inspector?' he asked finally, trying to ensure that his voice sounded as even as he could make it.

Had they traced some of the pornographic videos he'd bought?

Grant turned away from the window and sat down opposite him.

Chapman blanched slightly beneath the inquisitive

gaze of the policeman and, despite efforts not to, he lowered his eyes slightly.

Grant looked across the banker's desk. He took in details like the half-drunk cup of tea, the computer screen filled with numbers, the pad and pen that lay in front of Chapman, numbers and names scrawled on the paper. Then, finally, he looked directly into the other man's eyes.

'Can I get you coffee?' Chapman asked.

Grant shook his head. 'I won't waste your time,' he said tersely. 'We're both busy men. I need you to answer some questions.'

'Whatever I can help you with.'

'How long have you been having psychiatric treatment?'

Chapman swallowed hard.

How did they know?

'You were being treated for, what was it, an addiction, a reliance on pornography. That's right, isn't it?'

Chapman's ability to control his breathing was vanishing rapidly. He sucked in several deep breaths, trying to calm himself.

'You were being treated by Charlotte Kilbride at her Harley Street practice, weren't you?'

'How do you know?'

'I *am* a detective, Mr Chapman. How long have you been seeing her?'

'A year. I can't remember exactly how long.'

'What made you go to her in the first place?'

'What do you mean?'

'Why seek psychiatric help? Looking at a few dirty books never hurt anybody. Did it?'

'There was more to it than that.'

'Like what?'

'I was spending a fortune every month on books and videos. Visiting peep shows.'

'And prostitutes?'

'Occasionally.'

'Did your wife know?'

'No. It would finish her if she did. It would finish *me* if anyone here found out. That was why I needed help.'

'Were you and Charlotte Kiloride close?'

'Meaning what?'

'Did you fancy her? She was an attractive woman. It would have been understandable.'

'I didn't notice.'

'Oh, come on, Mr Chapman. You saw her once a week for a year and you never noticed that she was attractive. You were being treated for a condition that meant your main obsession in life was staring at naked women, either on paper, in films or in the flesh, and you're trying to tell me you never noticed that Charlotte Kilbride was attractive?'

'I suppose she was, I mean, I *did* notice, yes.'

'Did you ever come on to her?'

'No. Never.'

'You never made a move on her? So she never rejected you? You weren't having an affair with her?'

'What the hell is all this about, Inspector?' snapped Chapman, his initial fear turning to confusion.

'Have you ever had an AIDS test?' Grant continued.

'Why would I?'

'You were sleeping with prostitutes.'

'I wasn't sleeping with them, I . . .'

'And you weren't sleeping with Charlotte Kilbride?'

'No, now could you please tell me what's going on?'

'Charlotte Kilbride was murdered last night. Some patient files were stolen from her office. One of them was yours.'

Grant watched as the colour drained from the banker's face. Chapman tried to swallow but it felt as if his throat was being constricted. His mouth opened and closed soundlessly for a second.

Got you, you bastard, thought Grant, glaring even more intently at his quarry.

'She was murdered between ten and twelve last night,

Mr Chapman,' he persisted. 'Can you account for your movements between that time?'

Chapman lowered his head even more.

'Could your wife supply you with an alibi?' Grant continued.

Turn that screw a little more.

'Please don't tell my wife,' Chapman blurted, his eyes bulging in their sockets.

'Don't tell her what? That you're a suspect in a murder case? She's going to find that out soon enough anyway.'

'She doesn't know about any of this. The therapy or my problem. Please don't tell her.'

For a second, Grant thought the other man was going to burst into tears.

'You're worried about your wife finding out that you read dirty books and *I'm* telling you you're a murder suspect. Which is worse?'

'I didn't kill Charlotte Kilbride? Why should I?'

'Because she was convinced that *you* were the killer who's been topping pimps, pushers, prostitutes and all the others. She wanted to crack the case herself.'

'How do you know that?'

'Because it's in your file. All her notes about you. Her thoughts. Her suspicions. Now, why would she think you were the sort of man who could kill seventeen people, Mr Chapman? Or is it eighteen now?'

'That's ridiculous,' Chapman said, his face milk-white.

'She was on to you so you killed her. You knew that all her theories were in your file so you stole it to protect yourself and you killed her. You just forgot that she kept duplicate files, didn't you?'

'Are you charging me?'

'I'm just talking to you.'

'I'm not sure I want to say anything else without a lawyer here.'

Grant got to his feet.

'Fair enough,' he said. 'I've said what I came to say

anyway. Where would you like to do the next interview? Here, at New Scotland Yard or at home?' Grant
smiled again.

'I didn't kill her,' Chapman said, also standing up.

'Well then, you won't mind if we talk again and there's
something else. I need you to take a blood test.'

'What for?'

'Just routine procedure,' Grant told him, opening the
office door.

As he stepped out he saw faces turned towards
Chapman's office. One of them, a tall man with grey
hair, ran curious eyes over the policeman.

Chapman followed Grant out and saw the grey-haired
man. He nodded hesitantly towards him, his mind spinning. Duncan Scott had been manager of the branch ever
since Chapman had worked there. Nothing happened in
the bank without him knowing.

Scott watched for a moment longer then wandered into
his own office further down the hall.

'I'll be in touch,' said Grant, and headed for the escalator that would take him back to street level.

Chapman was aware of the faces turned in his direction. Of cashiers watching him from behind their glass
partition. Of secretaries casting furtive glances from the
other side of their desks.

He retreated quickly back into his office and closed the
door, aware of the perspiration that had beaded on his
forehead.

He sat down, his hands shaking, his head reeling. He
stared blankly ahead, his mind unable to focus on any one
single thought. Fear enveloped him and crushed him like
a powerful fist. For fleeting seconds he thought he was
going to be sick.

His phone rang. An internal call.

He sucked in a couple of deep breaths then lifted the
receiver.

'Andrew Chapman,' he said, trying to sound unconcerned.

'Andrew, it's Duncan Scott,' said the voice at the other end of the line. 'Could you spare me a moment or two in my office now, please?'

'I'll be straight down, Mr Scott,' Chapman said, replacing the receiver.

What now? How much worse could it get?

'He's cracking already,' said Grant, sliding into the passenger seat of the car.

Stuart Lawrenson looked across at his superior.

'I want surveillance on him,' Grant continued. 'Assign two men, day and night, and let the bastard *know* they're there. I want him to know we're watching him. Get phone taps sorted out too. One for this office line and one for his home phone. If Chapman has a shit I want to know about it. We've got him and he knows it. I'll have him charged within three days, you'll see.'

Seventy-Seven

Amy stretched on the sofa and looked down at Webber, who was sitting on the floor with his back to her, poring over some paperwork.

She leaned forward and gently massaged his shoulders, feeling the stiffness there.

'You're tense,' she said softly, kissing his ear lightly.

'That's the story of my life,' said Webber, smiling at her. He looked back at the file he'd been reading.

'Do you think that this Chapman bloke is the killer?' she asked.

'You mean do I think Grant is right?'

'*Do* you?'

'He's convinced.'

'But you're not?'

'He wants *someone* for these killings. There's pressure on him from the top brass and the media. Everyone wants the geezer caught.'

'But?'

He picked up one of the other files.

'The killer, supposedly, picked his victims because they had some kind of disease, right. So, that would indicate someone with a pathological hatred or fear of illness and disease.'

She nodded in agreement. 'I'm with you so far, Sherlock,' said Amy, smiling.

'"James Cavernar,"' he read from the file. '"Aged forty-two. Single. Diagnosis: mysophobia and nosophobia. Clinical fear of dirt and disease."'

'You think it could be him?' Amy asked.

Webber dropped the file.

'Perhaps I just *want* it to be him,' he said wearily. 'Perhaps I just want it to be anyone except Andrew

Chapman. Because I want Grant to be wrong. Does that sound childish?'

She continued massaging his shoulders gently.

'The bastard's convinced it's Chapman,' Webber continued. 'He's had tails on him for the last forty-eight hours. Questioned him five times. He says he's waiting for him to crack.'

'Would it matter so much if he *was* right about Chapman?'

'Fuck him. Let him get his conviction if he wants it. I want this killer off the streets as much as he does.'

'So, you were right about Roy? His calls were fake.'

'I'm sure he's not the killer, whoever he is, but he still threatened *you*.'

'I haven't heard from him for three days. Do you think that Chapman could have called in as Roy?'

'It's possible but I doubt it. I tell you what though, the thing that puzzles me is why he killed Charlotte Kilbride the way he did. If Chapman *is* the killer, why didn't he just strangle her like the others? By battering her first he risked getting blood on his clothes or himself. Strangling her would have been easier. Cleaner. And taking the files was clumsy – he must have known it would point us in his direction. I don't get it.'

'Aren't all murderers supposed to secretly *want* to be caught? That's what the experts always say in films.' She smiled.

He chuckled. 'Maybe but, like the man said, if it don't gell it ain't aspic. And this ain't gelling.' He picked up another file, flicked through it and discarded it.

'I'm sorry,' he said.

'For what?'

'I've been going on about this fucking case when you've got other things on your mind. More important things.' He turned and kissed her gently on the lips.

'Jake, I'm grateful for anything that takes my mind off my problems.'

She rolled on to her back, arms folded behind her head, her gaze fixed on the ceiling.

'What will you do when this is all over?' she asked.

'What do you mean?'

'Once the investigation is finished. You'll be moving out, won't you?'

'I couldn't afford one of these flats on *my* salary, Amy. I'm just a humble copper. Like Grant said, it's the taxpayers who've paid for this.'

'So where will you go?'

'Back home. Where else am I going to go?'

'And what about us, Jake? When you pack up and put your stuff back in boxes, what do you do with our relationship? Pack that up and put it in a crate too?'

He turned to face her, kneeling beside the sofa, one hand resting on her thigh, the other gently caressing her cheek.

'Is that what you want?' he asked quietly.

'I want *you*,' she whispered and pulled him down to her, their lips meeting.

He responded fiercely.

When they broke the kiss they were both breathing heavily.

'You're not getting rid of me,' he said, smiling. 'I told you before, I lost one thing I loved. I won't lose another.'

She enfolded her arms around his neck and pulled him tightly to her.

From the coffee table close by, the photograph of Andrew Chapman fluttered to the floor, displaced by Webber's movements. Blind monochrome eyes gazed upwards.

Seventy-Eight

Jo Parker watched as her brother pulled on his leather jacket.

'Out again, Billy?' she said wearily.

'Looks like it.'

'Where to?'

'It's not important.'

'Do you really hate me that much?'

'What the fuck are you going on about?'

'You must hate me. You never talk to me. You never share things with me. Have I been *that* awful to you since you came to live with me?'

Billy laughed. 'I get it,' he said, 'we've had the "angry older sister demanding to know where her no good brother is going" routine and that didn't work. So now you're trying the softly, softly approach. Is that it?'

'This isn't any *routine*, Billy,' Jo told him angrily. 'I care about you. I'm sick of telling you that.'

'And I'm sick of hearing it. Get off my fucking back, will you?'

'Don't you know what's going on out there?' she demanded, pointing towards the window. 'There's a killer on the loose. How do you know you won't be next?'

'How do you know *you* won't?'

They faced each other for interminable seconds.

'What is your fucking problem, Jo?' he said finally. 'Have I been sponging off you since I got here? No. I've put money in your pocket.'

'I just want to know where that money's come from.'

'Where do you *think* it's come from?'

She had no answer as he took a step closer to her.

'Well, go on, tell me,' he persisted. 'Where do you think

it comes from?' He stuck his hand in the pocket of his
jeans and pulled out a thick wad of ten-pound notes.

'Drugs,' she said flatly.

'You think I'm pushing?'

'How else could you earn *that* sort of money?'

'I'm a very resourceful lad,' he told her sneeringly.

'Tell me, Billy.'

He turned away, but Jo shot out a hand and gripped
his wrist.

'Tell me,' she rasped.

'It doesn't matter,' he snarled, shaking loose. 'Nothing
matters any more.' She saw his hand go to his inside
pocket where he pulled a piece of paper free. 'Here,
read this, you'll see what I mean.' He hurled it in her
direction then turned and headed for the door, wrenching
it open.

'Billy,' she called after him, stooping to pick up the
paper. She heard his footsteps receding down the stairs.

Jo unfolded the carefully folded sheet and glanced at
it. At the headed paper.

THE HOLMWOOD CLINIC

She skimmed the typed letter, only the odd word catching
her attention.

'Dear Mr Parker . . .'

Jo found that she was quivering slightly.

'HIV test . . .'

She could not swallow.

'. . . Regret to tell you . . .'

She had to hold the paper in both hands now to
steady it.

'. . . Positive . . .'

'Oh, God,' she murmured.

'Test result was positive . . .'

'Billy!' she shouted again.

Jo tossed the letter aside, snatched up a jacket and
rushed out of the flat, slamming the door behind her.

She took the steps two at a time, almost stumbling near the bottom, but she hurtled out into the small hallway, then dashed on and out into the street.

Frantically she looked right and left, searching for any sign of Billy in the street.

'Billy,' she whispered under her breath.

She saw him. On the other side of the road, about to turn left.

Calm down. Don't get too close. Don't let him see you.

He made his way briskly down Corfield Street then turned right.

Jo was relieved to see that there were more people in Bethnal Green Road. It would give her more places to hide. Not that Billy would have any idea she was following him. She darted and weaved past fellow pedestrians as if she was competing in some kind of bizarre slalom, never taking her eyes from her brother. He was crossing the road again, heading into the tube station itself.

She scurried across the road, slowing her pace slightly, allowing him to put more distance between them. Using a concrete pillar as cover, she saw him feeding small change into a ticket machine.

As he passed through the barrier she scurried across to the machine herself, hand fumbling in her pocket. No change. She would lose him.

Her heart thudded even harder against her ribs. She tried the other pocket, found coins and fed them in, punched one of the buttons and grabbed the ticket.

When she reached the escalator there was no sign of him. She hesitated a moment, knowing that the Central line ran through Bethnal Green. But which platform was he on?

She decided to try westbound. *A hunch? Desperation?*

As the escalator carried her down she heard the rumble of an approaching train; she hurried down the last few moving steps and through the archway that led her to the westbound platform. The train was just pulling in.

Again she looked right and left.

Where the hell was Billy?

People were spilling off the train from most carriages.

She took a few paces to her left, eyes scanning the many figures waiting to board, mingling with those leaving.

Jo spotted him. He stepped on three or four cars down to her right.

She pushed past a middle-aged man who muttered something at her as she barged through and jumped on to the carriage next to the one where Billy was seated.

Someone had left a copy of the *Evening Standard* on a seat opposite and she snatched it up, banking on it giving her at least a little cover should he look her way.

Her hands were quivering as she turned the pages, aware of the ludicrousness of this entire episode. For all she knew he might have known she was following. Even now he might be preparing to jump off and leave her stranded on the train.

She cast an anxious glance in his direction. He was still there in the next carriage, head tilted back, head resting against the window. Waiting.

Where are you going?

The automatic doors slid shut and the train moved off.

Seventy-Nine

As the taxi pulled up outside the studios in Bedford Square, Amy was surprised to see Mike Osborne standing in the reception area.

She walked across to the main entrance, her eyes never leaving the producer, who was standing, statue-like, arms folded across his chest, his face set in stern lines.

Amy was barely through the main doors when he began talking.

'Where the hell is she?' he demanded angrily.

'Who?' Amy asked, signing in.

'Your bloody friend, Jo.'

They walked to the lifts.

'Hasn't she come in?' Amy asked as the producer pressed the Call button.

'Why the fuck do you think I'm standing down here?' he snapped.

'Look, I'm her friend, not her keeper, Mike,' Amy said irritably, stepping into the lift behind the producer. 'Hasn't she rung in?'

'No. And she's not answering her phone either, I've been trying for the last half-hour.'

The lift bumped to a stop at the appointed floor and they both stepped out.

'*I'm* going to have to work the fucking calls tonight,' Osborne said angrily.

He pushed open the production-room door and barged his way in.

'She could have had an accident or anything and all you're worried about is having to answer the phone?' Amy said.

'Well if it *is* an accident, it better not be anything

trivial,' he said. 'I hope she realises the mess she's dropped us in.'

'It's nothing we can't handle. I just hope she's all right.
I'll try her flat again.'

Amy reached for the phone.

'Well, get a move on, you're on the air in ten minutes.'

Amy waved away his protestations and jabbed the
digits she wanted.

'I've told you, there's no one there,' he said.

Amy waited.

It was ringing.

'I'm telling you, Amy, she'd better have a bloody good
explanation for this,' he continued.

Still ringing.

'Come on, Jo,' Amy murmured.

Ringing.

'Nothing,' Amy said finally, gently replacing the
receiver.

'I've already told you that. It's probably something to
do with her brother.'

'What did she say to *you* about her brother?'

'I overheard her talking to your boyfriend the other
night about him. He sounds like a fucking waster to me.'

Amy was dialling another number.

'Eight minutes to show-time, Amy,' he reminded her.

She ignored him, waiting for the call to be answered.

When it was, she recognised Webber's voice immediately.

'Jake, it's me. Listen, Jo hasn't turned up for the show
tonight and there's no reply from her flat. It's probably
nothing but it's not like her. I just wanted to check she
was okay.'

'I wouldn't worry,' Webber told her.

'That's exactly what I *am* doing, Jake. Please check it
out for me, will you?'

'I'll meet you there after the show,' he said. 'I've
got to go.'

'See you.'

She hung up.

'Jake's going to check she's all right,' Amy said, getting to her feet.

'Well then I'm sure everything will be fine if *Jake* is on the job.'

'Fuck you, Mike.'

'I'll have her job for this, Amy, unless she's got a good excuse,' he said threateningly.

'And I'll have *yours* if you fuck up those calls,' Amy snarled.

She made her way into the studio. Six lines were already lit up.

Eighty

Jo became more agitated with each successive station the train passed through.

Liverpool Street.

She glanced from behind her paper and saw that Billy hadn't moved.

Bank.

Still he remained in his seat.

Did he know she was in the next carriage?

St Paul's.

Two youths got on and stood by the door, talking loudly. They were blocking her view of the next carriage.

Jo thought about changing seats but, even if she sat on the seat opposite, her view would still be blocked. By now the youths had noticed she was constantly looking in their direction. One of them leaned close to his companion to whisper something.

The second youth laughed loudly and also looked at her, licking his lips.

Jo lowered her gaze, glancing at the paper again as if engrossed. It didn't seem to matter that she hadn't even turned a page for the last fifteen minutes.

The youths got out at Chancery Lane, still laughing loudly.

Jo chanced a look into the next carriage, checking to see if her brother was also there. He was.

Holborn came and went and he still hadn't moved, had barely shifted position in fact.

Glancing at the map opposite, she noticed that the next stop was Tottenham Court Road.

Here perhaps?

The train was getting busier with each stop, mor

people spilling on and off as it penetrated deeper into the heart of the West End.

Again she chanced a look into the next carriage. He looked up.

For one frantic second, Jo thought that he'd seen her. She felt sure that their eyes had met.

And what if they had? What would he do?

He was still on the train as it pulled away, laden with yet more travellers, heading towards Oxford Circus.

Jo was gripped by the unshakeable feeling that Billy knew she was following him, that, at one stop or another he would simply weave in and out of the crowd, give her the slip and leave her stranded. What had made her think she could carry on this ridiculous behaviour anyway? Things like this only worked in spy films. This was real life. Uncomfortably real.

The train slowed down as it pulled into Oxford Circus and, at last, Billy got to his feet.

She swallowed hard.

What now? Get up and step off the train at the same instant? Walk straight into his arms?

She sat still and waited for the train to stop.

It juddered slightly and the doors slid open. Still she waited.

How long would the doors remain open? Ten seconds? Fifteen?

She saw Billy pass by on the platform.

The doors would be closing any second.

She had to get off now. If she didn't she'd be left on the train.

But was he far enough away not to see her?

She moved slightly, heart thumping madly.

Move now or you'll lose him.

She heard a metallic rumble.

Move.

The doors were beginning to close.

She leaped to her feet and managed to squeeze through

the narrowing gap just in time. She landed on the platform and spun round, eyes searching the crowd.

She took a few paces in the direction that he'd walked, slipping past a couple of other travellers. No sign of Billy.

Up ahead there were two archways, one of them an exit the other leading to the Jubilee Line.

Which one to take?

She sped towards the one marked Exit, slowing her pace slightly as she reached the bottom of the stairs.

He wasn't there. Surely he couldn't have climbed the flight so quickly? She decided to try the connection to the other line.

As she moved breathlessly through the throng of people Jo continually scanned the bodies moving in front of her, her anxiety building to a crescendo. She had lost him she was sure of it. How could she ever have hoped to catch him when . . .

Billy was ahead of her. About twenty yards away. He was standing on an escalator glancing at the panels advertising books, films, museums and art galleries that flanked each moving stairway.

Jo stepped on to the escalator behind a tall man in a dark suit and lowered her head slightly in case her brother should look back.

Unless he already knows you're there.

She forced the thought aside. She had to believe that he didn't know. Had to convince herself that this subterfuge would be worth it. She began to worry about what she might find when she reached his destination. Perhaps it would be better to turn back now. Maybe she was better off not knowing where he was going.

He stepped off the escalator and, moments later, so did Jo.

Don't give up now.

Billy wandered through on to the southbound Jubilee Line platform.

She loitered at the bottom of the escalator, pretending

to tie her trainer, giving him time to move down the platform.

She could hear a train coming. Only then did she scurry through on to the platform.

She spotted him as he stepped on to the waiting tube and, again, she boarded one carriage away from him. This time he stood, holding on to one of the overhead rails, looking around him at the other passengers.

If he was standing, she surmised, this leg of the journey must be a short one.

She was right. Billy got off at the first stop. Green Park.

Jo followed.

Eighty-One

Andrew Chapman sat at his desk, the silence around him total. Even the sound of traffic outside in Piccadilly sounded muted, unreal. Everything had seemed unreal for the last three days. Seventy-two hours in which he had seen his life collapse around him. That was all it had taken for his world to be destroyed, his existence to be shattered. The police interrogations. The confession to his wife about his psychiatric visits and their nature. The fact that he was suspected of murder. The recriminations. The tears.

And this very morning, the redundancy notice.

The final nail.

He sat at his desk looking at it. Something else to break to Laura when he got home. If she would listen to him. They'd barely spoken a dozen words in the last thirty-six hours. She had cried a lot. Her sobbing was her only communication at present. Even his children had not spoken to him since the first police visit to his house.

And, as if that wasn't bad enough, there was the surveillance.

The unmarked police car followed him everywhere he drove. It parked outside his house at night. It remained close to the bank all day. The men who occupied it made no secret of their presence. One had even nodded a greeting to him the day before.

He knew it was parked out there now. Somewhere, hidden in the gloom but waiting for him. When he drove away it would follow, keeping a none too discreet distance until he arrived home, then it would carefully park up opposite his house, just like it always did.

In the gloom of his office he looked at his watch.

12.04 a.m.

He was alone in the building.

He was alone in the world.

There was no rush to get home. Laura and the children would be in bed. She would be sleeping in the spare room. Anxious to be away from him. He would have to find some way of telling her about the redundancy notice. Some way of telling her that the house repayments could not be maintained unless he got another job quickly. And what chance of that with a possible court case hanging over his head?

True, he hadn't been charged yet but it seemed just a matter of time.

He'd stayed on at the bank ostensibly to finish some work but really because there was nowhere else for him to go. In this office he was not watched by prying eyes, not subject to whispered scandal as he passed, not stared at the way he was when he emerged periodically during the working day.

He had felt many emotions during his life but never anything like this, never a sense of such utter helplessness and worthlessness. It was intolerable and it was unrelenting.

He got to his feet, pushed the redundancy notice into his inside pocket then walked to the office door and locked it behind him.

The lift was to his left. He pressed the Call button and stepped in, hesitating for a moment. It was a small, private lift for employees' use only, barely large enough to carry two people.

He pressed 3 and the lift rose. He stood motionless, eyes gazing blankly ahead, finally stepping out at the appointed floor when the car bumped to a halt.

A long corridor stretched away in front of him and, at the end of it, a locked door.

He strode down the corridor and unlocked the door. Management had keys to this door and, at least until the end of the week, he was management.

The end of the week.

He opened it and ascended the narrow flight of stairs that led to the roof.

He moved purposefully, eyes fixed ahead, tears forming in his eyes as they scanned the neon skyscape of Piccadilly. Around Eros, dozens were gathered. Traffic passed through. The night was filled with the sound of beeping hooters, car engines, disembodied chatter. Laughter. It was an alien sound to him now.

The breeze up on the roof was strong, it ruffled his hair as he stood by the parapet, looking down into the street wondering where the police car was parked. The car that waited for him.

He stood there, eyes closed, a single tear rolling down one cheek.

One reason to go on living?

There wasn't one.

He jumped.

Eighty-Two

As Jo emerged from Green Park tube station into Piccadilly she heard the wail of sirens, but she was more concerned with keeping as close to Billy as she could. The thoroughfare was busy even for such a late hour, and for that she was grateful.

He crossed the road and walked along in front of The Ritz, illuminated by the lights that shone beneath its frontage.

Jo waited a second then hurried across behind him, narrowly avoiding an onrushing Nissan that sounded its hooter at her. She ignored it and settled into a more measured stride about twenty yards behind Billy.

He had both hands dug into his pockets and walked without obvious concern. If he knew she was following he certainly gave her no indication. And surely, if he had known, he would have confronted her by now.

Wouldn't he?

There would have been a loud row in the middle of the street and he would have run off, leaving her to ponder about his destination and the nature of his business at such a late hour.

But no, he kept on walking, turning right into St James's Street.

Jo followed at a more cautious distance. It was less crowded here and her only hope of avoiding being seen would be to sneak into a doorway. However, he didn't turn. Just kept walking.

He turned again. Into Park Place. A dead end.

What the hell was going on?

Jo hesitated, pausing on the corner of the street, watching as Billy walked further along the darkened cul-de-sac.

He *had* seen her, she was growing more certain of that by the second. He would wait until she followed him down this dimly lit place, then he would confront her and tell her that he'd known from the beginning that she'd been tailing him.

And yet he continued on.

Jo darted into a doorway, enveloped by the blackness, squinting to see Billy now.

She moved a few yards further down. Getting closer.

He had stopped beside a car.

Oh, no. He was going to steal it. That was where the money was coming from.

It suddenly became so clear. So . . .

No.

The car door opened, light from inside suddenly spilling into the street as the driver stepped out to talk to Billy.

Jo watched mesmerised, her gaze drawn to the driver of the vehicle. There was something familiar about him.

The driver embraced Billy. They kissed passionately. The man touched his cheek then kissed him again, more deeply this time.

And she understood.

Now she knew where the money came from and it thundered in her head like an explosion. The realisation was there before her.

'Rent boy,' she whispered to herself.

It felt as if every muscle in her stomach had knotted into a ball.

Rent boy.

She saw Billy slide into the passenger seat of the car and something else struck her. Struck her like a thunderbolt.

Seconds before the driver's door was closed, while the car's interior was still illuminated, she saw the man kiss Billy again. And in that split second she knew who the driver was.

David Albury.

Eighty-Three

Amy left the studio and headed straight for the lift. She didn't even wait to say goodbye to Osborne, who was shouting something incomprehensible at her.

She rode the lift to the ground floor and asked the security guard to call her a cab.

She glanced at her watch.

It should be here in less than ten minutes, he told her.

Amy nodded, reaching for a cigarette.

She waited.

'What time was he found?' Webber asked, peering at the pulped face of Andrew Chapman.

'About fifteen minutes ago,' a uniformed officer informed him, turning away from the bloodied mess that had once been Chapman's head. He had noticed, with a tremor in his belly, that portions of pinkish-white brain matter had spilled from the ruptured skull.

An ambulance, its lights turning silently, was blocking one end of the street, a police car the other. Officers, uniformed and plainclothes wandered around the scene, all presumably engaged in some kind of meaningful activity.

Webber saw Grant talking to the two men who had been tailing Chapman for the past forty-eight hours. Grant was nodding, even smiling occasionally as he spoke to the other policemen. Webber finally got to his feet, glancing back one last time at Chapman's corpse before the waiting ambulancemen covered it with a plastic sheet and carried it to the waiting emergency vehicle, leaving a pool of blood fully twelve feet across in the corpse's wake.

'I think we can close this case,' said Grant smugly.

Webber didn't answer, merely took a drag on his cigarette.

'I told you he'd crack,' Grant continued.

'I didn't think he'd kill himself,' Webber announced.

Grant could only shrug. 'Who gives a shit? One way or the other this is over. Done deal.'

'So you were right?'

'Looks like it, Jake. Why sound so surprised?'

'What about the blood test?'

'That'll be done when they get the body to pathology. A match with the blood on the glass at Charlotte Kilbride's place and bingo. I'll call a press conference in the morning and announce that the investigation is over. The killer is dead.'

Webber sucked on his cigarette, blowing a stream of smoke out into the air.

Grant was heading back to his waiting car.

'It's over, Jake,' he called, smiling.

'What if you'd been wrong?'

'I'd have resigned. But I *wasn't* wrong, was I?' He slid into the passenger seat. 'I win again, Jake.'

The car pulled away.

She could take no more.

The lies. The deceit.

The pain.

Jo wanted no more.

As she stuffed Billy's clothes into his duffel bag she had to force back the tears.

Tears of anguish?

She didn't *want* to throw him out. Not now. Not now he *knew* he was dying.

Tears of sorrow.

He was her brother. No matter what he had done, or what he was doing, he was still her flesh and blood. Except that flesh and blood was diseased.

Tears of disgust.

He knew that he had AIDS and yet he was prepared to spread the virus. His words echoed in her head.

'I'll take as many with me as I can. If I'm going to die then so are a lot of other people too.'

How many had he infected? How many men who had paid to use his body and he theirs? How many would die?

Jo had run back to Green Park tube, fighting back her tears caused lay the vision of her brother and Albury together.

Albury. That two-faced bastard.

She had returned to the flat and begun packing Billy's things up immediately. She could take no more.

As she pushed the sofa back to look for any stray socks that may be hidden beneath she saw the carrier bag. A simple grey HMV bag. Billy's.

She picked it up, ready to stuff it into the duffel bag with the rest of his things. Things she didn't want in her flat any longer.

She saw an envelope inside. Larger than A4 size and thick.

Jo took it out and saw that the top was undone. She pulled at what was inside. Files. Brown, manilla files. There were about twenty of them. Too many for the envelope to confortably hold.

She pulled one free and opened it. It was a psychiatric report. There were other notes inside it. Prescriptions. A case history. One of the letters inside was signed in a sweeping hand.

Charlotte Kilbride.

'Oh my God,' Jo murmured, the colour draining from her face.

She stood motionless, the file gripped in her shaking hand. It was then that she heard a key in the lock.

Eighty-Four

When Billy walked in he saw Jo standing transfixed, one of the files still held in her hand.

'What are you doing with that?' he asked, closing the door behind him.

'You killed her, didn't you?' said Jo flatly. 'You killed Charlotte Kilbride.'

'I didn't want to,' he said almost apologetically.

'Why, Billy?'

'Does it matter?'

'You murdered someone and you ask me if it *matters*?' She shouted the last word, flinging the file at him. 'And how many others have you killed?'

'What the fuck are you talking about?'

'I saw you tonight.'

He looked puzzled.

'I followed you. I know where your money's been coming from. Did they all pay you as well as David Albury? Are all your clients as generous? How many have there been, Billy?'

'I didn't keep a list. Thirty, forty, maybe more.'

'You infected them. You knew you had AIDS but you still went with them.'

'That's *their* problem. Anyone picking up rent boys knows they're taking risks. If they wanted to do it without condoms and pay me extra I wasn't going to refuse. What's that old saying about a fool and his money?'

'You murdered them.'

'Don't be so fucking stupid.'

'You might as well have put a gun to their heads.' She ran a hand through her hair. 'Why Charlotte Kilbride?'

'I was paid to do it.'

'Who by?'

'David Albury.'

'Why?'

'He didn't want anyone to know that he'd been treated by her. He thought it might fuck up his political career. When she started going on television and talking about the murderer and how she could help the police, Albury got nervous. He thought if the police investigated her then they'd find out about her patients.'

'So he hired you to kill her?'

'He paid me to break into her place and steal his file. But then she walked in while I was doing it. I didn't know what to do. I was out of my skull and desperate not to get caught. I panicked.'

'Why did Albury pay *you*?'

'He was a regular. He trusted me.' Billy laughed and it had a hollow, empty sound. 'The old tosser's got it bad. I think he's in love with me.'

'Does he know you've got AIDS?'

'Like I was going to fucking tell him. I'm not stupid, Jo. He pays too well. I'd have to get fucked by *ten* blokes to match the money he pays.'

'How much *does* he pay?'

'Two hundred a time. Easy money for sucking his limp old dick.'

They regarded each other in silence for a moment then Billy spoke again. 'What are you going to do, Jo? Shop me?'

She had no answer.

'You've already packed my stuff,' he continued. 'Let me have it. I'll walk away. I'll walk out of your life. There's no need for you to get involved in this.'

'I *am* involved,' she snarled. 'What am I supposed to do? Just forget about what I've seen and heard?'

'Give me my stuff, Jo. You'll never see me again, I promise.'

'I can't do that, Billy,' she said, tears forming.

'Why? You wanted me out anyway. I'm offering to go.'

He watched a single tear roll down her cheek.

'You're ill too,' she said, softly. 'I can't let you walk out in your condition, knowing you're going to suffer. I couldn't live with myself.'

'I'll manage. Give me the bag.' He held out a hand for the duffel bag.

'And these?' she said, indicating the files.

'I'll take those too.' He still had his hand outstretched.

Jo wiped tears from her face and passed him the bag. He took it and smiled wanly.

'Time to go,' Jo whispered, her voice cracking.

Eighty-Five

Amy paid the taxi driver, and while he was preparing to hand her some change she hurried from the car and disappeared into the main door, taking the stairs to Jo's first-floor flat. She didn't care that she'd given him ten pounds for a six-pound fare. She was probably worrying over nothing, she told herself, but it was unusual not only for Jo not to turn up, but also for her not to phone in a reason.

She reached the flat door and pressed the buzzer.

It was answered almost immediately.

'Jo! Are you okay?' A smile of relief spread across Amy's face.

'I'm fine, why?' Jo said flatly, ushering Amy inside.

'When you didn't turn up for the show and I couldn't get hold of you I thought there was something wrong.'

Jo didn't answer, just sat down on the sofa beside Amy, who could see that her eyes were red-rimmed and puffy.

'There *is* something wrong, isn't there?' Amy persisted. 'Please tell me, Jo.'

'It's Billy,' the younger woman said, swallowing hard. 'He found out that he has AIDS.'

'I'm sorry, Jo. Why didn't you say something?'

'I only found out myself tonight. That and a couple of other things,' Jo continued, smiling crookedly.

'Where is he?'

'In my room. Perhaps you'd like to see him.'

'If you think it would help.'

Jo got to her feet and walked across the sitting room to a narrow hallway.

Amy followed, moving slowly, almost reverentially, into the room that Jo indicated.

Billy Parker lay on the bed, legs splayed, arms stretched out on either side of him in a cruciform position. His eyes were still open, bulging in the sockets, some of the blood vessels having ruptured in the whites. The skin of his face had a bluish tinge, especially his lips. A swollen tongue protruded from his mouth, which was stretched in an awful rictus. Blood had spilled down his chin and on to his chest where he'd bitten the inside of his cheek.

There was a length of cord around his neck that, at first glance, appeared to have come from a bathrobe. It had cut so deeply into the flesh that Amy thought it might have severed the head if it had been drawn any tighter.

She stared, transfixed, at the corpse.

'He was dying anyway,' said Jo, also looking at the body, her head tilted to one side, her expression blank. 'I saved him from more pain. Just like the others.'

Amy suddenly snapped out of her hypnotic gazing.

'The others?' she said, her voice, barely a whisper, betraying her fear.

'Those two girls, the prostitutes. They were ill,' Jo continued, monosyllabically. 'So was the pimp *and* the drug pusher. I only had to look at them. And what kind of life did those people in the hospice have to look forward to? Just day after day of pain. I stopped their pain. All of them. I stopped their suffering. Just like I stopped Billy's suffering.'

'Oh God, Jo,' Amy murmured, the full realisation hitting her.

She could smell something pungent in the air and realised it was excrement, the odour rising from Billy Parker's corpse.

'My other brother, Danny. He died in pain but there was nothing I could do about that,' Jo said, looking directly at Amy. 'I wasn't going to let Billy suffer the same way. I did what I did because I loved him.'

'And what about the other people you killed?'

'I didn't kill them,' Jo hissed. 'I *helped* them. I read up on all kinds of diseases. AIDS, multiple sclerosis, cancer.

All of those that had no cure, all of those that caused suffering. I couldn't bear to think of people with those illnesses suffering the way my brother Danny suffered. The way Billy was suffering.' She looked directly at Amy. 'The way *you're* suffering.'

Amy took a step backwards.

'I can't let you suffer too, Amy,' Jo said. 'I think too much of you for that.'

She lunged at Amy.

The attack was sudden and unexpected and Amy couldn't avoid it. The two women crashed to the ground, Jo thrusting out her hands in an attempt to close her fingers around Amy's throat.

Amy knocked one of her hands away and drove her fist into Jo's face, striking hard against the other woman's cheek.

A livid mark appeared immediately.

Jo hissed and struck back, splitting Amy's lip.

Amy tasted blood in her mouth and the coppery tang seemed to galvanise her even more. Using all her strength, she grabbed on either side of Jo's head and hurled her to one side. Jo crashed into the bedside table.

Amy leaped to her feet and sprinted from the room but Jo rolled over with incredible speed and lashed out, catching Amy's ankle.

Amy went crashing to the floor, the wind momentarily knocked from her but, as Jo came at her, Amy managed to drive a foot hard into her stomach with enough force to double the younger woman up.

Amy took advantage of the respite and swung another foot, cracking it with tremendous power into Jo's face. One front tooth snapped and tore through Jo's upper lip.

Blood spilled down her face as she opened her mouth to vent her rage.

Again she launched herself at Amy, the impact knocking Amy backwards over the sofa.

This time it was Jo who was first on her feet, grabbing Amy's hair and lifting her bodily to her feet.

Amy screamed in pain as she felt a clump of hair torn from her scalp. She was both amazed and horrified at Jo's strength. The power in those hands and arms was colossal.

Jo lifted her by her throat now, raising Amy from the ground, thumbs pressing with incredible force into her windpipe.

Amy felt her head beginning to spin, it was as if someone was pumping it full of air. Spittle and blood flew into the air, some of it spattering Jo who continued to squeeze, her face contorted with the effort.

Amy struck out and drove two fingers into Jo's right eye, part of the eyelid ripping.

Amy fell to the ground as the pressure on her throat was relaxed.

She struggled to her feet and kicked twice at Jo. The first blow caught her in the side and Amy heard the crack of a snapping rib. The second struck her on the shoulder, the impact enough to unbalance her.

Amy staggered towards the door, desperate to get out.

Jo reached her as her hand was tightening on the lock.

The younger woman grabbed Amy by the wrist and used all her strength to swing her around, driving her into the wall with incredible power. Amy's head snapped backwards and slammed into the plaster. She felt her knees beginning to buckle.

Jo struck out at her, the punch catching her in the mouth, opening the gash in her lip even wider. Fresh blood spilled from it.

Amy fell sideways, dimly aware through a haze of pain, that Jo was locking the flat door.

She tried to rise but Jo grabbed for her again and the two women fell back into the kitchen, crashing against a work top. Half-a-dozen plates, a knife block and the electric kettle all went hurtling to the floor, two of the plates shattering, knives skittering across the lino.

Amy rolled over on to her belly, grabbing for one of the knives. She swung wildly with it and the razor-sharp blade sliced effortlessly through Jo's calf. Blood erupted from the wound, some of it spattering Amy, who tried to haul herself upright.

Jo grabbed for the knife, missed and hissed in pain as the blade laid her palm open. Lunging further, she picked up the kettle lead, wrenching it from the wall and, with one expert flick, she looped it around Amy's neck and grabbed the other end.

Amy felt incredible pressure around her throat and dropped the knife, trying to pull at the flex that was choking her. Her head was swimming and, with horror, she realised that Jo was straddling her, using her weight to keep her pinned down while she tugged ever-tighter on the flex.

Amy felt her head being tugged back even harder. Her eyes were throbbing in their sockets, her tongue lolling from her mouth as she gasped for air. She was beginning to lose consciousness.

Eighty-Six

Webber was at the bottom of the stairs when he heard the crash coming from the first floor. He hesitated a second then sprinted up the flight, taking the steps two at a time, the din growing louder as he drew closer to Jo's flat.

He stood beside the door for a moment, certain now that the murderous cacophony of sound was coming from within.

'Jo!' he shouted, banging on the door.

Nothing. Just the sound of shattering crockery.

He drove one foot against the door. Then another.

Inside there was another crash then a shout of pain.

He slid his hand inside his jacket and pulled the .459 Smith and Wesson automatic from its shoulder holster.

He kicked the door again, mustering every ounce of strength he had.

Still it wouldn't budge.

Through a haze of pain and a steadily rolling tide of blackness, Amy heard the thudding of something heavy against the flat's door.

It meant nothing.

All she was aware of was the incredible force being exerted on her throat as Jo tugged with greater ferocity on the kettle lead, digging one knee into Amy's back to provide more leverage.

Amy's hands flailed helplessly then towards the knives spilled across the carpet.

With what little strength she had left she managed to pull one towards her by the handle. At last she was able to close her fingers around it and then she struck backwards with a power born of desperation.

The blade tore through Jo's thigh, ripped a path

through the quadriceps muscle and, driven with such desperate force, it struck bone, rasping against the femur.

Jo shrieked, and Amy felt the excruciating pressure around her throat ease as her assailant toppled backwards, the knife jammed firmly into her leg.

She gripped the handle, made sticky by gouts of blood spurting from the wound, and tried to tug the razor-sharp blade free but it remained stuck, the muscles having contracted around it.

Amy coughed, spat blood and tried to call out but realised that something in her throat had ruptured. Blood was spilling over her lips, forming small pools as she crawled towards the sitting room. Towards the sound of the thudding against the door.

She rose up on to her knees, dragging herself up by pulling on the back of the sofa.

As she did, the door exploded inwards, finally succumbing to the ferocity of Webber's assault.

He burst in, gun levelled. Immediately he froze, transfixed by the sight before him. The wrecked room.

The blood.

Amy was on her knees looking at him, her face and clothes covered with the crimson fluid. Her eyes bulging wildly in their sockets.

She tried to speak, to warn him but all she could manage was a guttural sound deep in her throat.

He took a step towards her.

There was a banshee-like wail as Jo hurtled from the kitchen, hobbling on her injured leg.

Again he hesitated. Shocked by the vision that was charging towards him.

He saw her rip the blade from her thigh and raise it above her head.

Before he could react, she had driven the knife forward with all her strength.

The aim was appallingly accurate.

The steel tip pierced his wrist, cut the flexors to his and and snapped the ulna bone.

The blade erupted a full three inches from the other side of his arm, pinning his arm to the wood of the door as surely as if it had been nailed there.

He lost all feeling in his hand and the gun dropped to the floor.

Amy reached for it but Jo got there first.

She swung it up with both hands, pressed the barrel hard against his forehead and for fleeting seconds they were gazing into each other's eyes, only inches apart.

Webber saw the madness in Jo's eyes.

Then she pulled the trigger.

Eighty-Seven

Webber roared something unintelligible, expecting the deafening blast of the weapon to take his life.

Jo smiled crookedly, blood smeared across her face.

The hammer slammed down.

Nothing happened.

Jo squeezed the trigger again. And again.

Amy hauled herself upright and aimed a kick at Jo's injured thigh, slamming her instep against the spouting wound.

Jo dropped the pistol and Webber realised why it hadn't gone off. The safety catch was still on.

Gritting his teeth, and using his other hand, he pulled the knife pinning his arm from the door, then pulled the knife out of his arm. He shrieked in agony but he was free of the impaling blade.

He fell to the floor, his right hand crumpling beneath him uselessly but with his left he grabbed the automatic as he saw Jo rising above him once again, her face contorted.

Webber swung the pistol up and fired.

From point-blank range he couldn't miss and squeezed off four rounds in quick succession.

The thunderous discharge was deafening in such a small room; with the smell of cordite filling the air, the bullets – travelling at over fifteen hundred feet per second – slammed into Jo.

Each impact jerked her body backwards a few inches, the first shot drilling through her chest and erupting from her back. The second hit her in the shoulder. The third powered into her midriff, just below the sternum and the fourth caught her in the forehead. It stoved in portion of bone before tearing through her brain and exploding from the back of her head, carrying a flux of greyish-red material with it.

Jo dropped to the floor in a bloodied, untidy heap.

'Jesus,' gasped Webber, the pain in his right arm agonising.

He looked round to see Amy stumbling towards him, her face and blond hair spattered with blood.

'Jesus,' Webber repeated, pulling her close to him with his good arm.

She was weeping uncontrollably, even though no sound would escape her battered throat. They held each other tight, ears ringing from the thunderous blasts of the .459. Webber still had it drawn, gripped in his fist.

A door opened across the hallway and a terrified face peered out. A man in his twenties.

'Call the police and an ambulance,' Webber shouted to him, watching as the man stared fixedly at the scene of carnage.

The man disappeared back inside his flat again.

Webber helped Amy to her feet, supported her against him, his right arm dangling at his side. The entire limb felt numb and a steady stream of blood was flowing from the wound in his wrist, trailing down his fingers and dripping on the floor.

He made sure that Amy was comfortably settled on the sofa, then he perched beside her.

Amy gripped his good hand in a vice-like hold, clinging on as if she never wanted to let go.

Neither of them spoke. Webber merely stroked her hair gently. Reassuringly.

The room smelled of blood and sweat.

They waited patiently.

Eighty-Eight

It took time for everything to sink in.

Jo's death.

What she'd done.

What had happened at her flat that night.

Some of it had blurred into one waking nightmare for Amy. There were details she couldn't remember no matter how hard she tried. Perhaps, she told herself, she didn't *want* to remember them. Didn't want to think how close to death she had come at the hands of a woman she had always regarded as such a close friend.

A woman who had been a murderer.

It still seemed unbelievable.

Webber watched her as she paced the office, his right arm still heavily bandaged and in a sling. He saw the hard lines etched across her face and he knew what she was thinking about. He didn't have to ask. He'd seen that look many times during the past couple of days.

Amy looked at her watch. 'Where is he?' she said, her voice still a little hoarse.

As if in answer to her question, Dr Alan Davidson entered the room carrying several files, one of which he selected and laid on his desk.

'Sorry to have kept you,' he said cheerfully.

Amy wondered if the smile on his face was manufactured. An attempt to soften the news he was about to give her.

She sat down beside Webber, her hand seeking his.

'We got the biopsy result,' Davidson said at last.

Amy squeezed Webber's hand more tightly.

The doctor coughed.

'It was positive,' he said flatly. 'The cells we removed ere malignant.'

Amy gripped even more tightly on to Webber's hand and he responded.

'However, the growth was very small and there doesn't appear to be any evidence of secondary tumours or any spread,' he continued.

'Will I need more surgery?' Amy asked.

'It's unlikely,' Davidson told her.

'A mastectomy?' she persisted.

'No,' the doctor said, smiling. 'I want to keep a close eye on you for the next six months but, all in all, I'd say the prognosis is very encouraging. We caught it early enough.'

Amy relaxed her grip slightly.

'So I'll be okay?' she said, wanting to hear him say it.

'Like I said, I'll need to monitor your progress closely for the next six months, perhaps longer, but you'll be fine. Drugs and a little radiotherapy will eradicate any cells that might be left.'

'I'm not going to lose my hair, am I?' Amy said.

'You're not going to lose anything,' Davidson said, smiling.

'Is that it, then?'

'Make an appointment for two weeks' time, and I'll see you then.'

Amy and Webber got to their feet.

'Thank you, doctor,' she said, still gripping Webber's hand.

They left the surgery together. Outside he embraced her, ignoring the pain from his injured arm.

'It would have been ironic, wouldn't it?' she said. 'You stopped me from being killed by Jo but you couldn't have stopped the cancer killing me.'

'Forget about that shit now,' he said. 'You heard what the doctor said – you're going to be fine.'

She kissed him.

'What was that for?' he asked, smiling.

'Do I need a reason?'

'No. Feel free any time.' He touched her cheek gentl

'Look, I've got to go. I've got to get back to the Yard. There's a press conference in an hour and there's something else I want to see.'

'What?'

'Grant's resigning today.' He winked at her.

'Are you in line for his job?'

'We'll see. I'll tell you later. See you.'

He stuck out his hand and hailed a cab that pulled over to the kerb.

'Jake,' she called.

He turned as he prepared to climb into the taxi.

'I love you,' she said, smiling.

'I love you too,' he told her. 'See you tonight.'

She watched as the taxi pulled away.

Eighty-Nine

Amy sipped at her coffee, wincing slightly as she swallowed. Her injured throat still burned a little but it was more discomfort than pain.

On more than one occasion she had seen Osborne standing in the window of the production booth watching her. Checking on her. Each time she saw him she raised a hand to signal that she was okay.

Until someone was found on a permanent basis to replace Jo they had hired a temp to work the switchboard and put through the calls. She was a bright, cheerful girl in her late twenties. Lorraine. Her friends, she had informed them, called her Loz.

Amy checked the screen next to her and saw a number of names glowing there.

Alison from Clapham.

Gary from Mile End.

Roy.

She shuddered involuntarily.

When she looked up she saw Osborne looking at her again. He was shaking his head.

Nonetheless Amy took the call.

'Roy,' she said. 'Where have you been hiding?'

Silence.

'Come on, you haven't gone bashful on me, have you?' Amy persisted. 'What have you been up to?'

'You must think you're a hero,' said Roy. 'Helping to catch the murderer.'

'I do my best.'

'So one is gone,' Roy said flatly.

'What do you mean, Roy?'

'Out with the old, in with the new.'

He chuckled and, again, the sound raised the hairs on the back of her neck.

. . . And if I close my mind in fear,
please pry it open . . .'

Metallica

'I'm not with you, Roy.'

'Now it's *my* turn.'

'Roy?'

'I'll call again after I've started. After the first one. My style will be different.'

'Are you trying to tell me that you're going to start killing people, Roy? Now come on—'

'You'll hear from me soon,' he said.

There was a buzz of static.

'Roy?' she called.

She could hear him breathing.

'Roy?' Amy said more urgently.

Click.

Dead line.